THOSE JENSEN BOYS!
RIMFIRE

THOSE JENSEN BOYS!
RIMFIRE

William W. Johnstone
with J. A. Johnstone

PINNACLE BOOKS
Kensington Publishing Corp.
www.kensingtonbooks.com

PINNACLE BOOKS are published by

Kensington Publishing Corp.
119 West 40th Street
New York, NY 10018

PUBLISHER'S NOTE
Following the death of William W. Johnstone, the Johnstone family is working with a carefully selected writer to organize and complete Mr. Johnstone's outlines and many unfinished manuscripts to create additional novels in all of his series like The Last Gunfighter, Mountain Man, and Eagles, among others. This novel was inspired by Mr. Johnstone's superb storytelling.

All Kensington titles, imprints, and distributed lines are available at special quantity discounts for bulk purchases for sales promotions, premiums, fund-raising, educational, or institutional use. Special book excerpts or customized printings can also be created to fit specific needs. For details, write or phone the office of the Kensington sales manager: Kensington Publishing Corp., 119 West 40th Street, New York, NY 10018, attn: Sales Department; phone 1-800-221-2647.

PINNACLE BOOKS, the Pinnacle logo, and the WWJ steer head logo are Reg. U.S. Pat. & TM Off.

ISBN-13: 978-0-7860-3575-5
ISBN-10: 0-7860-3575-7

First printing: May 2016

10 9 8 7 6 5 4 3 2 1

Printed in the United States of America

First electronic edition: May 2016

ISBN-13: 978-0-7860-3576-2
ISBN-10: 0-7860-3576-5

CHAPTER ONE

"Let's take a ride on a riverboat, you said," Ace Jensen muttered to his brother as they backed away from the group of angry men stalking toward them across the deck. "It'll be fun, you said."

"Well, I didn't count on this," Chance Jensen replied. "How was I to know we'd wind up in such a mess of trouble?"

Ace glanced over at Chance as if amazed that his brother could ask such a stupid question. "When do we ever *not* wind up in trouble?"

"Yeah, you've got a point there," Chance agreed. "It seems to have a way of finding us."

Their backs hit the railing along the edge of the deck. Behind them, the giant wooden blades of the side-wheeler's paddles churned the muddy waters of the Missouri River.

They were on the right side of the riverboat—the starboard side, Ace thought, then chided himself for allowing such an irrelevant detail to intrude on his brain at such a moment—and so far out in the middle of the stream that jumping overboard and swimming for shore wasn't practical.

Besides, the brothers weren't in the habit of fleeing from trouble. If they started doing that, most likely they would never stop running.

The man who was slightly in the forefront of the group confronting them pointed a finger at Chance. "All right, kid, I'll have that watch back now."

"I'm not a kid," Chance snapped. "I'm a grown man. And so are you, so you shouldn't have bet the watch if you didn't want to take a chance on losing it."

The Jensen brothers were grown men, all right, but not by much. They were in their early twenties, and although they had knocked around the frontier all their lives, had faced all sorts of danger, and burned plenty of powder, there was still a certain . . . *innocence* . . . about them, for want of a better word. They still made their way through life with enthusiasm and an eagerness to embrace all the joy the world had to offer.

They were twins, although that wasn't instantly apparent. They were fraternal rather than identical. Ace was taller, broader through the shoulders, and had black hair instead of his brother's sandy brown. He preferred range clothes, wearing jeans, a buckskin shirt, and a battered old Stetson, while Chance was much more dapper in a brown tweed suit, vest, white shirt, a fancy cravat with an ivory stickpin, and a straw planter's hat.

Ace was armed with a Colt .45 Peacemaker with well-worn walnut grips that rode easily in a holster on his right hip. Chance didn't carry a visible gun, but he had a Smith & Wesson .38 caliber, double-action

Second Model revolver in a shoulder holster under his left arm.

However, neither young man wanted to start a gunfight on the deck of the *Missouri Belle.* It was a tranquil summer night, and gunshots and spilled blood would just about ruin it.

The leader of the group confronting them was an expensively dressed, middle-aged man with a beefy, well-fed look about him. Still pointing that accusing finger at Chance, he went on. "Leland Stanford himself gave me that watch in appreciation for my help in getting the transcontinental railroad built. You know who Leland Stanford is, don't you? President of the Central Pacific Railroad?"

"We've heard of him," Ace said. "Rich fella out California way. Used to be governor out there, didn't he?"

"That's right. And he's a good friend of mine. I'm a stockholder in the Central Pacific, in fact."

"Then likely you can afford to buy yourself another watch," Chance said.

The man's already red face flushed even more as it twisted in a snarl. "You mouthy little pup. Hand it over, or we'll throw the two of you right off this boat."

"I won it fair and square, mister. Doc Monday always says the cards know more about our fate than we do."

"I don't know who in blazes Doc Monday is, but your fate is to take a beating and then a swim. Grab 'em, boys, but don't throw 'em overboard until I get my watch back!"

The other four men rushed Ace and Chance. With their backs to the railing, they had nowhere to go.

Doc Monday, the gambler who had raised the Jensen brothers after their mother died in childbirth, had taught them many things, including the fact that it was usually a mistake to wait for trouble to come to you. Better to go out and meet it head-on. In other words, the best defense was the proverbial good offense, so Ace and Chance met the charge with one of their own, going low to tackle the nearest two men around the knees.

The hired ruffians weren't expecting it, and the impact swept their legs out from under them. They fell under the feet of their onrushing companions, who stumbled and lost their balance, toppling onto the first two men, and suddenly there was a knot of flailing, punching, and kicking combatants on the deck.

The florid-faced hombre who had foolishly wagered his watch during a poker game in the riverboat's salon earlier hopped around agitatedly and shouted encouragement to his men.

Facing two-to-one odds, the brothers shouldn't have been able to put up much of a fight, but when it came to brawling, Ace and Chance could more than hold their own. Their fists lashed out and crashed against the jaws and into the bellies of their enemies. Ace got behind one of the men, looped an arm around his neck, and hauled him around just in time to receive a kick in the face that had been aimed at Ace's head, knocking the man senseless.

Ace let go of him and rolled out of the way of a dive from another attacker. He clubbed his hands and brought them down on the back of the man's neck. The man's face bounced off the deck, flattening his nose and stunning him.

Chance had his hands full, too. His left hand was clamped around the neck of an enemy while his right clenched into a fist and pounded the man's face. But he was taking punishment himself. His opponent was choking him at the same time, and the other man in the fight hammered punches into Chance's ribs from the side.

Knowing that he had only seconds before he would be overwhelmed, Chance twisted his body, drew his legs up, and rammed both boot heels into the chest of the man hitting him. It wasn't quite the same as being kicked by a mule, but not far from it. The man flew backwards and rolled when he landed on the deck. He almost went under the railing and off the side into the river, but he stopped just short of the brink.

With the odds even now, Chance was able to batter his other foe into submission. The man's hand slipped off Chance's throat as he moaned and slumped back onto the smooth planks.

That still left the rich man who didn't like losing.

As Ace and Chance looked up from their vanquished enemies, they saw him pointing a pistol at them.

"If you think I'm going to allow a couple gutter rats like you two to make a fool of me, you're sadly mistaken," the man said as a snarl twisted his beefy face.

"You're not gonna shoot us, mister," Ace said. "That would be murder."

"No, it wouldn't." An ugly smile appeared on the man's lips. "Not if I tell the captain the two of you jumped me and tried to rob me. I had to kill you to protect myself. That's exactly what's about to happen here."

"Over a blasted watch?" Chance exclaimed in surprise.

"I don't like losing . . . especially to my inferiors."

"You'd never get away with it," Ace said.

"Won't I? Why do you think none of the crew has come to see what all the commotion's about? I told the chief steward I'd be dealing with some cheap troublemakers—in my own way—and he promised he'd make sure I wasn't interrupted. You see"—the red-faced man chuckled—"I'm not involved with just the railroad. I own part of this riverboat line as well."

Ace and Chance exchanged a glance. If the man shot them, his hired ruffians could toss their bodies into the midnight-dark Missouri River and no one would know they were gone until morning. It was entirely possible that a man of such wealth and influence wouldn't even be questioned about the disappearance of a couple drifting nobodies.

But things weren't going to get that far.

Ace said in a hard voice that belied his youth, "That only works if you're able to shoot both of us, mister. Problem is, while you're killing one of us, the other one is going to kill *you*."

The man's eyes widened. He blustered, "How dare you threaten me like that?"

"Didn't you just threaten to kill us?" asked Chance. "My brother's right. You're not fast enough . . . and your nerves aren't steady enough . . . for you to get both of us. You'll be dead a heartbeat after you pull the trigger."

The man's lips drew back from his teeth in a grimace. "Maybe I'm willing to take that risk."

Well, that was a problem, all right, thought Ace. Stubborn pride had been the death of many a man, and it looked like that was about to contribute to at least one more.

Then a new voice said, "Krauss, I guarantee that even if you're lucky enough to kill these two young men, you won't be able to stop me from putting a bullet in your head."

The rich man's gaze flicked to a newcomer who'd stepped out of the shadows cloaking the deck in places. Wearing a light-colored suit and hat, he was easy to see. Starlight glinted on the barrel of the revolver he held in a rock-steady fist.

"Drake!" exclaimed Krauss. "Stay out of this. It's none of your business."

"I think it is." Drake's voice was a lazy drawl, but there was no mistaking the steel underneath the casual tone. "Ace and Chance are friends of mine."

Krauss sneered. "You wouldn't dare shoot me."

"Think about some of the things you know about me," said Steve Drake, "then make that statement again."

Krauss licked his lips. He looked around at his men, who were starting to recover from the battle with the Jensen brothers. "Don't just lie there!" he snapped at them. "Get up and deal with this!"

One of the men sat up, shook his head, and winced from the pain the movement caused him. "Mr. Krauss, we don't want to tangle with Drake. Rumor says he's killed seven men."

"Rumor sometimes underestimates," said Steve Drake with an easy smile.

"You're worthless!" Krauss raged. "You're all fired!"

"I'd rather be fired than dead," one of the other men mumbled.

Steve Drake gestured with the gun in his hand and told Ace and Chance, "Stand up, boys."

The brothers got to their feet. Chance reached inside his coat to a pocket and brought out a gold turnip watch with an attached chain and fob. "I don't want to have to be looking over my shoulder for you the rest of my life, mister. This watch isn't worth that."

"You mean you'll give it back to me?" asked Krauss.

Ace could tell from the man's tone that he was eager to resolve the situation without any more violence, now that it appeared he might well be one of the victims.

"I mean I'll sell it back to you," said Chance.

Krauss started to puff up again like an angry frog. "I'm not going to buy back my own watch!"

"I won it from you fair and square," Chance reminded him. "Unless you think I cheated you . . ." His voice trailed off in an implied threat.

Krauss shook his head. "I never said that. I suppose you won fair and square." That admission was clearly difficult for him to make. "What do you want for the watch?"

"Well, since it came from a famous man, I reckon it must have quite a bit of sentimental value to you. I was thinking . . . five hundred dollars."

"Five hun—" Krauss stopped short and controlled

an angry response with a visible effort. "I don't have that kind of money on me at the moment. That's why I put up the watch as stakes in the game."

Steve Drake said, "We'll be docking at Kansas City in the morning. I'm sure you can send a wire to your bank in St. Louis and get your hands on the cash. That's the only fair thing to do, don't you think? After all, you set your men like a pack of wild dogs on to these boys, and then you threatened to murder them and have their bodies thrown in the river like so much trash. You owe them at least that much."

"Nobody's going to take their word over mine," said Krauss, trying one last bluff.

"Captain Foley will take *my* word," Drake said. "We've known each other for ten years, and I've done a few favors for him in the past. He knows I wouldn't lie to him. You wouldn't want it getting around that you were ready to resort to murder over something as petty as a poker game, would you? Seems to me that would be bad for business."

"All right, all right." Krauss stuck the pistol back under his coat. "It's a deal. Five hundred dollars for the watch."

"Deal," Chance said.

The rich man laughed. "The watch is worth twice that. You should have held out for more."

"I don't care how much it is. I just want you to pay to get it back."

Krauss snorted in contempt, turned, and stalked off along the deck. His men followed him, even though he had fired them. Evidently that dismissal wouldn't last, and they knew it.

A man with a temper like Krauss's probably fired

people right and left and then expected them to come right back to work for him once he cooled off, Ace reflected.

Once Krauss and the others were gone, the Jensen boys joined Steve Drake, who tucked away his gun under his jacket and strolled over to the railing to gaze out at the broad, slow-moving Missouri River.

The gambler put a thin black cheroot in his mouth and snapped a match to life with his thumbnail. As he set fire to the gasper, the glare from the lucifer sent garish red light over the rugged planes of his craggy face under the cream-colored Stetson.

"We're obliged to you, Mr. Drake," Ace said. "You're making a habit out of pulling our fat out of the fire."

"Yeah," Chance added. "If you hadn't come along when you did, we might've had to kill that obnoxious tub of lard."

"Krauss's gun was already in his hand," Steve Drake pointed out, "and yours were in your holsters. He might have gotten one of you, just like you said."

"Yeah, and he might have missed completely," said Chance. "We wouldn't have had any choice but to drill him, though."

"And then we would have been in all kinds of trouble," put in Ace. "The odds of hanging are a lot higher if you kill a rich man instead of a poor one."

"You sound like you have a low opinion of justice," said Steve Drake with a chuckle.

"No, I just know how things work in this world."

The gambler shrugged and blew out a cloud of smoke. "You may be right. We all remember what happened back in St. Louis, don't we?"

CHAPTER TWO

St. Louis, three days earlier

Neither Ace nor Chance was in awe of St. Louis. They had seen big cities before. Traveling with Doc Monday when they were younger had taken them to Denver, San Francisco, New Orleans, and San Antonio, so the buildings crowded together and the throngs of people in the streets were nothing new to the Jensen brothers.

It had been a while since they'd set foot in such a place. They reacted to it totally differently.

Chance looked around with a smile of anticipation on his face as they rode along the street, moving slowly because of all the people, horses, wagons, and buggies. He was at home in cities, liked the hubbub, enjoyed seeing all the different sorts of people.

Because Doc Monday, their surrogate father, made his living as a gambler, he had spent most of his time in settlements. That was where the saloons were, after all. And although Doc had tried to keep the boys out of such places as much as possible while they were growing up, it was inevitable that they had spent a great deal of time in those establishments.

Chance had taken to that life, but Ace had reacted in just the opposite manner. He didn't like being hemmed in and preferred the outdoors. He would rather be out riding the range any day, instead of being stuck in a saloon breathing smoky air and listening to the slap of cards and the raucous laughter of the customers. If he had to spend time in a settlement, the smaller ones were better than the big cities. To Ace's way of thinking, a slower pace and more peaceful was better.

Ever since Doc had gone off to a sanitarium for a rest cure, the boys had been on their own, and they had packed a lot of adventurous living into a relatively short amount of time. Chance was always happy when they drifted into a town, while Ace was ready to leave again as soon as they replenished their supplies and his brother had an opportunity to win enough money to keep them solvent for a while.

St Louis was the farthest east they had been in their travels, with the exception of New Orleans. There was no particular reason they were there, other than Chance deciding that he'd wanted to see St. Louis.

Ace figured Chance might have assumed St. Louis was like New Orleans, the city he loved, with its moss-dripping trees, its old, fancy buildings, its music, its food, its saloons and gambling halls, and especially its beautiful women. After all, both cities were on the Mississippi River.

He seemed somewhat disappointed in their present

surroundings, which led him to look around and ask, "Is this it? A bunch of people and businesses?"

"That's generally what a big city is," Ace reminded him.

"Yeah, but it doesn't even smell good! In fact, it smells sort of like . . . dead fish."

"That's the waterfront," Ace said with a smile. "New Orleans smelled like that in a lot of places, too. You just didn't notice it because you liked all the other things that were there."

"Maybe," said Chance, but he didn't sound convinced.

"I guess we'd better find a place to stay. We've still got enough in our poke for that, haven't we?"

Chance grunted. "Yeah."

Something else caught his attention and he pointed to a large saloon with a sign on the awning over the boardwalk out front announcing its name. RED MIKE'S. "I think we should have a look inside that place first."

The place took up most of the block on that side of the street. A balcony ran along the second floor. Ace wouldn't have been surprised to see scantily clad women hanging over the railing of that balcony, enticing customers to come up, but it was empty at the moment.

The hitch rails in front of the saloon were packed. The Jensen brothers found space to squeeze in their horses and dismounted, looping the reins around the rail. Chance bounded eagerly onto the boardwalk with Ace following at a more deliberate pace. He would have preferred finding a place to stay first, maybe even getting something to eat, but once

Chance felt the call of potential excitement, it wasn't easy to stop him from answering.

Considering the number of horses tied up outside, Red Mike's was crowded with customers. Men of all shapes, sizes, and types lined up at the bar and filled the tables. Ace saw buckskin-clad old-timers and burly men in canvas trousers, homespun shirts, and thick-soled shoes who probably worked on the docks or the riverboats. Also in attendance were cowboys in boots, spurs, and high-crowned hats, frock-coated gamblers who reminded him of Doc, and meek, suit-wearing townsmen.

Circulating among the men were women in low-cut, spangled dresses that came down only to their knees. Some of them looked fresh and innocent despite the provocative garb, while others were starting to show lines of age and weariness on their painted faces. All of them sported professional smiles as they delivered drinks, bantered with the customers, and occasionally perched on someone's knee to flirt for a minute before moving on.

In each front corner of the big room was a platform with steps leading up to it. A man holding a Winchester across his knees sat on a ladder-back chair on each platform. They were there to stop any trouble before it got started.

The tactic seemed to be working. While Red Mike's place was loud, even boisterous, it was peaceful enough in the saloon. Everyone seemed to be getting along.

Ace leaned closer to his brother and said over the hubbub, "It's too busy in here. We'd better move along and come back later."

"No, there's a place at the bar," Chance replied, pointing. "Come on."

Ace followed, unwilling to let Chance stay by himself. It wasn't that he didn't trust his brother, but sometimes Chance could be impulsive, even reckless . . . especially in such surroundings.

They weaved through the crowd to the bar. By the time they got there, the space Chance had noticed was smaller than it had been. There was still room for one of the brothers, but not both of them.

That didn't stop Chance from wedging his way into the opening and then using a shoulder to make it wider by pushing one of the flanking men aside. Ace winced a little when he saw that, because he knew what was liable to happen next.

Chance turned his head and beckoned to his brother. "Come on, Ace. There's room now."

No sooner were those words out of his mouth than a big hand clamped down on his shoulder and jerked him around. The man Chance had nudged aside glared down into his face and demanded in a loud voice, "Who do you think you are, boy?"

"My name's Chance Jensen," Chance said coolly. "If this is a formal introduction, you can go ahead and tell me your name."

The man ignored that. "You can't just push a man around like that and expect to get away with it, *boy*. You done left school too early. You ain't been taught all the lessons you need."

"From the sound of it, I have considerably more education than you do."

The big man's face darkened with anger. He was several inches taller than Chance, about the same height as Ace, and probably weighed fifty or sixty pounds more than either brother. His rough clothes and a shapeless hat jammed down on a thatch of dark hair indicated that he probably worked on the docks. Not the sort of hombre to mess with unless it was absolutely necessary, that was for sure.

The man leaned closer and growled. "Listen to me, you little son of a—"

Ace managed to get a shoulder between the two of them and said quickly, "My brother and I aren't looking for any trouble, sir. Maybe we can patch this up by buying you a drink."

Chance began, "We don't have enough money to throw it away buying drinks for—"

Whatever Chance was about to say, it wasn't going to help matters any, Ace knew. He pushed in between them harder, which made Chance take a step back and bump into the man behind him.

Being jostled made the man spill his beer down the front of his shirt. With an angry shout, the fellow twisted around, brandishing the now-empty mug like a weapon. "What in blazes?" he roared. "I'm gonna—"

The place went quiet, but not because of the man's shout.

Ace heard the familiar sound of a rifle's lever being worked and glanced around to see that both men on the elevated platforms in the front corners of the room were on their feet. Their Winchesters were socketed firmly against their shoulders, and the barrels were leveled at the group involved in the confrontation at the bar.

The dockworker who'd been glaring at the Jensen boys swallowed hard and unclenched his big fists.

"Blast it, Mike. Tell those killers o' yours to hold their fire."

A man wearing a gray tweed suit moved along the bar until he was across the hardwood from Ace, Chance, and the other two men. He was short and broad and the color and coarseness of his hair made it resemble rusty nails. "You know the rules, Dave. No fighting in here. My grandfather didn't allow brawling and neither did my father. Neither do I."

Dave glowered at Chance and accused, "This obnoxious little sprout started it, not me."

"Obnoxious," repeated Chance. "That's a longer word than I thought you'd be able to handle."

From the corner of his mouth, Ace told his brother, "Just be quiet, all right?"

Chance looked offended, but Ace ignored him.

"Sorry for causing trouble," Ace went on to the man on the other side of the bar. Judging by the man's attitude and the fact that the dockworker had called him Mike, Ace figured he was the owner of the place, Red Mike himself. "We just wanted to get a quick drink, and then we'll be moving on."

"Speak for yourself," said Chance. "I might like it here. I don't so far, not particularly, but I might."

Mike nodded to the brothers and asked the two offended parties, "If these youngsters were to apologize, would that take care of the problem?"

"Hell, no," replied the man who had spilled his drink when Chance jostled him.

Mike pointed a blunt thumb toward the batwings. "Then there's the door. Get out."

The man stared at him in disbelief. "You're kickin' *me* out? I wasn't doin' anything but standin' here enjoyin' a beer when this little pissant made me spill it all over myself!"

"Come back tomorrow and your first drink is on me," Mike said. "That's the best offer you're going to get, Wilson."

The man glared and muttered for a moment, then snapped, "All right, fine." He thumped the empty mug on the bar with more force than necessary, then turned and walked out of the saloon, bulling past anybody who was in his way.

"Now, how about you, Dave?" Mike went on. "Will an apology do for you?"

"No," the dockworker said coldly. "It won't. But I don't want those sharpshooters of yours blowin' my brains out, so I'll leave. I reckon that same free drink offer applies to me, too?"

"It does," Mike allowed.

Dave nodded curtly. "You shouldn't take the side of strangers over your faithful customers, Mike. It's these two as should be leavin'."

"You're probably right. Make it two free drinks."

That seemed to mollify Dave somewhat. He frowned at Ace and Chance one more time and said, "Don't let me catch you on the street, boys. You'd be wise to get outta town while you got the chance." With that, he stomped out of the saloon.

The two guards on the platforms sat down again. The noise level in the place swelled back up.

Mike looked at Ace and Chance and asked harshly, "Do you two cause so much trouble everywhere you go or did one of my competitors pay you to come in here and start a ruckus?"

"We're sorry, mister," Ace said. "Things just sort of got out of hand."

Chance looked slightly repentant as he added, "Sometimes my mouth gets away from me."

Mike grunted. "See that it doesn't again, at least not in here." He shook his head. "I don't care what you do elsewhere or what happens to you, either. You said you wanted a drink?"

"A couple beers would be good," Ace said.

Mike signaled to one of his aproned bartenders. "Don't expect 'em to be on the house, though. Not after the way you acted. In fact, I ought to charge you double . . . but I won't."

Ace dug out a coin and slid it across the hardwood. Mike scooped it up with a hand that had more of the rusty hair sprouting from the back of it.

The bartender set the beers in front of them.

Since Mike didn't seem to be in any hurry to move on, Ace started a conversation after picking up a mug and taking a sip from it. "You mentioned your father and grandfather. Did they own this saloon before you?"

"What's it to you, kid?" asked Mike as his eyes narrowed in suspicion.

"Nothing, really," Ace replied honestly. "I'm just interested in history, that's all."

A short, humorless bark of laughter came from the saloonkeeper. "Red Mike's has got some history, all right. The original tavern, back in the days when all the fur trappers and traders came through St. Louis on their way to the Rockies, was over by the docks, almost right on the river. A hell of a place it was, too. Men were men back in those days, especially those fur trappers. Always ready to fight or drink or bed a wench. My grandpap ruled the place with an iron fist. He had to."

"His name was Mike, too?"

"The name's passed down to me from him," the saloonkeeper confirmed. "My pa, whose name was Mike as well, moved the tavern a couple blocks in this direction. When I took over, I figured it was time to make a regular saloon out of the place and moved it again. I kept the name, though." He laughed again, but he sounded more genuinely amused this time.

"A while back, one of those old mountain men wandered in. Claimed he knew my grandpap and used to drink in his tavern, more than forty years ago. I figured he was probably crazy, but there was just enough of a chance he was telling the truth that I bought him a drink for old time's sake. Can't remember what he said his name was. Deacon or something like that."

Chance inclined his head toward the guards on the platforms. "Would they have really started shooting if somebody threw a punch?"

"Damn right they would have," snapped Mike, losing his slightly more jovial attitude. "Both of those boys can hit a gnat at a hundred yards."

Ace wasn't convinced that the saloon owner would resort to execution to break up a fight, especially with so many innocent bystanders around . . . but as long as people believed it was possible, they would be a lot more likely to behave.

"Now drink up," Mike went on, "and then get out."

"You're giving us the boot, too?" asked Chance, sounding surprised.

"That's right. I don't want you hotheads starting anything else."

Ace was equally determined that wouldn't happen, so he didn't argue with the saloonkeeper's edict. He wanted to leave and find a place to stay for the night. He had already seen enough of St. Louis to satisfy any curiosity he had about the city. He drained the rest of his beer and told Mike, "Again, sorry for the trouble."

"Let's just go," Chance muttered after swallowing the last of his beer.

They headed for the entrance, moving past several tables full of drinkers and a couple poker games. Chance pushed through the batwings first with Ace right behind him. They went to the hitch rail, untied their horses, and started along the street leading the animals.

Ace was looking around for a hotel that might be a place they could afford to stay when hands suddenly grabbed him and jerked him away from his horse, flinging him along a narrow alley between two buildings. The hour was late in the afternoon and shadows already gathered in the alley, but as Ace stumbled and then caught his balance, he could see well enough to make out several figures blocking his way back to the street.

A couple of the men had grabbed Chance, too, and dragged him into the narrow alley space. They gave him a hard shove that made him go to one knee. He cursed bitterly as Ace took hold of his arm and helped him up.

"Look what I landed in!" Chance exclaimed.

Ace was less worried about that than he was about the fact that they were surrounded. He recognized not only the burly dockworker called Dave but also the man who had spilled his drink when Chance bumped into him.

"So the two of you are friends," Ace said.

Dave shook his head and grinned. "Naw, I don't even know this fella. But we both have friends of our own, and we both know you two need a good stompin'. So that's what we're gonna give you."

With fists flying, the ring of attackers closed in around the Jensen boys.

CHAPTER THREE

In the opening seconds of the battle, Ace realized that the alley's narrow confines actually worked in favor of him and Chance. Their enemies couldn't all come at them at once. He ducked a wildly swung haymaker from Dave, leaned closer, and hammered a punch into the dockworker's midsection. It felt a little like hitting a wall, but at least the blow slowed down Dave's charge.

Next to Ace, Chance weaved to the side and let a fist fly harmlessly past his ear. His right arm shot straight out. The jab landed squarely on the man's nose. He jumped back and yelped as blood spurted from the injured member.

"I've had pugilistic training—" Chance began.

Ace grabbed his brother's shoulder and hauled him backwards. They couldn't go very far before their backs thumped against the wall of the building behind them, which prevented anyone from attacking them from that direction and cut down the number of foes they had to deal with at one time.

The attack didn't lessen in its intensity. Men jostled

each other for position as they crowded forward, eager to throw punches at the Jensen brothers.

Ace and Chance blocked the blows they could and tried to absorb the punishment from the ones they couldn't. At the same time, they dished out damage of their own. Their fists cracked solidly against jaws and chins.

They were heavily outnumbered. Every time one of them knocked a man down, there was another one—or two—right there to take his place. Inevitably, they would wear down, and then the bruisers they battled would get hands on them, drag them down to the hard-packed dirt of the alley, and kick and stomp them half to death . . . if they were lucky.

If they weren't, they wouldn't leave the alley alive.

Ace didn't know how many men were armed, if any of them were. He remembered from the confrontation in Red Mike's that Dave and Wilson hadn't been carrying guns, at least not that Ace had seen.

He and Chance both packed iron, and Ace knew they could pull their guns and maybe blast their way clear of the fight. But if they killed any of the men, a judge would likely consider it murder, especially since they were strangers in town. They would wind up dangling from hang ropes.

Either way, it was starting to look like their luck had run out.

Then once again, he heard the sound of a rifle being levered, and a deep, powerful voice called out, "Step away from those boys or I'll start shooting!"

The attackers froze with fists raised and poised to lash out. Ace and Chance stood in defensive postures.

Ace looked toward the alley mouth and saw a man standing there holding a Winchester like the ones Red Mike's sentinels used.

Ace couldn't make out many details in the twilight. He saw only the stranger's general shape, topped by a broad-brimmed, flat-crowned hat.

The newcomer advanced toward the knot of men in the alley. Dave, Wilson, and their friends moved back, instinctively drawing away from the menace of that leveled repeater.

"This way, boys." The stranger's voice was resonant yet friendly, maybe even a little amused by the situation. "Time to leave this little dance behind." He was coolheaded and absolutely unafraid.

Ace could tell that for sure.

"I know you," one of the men blurted. "You're that gambler—Drake."

Once Ace heard that, he realized he had seen their rescuer at one of the poker tables he and Chance had passed on their way out of Red Mike's.

"That's right," acknowledged the man with the rifle. "I'm Steve Drake."

Ace realized that Steve Drake was introducing himself to them. He replied quickly, "My name's Ace Jensen, and this is my brother Chance."

Steve Drake chuckled. "Ace and Chance, eh? I like that. You must have been given those monikers by another knight of the green felt."

Ace frowned.

"A poker player," Drake added in explanation.

"Yeah," said Chance. "A fella named Doc Monday."

"Doc! I know him. We've sat down at many of the

same tables over the years, although I haven't seen him in a long time. He's your father?"

"No, sir," said Ace, "but he raised us."

"Doc's a good man, as I recall."

"That's right, Mr. Drake," Ace said. "He'd be obliged to you for giving us a hand."

Dave stabbed a blunt finger at them. "You got no right mixin' into this, Drake. These boys deserve what we were handin' 'em."

"Beating them to death? Or close to it?" Drake said coolly. "What did they do to deserve that? Bump into you? Spill a beer? Remember, I was in Mike's place. I saw everything that happened. That's why I borrowed a rifle from one of Mike's men and followed them out here. I figured you and your friends might be ugly and brutal enough to do something like this."

So the Winchester Steve Drake held wasn't *like* the ones the saloon guards used. It actually was one of the same rifles, Ace mused. The gambler and Red Mike had to be friends for the saloonkeeper to have allowed that.

"Let's go," Drake went on, addressing the Jensen boys. "The rest of you leave these youngsters alone. If you don't, you'll answer to me. In fact, if anything happens to them while they're in St. Louis, no matter who's responsible, I'll be looking you up, Dave. And you, too, Wilson."

"That ain't fair!" Wilson exclaimed.

"Maybe not, but it's the way things are." Drake inclined his head toward the street and backed away. Ace and Chance went with him, moving ahead so that they reached the street first.

Ace spotted their horses standing a few yards from the alley with their reins dangling. He and Chance claimed the animals as Drake lowered the Winchester. Ace was glad no one had stolen them while he and his brother were busy being attacked.

"Aren't you afraid they're liable to bushwhack you?" Chance asked the gambler.

"That bunch?" Drake chuckled and shook his head. "There's not a gunman among them. They fight with their fists and feet. I doubt if any of them could hit the side of a barn with a shotgun." He pointed along the street. "Come with me. I'll take you to the hotel where I'm staying. I'm pretty sure there's an empty room there."

"Don't you need to take that rifle back to Red Mike's?" asked Ace.

"I'll do that later. Mike and I have known each other for years. When I was starting out in this game, I knew his father, too. He trusts me."

Ace and Chance led their mounts while Steve Drake walked along the street with the Winchester tucked casually under his left arm. He wore a good brown suit and a cream-colored Stetson. The brown hair under the hat was liberally streaked with silver.

In the light from the buildings they passed, Ace saw that the older man's face had a rugged, rough-hewn look about it, as well as a deeper tan than most gamblers possessed. Obviously, Steve Drake didn't spend all his time in saloons.

When they came to the Halliday House, Drake said, "It's not the fanciest hotel in St. Louis, I'll grant you that, but it's clean and comfortable."

"It may be too fancy for us to afford," Ace said.

"Are you going to be in town for a few days?"

"I don't really know. We don't have any plans."

Steve Drake waved a hand. "Then don't worry about it. I'll make up the difference if I need to, but I doubt if that will happen." He looked at Chance. "You enjoy a good game of cards, don't you? You have that look about you."

Chance grinned. "Not much I like better than a good poker game, although a girl might tempt me away from one . . . if she was pretty enough."

"A man with his priorities in order," Steve Drake said with a grin of his own. "I like that. You'll do fine. You boys *are* looking for a stake, aren't you?"

"We could use one," admitted Ace.

"Then come on. We'll get you settled, take these horses to the livery, have a good meal, then find a game so Chance here can get started on it."

"Maybe not at Red Mike's," Ace said. "He told us to stay out of there."

"There are plenty of other places in St. Louis," Drake said.

They left their horses at the hitch rail, carried their rifles and warbags into the Halliday House, and checked into the hotel. The clerk seemed to know and like Steve Drake.

The gambler appeared to have friends all over town, thought Ace.

That was confirmed a short time later when the proprietor of the livery stable greeted them with a big grin and a booming, "Howdy, Mr. Drake!"

"Hello, Gil," Steve Drake said as he returned the grin. "Take good care of these boys' horses, will you?"

"Why, sure thing, Mr. Drake," the burly stableman agreed.

The three of them proceeded to a café.

The people who worked there also were friendly, especially the blond, curly-haired waitress who hovered over the table. "Is there anything else I can get you or do for you, Mr. Drake?"

"Not right now, darlin'," he replied, his Southern drawl even thicker than before, "but if there is, I'll be sure and let you know right away."

While they were eating bowls of thick beef stew and chunks of fresh bread, washed down with hot, strong coffee, Ace asked the gambler, "Where are you from, Mr. Drake?" Then, because some men didn't like being asked that question, he added, "Not that I mean to pry or anything."

"That's all right, lad," said Steve Drake. "I don't mind telling you. I was born in Virginia. The Old Dominion."

"Were you in the war?" asked Chance.

The older man's rugged face tightened slightly. "Now that's something I *don't* like to talk about. The way I see it, the war's over and done with, and the sooner we all put it completely behind us, the better." He sighed. "Unfortunately, a lot of folks have a hard time doing that."

"We were born in Denver," Ace said, thinking it might be best to change the subject.

"I'm sure your mother and father must have been very proud of a couple fine, strapping boys like you."

Chance shook his head. "We never knew our mother."

"Or our father," added Ace. "Like we told you, we were raised by a man named Doc Monday."*

Steve Drake nodded. "Oh, yes, of course. I remember now."

"He may not have been our real pa, but he did a good job of bringing us up." Chance grinned. "Although most folks probably wouldn't think so, considering how much time we spent in saloons and gambling dens or out on the trail."

"There are some fine people in those places," said Steve Drake. "Although you *do* have to know where to look for them."

After they were finished with the meal, they left the café and headed toward a different saloon—one called The Royal Flush. Despite the rather gaudy name, the establishment was small and on the sedate side.

Chance frowned as they went in and commented quietly, "This place doesn't look like it'll be very entertaining."

"Do you want entertainment," asked Steve Drake, "or the chance to win some money at poker?"

"You know my name," Chance replied with a smile.

"I'll be at the bar." Ace left the card-playing to his brother. He preferred to nurse a beer and just sort of keep an eye on things while Chance sat in on the games.

---

*For the full story of the Jensen brothers' family history— which they themselves are unaware of at this point in their lives—see the novel *Those Jensen Boys!*

Chance and Drake went to a table in the back of the room where four men sat with cards in their hands and money in the center of the green felt. Evidently the Virginian was known to all of them, because they gave him friendly nods. When the hand was over, the two newcomers were invited to join the game.

"Get you something, young fella?" a balding bartender asked Ace at the bar.

"Beer will be fine."

The drink juggler nodded toward the table as he filled a mug from a tap. "You boys friends with Mr. Drake?"

"Well, I guess so. We only met him earlier this evening, but I reckon you could say he's sort of taken us under his wing. He seems to be a fine hombre."

"Oh, he is, definitely." The bartender set the beer on the hardwood in front of Ace. "In fact, if you're friends with Steve Drake, that's good for a free drink. This one's on the house."

Surprised, Ace said, "I'm obliged to you."

"No, to Mr. Drake. He helped me come up with the money to start this place. I offered to make him a silent partner, but he didn't want that. Said he didn't want to be tied down in one spot for too long."

"I can understand that feeling." Ace stood with one elbow propped on the bar while he sipped his beer and watched the game in progress. Several other men were drinking in the saloon, but none of them bothered him. There were no gaudily dressed saloon girls or women of any sort in there.

Ace trusted his instincts and his judgment of Steve Drake's character, but in the back of his mind lurked the worry that the gambler had befriended them and brought them there only to try to fleece them of whatever funds they had left.

As he watched the game, he could tell that wasn't the case. Chance won some hands and lost others, but he seemed to be playing more cautiously than usual and didn't appear to have any big losses. Maybe he was following Steve Drake's example and learning from the older man.

The pile of bills and gold pieces in front of Chance grew slowly but steadily. Ace figured it wouldn't be long until they had enough to stay in St. Louis for a few days and then stock up on supplies before heading out on the trail again. Hearing heavy footsteps from the boardwalk outside, he looked in that direction.

The batwings swung back and several men entered the Royal Flush, stopping just inside the door. The one in the lead wore a cheap brown suit and a derby. His mustache curled up on the tips. He had a good-sized belly, but he didn't look soft. Just the opposite, in fact. The fabric of his suit bulged more from muscle than with fat. The men with him, although they were all different shapes and sizes and dressed differently, had the same sort of cheap but tough look about them.

They were trouble, Ace realized instantly. Hired muscle looking for someone.

So he wasn't all that surprised when the leader stepped forward, glaring at the table in the back of the room. "There you are, Drake! You're comin' with us!"

CHAPTER FOUR

Moving deliberately, seemingly unbothered by the intrusion, Steve Drake placed the cards in his hand facedown on the table in front of him and raised his head. "Hello, Bennett. "I'll be with you shortly."

"You'll be with me right now, blast it," responded the tough called Bennett. "Mr. McIsaac sent us to fetch you, and that's just what we're gonna do."

"When I'm finished with this game."

"No. Now."

Bennett's ham-like hands clenched into fists as he started toward the table with his cronies close behind him. Other customers quickly got out of their way.

The four men in the game when Drake and the Jensen boys had entered the saloon looked like they wished they were somewhere—anywhere!—else. Chair legs scraped on the floor as they put down their cards and pushed away from the table.

Chance stayed where he was, sitting forward tensely. "Mr. Drake . . ."

The gambler casually lifted a hand and gestured

for Chance to stay where he was. "I'll reason with these fellows."

"Not gonna be any reasonin'," declared Bennett. "We're takin' you out of here, mister, if we have to drag you by the heels to do it. Or by the neck, as long as we don't kill you." He sneered. "Mr. McIsaac didn't say what sort of shape you had to be in when we take you to his house."

Ace had seen and heard just about enough. He stepped away from the bar, palmed out the Colt on his hip, and eared back the hammer as he pointed it at Bennett and the others. The metallic ratcheting made all of them freeze.

"That's far enough," Ace said. "Hold it right there."

At the table, Steve Drake pursed his lips slightly as if he wasn't happy that Ace had stepped in to help him.

Ace saw it and thought that was just too bad. The gambler had saved him and Chance from that trouble earlier in the evening, so they owed him.

Bennett looked back over his shoulder and rumbled, "Kid, you won't want to get mixed up in this."

"That's where you're wrong," said Ace. "I don't know what you think Mr. Drake has done, but he's my friend and I'm not going to let you take him anywhere he doesn't want to go."

"Ace, I appreciate the sentiment, lad," said Steve Drake, "but Bennett here is right. This is a private matter between me and his employer."

"That fella McIsaac he mentioned? I don't know anything about that. All I know is that you saved our bacon a while ago, and I intend to return the favor if I can."

Steve Drake sighed. "There's no way I can talk you into putting away your gun and backing off, I suppose?"

"No, sir," said Ace.

"Or me, either," added Chance. His hand was close to the opening of his coat, where it could dart inside and snatch the revolver from his shoulder holster with blinding speed if necessary.

How the confrontation might have ended was destined to remain unknown. One of the men with Bennett stealthily reached over, grasped the back of an empty chair, then suddenly jerked it up, whirled toward Ace, and let it fly.

Ace tried to duck away instead of opening fire, but the chair crashed into him and knocked him back against the bar. It jolted his arm upward so that when his finger tightened involuntarily on the Colt's trigger, the bullet went harmlessly into the ceiling.

The man who had flung the chair charged right behind it. He tackled Ace while the young man was still off balance. The man's fingers closed around the wrist of Ace's gun hand and kept it pointing up. At the same time, he rammed his shoulder into Ace's chest and drove him into the bar again. The painful impact against the small of his back made Ace groan as he fought to stay on his feet.

With surprising speed, Bennett charged the table where Chance and Drake sat. Chance reached for his gun, but Bennett plowed into the table first, upsetting it and knocking Chance's chair over backwards. As Chance hit the floor, a couple of Bennett's companions leaped at him. Bennett pivoted toward Drake and lunged at him, hands outstretched.

Drake was on his feet to meet Bennett's attack. The gambler grabbed Bennett's right arm with both hands, twisted at the waist, and threw a hip into Bennett's onrushing form. Using his attacker's own momentum against him, Drake bent and heaved. Bennett flew into the air, flipped over, and slammed down on his back.

Over at the bar, Ace hooked a left into his opponent's belly. The powerful blow made the man double over as whiskey-laden breath gusted out of his mouth. His grip on Ace's gun hand began to slip.

As the man bent toward him, Ace lowered his head and butted the hombre in the face, knocking him loose completely. Ace brought his gun arm down swiftly, reversing the Colt and clipping the man on the head with the butt. His knees folded up, dropping him to the sawdust-littered floor.

Chance struggled to get to his feet as the pair of foes closed in on him. He hadn't made it when one of the men aimed a kick at his head. Chance jerked aside, avoiding a broken jaw or worse, but the kick still caught him on the shoulder and knocked him down again.

The second man was ready to strike, rushing in with a foot lifted so he could drive his heel down viciously into Chance's face.

Chance's reflexes were fast as his hands shot up, grabbed hold of the foot, and heaved. Balanced only on the other foot, the man couldn't stop himself from toppling over with a startled, angry yell.

Chance rolled into the other man's legs, reached up, caught hold of his belt, and pulled him down.

With both of his foes floundering on the floor, he scrambled to his feet.

One of the men tried to get up and ran into a powerful right hook to the jaw that stretched him out and left him too stunned to rise again for a few minutes. The second man made it to his feet and even managed to throw a punch, but Chance avoided it and landed a counterblow that knocked the man to the floor next to his ally.

Having disposed of their opponents at roughly the same time, Ace and Chance looked toward Steve Drake and saw that the gambler was standing over Bennett with a nickel-plated revolver in his hand.

The gun must have been under his coat, Ace thought, because he hadn't seen it.

Bennett's face was flushed dark red with fury, but clearly he understood the threat of the gun in Drake's hand and didn't want to buck it. "You'll be sorry about this, Drake," he raged, spittle flying from his mouth. "Damn sorry!"

Drake backed off a little and motioned with the gun for Bennett to get up. "You're going to have to take something back to Joshua McIsaac, Bennett, but it won't be me, so deliver this message instead. I never led his daughter on, and I certainly never promised to marry her. That's all in her imagination. If she actually believes it . . . well, she's fooled herself into thinking it's true."

Bennett clambered to his feet and growled, "You expect me to tell him that? The old man dotes on that gal. He believes every word that comes outta her mouth!"

"I'm sure he does, but that doesn't change the

facts of the matter. I never asked Lydia McIsaac to marry me. I promise you, I have no interest in taking a wife!"

Bennett brushed sawdust off his clothes, then bent and picked up the derby that had come off his head. "You ain't heard the last of this."

"I sincerely hope I have."

Chance had drawn his gun, and Ace still held his. The brothers backed off to cover Bennett's battered henchmen as they climbed to their feet, shaking their heads and grimacing from bruises that were starting to form.

Bennett jerked his head toward the door, and with plenty of murderous glares directed at Ace and Chance, the men headed in that direction. Bennett followed them, muttering curses under his breath.

When the troublemakers were all gone, Drake looked over at the Royal Flush's proprietor. "I'm sorry for the commotion. I'll cover any damages—"

"No, you won't," the balding man said. "I owe you a lot more than got busted up in this fracas. Anyway, I figure I'll send a bill to Joshua McIsaac. It was his men who started the trouble."

"That's true," Drake said with a slight smile. He slipped his gun into a holster under his coat and turned to Ace and Chance, who pouched their irons as well. "It appears the game has broken up for the night. Gather your winnings, Chance. We'll leave the rest of the pot here for those gentlemen to come back and collect later."

"You could take the whole thing," Chance pointed out. "They ran out and left you to face those bruisers."

Drake gave a little shrug. "It wasn't their fight. Nor was it yours and your brother's, but I appreciate the help anyway." He tucked away some of the money that had been scattered on the floor. "Let's have another drink, then head back to the hotel."

The bartender set shot glasses on the bar and splashed whiskey into them. "I figure you're going to want something stronger than beer after that little dustup."

Steve Drake nodded gratefully. "Thank you, Ben."

Ace and Chance weren't big drinkers, but they agreed the whiskey would have a bracing effect.

As they sipped the drinks, Chance asked, "What was that all about?"

"Probably none of our business," Ace cautioned his brother.

"Perhaps not," Steve Drake agreed, "but the way you boys stepped in to give me a hand, I think you've earned the right to know why you were fighting."

"I know why," said Ace. "Because you're our friend."

"Well, I appreciate that," Drake said, smiling faintly. "But you probably heard enough of Bennett's bluster to make a pretty good guess as to the rest of it, anyway."

"That fella McIsaac thinks you proposed to his daughter and then backed out on it and broke her heart."

"That's right. That's what Joshua McIsaac thinks. But it's not what really happened. All I ever did was smile at the girl, make some pleasant small talk, and dance one dance with her at a party. Evidently she took that to mean a lot more than it actually did."

"Is this girl an old maid?" asked Chance. "So homely she's gonna have a hard time finding a husband?"

"On the contrary. Lydia McIsaac is quite beautiful. *And* her father has a great deal of money, to boot. She shouldn't have any trouble at all making a good match with a suitable young man."

Chance laughed. "Maybe you should introduce me to her."

"Oh, I wouldn't do that to you, my young friend. You see, while her father thinks of her as an angel, in reality Lydia is, well, a bit of the opposite. She tends to make life a living hell for any man who decides to court her. It didn't take long for some of her disgruntled suitors to spread the word."

Ace frowned. "I'm a mite confused about something. You said you danced with this girl at a party . . . ?"

"And you're wondering how a disreputable fellow like me ever got invited to a soiree at the home of the richest man in town?" Drake threw his head back and laughed.

Ace looked a little embarrassed.

The gambler went on. "Don't worry, Ace. I'm not offended. It's true that I'm a drifting gambler, but back in Virginia, my family is quite the upper crust of society. I'm the proverbial black sheep. McIsaac knows that and probably hopes that the love of a good woman will reform me. Unfortunately, his daughter doesn't fit that description."

"But he believes you broke your word to her and now he's going to force you to marry her."

Steve Drake nodded slowly. "That's just about the size of it, all right."

"Shoot," said Chance, "why don't you just get out of town? You said yourself that you're a drifter like us."

"I hate to let anybody make me run, but it may come to that. In fact, there's a riverboat heading up the Missouri in a couple days. I was thinking about taking it."

"A riverboat, eh?" Chance looked at his brother. "We haven't been on a riverboat since Doc took us on one when we were kids. Remember?"

"I do," Ace replied with a nod. "He was just there to gamble, but it was sort of fun."

"Why don't we go along? We wanted to head back west when we left here anyway, and that would be one way to get back out to the frontier without having to ride horseback all the way."

"Well, we haven't been invited," Ace pointed out.

Steve Drake waved a hand. "No invitation necessary, lads. Anybody can buy a ticket on the *Missouri Belle*. But for what it's worth, I think it's a fine idea. I plan to get off the boat in Omaha—have an old friend there I'm hankering to visit—but it goes all the way to Fort Benton in Montana. Quite a trip, if you'd like to make it."

"Can we take our horses?" asked Ace.

"You'll have to pay for space on the cargo deck for them, as well as their feed and care, but there are usually some animals on those boats. With Chance's winnings tonight, you should be able to afford it."

"And if the boat doesn't leave for a couple days, I can win even more," said Chance.

"Just don't get too overconfident," Drake said. "You're a good player. Doc Monday taught you well, but luck can turn against anybody, anytime. The key is being able to spot it when it happens and get out before too much damage is done."

"I'll be careful," Chance said.

Ace would have liked to believe that, but he knew his brother too well to be sure of it.

CHAPTER FIVE

The next night, when they returned to the Royal Flush, Ace was a little surprised to realize that Chance seemed to have taken Steve Drake's advice to heart. He took some risks as he played—it wouldn't have been called gambling if every hand was a sure thing—but he made his bets intelligently and didn't plunge when he had no business doing so.

In the process, he won enough money to cover their passage and that of their horses on the riverboat departing for Montana Territory the next day, with enough left over for supplies whenever they got off the boat.

Ace kept his eyes open and was alert for trouble, thinking that Joshua McIsaac might send men after Steve Drake again, but somewhat surprisingly, nothing of the sort happened. Maybe McIsaac had given up on forcing anybody to marry his daughter, although from the sound of it that might be the only way Lydia ever found herself a groom, no matter how attractive she was.

* * *

The *Missouri Belle* was scheduled to depart from the docks at ten-thirty in the morning. Ace was at the offices of the riverboat line to buy the tickets early. Chance had stayed back at the Halliday House to finish packing their gear.

"Headed for Montana, eh, son?" the ticket clerk asked.

"Yes, sir. All the way to Fort Benton." The Jensen brothers hadn't decided where they would leave the boat, but they figured if they bought passage all the way to the end of the line, they would be safe. If someplace struck their fancy before they got there, they wouldn't lose enough money to worry about.

Besides, Chance could always win more.

"Rugged country up that way," said the talkative clerk. "Plan to do some prospectin'? Or maybe work on one of those big cattle ranches they got up there?"

"Don't really know yet," Ace told him. "I reckon my brother and I will figure it out once we get there."

The clerk sighed and shook his head. "Ah, to be young again! When my job here is finished for the day, you know what I'll do?"

"No, sir."

"I'll walk home, eat supper, talk to my wife a little if she's in a good mood, read the paper, and go to sleep. Then tomorrow morning I'll walk back here, work all day, walk home and do the same things I'll do this evening. It just all starts over again every morning. How's that sound to you?"

It sounded like hell on earth, but Ace wasn't going

to say that. "Uh, fine, I reckon, if that's what you want to do."

The clerk laughed. "Most of the time, son, life doesn't have a damn thing to do with what a fella wants. Enjoy it while you can."

"Yes, sir." As Ace left the office, he felt the weight of the clerk's cloud of gloom lifting from his shoulders.

He stuck the tickets and the receipt for them and the space on the cargo deck for the horses into his pocket and headed for the hotel. His step was lighter as he reached the Halliday House. Anticipation for the journey filled him. It always felt good to be on the move again, going new places and seeing new things.

When he went upstairs, he found that the room he and Chance had shared for the past two nights was empty, although their rifles and warbags were still there. Chance might have gone down to the dining room, or he might be in Steve Drake's room, which was on the other side of the upstairs hall, three doors down. Ace decided to check there first.

When he rapped on the door of the gambler's room, at first there was no response.

Then Steve Drake's voice asked cautiously, "Who's there?"

"It's me, Mr. Drake. Ace Jensen. Is Chance in there?"

Before Drake could answer, Chance shouted, "Don't come in, Ace! Run!"

Ace could tell that his brother was in trouble, so he wasn't about to run. He reached for the doorknob with his left hand while his right dropped to the butt of the holstered Colt on his hip.

A gun blasted inside the room. Ace felt the wind-rip of a bullet past his ear as the slug punched through the door and nearly hit him. A split second later his hand closed around the knob and twisted it, but the door was locked.

He heard the sounds of a struggle inside the room. A piece of furniture crashed on the floor as somebody knocked it over. Another shot rang out, but the bullet didn't come through the door.

Maybe because it had lodged in the body of either Chance or Steve Drake.

Ace lowered his shoulder and rammed it against the panel with as much strength as he could muster. Wood splintered as the lock tore out from the jamb and the door flew open. He stumbled a little as his momentum carried him into the room.

He caught his balance, looked around, and saw Steve Drake wrestling with a woman. She had the gun, but the gambler had hold of her wrist and kept the weapon pointing toward the ceiling.

Chance stood to one side with a worried expression on his face. Ace didn't see any blood on his brother's clothes, but he gripped Chance's arm anyway and asked, "Are you all right?"

"Yeah, that second shot of hers went into the ceiling," Chance replied. "But what about you? She fired right through that door at you!"

"It missed . . . by a whisker. Is that—?"

"Yeah. Lydia McIsaac."

Drake got an arm around the young woman's waist and twisted her so that she was facing away from him. He bent the arm of her gun hand until she finally cried out and dropped the gun. A kick from Drake sent it sliding across the floor toward the Jensen boys. Chance bent and scooped it up.

"If I let go of you, are you going to behave yourself?" Drake asked his captive.

"Go to hell!" Lydia screamed. "If you think I'm going to let you get away with humiliating me, you're crazy!"

As Drake had said, she was beautiful, or at least she would have been if her face hadn't been so contorted with rage. Glossy black hair whipped around her head as she struggled to break free, writhing in the gambler's grip.

"How in blazes did this happen?" asked Ace.

Chance looked and sounded annoyed. "It was my fault. I'm the one who opened the door. I was in here talking to Mr. Drake when she knocked and said she was one of the maids from the hotel. I reckon she was trying to disguise her voice, but Mr. Drake caught on anyway and tried to warn me. It was too late. I opened the door and she stuck a gun in my face."

"And just think, night before last you were saying you wanted Mr. Drake to introduce you to her." Ace couldn't resist needling his brother.

Chance winced. "Don't remind me."

Steve Drake said, "Are you two going to stand there jawing all day or are you going to give me a hand here?"

"What do you want us to do?" asked Ace.

"Come grab hold of this hellcat and hang on to her so I can try to talk some sense into her head."

"I'll never forgive you for this, Steve!" Lydia cried. "Never!"

"Well, I reckon I'll just have to live with myself," the gambler said. "Now settle down!"

Ace and Chance moved in, each of them taking

hold of an arm. Ace didn't like manhandling a woman, even one who was loco, but Lydia McIsaac wasn't giving them much choice.

Once the Jensen boys had hold of her, Drake let go and moved around in front of the distraught female so he could look into her eyes. "Lydia, you've got to understand. I never had any intention of marrying you."

"Then why did you court me?" she demanded, a little breathless. "Why did you propose to me?"

"I never did any such thing. I didn't court you, either. We talked for a few minutes and I danced one dance with you. That's all."

"You know as well as I do that it was love at first sight!"

Drake sighed and shook his head. "That's not the way it happened, and I think you know that, deep down. I'm sorry that things in your life haven't gone the way you wanted them to, but you can't run around trying to force men at gunpoint to get them to marry you!"

"I'll do whatever I have to," she said as she strained against the grip of the brothers on her arms.

The broken door still stood open. A heavy footstep from that direction made Ace turn his head and look over his shoulder.

The big man named Bennett stood there with a scowl on his face. A tense second ticked by, then Bennett roared, "Let go o' her!" and charged toward Ace and Chance.

"Hang on to her!" Ace snapped at his brother, then released Lydia's arm and turned to meet Bennett's charge. He ducked under the man's round-house punch and jolted a left and a right to Bennett's ribs. The punches slowed the big man down a little but didn't stop him.

An uppercut caught Ace on the chin and rocked his head back. Bennett crashed into him and wrapped him up in a bear hug.

Ace felt his ribs creak as Bennett applied incredible pressure to them. With his arms pinned to his sides, the only way he could strike back was by lifting his knee into Bennett's groin. Ace didn't like fighting like that, but the alternative was broken ribs.

Bennett groaned in pain and his grip slackened. Ace tore his right arm free and rocketed a punch into Bennett's face. The big man let go of him completely and roared furiously, like a maddened bear. He swung wild punches, first a right and then a left, and Ace managed to avoid both of them by the skin of his teeth. He chopped the sides of his hands against Bennett's bull-like neck where it met the broad shoulders.

That seemed to paralyze Bennett momentarily. Ace snapped a left jab into the man's face then lifted an uppercut of his own that smashed against Bennett's jaw. Bennett went to one knee, then slewed on over and fell to the floor, breathing harshly, seemingly too stunned to rise.

Ace stepped back. His fists ached from the pounding and he was breathless from having most of the air squeezed out of him. But the big man was down and didn't seem on the verge of getting up again anytime soon.

Bennett was able to lift his head and peered around, his gaze unfocused until it landed on Lydia McIsaac, who was still being held firmly in Chance's grip. Bennett lifted a trembling hand toward her.

"Miss . . . Lydia," he gasped, "I . . . I'm sorry . . . Gimme . . . a minute . . . I'll wallop these varmints . . . who hurt you."

The dog-like devotion in the man's eyes as he looked at Lydia made Ace realize something that hadn't occurred to him before. Bennett had feelings for Lydia McIsaac. It was possible he had fallen in love with his employer's daughter . . . a relationship that more than likely a man like Joshua McIsaac would never endorse.

More heavy footsteps sounded in the corridor outside the broken door. Ace tensed, thinking that it might signal the arrival of more of McIsaac's men, but it was a pair of uniformed police officers who peered through the opening.

"What the devil is going on here?" demanded one of them. "We've had reports of gunshots, not to mention one that said it sounded like somebody was trying to tear down the place!"

"Arrest these men!" Lydia cried. "They're trying to hurt me!"

The way the officer looked at her and said, "Uh . . . Miss McIsaac, isn't it?" indicated that he had had dealings with her before. The man glanced over at his companion, who shrugged. Clearly, both of them wished they hadn't landed in the middle of whatever was going on, but they couldn't very well ignore the ruckus.

The one who seemed to be in charge frowned at Chance. "You there, let go of that young woman."

Chance frowned back at him. "I don't know if that's a good idea—"

"I said let go of her!"

"All right." He let go of Lydia's arms and stepped back quickly away from her, in case she turned around and came after him.

She whirled and flung herself at Drake with hands upraised and fingers hooked to claw out the gambler's eyes. Ace was ready for that and made a leap, catching her around the waist and hauling her back before she could reach her target. Her arms still flailed in Drake's direction.

"Maybe you fellas ought to take charge of her!" he suggested to the two police officers.

They didn't want any part of that. The one who had hung back suddenly said, "Why don't you stay here and keep an eye on things, Bob? I'll fetch the chief!"

The first officer jerked his head around. "Don't you go off—"

But it was too late. The second officer had already moved down the hall toward the landing practically at a run, judging from the rapidity of his footsteps.

The first officer sighed and told Ace, "All right, hang on to her. Maybe both of you better do that. But be careful. Her father's an important man in this town. Don't hurt her."

"We'll be as gentle as we can," promised Ace.

It wasn't easy. Lydia continued to struggle, as well as unleashing a torrent of profanity that might have shocked a muleskinner. Despite everything that had happened, Ace was starting to feel sorry for her. It was obvious she wasn't right in the head.

After a few minutes, Lydia's cursing seemed to run out of steam. She let her head sag forward and began to sob. That was almost more disturbing. Like most men, none of the hombres in the room reacted well to a woman's tears.

For that reason, all of them were relieved when another uniformed man bustled into the room, trailed by several more officers.

"Good Lord, Bob," he boomed to the first officer, "from what I heard, I expected a war over here. Instead, I find one woman and a bunch of men standing around looking like they're afraid of—" He stopped short and peered at Lydia, then nodded. "Oh. I understand now."

"That's right, Chief. I figured you'd want to handle this personally."

The St. Louis chief of police cleared his throat. "Well, it's not so much that I *want* to . . . but I suppose I had better, under the circumstances." He looked over at the gambler. "Drake, what do you have to do with this?"

For the next few minutes, Steve Drake explained the situation, with comments added every now and then by Ace and Chance. Ace expected Lydia to perk up and start arguing again, but all the fight seemed to have gone out of her.

He sure as blazes wasn't going to complain about that.

When the story was finished, the chief of police nodded slowly. "It seems to me that there's only one thing to do here. Drake, you and your young friends need to get out of town."

"Wait a minute," exclaimed Chance. "We didn't do anything wrong—"

Steve Drake held up a hand to stop him. "We were

already leaving in less than an hour," he reminded Chance.

"Yeah, but I don't like being run out of town," said the younger man with a frown.

The chief said, "You know good and well I can't lock up Miss McIsaac or anything of that sort. Her father wouldn't stand for it, and he and the mayor are best friends."

"I understand," said Drake. "She really does need someone to look after her, though, for her own good."

Bennett had gotten to his feet, shaking off the grogginess he had displayed earlier. With a scowl directed toward the gambler and the Jensen boys, he said, "I'll make sure she's all right. Her father pays me to take care of things for him. I . . . uh, I reckon this can be one of 'em."

"More power to you, my friend," said Drake.

"We ain't friends, and don't get the idea we are." Bennett paused as his brawny shoulders rose and fell in a shrug. "But I guess it ain't all your fault. I can see that now."

"Take Miss McIsaac home," the chief told him.

Bennett nodded and put an arm around Lydia as Ace and Chance let go of her. Ace watched her closely in case she tried to attack one of them again, but the spell that had gripped her earlier, whatever it was, appeared to be over. Bennett steered her toward the door, and she went along meekly.

"I don't envy that fella his job," Ace said.

The chief of police turned to Drake and the brothers. "Get your things and move on out while you've got the chance."

"It still feels like we're being railroaded," Chance complained.

"Not railroaded," Drake said with a smile. "*Steamboated* is a more accurate description."

"Whatever you call it, it's not fair."

"You may be young, my friend, but you're old enough to know that life seldom is."

Aboard the Missouri Belle

"We didn't waste much time getting in trouble again, did we?" said Ace as he and Chance stood at the railing with Steve Drake. "Haven't even been gone from St. Louis for twelve hours, and we were already fighting for our lives again."

"And having our bacon saved by you, Mr. Drake," added Chance.

"I think we've all done enough for each other that things are square between us," the gambler said. "And perhaps now that we've left St. Louis behind, we've left all our troubles behind as well."

Ace grunted. "I'll believe that when I see it."

"You know," mused Chance, "I never would have thought that having a beautiful girl come after you would be such a problem."

"You can always have too much of a good thing," Drake pointed out.

"Too much of a beautiful girl?" Chance shook his head. "You know, even after everything that happened back there, I'm not so sure I believe such a thing is possible!"

CHAPTER SIX

Some of the cabins on the *Missouri Belle* were large and opulent, while others were small and cramped.

To save money, Ace and Chance had decided to take one of the smaller cabins. They were a little crowded, but they could put up with the close quarters for a while, until they were ready to leave the riverboat.

Steve Drake had a larger cabin on the same deck, several doors away from the one where the Jensen brothers were staying. He was lounging at the rail, smoking a cheroot, when the younger men emerged from their cabin the next morning.

"We'll be docking in Kansas City soon," he told them after saying good morning. "Then you can finish conducting your business with Edward Krauss, Chance."

"I don't like that fella," said Chance. "I hate a sore loser."

"Krauss hasn't had to deal with losing very often in his life. He's a rich, powerful man. People go out of their way to make sure that he's kept happy."

"Not me."

"Or me, either," said Drake with a smile. "Why don't we go have some breakfast in the dining room? We should have plenty of time for that."

The boat docked while they were eating. They were still sitting at one of the tables covered with a white linen cloth, sipping coffee with empty plates in front of them, when Krauss and a couple men who had been with him the night before came into the dining room.

Both of Krauss's men had bruises on their faces, Ace noted with some satisfaction. Of course, he and Chance were a little sore as well.

"I've been to the telegraph office and the bank," Krauss said without any greeting or other small talk. He reached inside his coat, took out an envelope, and slapped it down on the table in front of Chance. "There!"

The gesture was vehement enough that some of the other passengers at surrounding tables looked around to see what was going on. Chance picked up the envelope, looked inside, and smiled. Then he reached inside his coat and brought out the gold watch with its attached chain. "I believe this is what you want."

Krauss snatched it out of his fingers, practically slapping Chance's hand aside in the process.

"Take it easy, Krauss," warned Drake.

Krauss studied the watch, turning it over in his fingers as he examined the front and back of it then opened it to check the face. He snapped it shut and grunted in satisfaction. "These two young scoundrels aren't worth holding a grudge against, but I'm going to remember what you did, Drake. There'll come a time when you'll regret defying me."

Drake smiled. "I've had a few regrets in my life. I doubt very seriously that this is going to turn out to be one of them."

Krauss gave a contemptuous snort and turned away as he put the watch in his vest pocket. He stalked out of the dining room with his men trailing him.

Ace said, "If he's as rich as you say he is, Mr. Drake, he might be able to cause some trouble for you."

"He might try, but I have enemies who worry me a lot more than Edward Krauss does," Drake said. "Besides, he'd have to find me first, and that's not easy. It's hard to predict where a man will be when he doesn't even know that himself . . . as you boys should be aware, if you're as fiddlefooted as you seem to be."

The *Missouri Belle* stayed docked in Kansas City long enough for some of the cargo to be unloaded and more taken on. Some of the passengers disembarked, too, while others boarded.

Then, with a shrill blast of its steam whistle, the riverboat was on its way again, the big paddles churning the water as it pulled away from the wharves and maneuvered back into the middle of the broad, muddy stream.

The rest of the day passed pleasantly enough. Chance spent most of it in the salon with Steve Drake, while Ace checked on their horses from time to time and explored the riverboat from top to bottom, at least the areas in which he was allowed.

The texas deck, just below the pilothouse, was the highest point he could reach, and from there he was able to see far out on both sides of the river. The terrain was largely flat, although broken up somewhat by rolling hills here and there. It was still agricultural land, and Ace decided he would be glad when the boat reached open range—someplace where cattle roamed and a man could see mountains and trees.

That evening in the salon, Chance and Steve Drake were involved in a poker game again. Standing nearby watching the game, Ace realized Edward Krauss was not playing. Ace didn't see him anywhere and in fact hadn't seen him since that morning. Evidently, he had either left the boat in Kansas City or was staying away from the salon.

It would be fine with him if they never saw the rich, obnoxious businessman again, Ace thought.

One of the other players was a well-dressed man with white hair and a thin white mustache. The smoothness of his face indicated that the hair color was premature. Ace figured the man was still in his thirties.

As Ace followed the progress of the game, it became obvious to him that in ability, Chance, Steve Drake, and the white-haired man were at least a notch above the other players at the table.

At one point, when several of the others had dropped out, Drake raised the bet and said, "That's a hundred to you, Mr. Haggarty."

Ace hadn't seen the man earlier and figured he must have boarded the *Missouri Belle* at Kansas City.

Haggarty's face was unreadable as he studied his cards. After a moment he said, "I'll see your hundred, Mr. Drake."

"I won't." Chance tossed his cards facedown into the center of the table. "It's between the two of you."

Steve Drake turned over his hand, revealing a full house.

Haggarty grimaced, but the expression was a fleeting one. He allowed emotion onto his smooth features only for a second. "You have me beat, sir," he said as he threw in his hand. "I honestly didn't believe you'd landed that third nine."

Steve Drake gathered in the pot. "Good fortune was with me."

"Fortune favors the bold"—Haggarty took a cigar from his vest pocket, bit off the tip, and then put the cigar in his mouth, leaving it unlit—"but luck always turns sooner or later."

"Indeed it does," agreed Steve Drake. "Shall we see how loyal it is tonight?"

Haggarty took the cigar from his mouth and gestured expansively with it, indicating that Steve Drake should go ahead.

Haggarty won the next hand, then Chance took two after that.

Ace got bored, as he usually did whenever he watched poker for very long, and wandered back out on the main deck. It was a warm night, but there was enough breeze caused by the boat chugging along the river that it was pleasant on deck. He strolled toward the bow and spotted someone standing at the railing.

Even though there was enough light from the moon and stars for the riverboat's pilot to keep it moving instead of tying up for the night, shadows lay over that part of the deck and Ace couldn't tell much about the person who seemed to be staring out wistfully over the water.

Whoever it was heard his footsteps on the deck,

turned, and vanished into the deeper darkness along the row of cabins.

Ace heard what sounded like the swish of skirts, then a door opened and closed. He felt a little guilty because clearly it had been a woman standing at the railing, enjoying the evening, and he had come along and spooked her. There was nothing he could do about it, so he continued his stroll, making several circuits of the deck before he went back to the cabin he shared with his brother and turned in for the night. Chance would be playing cards in the salon until late, and Ace wasn't going to wait up for him.

He hadn't seen any more sign of the mysterious woman.

The next day, the riverboat docked in Omaha, and Steve Drake took his leave of the Jensen brothers. "Enjoy the rest of your trip, boys," the gambler told them as they all shook hands at the top of the gangplank connecting the *Missouri Belle* to the dock.

"We appreciate everything you've done for us, Mr. Drake," Ace said.

"When we meet again—and I'm sure we will, since the frontier is a smaller place in many ways than most people would believe—I'll regard it as a reunion of old friends. You should call me Steve."

"All right," Ace said with a nod. "I reckon I can do that."

Chance said, "I appreciate the tips you've given me about cards."

Drake waved a hand. "That didn't amount to much, I'm afraid. Doc Monday taught you well. Just remember . . . there's a time to be reckless and a time to cut your losses. The key is knowing which is which."

"Yeah, being reckless is a problem sometimes," Ace said dryly as he looked at his brother.

"I prefer to think of it as being daring," said Chance.

Drake chuckled. "So long, boys." He headed down the gangplank.

The Jensen boys watched him go until he disappeared among the crowded streets. Ace was a little sorry to see the older man go. He had pulled them out of bad trouble a couple times, and he had been a good friend and temporary mentor. In some ways, the past few days had been like revisiting all those years Ace and Chance had spent with Doc Monday.

Doc had made a few attempts to give up his roving ways and settle down, but those efforts had never lasted long before his restless nature got the best of him. Ace knew that Steve Drake had much the same sort of nature, always needing to be on the move and see something new.

The Jensen boys were the same way. The whole sweeping breadth of the frontier was waiting for them—along with all the potential adventures it contained.

Ace was looking forward to getting there.

CHAPTER SEVEN

First, though, was the rest of the trip up the Missouri River. The days passed slowly but peacefully. Taking a riverboat was a leisurely way to travel. At least, the landscape placidly rolling past made it seem that way. In reality, taking a riverboat was faster than either horseback or wagon.

Sioux City and Yankton fell behind the *Missouri Belle* as the river angled northwest through Dakota Territory. Ace and Chance had been in that part of the country before, although they had never traveled through it by boat.

When they were youngsters, Doc had taken them to Deadwood, over in the Black Hills, during the era when that rude mining camp was turning into a violent, colorful boomtown. Ace had never forgotten seeing Wild Bill Hickok sauntering along the street, the famous prince of pistoleers with his long, flowing hair, his fancy clothes, and his pair of revolvers tucked into the sash around his waist. It was the most impressive sight Ace had ever seen.

Nor had he forgotten hearing about Hickok's

murder at the hands of the craven coward Jack
McCall in the Number 10 Saloon. Doc had left Deadwood not long after that, taking the boys with him.
The lid was about to come off the place, he had said,
and he didn't want them to be there for it.

In the decade since then, Deadwood had tamed
down a lot and become a respectable city, or so Ace
had heard. He didn't know for sure since they hadn't
been back since those wild days.

The river curved more to the west at Bismarck.
Fort Benton was only a few days away. The Jensen
brothers had decided to stay with the riverboat all the
way to the end of the line. The *Missouri Belle* couldn't
go any farther than Fort Benton because not far
beyond it were the Great Falls of the Missouri, which
blocked navigation except for canoes, which had to
be portaged around the falls.

Chance played poker every night in the salon. His
luck hadn't turned on him yet. He won steadily, if not
spectacularly, and had accumulated a big enough
stake to keep the brothers in supplies for quite some
time. They wouldn't have to worry about finding jobs
when they reached Fort Benton. They could afford
to just drift for a while, and the prospect sounded
mighty appealing to Ace.

Jack Haggarty was in the game every night as well,
but he hadn't had the same good fortune as Chance.
He lost, recouped some of his funds, then lost again,
repeating that pattern until his money had slowly
drained away.

At least, that was according to the complaints he
made during the game the last night before the boat
reached Fort Benton. "Can't seem to get a break."

Haggarty threw in his cards after another losing hand. "At least that pot wasn't too big. I'm getting close to tapped out."

"That's a shame." Chance had won more from Haggarty than from any of the other card players on the boat, although he had done a good job of beating them consistently, too.

Haggarty chuckled. "I'm sure you're just being polite, since more of my money has wound up in your pockets than anywhere else. Or maybe you think it's a shame because soon I won't have anything left for you to win from me."

Ace was sitting nearby on a chair he had turned around and straddled. He thought for a second that Haggarty was angry, but he was still smiling and didn't seem put out. He was the unflappable sort of gambler who greeted every turn of the cards the same way, whether it was good or bad for him.

"That's not what I meant," Chance said. "I've enjoyed playing against you, Mr. Haggarty, not because of who won or lost but because you've been good company."

"Well, I've always said that gambling is too uncertain a way to make a living unless you really enjoy it, so I try to find pleasure in what I do." Haggarty shrugged. "Admittedly, winning makes it more pleasant. So here's what I'd like to do, young fella, if it's all right with everyone else. Since I'm low on funds, I propose one more hand, you against me, and these other gentlemen will sit it out."

Ace straightened from his casual attitude when he heard that. Anytime somebody at a poker table proposed something out of the ordinary, players had to be careful. Ace remembered that from Doc's teachings, even though he wasn't much of a poker player himself. A change in the game often meant an attempt to try something slick. Haggarty looked and sounded sincere, but that didn't mean anything.

Chance's eyes narrowed, indicating that he was suspicious, too. But with the confidence he felt in himself, it was no surprise that he said, "I'd be agreeable to that, as long as everyone else is."

Haggarty looked around the table at the other four players and raised his eyebrows.

A couple men shrugged, one nodded, and the fourth man said, "It's fine by me, as long as we can watch."

"By all means, gentlemen." Haggarty asked Chance, "Would you like a fresh deck?"

"This one's been straight enough so far. I reckon it'll stay that way."

"Then I believe it's your deal," said Haggarty.

Chance gathered up the cards, shuffled, let Haggarty cut, and then said, "Five card draw." He dealt without any wasted motions, then picked up his cards and studied them while Haggarty did likewise.

Ace was sitting where he could see his brother's cards but no one else's; it wouldn't have been polite for him to sit anywhere else if he was going to watch the game. Somebody might have thought he was trying to tip off Chance to the other players' hands.

Ace leaned his head a little to one side to get a better look at Chance's cards. He kept his face expressionless, which wasn't very hard to do. Chance didn't have much except a pair of deuces. An ace was among the other cards, but it wasn't any help with a six and an eight.

Haggarty pushed a sizable percentage of the money in front of him into the center of the table.

"Trying to run me off right from the start, eh?" said Chance.

"Not at all," the older man replied. "I'm just not in a position to play it safe."

"All right. I can match that." Chance picked up some of the bills in his pile, riffled through them to make sure he had the right amount, and tossed them into the pot. "Cards?"

"One," said Haggarty.

That provoked a reaction from the other men at the table. A couple of them leaned forward to watch more intently, while one man chuckled.

"I still think you're bluffing," Chance said. He dealt the single card Haggarty had requested. "Dealer's taking three."

Ace had thought his brother might keep the ace and throw in the other four cards, but Chance kept the twos. He picked up a queen, a ten . . . and a third two.

"Your bet," he said calmly to Haggarty.

Ace was trying to figure the odds in his head— something he'd never been particularly good at. He reasoned that since Haggarty had taken only one card, he was trying to fill a straight, a flush, or a full house, any of which would beat Chance's three deuces. There was also a chance that if he was trying for a full house, he had three of a kind already, and they had to be higher than what Chance held. Pushing the bet wouldn't be all that reckless on Chance's part, but Ace figured the odds were slightly against his brother.

Haggarty pushed more money into the pot, then added the rest of his stack, leaving the table in front of him empty.

"That's a couple hundred to me," said Chance.

"Two hundred and twenty-five, to be precise."

Chance nodded. "Two twenty-five. But you're all in, Mr. Haggarty. I can raise you right out of the game."

"I hope you wouldn't do that. You know, in the spirit of the game. Besides, I can give you a marker . . ."

Chance frowned. "My brother and I are getting off the boat at Fort Benton."

"We're *all* getting off the boat at Fort Benton. That's the end of the line."

"Yeah, but I'd just as soon not have any unresolved business hanging over our heads. It's just simpler that way. No offense."

"None taken," Haggarty said easily. "I was hoping not to have to do this, but I have something else I can wager. I'm something of a collector, I suppose you could say, of beautiful objects. Specifically golden objects. *Treasure from the Orient*, for want of a better term."

"You have some Oriental treasure you want to bet?" Chance sounded skeptical.

For the first time during the trip, Haggarty seemed a little irritated. "If you don't believe me, you can force me to fold, but it's not very sporting of you."

Chance placed his cards facedown on the felt. "What's this treasure of yours worth, anyway?"

"Well, it's difficult to assign a value to something like that—"

"Yeah, I thought so."

Haggarty was definitely angry, Ace thought.

The gambler snapped, "I've been offered two thousand dollars."

One of the other men at the table let out a whistle. "Two grand is a lot of money."

"Can you cover that much?" Haggarty asked Chance with an insolent edge in his voice.

Chance looked at the money on the table in front of him. "I don't have that much with me, but I can cover it."

"And *I'll* be happy to take your marker, if it comes to that," Haggarty said.

Ace's hands tightened on the back of the chair he was straddling. If Chance folded, they would lose a chunk of money, sure, but they would have enough left for provisions and other supplies before they set out from Fort Benton.

On the other hand, if he called Haggarty and lost, it would wipe out most of their stake. They might have to look for jobs right away. That wasn't an appealing prospect.

Ace cleared his throat, hoping that his brother would turn around and look at him, but Chance just sat there stiffly until Haggarty spoke.

"What's it going to be, Jensen?"

"You're betting this golden Oriental treasure of yours?"

"That's right."

"And it's worth two thousand?"

"At a bare minimum," Haggarty said. "But we'll call it that for purposes of the bet."

"All right," Chance said. "I call."

Ace tried not to grimace.

Chance laid down his cards and said, "Three deuces."

Haggarty stared at the cards for a long couple of seconds, then a smile began to spread across his face. Ace's heart sank.

"I honestly thought I had you beat," Haggarty said as he placed his own cards on the felt. Ace stood up to see them better, then realized he was looking at two jacks and two nines.

Chance leaned back in his chair and blew out a relieved breath. "Sorry if that cleaned you out."

"Part of the game, my boy, part of the game," Haggarty assured him. He was trying to put up a brave front, but his eyes were bleak.

Chance gathered in the pot but left a twenty-dollar gold piece on the table. He nodded toward the double eagle and said, "I don't believe in leaving any man busted, and I hope you'll take that in the spirit it's meant, Mr. Haggarty. One card player to another."

"I will, and I'm obliged to you." Haggarty picked up the coin. "If I could ask one more favor of you . . ."

"Sure."

"We'll be docking at Fort Benton in the morning. I'd like to turn over that bit of treasure to you then, if that's all right. It has some sentimental value to me. I'd like to keep it with me for one more night."

When Chance frowned and hesitated, Haggarty continued quickly. "I give you my word I'm not trying to get out of the bet. Anyway, where could I go? We're in the middle of the river, and I assure you, I don't intend to slip overboard and swim ashore. I've heard too many stories about areas of quicksand along here to risk that." He straightened his lapels. "Besides, it would ruin my jacket."

"Well, all right," Chance said. "My brother and I will come to your cabin first thing in the morning to collect."

"I appreciate that, I really do."

Ace said, "I don't want to butt in, but I have a question. How big is this treasure of yours, Mr. Haggarty? Can we carry it on horseback?"

"Oh, yes, of course. That won't be any problem. Did you think I was going to stick you with some huge statue of Buddha or something?"

"I don't know this Buddha hombre," Chance said.

"No, this object is small and delicate and very, very beautiful. I promise you, you'll be pleased with it."

"All right. We'll see you in the morning."

Haggarty stood up and nodded to the men at the table. "Gentlemen, it's truly been a pleasure, despite the outcome. Perhaps we can play again sometime." He left the salon.

Chance twisted around in his chair and looked at Ace, who knew what his brother was thinking. Despite what Haggarty had said about not running out on his debt, it might be a good idea to keep an eye on him.

He might decide that he would rather risk the river than accept being broke.

CHAPTER EIGHT

Ace reached the deck in time to see Haggarty let himself into one of the cabins near the boat's bow. As far as he knew, all the cabins on the *Missouri Belle* were set up the same, with only one door and no windows.

So there was only one way in or out. Ace intended to watch that door all night if he had to. He walked along the deck until he was even with the door, then propped a hip against the railing and crossed his arms over his chest.

It would be a mite embarrassing if Haggarty came out and found him watching the cabin—but not as embarrassing as letting the man make fools of him and Chance.

The night passed slowly. Ace found his eyelids drooping more than once, but he managed to stay awake.

After several hours, Chance came along the deck, wearing his straw planter's hat. "I'll relieve you," he told his brother. "I got some sleep, so I'll be good for the rest of the night."

"Are you sure?" Ace asked.

"Yeah, you go on. You won't be far away if I need help." That was true. Their cabin was on the same side of the boat, although down at the far end toward the stern.

"All right," said Ace. "But you fetch me right away if there's any trouble."

"You've got my word on that," promised Chance.

Ace went back to their cabin and took off his hat, boots, and gunbelt, but that was all he removed before he stretched out on the bunk. He wasn't expecting trouble, but he wanted to be ready for it if it came.

He fell asleep quickly, and his slumber was deep and dreamless for a while. He didn't know how much time had passed before shouts and the thud of running footsteps on the deck outside the cabin door jolted him awake.

Ace sat up quickly, yanked his boots on, and grabbed his Colt from the holster where his gunbelt hung over the back of a chair. Without taking the time to do anything else, he charged out of the cabin and turned toward the bow. His first priority was making sure that Chance was all right.

The sky over the river was pale gray, but to the east an arch of gold lit up the heavens, indicating that dawn wasn't far off. Ace could see wreaths of smoke hanging around the boat, and some of the people rushing along the deck—a mixture of passengers and crew—shouted, "Fire!"

An out-of-control blaze was one of the most feared things on a riverboat. They had been known to burn right down to the waterline, forcing everyone onboard to swim for their lives. Ace didn't see any flames, but he could certainly smell the smoke as he pushed his way through the panicky crowd to the spot where he had left his brother. Chance still stood there, looking around worriedly.

Ace gripped his arm and asked, "Are you all right?"

"Yeah, I'm fine. But I thought I caught a glimpse of Haggarty in this mob, and now I can't see him anymore!"

"Don't worry about Haggarty," said Ace. "Where's the fire?"

"I don't know. I just started smelling smoke a few minutes ago, and so did everybody else. Blast it, he'd better not try to take advantage of this to run out with that treasure I won!"

Ace was more concerned with their safety and the safety of everyone else on the *Missouri Belle*, but he understood why Chance was upset. They would have to worry about that later, however. The most important thing was to find out just how bad the situation was. If the riverboat was in danger of burning or sinking, they would need to help as many people as possible reach the shore safely.

Ace grabbed one of the crew members hurrying past. "Where's the fire?"

"Nobody knows," the man replied with a frightened edge in his voice. "Smoke just started coming out of the ventilation shafts. It doesn't seem to be coming from the engine room, though, so maybe the boilers won't explode."

Chance grunted. "That'd be good. Nobody's seen any flames or knows where it started?"

The crewman shook his head.

Frowning, the Jensen brothers looked at each

other. Something was suspicious. They had no reason to think that Jack Haggarty had anything to do with it, but on the other hand, if the gambler wanted to slip away from the boat, the uproar would provide a mighty nice distraction for him to do so.

"Let's take a look in Haggarty's cabin," Ace said grimly.

"Just what I was thinking," agreed Chance.

They went to the door and Ace rapped sharply on the panel. "Mr. Haggarty!"

There was no response, although it might have been difficult to hear with all the commotion on deck. However, Ace was pretty sure no one said anything in the cabin.

Chance slapped the door hard with his open palm. The crack sounded a little like a gunshot. He leaned close to the door and shouted, "Haggarty, if you're in there, open up!"

Still nothing happened. Ace grasped the knob and tried it, but it wouldn't turn. "Locked."

"We can take care of that," snapped Chance. He backed off slightly, raised his right foot, and drove the heel of his boot against the door beside the knob. With a splintering of wood, the catch tore out of the jamb and the door flew open.

A crew member passing by exclaimed, "Hey! You're gonna have to pay for that!"

A gout of smoke rolled out of the cabin. Ace said, "The fire must be in there!"

The smoke kept them from seeing in. Ace snatched his broad-brimmed hat off his head and whipped it back and forth, shredding the gray cloud to a certain extent. It was also thinning because with the door open it had somewhere to go.

Ace thought Haggarty might be in there, possibly overcome by the smoke while he was sleeping. He pressed the hat over the lower half of his face, trapping a bit of breathable air inside it, then plunged into the cabin to see what he could find.

"Be careful, Ace!" his brother called after him.

Ace shoved his gun into the waistband of his trousers as he stumbled through the smoke. It stung his eyes and made them water, which blurred his vision. He saw flames leaping up in front of him, but they didn't appear to be spreading. In fact, they seemed contained, which struck him as odd.

The next moment he understood as his foot bumped into something and made it scrape across the floor. He looked down and saw that the flames were burning in a metal bucket of the sort that was used to carry hot coals. Thick black smoke came from it.

Ace knew he couldn't pick up the bucket, but he shoved it toward the door with his foot and called to his brother. "Chance, we need a bucket of water!"

A minute later, one of the crewmen appeared with a wooden bucket full of muddy water dipped out of the river. He threw it onto whatever was burning in the metal bucket, which caused even more smoke to billow up for a moment. But then the air began to clear since the fire was out.

Men—including Chance and several members of the crew—crowded into the cabin. The lingering smoke made them cough and wipe their stinging eyes.

One of the crewmen looked into the bucket. "Looks like what's left of a bunch of greasy rags! Somebody did this on purpose."

"Whose cabin is this?" asked another of the crew.

"It belongs to a man named Haggarty," said Chance. "Ace, did you see him in here?"

Ace shook his head. "Not a sign of him. Of course it was hard to see much of anything with all that smoke."

"Well, it's getting better now, and he's still not here." In a disgusted voice, Chance added, "He must have slipped out when everybody started running around on deck."

Ace knew his brother was right. A ventilation shaft ran through all the cabins, and with this one's position near the bow, the air moving through it had carried the smoke from the bucket to all the cabins farther astern. Haggarty must have known that the smoke would cause a panic, affording him a chance to escape.

It seemed like a lot of trouble to go to in order to avoid paying a debt, but maybe he was really attached to that treasure he owed to Chance.

With only a little smoke remaining in the air, Chance cleared his throat and said, "Let's look for him."

One of the crewmen said angrily, "If you find the man responsible for this, you'd better turn him over to the captain. He could have set the whole boat on fire. He deserves to be in jail!"

"After he gets a good beatin'!" added another member of the crew.

The Jensen boys couldn't argue with that. They set off to search for Haggarty. Some of the crew spread out to look for the gambler as well.

When the alarm had gone out about the smoke circulating through the boat, the man at the wheel in the pilothouse had sent the *Missouri Belle* angling toward the closest shore, so the passengers wouldn't have to swim as far if they had to get off.

With the fire out, the smoke clearing, and word relayed to the captain that the boat wasn't in any real danger, it chugged back out to the deepest part of the stream where it wasn't as likely to get hung up on a sandbar, which could be a real problem in the upper reaches of the Missouri.

By the time the sun was up, it was obvious that Jack Haggarty was no longer onboard. The fact that the riverboat had kept moving meant it was well upstream from where he had left the boat. Tracking him would be just about impossible, even if Ace and Chance were able to convince the captain to turn back, which was highly unlikely.

Chance fumed as he paced up and down the deck. "It's not so much the value of that so-called treasure. I just hate to let somebody get the best of me."

"Like that fella Krauss and his watch from Leland Stanford, back at the beginning of this trip?" Ace suggested.

"It's not the same thing at all," snapped Chance, then he stopped his pacing and grinned ruefully. "Well, I guess it's kind of the same, isn't it?"

Ace returned the grin and shrugged. "At least

you've still got the money you won off Haggarty, plus the rest of your winnings."

Thinking about that seemed to make Chance feel better. "Yeah, it's been a pretty profitable trip so far, hasn't it? I reckon we've got a bigger stake right now than we've had for a long, long time. We won't have to worry about money again for at least six months."

"If we were careful, I'll bet we could make it last a year," said Ace.

"Yeah, but where's the fun in being careful?"

Ace didn't have an answer for that question, and the fact that Chance had asked it was a good example of the fundamental differences between the brothers, even though they were twins. That kinship didn't mean they thought alike. Probably, they never would.

"We should reach Fort Benton in another hour or so," Ace said. "I guess we should go back to our cabin and get all our gear together."

Chance nodded in agreement. As they walked along the deck, he said under his breath, "I still wonder what that blasted treasure was."

"I don't reckon we'll ever know," Ace said.

"Unless we run into Haggarty again one of these days. It could happen."

It certainly could, thought Ace, remembering what Steve Drake had said about the frontier being a smaller place in many ways than people would have expected.

He hadn't locked the cabin when he rushed out earlier to see what all the commotion was about. He hoped nobody had gotten in there and stolen any of their things. There wasn't anything all that valuable in the cabin—Chance carried their stake in a money belt strapped around his waist, under his clothes— but Ace didn't want to lose his hat or his rifle or his gunbelt. He had some books in his warbag he probably wouldn't be able to replace in Fort Benton, either.

The door was closed as they approached. Had he left it that way? He couldn't remember, but he thought he had been in such a hurry that he'd left it open. That didn't bode well, he thought with a slight frown.

Somebody might be in there, pawing through their things, he realized, making him close his hand around the butt of the Colt tucked in his waistband.

"What's wrong with you?" asked Chance.

"I'm pretty sure I left the door open."

"Well, that wasn't a very smart thing to do, was it?"

"Maybe not, but I was kind of in a hurry. You know, thinking the boat was on fire and all."

"Yeah, that could make a fella act a mite hasty, all right." Chance moved his coat aside a little to make it easier to reach the gun in his shoulder holster. "You're thinking somebody might be in there? A thief, maybe?"

"Can't rule it out. Let's keep our eyes open when we go in."

Chance nodded. He hung back a little as Ace wrapped his fingers around the knob then looked at him. Chance nodded for him to go ahead.

Ace twisted the knob, threw the door open, and went through it fast, ready to pull the revolver if he needed to. His brother was close behind him. Ace stopped so abruptly that Chance bumped into him.

Chance exclaimed, "What—" He fell silent as Ace moved aside a step to let him see what was waiting for them inside the cabin.

A young woman sat on the bunk staring at them, her dark, almond-shaped eyes wide with surprise and fear.

CHAPTER NINE

"P-Please," she said, her English slow and halting. "Do not . . . shoot this lowly one."

"Son of a—" exclaimed a startled Chance, stopping himself just before the rest of the oath escaped from his lips.

Ace could only stare back at the young woman. He was just as surprised as she and his brother obviously were.

The fact that a woman was in their cabin where she didn't belong was unexpected enough. The fact that she was young and very attractive made the situation even more astonishing. Throw in her long, sleek hair which was as dark as a raven's wing, her delicately slanted eyes, her intriguingly lovely face, her smooth golden skin, and the odd-looking trousers and tunic she wore, and the whole thing was downright flabbergasting.

"You're Chinese," Chance said as if he had just figured out a great mystery.

"An Oriental . . ." Ace mused. His eyes widened

even more as he looked over at his brother just as Chance looked at him. They said the next words together. "A golden Oriental treasure!"

From the bunk, the young woman said, "You are not going to . . . shoot this one?"

"Wait. What?" Chance said. "Of course we're not going to shoot you! Where'd you get a loco idea like that?"

Ace looked down and realized he still had his hand wrapped around the Colt's butt. He let go of it in a hurry and held up both hands, palms out toward the young woman. "Don't worry, we're not going to hurt you. You, uh, do speak English, don't you?"

"Of course she speaks English," said Chance. "She's been asking us not to shoot her, hasn't she?"

The young woman nodded. "This one speaks English." She didn't seem quite as scared, although her body was still tense and stiff as she sat on the bunk watching the Jensen brothers. Her eyes darted back and forth between them.

"What are you doing here?" asked Chance, speaking slowly and a little more loudly than necessary.

"You do not have to shout, kind sir. This one understands you quite well."

"Oh. Uh, sorry," Chance said, looking a mite sheepish.

"You still need to tell us what you're doing here." Ace could tell from the way his brother was looking at the woman that he found her attractive. Most any man would, but pretty girls tended to distract Chance quite a bit.

"This one was told to come here and wait."

"Told by who?" asked Ace.

"Jack Haggarty, I'll bet," said Chance.

The young woman nodded. "It was Mr. Jack. He was this one's master."

"Master?" Chance repeated.

"Yes. This one belonged to Mr. Jack. This one was his . . . how do you say it? His slave."

"Oh, no," Chance responded as he started to shake his head. "This is America. We don't have any masters and slaves. We fought a whole war amongst ourselves about that."

"And other things," Ace added. "But my brother's right about us not having slaves anymore. If Haggarty told you that we do, he was lying to you."

The young woman's face and voice were tightly controlled as she replied, "In this one's homeland, there are few masters and many slaves. It is the custom of our people, and where we are makes no difference."

"The hell it doesn't!" Chance took off his hat and scrubbed a hand over his face. "Let me get this straight. *You're* the Oriental treasure he bet in that poker game last night?"

"Good fortune was not with him. He told this one that she now belongs to you, in payment of the debt he owed you."

"Belongs to—wait. No, this is crazy!"

"You are the one called Chance Jensen, are you not?"

"Yeah, but—"

"Then this one is now yours to do with as you will," she said, smiling serenely, evidently happy that the matter had been settled, at least in her own mind.

Chance turned to his brother. "Ace, what in blazes are we gonna do about this?"

Ace rubbed his chin and frowned in thought. After a moment he asked, "What's your name?"

"This one is called Ling."

"I'm Ace, and you already know this is my brother Chance. Now listen, Miss Ling—"

"Just Ling," she told him. "You should not refer to this lowly one with a term of respect."

"Well, we were raised to respect women," Ace explained. "All women."

"Not slaves," Ling said with a stubborn shake of her head.

"But you're not a slave."

"This one cannot change the fate to which she was born." She looked intently at Chance and went on. "Mr. Chance, this one will be your slave from now until the day she dies, unless you sell her or trade her first."

"Well, that's just . . . Arrgghh!" Chance threw his hands in the air in exasperation. "It's not the way we do things here! Anyway"—he clapped his hat back on his head, pushed his coat back, put his hands on his hips, and glared at her—"I was promised a treasure worth two thousand bucks."

Ling's bottom lip quivered as she said, "This one will endeavor to be a suitable payment of Mr. Haggarty's debt. This one is an excellent servant and can cook and clean and mend clothing and . . . and"—she lowered her gaze to the floor as she went on in a whisper—"and there are other services this one can perform as well, if needed."

Chance's eyes widened. He opened his hands and

thrust them out toward her as if to push her away as he said, "Now wait just a minute! Nobody, uh, nobody said anything about anything like that! We may not be the most respectable hombres you ever ran into, but we're gentlemen, dadblast it!"

"One of us is, anyway." Ace didn't know whether to be confounded or amused or troubled by this situation, so he settled for being a little of all those things.

"You're not helping," Chance said through clenched teeth.

"All right. Let's figure this out. Haggarty knew you wouldn't accept this young lady as settlement of your bet, so he set those rags on fire in that bucket to smoke up the boat and raise a ruckus. He slipped away in the confusion and swam ashore after telling Miss Ling to come down here and wait for us." Ace frowned. "Why didn't he just take the girl with him?"

He hadn't directed the question to Ling, but she answered anyway. "This one cannot swim," she said solemnly. "And she believes that Mr. Haggarty had grown tired of her and no longer wished for her to be his slave."

"Well, if that's true, then he's a damn fool," said Chance. "I mean . . . I don't mean—I mean, he shouldn't have wanted you to be his slave, but as a, uh, traveling companion . . . well, any fella who didn't want somebody as pretty and charming as you around . . . he's a damn fool, like I said!"

"I guess it costs some to have a slave," Ace said. "You've got to feed 'em and all."

"This one does not eat much," Ling assured them. "This one is very . . . what is the word? . . . *inexpensive.*"

"Doesn't matter," Chance said, his voice curt. "We're not keeping you."

Ling stared at him for a couple heartbeats, then put her hands over her face and began to cry.

"Now, hold on, hold on!" Chance said hastily. He turned to look at his brother. "Give me a hand here, blast it. This whole mess has got me so bumfuzzled I can't think straight!"

"All right." Ace moved over to the bunk and raised his hand as if he were about to pat Ling on the shoulder. Then he thought better of it and lowered his arm. "Miss Ling, there's no need for you to cry."

Between sobs, she said, "But . . . if Mr. Chance is not this one's master . . . where will this one go? What will she do?"

"You know, it's really confusing when you talk about yourself like that," Chance told her, which just made matters worse because she started to cry harder.

Ace glared at him.

Chance spread his hands and asked, "What did I do?"

Ace ignored the question. "Miss Ling, if you'll settle down, we'll try to figure out what to do next. For one thing, the boat will be getting to Fort Benton soon. We'll all get off there and maybe talk to the law or something." He looked around. "Do you have a bag or any other personal belongings with you?"

Ling sniffled and reached under the bunk. She pulled out a canvas sack with a string tied around the top where it was gathered. "This is everything this lowly one owns in this world."

"All right, then. You just wait here and we'll come and get you when the boat docks."

She looked up at him with sudden terror in her eyes. "You will leave this one and not come back!"

Ace shook his head and assured her, "No, we won't. I give you my word."

"No one keeps their word to a slave," she said bitterly.

"Well, I'm not saying you're a slave—I just don't like that idea—but I keep my word no matter who I give it to."

"So do I," said Chance. "That's the way we were brought up. You don't have a thing to worry about."

That last statement wasn't strictly true, thought Ace, but at least Ling didn't have to worry about the Jensen boys lying to her.

He backed away from her and motioned for her to stay on the bunk. She looked anxious, like she wanted to follow him. Ace caught Chance's eye and jerked his head toward the cabin door.

"Do not abandon this one," Ling pleaded.

"We won't," Chance promised.

A shudder went through her. "This lowly one does not know how she would survive alone in such a strange, barbaric land."

"Well," Chance said with a shrug, "that's not necessarily a bad description of Montana Territory."

Ace rolled his eyes, took hold of his brother's shoulder, and steered him out the door.

CHAPTER TEN

Ace closed the door rather gingerly behind them. The deck wasn't anywhere near as crowded as it had been earlier, and the sense of panic had faded away along with the smoke.

Chance strode over to the railing, took his hat off, and raked his fingers through his close-cropped hair. "How in blue blazes do we get ourselves in messes like this?" he demanded.

"You're the one who's got himself a beautiful Chinese slave girl, not me," Ace pointed out.

"Hey, we're brothers, right? We're in this thing together!"

"Yeah, well, we'll see. Some things a fella's got to hash out on his own." Ace leaned against the rail and peered along the river ahead of them. "But I guess I can give you a hand with this, although for the life of me I can't think of what to do."

"We've got to convince that girl she's not my slave or anybody else's," Chance said as he put his hat back on.

"Yeah, but how? She seems pretty determined that she is."

Before Chance could answer that—although from the perplexed, irritated look on his face he didn't *have* an answer—someone hailed them, calling, "You two! Jensens!"

They turned to see a tall, spare man in blue trousers and black jacket striding toward them. He had a tanned, weather-beaten face and crisp white hair under the stiff-billed cap he wore. They recognized Matthew Foley, the captain of the *Missouri Belle*. Steve Drake had introduced him during the early days of the journey up the Big Muddy.

"What can we do for you, Captain?" asked Ace as Foley strode up to them with an intent, angry look on his hawk-like face.

"I'm told you two had something to do with that fire earlier," Foley snapped.

Ace shook his head quickly and emphatically. "No, sir. We knew the fella who seems to have set it, but that's all. I'm sure a lot of folks onboard knew him. Plenty played cards with him in the salon the past few nights, including my brother, but that's our only connection to him." He traded a quick glance with Chance, having not said anything about Haggarty's unorthodox way of settling a bet. More than likely, trying to explain about Ling would just confuse the issue.

"You're talking about Jack Haggarty?"

"That's right," said Chance. "From the looks of it, he set some greasy rags on fire in a coal bucket in his cabin, intending for the smoke to spread through the boat like it did."

Foley stroked his rather pointed chin. "Why the devil would he do that?"

"He didn't explain it to us, but we figure he was trying to get out of paying a gambling debt he owed to my brother." Ace didn't think they could avoid telling the captain that much, anyway.

"And where is he now?"

"We don't know, because his little trick worked," said Chance. "I caught a glimpse of him right after the stampede started, but then I never saw him anymore."

"He must have slipped overboard and swam ashore, since he's not on the boat," added Ace. "We've searched it from one end to the other, and so have some of your crewmen."

Foley nodded slowly and admitted, "That agrees with what I was told. But one of my men thought it was suspicious that you knew exactly where to look for the source of that smoke."

"I wasn't looking for the source of the smoke when I went into Haggarty's cabin," Ace said. "I was looking for Haggarty himself. But then I found the coal bucket, and it wasn't hard to figure out what he'd done."

"So you weren't in on it with him?" asked the captain, his voice sharp as he looked from brother to brother. "You're not covering up for him?"

"Covering up?" Chance repeated. "We want to find the cheat as much as you do!" He flung out a hand in frustration. "He's saddled me with that stubborn woman—" Chance stopped short as Ace winced, but it was too late. The damage was done.

"What woman?" Foley asked. His tone made it

clear he wasn't going to let them get away with not answering.

"Umm . . . Haggarty was traveling with a woman," Chance said. "He left her behind when he got off the boat."

"A gambler's woman, eh?" Foley's tone made it clear what he thought of such a person.

Ace said, "It's not really like that. Miss Ling . . . she's Chinese."

The captain's bushy white eyebrows rose. "A Celestial? I don't recall seeing one on the boat."

"He probably kept her face covered when they were boarding," Ace said. "Then she stayed in the cabin. You see, she claims that she was Haggarty's . . . slave."

Surprise and anger appeared on Foley's face. He exclaimed, "By God, there are no slaves on my boat! Or anywhere else in this country, for that matter."

Chance said, "We tried explaining that to her, but she wasn't willing to listen. She's got it in her head that Haggarty owned her."

The captain frowned. "Wait a minute. You said 'owned'?"

"Yeah." Chance shook his head. "Now she figures she belongs to me. Haggarty told her he was giving her to me to settle a bet he lost in a poker game last night."

"That's insane!"

"You try convincing her of that. My brother and I haven't had any luck at it."

With an exasperated sigh, Foley took off his cap and scratched at his head, much like Chance had done a few minutes earlier out of sheer frustration.

As the riverboat man clapped his cap back on, he said, "There's one good thing about this whole mess."

"What's that?" asked Ace.

"We'll be docking at Fort Benton in less than an hour, and I can wash my hands of the affair."

"But Captain—" Chance began.

Foley just shook his head. "That Celestial woman, whoever or whatever she is, is your problem now, Jensen."

Ling was still sitting on the bunk when Ace and Chance came into the cabin a few minutes later. She didn't appear to have moved since they'd left. She looked up at them with a mixture of fear and anticipation on her lovely face. "You came back."

"Of course we did," Chance replied. "We told you we would, didn't we?"

"Many men have told this one what they would do, but seldom did those things ever happen."

"Well, we do what we say we're gonna do," Chance insisted.

"And what is that?" she asked, gazing at him innocently.

"I, uh . . . Ace, what are we going to do?"

"We'll all get off the boat in Fort Benton, I guess, since that's as far as it goes," Ace said. "Unless you'd rather go back to St. Louis, Miss Ling. If you would, we'd be glad to pay for your return passage."

She looked frightened again as she shook her head in response. "This one does not know anyone in St. Louis. It would be impossible for this one to live there."

"You could get a job," said Chance. "Maybe work as a maid or something like that."

Ling drew in a deep breath and said solemnly, "I would have to go to one of the houses where . . . where women who have no one and nowhere else to go must find their fate."

Ace noticed that for the first time she didn't refer to herself as "this one." He took that to be an indication of how upset and afraid she was. Without hesitation he told her, "We're not going to let that happen."

Chance lowered his voice and said to his brother, "Wait a minute. What's to keep the same thing from happening if she stays in Fort Benton?"

"We'll be there to make sure it doesn't."

"I thought we were going to be moving on pretty soon."

"We will when we can," Ace said. "For now, it's more important that we get this settled. We can get Miss Ling a hotel room, so she'll have a safe place to stay."

She spoke up, saying, "If there is a stable, this one can sleep there with the horses."

"You're not sleeping with the horses," Ace told her with a shake of his head. "You'll have a decent hotel room, and we'll find you a good job before we ride out."

"You cannot leave without taking this one with you!"

"Now, dadgum it," Chance said, "there's no telling where we're going, and we can't be dragging around a woman!"

"This one will be no trouble. This one will do whatever she is told." She lowered her eyes. "This one is obedient."

"Blast it, that's not it. Life on the trail is just too rough for a woman."

Ling shook her head. "It cannot be worse than some of the things this one has already endured."

"All right. Let's just not worry about it right now. Chance and I will gather up our gear, so we'll be ready to get off the boat when it reaches Fort Benton."

Ling nodded and settled the canvas bag in her lap. "This one is ready."

The Jensen brothers didn't have much packing to do. Most of their possessions were still in their warbags. By the time the riverboat's steam whistle let out a shrill blast to alert passengers of the boat's arrival, Ace and Chance had their bags in one hand and their rifles in the other.

Ling stood up from the bunk. Suddenly, she gave in to impulse and hugged both of them, first Ace and then Chance. "Thank you," she murmured as she clung to Chance. "This one has always wished for such a kind master."

With his hands full, Chance couldn't pry her loose from him. All he could do was slowly turn red and say, "I, uh, I'm not your master, Ling. We keep trying to get that in your head. But I'll treat you nice as long as we're traveling together, I promise you that."

"It is all this one has ever hoped for." She let go of him, stepped back, and smiled. "Now, shall we go see this place Montana?"

CHAPTER ELEVEN

Fort Benton was the oldest settlement in the territory, having been established in 1847 by the American Fur Company as an outpost for fur trappers and traders.

Nearly four decades later, it was a small but thriving community located on a bend of the Missouri River. The terrain on both sides of the stream was flat, but numerous low gray hills and buttes were visible not far away. As the highest navigable point on the river, it served as the supply center for local mining interests as well as for the sprawling cattle ranches that had been established in the territory during the past twenty years.

A sturdy wharf had been built along the waterfront so the riverboats would have a place to dock. With the skill of a longtime river man, Captain Foley brought the *Missouri Belle* next to the wharf. Crewmen were waiting on deck to jump the narrow gap to the dock and tie the boat to sturdy wooden pilings, making the vessel fast with thick ropes.

Up in the pilothouse, Foley grasped the rope

attached to the whistle and gave it another tug. Townspeople waiting on the dock greeted the blast with cheers. The arrival of a boat was a welcome break in the all-too-frequent monotony of frontier life.

Once the boat was tied up, crewmen laid the gangplank in place so passengers could disembark and others could board. The *Missouri Belle* would remain in Fort Benton for several hours as cargo was unloaded. Before the day was over, however, it would be steaming downriver again.

Ling looked excited as she stood on the deck gazing at the town.

It really wasn't that much to see, thought Ace, but she seemed pleased that they were here. It could be the start of a new life for her . . . if she was willing to accept it.

The Jensen brothers started toward the gangplank. Ling hung back, and Chance paused to motion her forward with the hand that held his rifle. "Come on."

"This one will follow, as befits her lowly position."

Chance shook his head. "No, you're going down the gangplank with us."

"Chance is right," said Ace. "You're as good as anybody, and it's time you started acting like it."

Judging by her baffled expression, Ling still couldn't comprehend that concept, but the boys insisted and she moved up between them. The gangplank was wide enough for all three to walk down it together.

"This is very . . . odd," Ling murmured.

"You'd better get used to it," Chance said. "There's

not going to be any more of that crazy business about being a slave."

She might have wanted to argue but didn't. She was too busy looking around at the hustle and bustle of the busy river settlement.

Burly men were already unloading the cargo from the riverboat's deck. People came off the boat and greeted loved ones with hugs and kisses. Friends shook hands and slapped each other on the back. New passengers boarded, sometimes after tearful good-byes with relatives they were leaving behind.

"Let's get out of the way and put our gear down," Ace said, "and then I can go back aboard and get our horses."

Normally they would have saddled the horses and led them off the boat when they disembarked, but they had Ling to keep up with, too. She was such an innocent that the brothers didn't want her wandering off on her own. She probably wouldn't have gotten lost in the small town, but a young woman could easily find herself in trouble in a rough frontier settlement.

They found a good spot in front of a hardware store for Chance and Ling to wait.

Ace set his warbag down and leaned his Winchester against the wall of the building. "I'll be back." He headed to the boat to fetch his big chestnut horse and Chance's cream-colored gelding.

Chance had to smile as he watched Ling looking around with great interest at the town and the passersby. "You must have seen some big cities before. Where did the boat land when you came over from China? San Francisco?"

"That is right. This one has been to Denver as well, and a place called O . . . Omaha."

"I'm not sure what's so fascinating about a place like Fort Benton, then."

"If what you say is true, this is the first place I have ever been where I was not a slave." Her voice held a tone of awe as she spoke those words, as if she could hardly believe them.

Chance told her solemnly, "It's true, all right. You're no longer a slave, Ling. You're free to come and go as you please."

She looked quickly at him. "But it pleases me to be with you, Mr. Chance."

"That's all right, I suppose . . . for now. We'll have to figure somehow for you to make your way in the world without . . . without a master. For the time being, though, Ace and I will look after you."

"This one is so very grateful," Ling said.

The adoration on her face and in her voice made Chance a mite uncomfortable. He'd already felt the stirrings of desire when she'd hugged him earlier. He had never been good at resisting such temptations. In such a case, however, he knew it would be wrong for him to take advantage of such a trusting soul. Ace might not think Chance had much of a conscience, but he knew he had to draw the line somewhere, every now and then.

"Well, look here, Banjo. Looks like there's a brand-new China gal come to work in Miss Hettie's house." The voice was high-pitched and a little squeaky, but it definitely belonged to a man.

Chance looked around to see two men standing nearby in the street, staring at him and Ling.

Well, they were staring at Ling, to be honest, he thought. He couldn't really blame them. Even in the unflattering, pajama-like clothing, she was pretty enough to catch any man's eye.

The two men were unimpressive specimens. One was around medium height, with a sharply angled face that looked like it had been hacked out of wood with a dull hatchet. Carrot-colored hair stuck out from under a battered, stained hat worn with a Montana pinch in the crown.

The other hombre was shorter and stockier but just as roughly dressed. His red, swollen nose indicated that he was either a heavy drinker or someone had just punched him. Chance figured rotgut was to blame for the condition.

"You're right, Luther," the shorter man said, which pegged him as Banjo. "Gal who looks like her ought to make money hand over fist once she goes to work for Miss Hettie."

Ling moved closer to Chance and said quietly, "This one does not like those men looking at her."

"Hey, she speaks English!" Luther exclaimed. "That's even better. She'll understand when fellas tell her what they want her to do. They won't have to use Injun sign language."

Chance felt anger welling up inside him and tightened the reins on his temper. "You gents might be better off to just move along now."

Luther squinted at him. "Are you tellin' us what to do, boy?"

"Sounded to me like he was," Banjo put in.

Judging by their clothes, boots, and spurs, Chance thought they were probably cowboys from one of the ranches in the area. Heavy revolvers rode in holsters sagging from gun belts around their waists.

He wasn't afraid of a gunfight, even though the odds were against him, but he didn't want to start anything while Ling was with him and might get in the way of a stray bullet, so he said the thing that either he or Ace always said when they found themselves in a situation like that. "Listen, fellas, we're not looking for any trouble."

"We're not lookin' for trouble, neither," said Banjo. "But we are lookin' for a little lovin', and I got me a hankerin' for yaller meat. So why don't you jus' take the gal on over and get her set up with Miss Hettie, and we can commence to doin' business." He paused, then added, "Don't worry, kid. I'm sure you'll get your cut."

Luther chuckled and put in, "And it ain't like you're sellin' your sister or somethin'."

Normally, Chance would have taken hold of Ling's arm and steered her away, but with two warbags and two Winchesters to carry, he didn't think he could do that. They would have to wait until Ace got back from the boat with their horses. He glanced along the street toward the wharf, thinking that he might see his brother coming, but there was no sign of Ace.

Luther and Banjo swaggered closer. Chance could smell the whiskey on them.

Luther planted himself in front of Chance and hooked his thumbs in his gun belt while Banjo circled, getting around on Ling's other side. Their movements showed that even drunk, they knew what they doing when it came to starting trouble.

"Son, where'd you get this gal, anyway?" Luther asked. "Don't see all that many Chinamen around these parts."

Banjo snickered. "She ain't a China *man*. She's a China gal. You're blinder 'n an ol' bat if you can't tell that, Luther, even in that getup she's got on."

"Oh, I can tell," Luther said. "I wouldn't mind gettin' a closer look, though, just so's I could make sure."

"How close? The length o' your—"

"That's enough," Chance snapped. "You've had your fun. It's time for you to move on."

Luther's lips pulled back from his rotten teeth in a leering grin as he leaned closer. "Sonny boy, we ain't even *started* havin' our fun yet."

"But we're gonna," said Banjo as he reached out with a grimy hand and tried to touch Ling's glossy, raven hair.

She let out a soft little cry and pulled away from him.

Chance turned toward Banjo. "Hey, leave her alone—" He broke off as he realized that he had fallen for the shorter man's feint. From the corner of his eye, he spotted movement and tried to twist back toward Luther, but he was too late. He saw Luther's big, knobby-knuckled fist coming at him just before it landed on his jaw. The punch felt like the kick of a mule as it sent him flying backwards.

CHAPTER TWELVE

It didn't take Ace long to saddle the two horses. He led them across the broad gangplank used for unloading cargo onto the wharf, and then onto the hard-packed dirt street that ran along the riverfront. The first order of business would be to find a stable for the animals, then they could look for a suitable hotel where he, Chance, and Ling could stay while they figured out what to do about the young woman's situation.

She wanted to travel with them, and of course, logically, they could to afford to buy her a horse and saddle and more appropriate clothes for riding . . . assuming she was able to ride. Ace supposed they could get a buggy for her to drive, but that didn't seem very feasible to him. There were plenty of places out there where a buggy couldn't go.

Anyway, it wouldn't be proper by any stretch of the imagination for a young woman to be traipsing around the frontier with a couple young men unless she was married to one of them. Neither he nor Chance was in the market for a bride!

Ace hadn't come up with any answers as he approached the hardware store where he had left Chance and Ling. He was so deep in thought that at first he didn't notice the commotion taking place ahead of him. Suddenly, he realized people were running in that direction and shouting excitedly. He frowned as he craned his neck and tried to see what was going on.

He caught a glimpse of his brother just as Chance slammed a fist into the face of a rawboned cowboy. Chance's hat had been knocked off, and his clothes were covered with dust like he'd been rolling around in the street. Clearly the fight had been going on for several moments.

Another man leaped at Chance from behind and grabbed his arms, pinning them to his sides. "I got the sumbitch, Luther! Beat him good!"

"Hang on to him, Banjo!" the rawboned cowboy responded as he set himself and moved in, fists cocked to deliver pounding punishment to Chance.

Ace wasn't going to let that happen to his brother. He dropped the horses' reins and charged forward, shouldering aside some of the gathering crowd as he tried to reach Chance.

As Ace closed in, Ling stepped up behind the man holding on to Chance. Using both hands, she swung the canvas bag containing her belongings and yelled, "Unhand my master!" The bag thudded against the man's head and sent his hat flying.

His grip on Chance's arms slipped, and Chance was able to shrug him off.

That help didn't come in time to save him from a punch launched by Luther. His fist sunk into Chance's stomach and doubled him over. The hombre was about to lift an uppercut into Chance's jaw when Ace grabbed his vest from behind with both hands and slung him off his feet.

Spectators jumped back to give the man room to roll in the dirt as he landed. His hat flew off, revealing a thatch of carrot-colored hair. He came to a stop on his belly and tried to push himself upright.

"Just stay where you are, mister," Ace warned him, holding out a hand.

"You go to hell!" the man roared as he surged to his feet.

Meanwhile, Banjo had caught his balance after that unexpected blow from Ling. He turned toward her and yelled, "You damn hellcat! I'll get you for that!" He started after her.

She tried to retreat, but her back hit a hitch rail in front of the hardware store, making her hesitate for a second. She tried to duck under the rail, but the man grabbed one of the blousy sleeves of her tunic and jerked her toward him. She let out a frightened cry and swung the bag one-handed, but he blocked it with his free arm.

"Maybe we'll just rip them clothes offa you!" he cried. "You yeller whore!"

Chance was still doubled over. His face was gray and he was breathing hard from that punch to the belly, but he lifted his head as the man shouted at Ling, and resolve appeared on his features. He shook off the pain he was feeling and tackled the man from behind, knocking him away from the young woman. They both sprawled in the dust.

A few yards away, Ace had his hands full blocking the flurry of wild punches Luther directed at him. The attack was so furious Ace didn't have time to throw any punches of his own. He couldn't parry all the blows, either. One of them clipped him on the side of the head and made him dizzy for a second.

"Now I got ya!" the man bellowed as he lunged forward and clamped both hands around Ace's neck. He gouged hard with his thumbs. "I'll pop that gourd right off your shoulders!"

Ace doubted that, but the man might choke him to death, he thought as he was forced back. He turned the man's own momentum against him by going limp and falling backwards before he raised his right leg and rammed the sole of his boot into the man's belly. He levered him up and over, flipping him through the air. The man's choking hands slipped away from Ace's throat as people leaped out of the way, clearing a spot for him to crash down on his back with stunning force.

Ace rolled over and dragged air into his lungs as he fought his way to his feet. He looked over and saw that Chance was sitting on top of the other man, raining punches down on his face. That part of the fight looked to be just about over.

But then a *third* man came out of the crowd with a gun in his hand, looming behind Chance. He raised the revolver and was about to bring it crashing down on Chance's head in a vicious blow that might well prove fatal.

It wasn't just a street brawl any longer. It was deadly danger.

Ace let his instincts take over. His right hand flashed toward the holster on his hip. He hoped the Colt hadn't fallen out during the fracas.

It hadn't. His hand closed around the revolver's walnut grips. He palmed out the gun and brought it up with blinding speed. His thumb looped over the hammer and eared it back. "Drop it!" he called to the man about to pistol-whip Chance.

The blow never fell. Ace would have squeezed the trigger if it had started, even by a fraction. He aimed to shoot the hombre in the shoulder, but it was hard to say what would happen if guns started going off.

"Hold on, kid," the third man said. He was a lean, dour-faced individual. Like the other two, he wore range clothes that marked him as a cowboy. "Don't shoot."

"Then drop that gun," warned Ace.

"Sure, sure. Take it easy." Slowly, the third man lowered his arm and bent to let the revolver drop to the ground in front of him. While he was doing that, Chance sledged one final punch into the face of the man he had defeated, who now lay bloody and senseless.

"Back away from the gun," Ace told the third man.

The crowd had gone quiet, so he didn't have any trouble hearing a sound behind him. He recognized it as the twin hammers of a double-barreled shotgun being pulled back.

"You're the one who better drop your gun and back away from it," said a gravelly voice.

Ace glanced over his shoulder, saw a burly man in a dusty black suit and hat pointing the Greener at him. A five-pointed tin star was pinned to the man's vest.

Ace lowered his Colt but didn't drop it. "I was just trying to save my brother from getting his head stove in, Sheriff."

"I don't talk things over with fellas holdin' guns," the lawman rumbled. "Put it down."

From the ground where he was still astride the man he had battered into unconsciousness, Chance protested, "This isn't fair. They're the ones who jumped us."

"We'll hash it all out," said the sheriff. "In case you ain't noticed, I ain't alone, neither."

Ace looked around and saw that two more men had emerged from the crowd, which was scattering rapidly because of the possibility of gunplay. Each of the deputies carried a rifle and held it ready to use.

"All right." Ace put his gun on the ground and stepped back away from it.

"You there. Fancypants." The sheriff swung the shotgun toward Chance. "If you're packin' iron, get rid of it."

Grudgingly, Chance reached under his coat and took the revolver from his shoulder holster. He tossed it onto the ground next to his brother's Colt.

The man who'd been about to buffalo Chance said, "You need to lock these kids up, Sheriff. They're crazy. Look what they did to Banjo and Luther." He gestured toward his two friends.

The one Chance had tackled was still out cold.

Luther had rolled onto his side but couldn't get up. He just lay there groaning.

"Shut up, Kiley," the sheriff snapped. "They probably had it comin'. You McPhee men are always startin' trouble. What are you doin' all the way up here, anyway? Don't they have saloons down in Rimfire?"

"What we're doing here isn't really any of your affair, Sheriff," Kiley responded. "Banjo and Luther were just minding their own business—"

"That's a lie," Chance interrupted hotly before the man could go on.

"I told you, we ain't havin' this argument out here." The sheriff gestured with the twin barrels of his scattergun. "I want all five of you over in my office, now."

"Luther and Banjo can't even walk!"

"They'll manage all right once somebody's got a bucket o' water from the horse trough and thrown it in their faces." The lawman looked at one of the deputies and jerked his head in a curt nod.

The deputy lowered his rifle and hurried to carry out the order as the sheriff told the others, "Get movin'."

Ace and Chance looked at each other. There didn't seem to be anything they could do except go along with what the sheriff wanted. Maybe once things had calmed down, some of the bystanders would speak up and confirm that the Jensen brothers had just been defending themselves . . . and Ling.

At that moment, she stepped up beside Chance and took hold of his sleeve.

"Wait just a doggone minute," the sheriff said. "Who in blazes is this?"

"This one's name is Ling," she said with her eyes downcast. "Mr. Chance is my master."

The lawman stared at her and exclaimed, "He's what?"

"Hold on a minute, Sheriff," Chance said hastily. "You don't need to get the wrong idea here."

"Too late for that," the badge-toter snapped. "Get movin', the lot o' you!"

CHAPTER THIRTEEN

The Fort Benton sheriff's office and jail was housed in a sturdy stone building next to the brick courthouse. Ace worried that the sheriff might herd them all into cells before questioning them further, but the lawman settled for crowding them into the office and then placing the shotgun on top of the scarred wooden desk with a decisive thump.

According to what Chance had told him during a low-voiced conversation the Jensen boys had carried on while being marched over there, the two men who had started the fight were named Luther and Banjo. Their heads were soaked from the dousing one of the deputies had given them. They wore sullen, angry scowls as they stood on one side of the room with their friend Kiley. A deputy was behind them, keeping an eye on them.

The sheriff had directed Ace, Chance, and Ling to the other side of the room. The other deputy was posted next to them with his rifle tucked under his arm.

A nameplate on the desk identified the sheriff as

Bud Maddox. He looked back and forth between the two groups and said, "I'll give you one chance to explain what happened out there, and so help me God, if you all start talkin' at once I'll throw the whole bunch of you behind bars." He pointed a blunt finger at Ace. "You look reasonably smart. You go first."

"I, uh, wish I could, Sheriff, but the fight was already going on when I got there. I saw that two men had ganged up on my brother, so I jumped in to help him."

Maddox looked back and forth between the Jensens. "You two are brothers?"

"That's right." Ace didn't explain about them being twins. Whenever most folks heard that word, they expected to see identical twins.

"I can tell you what happened," said Chance. "Those two with the wet heads were very rude and insulting to this young woman. I was just defending her when the little one tried to lay hands on her."

Banjo said, "Little one? I ain't much shorter 'n you!"

"Don't start," Sheriff Maddox warned. He looked at Chance. "Go on . . . what's your name, anyway?"

"Chance Jensen. This is my brother Ace. And the young lady is Miss Ling."

Luther said, "He keeps callin' her a lady, but she's a China gal, and a harlot to boot."

Ling cringed at the harsh words and huddled closer to Chance.

"I'm not warnin' you again, Stebbins," the sheriff told Luther. "Open your mouth when you haven't been told to, and you're goin' in a cell."

Luther glowered, but he didn't say anything else.

"Go on, Jensen," Maddox told Chance.

"They mistook Miss Ling for a prostitute and said some terrible things to her. I told them to move on, then the little one tried to grab her, and the big one threw a punch and knocked me down." Chance shrugged. "I got up and fought back. Ace got there a minute later and joined in. That's the whole story, Sheriff."

"Not quite," Maddox said. "When I heard the commotion and got there with my deputies, there was a gun drawn." He leveled an accusing stare at Ace.

"That fella Kiley was about to hit Chance with his gun," Ace explained. "That might have hurt him really bad. So I wasn't going to let it happen."

"Even if it meant shootin' Kiley?"

"I was aiming for his shoulder."

"Yeah, and if you'd missed you might've hit him in the head." Maddox squinted at Kiley. "Not that it would've been any great loss, but I don't cotton to havin' anybody's brains splattered all over the street in my town."

"You haven't even asked for our side of the story," Kiley said bitterly.

Maddox swung toward the trio of cowboys. "All right. Are you claimin' it happened different from what these boys just told me? And remember, I can send my deputies out to get statements from witnesses if I have to. This ain't Rimfire, where Angus McPhee runs everything."

In a surly voice, Banjo answered, "Well . . . maybe it happened sorta like they said. But just look at the gal, Sheriff! How many China gals you see in these parts who *ain't* either washerwomen or harlots?

You can tell by lookin' at her that she ain't the sort to do laundry, so that only leaves one thing."

Luther added, "Look at the way that fella's dressed. He looks like a whoremonger, so we figured he'd brung the girl to town to sell her to Miss Hettie. It was a . . . what do you call it? A logical assumption."

"And you heard her say yourself that Jensen there is her master," Kiley put in with a smirk.

"That's not the way it is," Chance said hastily.

Maddox settled his suspicious gaze on Chance again. "Well, then, why don't you tell me how it is?"

For the next few minutes, Chance did so, explaining about the poker game on the *Missouri Belle* with Jack Haggarty and its unexpected outcome. "The boat should still be docked," he concluded. "You can go talk to Captain Foley if you want. He can tell you about the fire Haggarty started that panicked the whole boat and gave him a chance to get away."

"I don't reckon that's necessary," Maddox said with grudging acceptance in his voice. "The story you've told sounds reasonable enough to me. It's pretty clear you three ain't to blame for what happened."

Luther and Banjo started to protest, while Kiley just stood there with a sour look on his face.

"Shut up!" Maddox roared at them. "Lock 'em up, boys. They'll have to go to court for disturbin' the peace."

While the deputies prodded the three prisoners past a heavy, iron-strapped door into the cell block, Maddox took the guns belonging to Ace and Chance from behind his belt where he had tucked them away earlier. He placed the weapons on the desk and nodded toward them. "You can collect your hardware," he told the Jensens. "There's no law against carryin' guns in town, but if you pull iron you'd better have a damn good reason for it."

"Thanks, Sheriff," Ace said as he picked up his Colt and slipped it into its holster. "We were telling the truth about not looking for trouble."

"Then what does bring you to Fort Benton?" Maddox wanted to know. He squinted at Ling. "And if this gal is convinced she belongs to you, what're you gonna do with her?"

"We haven't quite figured that out," said Chance.

"She's starting to understand that she's not a slave, though," added Ace.

"Is that right, miss?" Maddox asked her.

Ling nodded tentatively. "It is all very confusing for this one. All of this one's life, she has had a master to tell her what to do. This one does not know if she can make up her own mind."

Maddox frowned at Ace and Chance. "She talk like that all the time?"

"Mostly," Chance said, nodding.

Maddox shook his head. "That would confuse the hell outta me. You have any business in these parts?"

Chance snugged his revolver back into the shoulder holster. "No business. We're just seeing the country, I guess you could say."

"Uh-huh," said Maddox. "Drifters, you mean. Saddle tramps." He looked at Ling again. "That's no life for a woman."

"We know that," Ace said. "That's why we're going to stay here for a while until we get her settled."

"You might point us to a decent hotel," suggested Chance.

"The Western Lodge is a good one. Fella name of Green runs it. You can tell him I sent you."

"Thanks, Sheriff," Ace said. "What about a livery stable?"

"Assuming nobody's run off with our horses," added Chance.

"Your mounts are fine. I don't allow any horse stealin' in Fort Benton, and folks know that. You'll find that somebody probably tied 'em to one of the hitch racks. Anyway, take 'em down to Patterson's Livery. Joe Patterson runs the best stable in town."

Ace nodded. "We're obliged to you. We're free to go, then?"

Maddox waved a hand. "Go on. Get outta here. And try to stay outta trouble while you're in town."

"We always try to stay out of trouble," Ace said.

The sheriff looked pretty skeptical about that, but he didn't say anything else.

When they stepped out onto the street again, Chance drew in a deep breath. "Always good to breathe free air."

"There are the horses," Ace said, pointing to the hitch rail where the animals were tied, just as Maddox had predicted. "Somebody put our warbags and rifles with them, too."

"The sheriff runs an honest town," Chance commented. He looked over at Ling, who still carried her canvas bag. "Say, what do you have in that sack of yours? It made a pretty good thud when you walloped Banjo in the head with it."

"Just some extra clothes. And this." She opened the drawstring, reached inside the bag, and brought out a small statue, no more than six inches tall.

Ace recognized the figure seated cross-legged. "That's Buddha," he told Chance. "Remember I mentioned him back on the boat?"

"Fat little fella, isn't he?"

Ace shook his head. "You shouldn't talk so disrespectful about him. He's part of their religion over there in that part of the world."

"Oh. I'm sorry. I didn't know."

"It is all right," Ling said. "Buddha is very forgiving."

"Is that gold?" Ace asked her.

"No. Merely paint. The statue is made of lead."

"Well, it's still good for walloping varmints in the head," Chance told her. "You'd better put it away, though. Somebody might see it and think it was made of gold. If it was, it would be worth a lot of money. Somebody might try to steal it."

"This one hopes not. Buddha has always watched over her and protected her."

Chance looked around the frontier settlement. "He's got his work cut out for him in a place like this."

Chapter Fourteen

The Western Lodge Hotel wasn't fancy, but not many places in Fort Benton were. The settlement had grown a great deal from the crude fur trading outpost it had started out as, but signs of its origins could still be seen in the many log and sod buildings in town. The Western Lodge was one of those log structures, but inside it was fairly nice.

Ling's room had a thick rug on the floor to go along with what looked like a comfortable bed, a ladder-back chair, a table with a basin on it, and a wardrobe. She looked around the room with wide eyes and said, "Mr. Chance and Mr. Ace will stay here with this one?"

"Uh, no, we can't do that," Ace said, trying not to look embarrassed.

"There is much space. This one can sleep on the floor. The rug is very soft." She bounced a little on the balls of her feet as if to demonstrate.

"You don't have to worry about that," Chance assured her. "We have our own room, and it's right across the hall if you need anything."

Ling shook her head in awe. "This one has never stayed in such a fine place."

"Not even in San Francisco or Denver?" asked Ace.

"This one's family in San Francisco lived in China-town. The quarters were very small and crowded. When this one's father sold her because the family had too many mouths and not enough food, she went to live in a house where the rooms were also small and had nothing in them but a bed." She'd been very matter of fact when she mentioned being sold by her father but looked down at the floor when she added, "That was all this one needed."

Ace and Chance glanced at each other. Ace already regretted asking her about her past. He sure wasn't going to press her for any details.

"Then Mr. Jack won this one in a poker game with the man who owned the house," she went on anyway. "When she traveled with him to Denver and Omaha, this one always stayed in a small room, befitting her status as a servant."

"You mean he didn't keep you on a tight rein all the time?" asked Chance. When Ling frowned in obvious confusion, he explained. "I mean, he didn't make you stay close to him so he could keep an eye on you?"

Ling shook her head solemnly.

"Then why in blazes didn't you run away?" he blurted out. "You must've had plenty of chances."

"A slave run away from her master?" Again Ling shook her head. "This one would not have known what to do if she were alone in the world."

That was difficult for Ace to comprehend. It seemed to him like almost anything would be better than being enslaved. However, he and Ling had been brought up in very different places. He couldn't expect her to look at things the same way he did.

"Well, you're free now," he told her. "And you don't have to sleep on the floor. You've got your own room, and nobody's going to bother you."

"Thank you, Mr. Ace. This one will be forever in debt to you and Mr. Chance."

"You can forget about that," Chance said gruffly. "You don't owe us a blasted thing."

Ling looked like she might have argued about that, but Ace didn't give her the opportunity. "We'll go out and get something to eat in a little while. It looked like there's a decent café across the street. You should try to get some rest. The way things have been changing all around you, you must be tired."

Ling smiled and nodded. "This one *is* weary," she admitted.

"We'll see you later, then," Ace said as he went to the room's open door.

Chance said, "If you need anything, just holler. I mean, shout. Call us."

She nodded. "This one will"—she looked around the room again—"but she does not see how she could ever need more than what she has right now!"

Once they were across the hall in their own room, Chance said, "After everything that girl's gone through, there's no way we can run out on her, Ace."

"Nobody said anything about running out on her. What we need to do is find her a job. A real job, not what she was doing back in San Francisco."

"Damn right. There's bound to be a Chinese laundry in town. You hardly ever see a frontier settlement without one."

"She ought to be able to do better than that, as smart as she is. Maybe she could cook in one of the cafés or work for a seamstress or something like that. She could probably even clerk in a store if she got over talking the way she does."

"Yeah, we're gonna have to work on that with her," Chance said. "So, it seems pretty obvious that we're going to be here in Fort Benton for a while."

"Reckon you'll be able to stand it?"

"Hey, I'm no more fiddle-footed than you are! Most of the time you're the one who gets worried first about grass growing under your feet."

Ace chuckled. "Yeah, that's probably true. In fact, why don't we go downstairs right now and see if there's anything happening in the lobby?"

"You expecting anything?"

"No . . . but you never know."

When they got to the lobby, however, it was empty except for the clerk dozing behind the counter and a man sitting in the corner reading a newspaper. Not a hint of anything exciting as far as the eye could see.

Something about the way the man was holding his newspaper caught Ace's attention. As he watched, the man lowered the paper slightly, glanced over it, then raised it again rather quickly to cover his face.

Ace almost laughed out loud but nudged his brother and nodded toward the man in the corner. Chance frowned in puzzlement.

Ace walked over to where the man was sitting in an overstuffed armchair. "You're going to have a hard time getting out of that chair in a hurry if there's any trouble, Deputy."

The man lowered the newspaper and glared at Ace. He was still in his twenties, a few years older than the Jensen brothers, and had a broad face that was flushed with embarrassment and annoyance at the moment. His hat was pushed back on fair hair that was already thinning despite his relative youth. The last time Ace and Chance had seen him, he had been ushering the three prisoners into the cell block.

"I dunno what you're talkin' about," he said sullenly. "I'm just sittin' here readin' the paper."

"You mean Sheriff Maddox didn't send you over here to keep an eye on us?" Ace asked.

"No," the deputy replied, but he didn't sound convincing at all.

Ace hooked a boot around one of the legs of a nearby chair, drew it closer, and sat down. "We'll make it easy for you. We'll just sit right here for a while."

"We sure will," Chance added as he drew up a chair, too. Now that he had caught on to what was happening, a grin stretched across his face.

The deputy looked like he was about to lose his temper, but then he let out a grunt of laughter. "You got me," the star packer admitted as he folded the newspaper. "The sheriff figured it would be a good idea for somebody to keep tabs on you. He said he had a hunch the two of you attract trouble like moths to a flame."

"Hey, we're peaceable men," Chance objected.

"Didn't look like it to me earlier this morning. It

looked like you were trying to whale the tar out of those no-account cowboys from Rimfire."

"Sheriff Maddox mentioned Rimfire," said Ace as he stretched his long legs out in front of him and crossed them at the ankles. "I take it that's the name of a settlement?"

"Yeah, a little cattle town about thirty miles south of here, between the Highwoods and the Little Belts."

Ace recognized the names of two mountain ranges that became more common the farther west a person went in Montana Territory, all the way to the great spine of the continent formed by the Rockies.

"It's right on this side of the Chouteau County line, so it lies in our jurisdiction and we have to take a ride down there every now and then," the deputy continued. "Don't let the sheriff ever hear that I said this, but the real law in Rimfire and thereabouts is a man named Angus McPhee."

"The rancher Luther, Banjo, and Kiley ride for," Ace guessed, remembering what the sheriff had said earlier.

The deputy nodded. "That's right. By the way, my name's Ernie Calloway."

"Pleased to meet you, Ernie," said Chance, "now that you're not pointing a rifle at us."

"Hey, the sheriff might've wanted to arrest you. Better to have the drop on a fella if you're fixin' to try to throw him in jail, don't you think?"

"Can't argue with that," Ace agreed. "Go on about Rimfire."

Deputy Calloway frowned slightly and asked, "How come you want to know?"

"Just curious. We haven't ever been there, that I recall."

"We might want to take a ride in that direction," Chance added.

"I don't see why you'd want to do that," Calloway said. "The range thereabouts is pretty good, but the town itself ain't much to look at or speak of. Just one street that'll choke you with dust in the summer and bog you down in the mud in the winter. McPhee owns most of the businesses, either outright or through loans, and he does what he pleases. That sticks in Sheriff Bud's craw, but all he's got is two full-time deputies and a couple part-timers to keep up with a big county. That ain't near enough firepower to take on a salty crew like McPhee's. Those three you tangled with—Ned Kiley, Luther Stebbins, and Banjo Doakes—they're just about the bottom of the barrel when it comes to that bunch. I reckon some of 'em rode the lonely trails and heard the owl hoot plenty of times, but as long as they do the job McPhee pays 'em for, he don't really care."

Chance said, "When your mouth gets wound up, it takes a while to run down, doesn't it?"

"I do like to talk. I'll admit that," said Calloway, nodding. "My ma was a talkin' woman, Lord, was she, so I never got a chance to speak up much when I was a kid."

Ace said, "If this fella McPhee has such shady characters working for him, is he an outlaw himself?"

Calloway pursed his lips for a second in thought, then said, "No, I reckon not. As far as I've ever heard, he built up his ranch—a spread called the Tartan—honest and aboveboard. Never known him to be accused of rustlin' or anything like that. He just rides roughshod over anybody who happens to get in his way. Seems to figure that whole valley between those mountain ranges is his little kingdom."

Ace nodded. He and his brother had run across high-handed cattle barons like that before. It was best to steer clear of them if at all possible.

Deputy Calloway opened his mouth to say something else, then stopped like that with his jaw sagging. He was looking at something on the other side of the lobby, and when Ace glanced in that direction, he saw what had transfixed the deputy's gaze.

Ling was coming down the stairs.

CHAPTER FIFTEEN

She was a sight to behold.

When she had said she had some spare clothes in her bag, Ace had assumed she meant more of the pajama-like garb she was wearing at the time.

But she had changed from the loose white trousers and tunic into a tight-fitting dress of blue-green silk. Ornate designs of golden thread had been worked into the fabric here and there to decorate it. Ling's long, glossy dark hair, which had been hanging loose earlier, was pulled back and fastened in wings on each side of her head by jade-colored combs.

She was beautiful, no doubt about that. Ace, Chance, and Deputy Calloway were all staring at her, and even the clerk behind the desk was wide awake and watching.

Ling stopped at the bottom of the stairs, rested one slim-fingered hand on the newel post where the banister started, and frowned in worry at the men. "Something is wrong with the way this one looks?"

Calloway stood up in a hurry. The folded, forgotten newspaper fell at his feet. He swallowed. "No, ma'am. There's not a thing wrong. About as far from it as you could get, in fact."

Ling shook her head. "This one does not understand."

Ace and Chance stood up as well and started toward her.

Ace said, "He just means that you look fine, Ling."

"Mighty fine," added Chance.

She smiled again. "This one is pleased. This one did not want Mr. Chance and Mr. Ace to be ashamed of her."

"I don't reckon that would ever be possible," Chance told her.

"You might be dressed a little fancy for Fort Benton, that's all," Ace said.

Ling gestured up the stairs. "This one could put on the clothes she wore earlier . . ."

"No, don't do that," exclaimed Calloway, then added sheepishly, "I mean, uh, no, you look fine just the way you are."

Ling smiled. "This one is pleased."

"Then we're pleased, too," Calloway said. "Ain't that right, fellas?"

"Pleased as punch," Chance agreed.

She came across the lobby toward them. Her stride didn't seem to be deliberately sensuous, but the four men couldn't help but watch her, anyway. She stopped a few feet short of them and looked intently at Calloway. "You are a lawman."

"Yes, ma'am, I am."

"Did the sheriff send you to arrest us?"

"What? No! No, not at all. He just, uh, wanted me to make sure there was no more trouble. That those terrible cowboys didn't come back to bother you again. That's all." He was making that up, of course.

In fact, all three men knew that Sheriff Maddox had said Kiley, Stebbins, and Doakes would remain in custody to face charges of disturbing the peace.

The story accomplished its purpose as the look of concern on Ling's face disappeared. "Then you are here to protect us and watch over us."

Calloway nodded emphatically. "Yes, ma'am. That's it."

"Like Buddha."

Calloway looked confused.

Ace told him, "Never mind, Deputy. It would take too long to explain."

"We are going to eat," Ling continued. "You must come with us, Deputy, since that is your job."

"Now hold on a minute—"

"Yes, ma'am. That's right," Calloway interrupted Chance. "I'll stick mighty close to you, and nobody'll bother you the least little bit while I'm around."

Chance frowned. "That's not necessary. My brother and I can take care of the lady just fine."

"No, sir. Orders is orders," insisted Calloway.

"Looks like we're stuck with the deputy's company," Ace told his brother. "Might as well make the best of it."

"Yeah, I suppose," Chance said with an obvious lack of enthusiasm for the idea.

The four of them left the hotel and headed for Plummer's Café across the street. Ling drew quite a few stares, which, considering her beauty and her colorful outfit, came as no surprise to Ace. No one accosted them, though, and soon they were sitting in the café with cups of coffee in front of them, waiting for plates of fried chicken, potatoes, and greens to arrive.

The deputy's talkative nature took a while to get started again, seeing as he was almost overcome with admiration for Ling, but once he started talking, he dominated the conversation. He told her all about the history of Fort Benton and delved into his personal history, explaining to her that he had left the family farm in Ohio and come to Montana Territory to prospect for a lucrative gold claim and make his fortune. When that plan hadn't worked out, he had drifted into wearing a badge.

"I probably could've picked up a ridin' job on one of the spreads hereabouts, but I'm not really cut out to be a cowboy. I can't stay in the saddle all day."

"So you'd rather ride a desk," said Chance, drawing a quick glower from the deputy.

"I feel like I'm doin' some good, you know," Calloway went on to Ling. "I mean by helpin' people and enforcin' law and order."

"You must be a fierce warrior," she told him.

"No, ma'am. Well, I mean, sure, when I have to be, when I need to corral some owlhoot or gunslinger. Mostly, I'm the gentle sort, when folks will let me be."

Chance rolled his eyes and looked away, muttering to himself under his breath. Ace tried not to chuckle at the way Ling was winding Ernie Calloway tightly around her little finger. Clearly, she knew how to get what she wanted out of men without even seeming to try.

He needed to remember that for future reference, Ace told himself. It might come in handy.

The food was typical cow country fare but it was good and there was plenty of it. Ling ate in a rather dainty fashion but still managed to put away quite a bit.

As they neared the end of the meal, Chance said, "Seeing as how you're here on official business, Deputy, maybe the sheriff's office would see fit to pay the bill for all of us."

Calloway frowned. "I dunno about that. I reckon Sheriff Maddox wouldn't go along with it."

Ace knew his brother was just giving Calloway trouble for horning in on their lunch. "We've got enough to take care of it."

"Yeah, but I wouldn't want to do anything to interfere with the law," Chance said.

"I've got it, I've got it," Calloway blustered. He dug around in a pocket, found a five-dollar gold piece, and slapped it down on the table. "There. All taken care of. This is on me, Miss Ling."

That confirmed he was just trying to impress her.

"You are very kind, Deputy Calloway," she told him with a smile. "This one is in your debt, as well."

"Oh, no, ma'am. Not at all. I'm happy to do it."

The hooded glance he threw toward the Jensen brothers indicated that he wasn't really all that happy with the way he'd been maneuvered in coughing up the money.

However, Chance seemed quite pleased with himself. As they left the café, he asked, "Do you plan on hanging around all day, Deputy?"

"I've got my orders," Calloway said.

Ace pointed across the street. "We'll be at the hotel,

then. Just so you'll know. That ought to make it a little easier for you."

"Doesn't matter whether it's easy or hard. I've got my job to do, and I intend to do it." Calloway hooked his thumbs in his gun belt and tried to look nonchalant yet vigilant, but then he suddenly stiffened as he turned his attention toward the riverfront.

Ace looked in the same direction and saw half a dozen men striding toward them. One member of the group was out in front by several feet and carried himself as if he belonged there. He was a little above medium height and had very broad shoulders stretching a buckskin jacket. A brown hat was crammed down on a thatch of curly, reddish-gray hair. He wasn't wearing a gun, but the five men following closely behind him were.

Even though Ace was sure he hadn't ever seen any of those men before, he recognized their type right away. They wore range clothes, but their hard, angular faces, their cold eyes, and the way their hands never drifted far from the butts of their guns told him they weren't regular cowboys even though they might be expected to do ranch chores.

The men were gun-wolves, hired more for their skill with their Colts than any talents they might have at roping and branding.

"Calloway!" the leader snapped as they all came to a stop. "I hear your boss has three of my men locked up in your jail." He had just a hint of a Scottish burr in his voice to show his ancestry.

Ace had no doubt it was Angus McPhee, owner of the Tartan Ranch.

Calloway confirmed that by saying nervously, "Uh, Mr. McPhee—"

"I want them turned loose! Now!" The tone of the cattleman's voice made it clear that he was accustomed to getting whatever he wanted, whenever he wanted it.

To Calloway's credit, he didn't back down, even though it was obvious he didn't relish this confrontation. "You'll have to take that up with Sheriff Maddox—"

"I'm taking it up with you," McPhee interrupted again. "You sorry excuse for a lawman."

Calloway's already flushed face turned even redder. "You've got no call to talk like that."

"I'll talk any way I please, you—" McPhee stopped short, but not because someone else had broken in to what he was saying. He fell silent, frowned, and leaned his head to one side to peer around the bulky figure of Deputy Ernie Calloway. "Good Lord in heaven, what do we have here?" he demanded as he stared at Ling.

Chapter Sixteen

Ace and Chance edged protectively closer to Ling standing between them.

Calloway said, "You were talking to me, Mr. McPhee—"

"Step aside, sonny," McPhee barked, brushing past him.

Once again Calloway wasn't allowed to finish his sentence. Acting out of instinct, his hand moved toward the butt of the gun on his hip. "You can't push around an officer of the law!"

Before he could touch the revolver, all five of McPhee's men stood tense with their hands poised over their own guns, ready to draw. Ace had no doubt that they were a lot faster than Calloway. If the deputy pulled iron, the air would be full of bullets in the blink of an eye.

Calloway realized he'd be endangering the whole town by pushing to a showdown and probably would be the first one to die. He froze with his fingers still several inches away from the gun butt.

McPhee didn't seem the least bit worried about

any gunplay. It was almost as if he felt like he would be protected somehow from the flying lead . . . like a bullet wouldn't dare touch him.

He stood in front of Ling and nodded politely. "Ma'am, I don't recall seeing any Chinese ladies around here lately. You don't work for Miss Hettie, do you?" He answered his own question. "No, you don't look the sort to be one of her girls. What brings you to a place like Fort Benton?"

She was saved from having to answer by the gravelly voice of Sheriff Bud Maddox, who rumbled, "McPhee! I heard you were in town. Looking to cause trouble, as usual."

McPhee swung around to glare at the sheriff as Maddox strode across the street toward the group of people gathered in front of the café. Maddox carried his shotgun as if he were ready to use it. McPhee's men backed off a little to give him room. Even those hardcases didn't want to tangle with a man wielding a double-barreled street-sweeper like that.

Ace had no doubt they could kill the sheriff if they wanted to, but more than likely he would blast most or all of them to kingdom come before he died.

McPhee lifted a hand in a slight motion that made his men retreat even more. He and Maddox glared darkly at each other, two powerful, stubborn men, neither of whom wanted to back down.

"I didn't come here to cause trouble," McPhee said after a moment. "I had a new safe shipped in on the riverboat, and my men and I are here to pick it up."

"A new safe?" repeated Maddox.

"The best they make," McPhee declared proudly. "Came all the way from New York."

"You wouldn't need a safe if you'd just put your money in the bank like normal folks."

The rancher blew out his breath contemptuously. "Why trust somebody else to look after my money when I can do it myself?"

"The bank here in Fort Benton's never been robbed," Maddox pointed out.

"And no one's ever stolen from me, either," McPhee shot back at him. "If anybody ever tried, he'd find himself decorating a limb on the nearest tree before he knew what happened to him."

"You can't take the law into your own hands—"

"A man's got a right to protect what's his!"

The two men clearly hated each other, thought Ace. While they were arguing and distracted, he figured it might be a good idea to slip away and get Ling out of McPhee's sight. The cattleman's scrutiny had made her uncomfortable.

He caught Chance's eye and inclined his head toward the hotel. Chance nodded his agreement, put a hand on Ling's arm, and steered her in that direction.

No one seemed to notice them leaving as Maddox and McPhee were still jawing at each other.

The sheriff asked, "Is that blasted safe of yours loaded on a wagon?"

"It is," replied McPhee.

"Well, then, there's nothing stopping you from getting out of town!"

"Nothing but the three men of mine you've got locked up for no good reason!"

"They were brawling. They have to answer to charges of disturbing the peace."

McPhee waved a hand dismissively. "That's just an excuse for you to cause trouble for me, and you know it!"

That was the last of the confrontation Ace saw over his shoulder. They had reached the hotel.

"What's going on out there?" asked the clerk as they walked through the lobby.

"None of our business," Ace replied.

The clerk looked out the window. "Oh, I see now. The sheriff and Angus McPhee are going at it again."

"Does that happen often?" Chance asked.

"Often enough. One of these days, things are really going to blow up between those two. I don't want to be around when it does!"

Ace felt the same way. Maybe they ought to rethink their plan to stay in Fort Benton for a while, he mused as he went up the stairs with Chance and Ling.

"I did not like the way that man looked at me," she murmured.

"Well, don't you worry about him," said Chance. "He won't bother you. Ace and I will see to that."

The rest of the day passed quietly enough. Ling said she was still tired and planned to lie down in her room. Ace and Chance spent the afternoon in their room across the hall, keeping the door open so they'd be able to see if anybody went up to Ling's door.

To pass the time, they played cards. Not poker, because that was business and Chance didn't relax by doing what he did for his livelihood. Doc Monday had taught them that.

Anyway, given Chance's skill at poker, that wouldn't

have been much of a contest. They played cribbage, and Ace was good enough at that to win from time to time, often enough to keep things interesting.

"Did you see the way that fella McPhee looked at Ling?" Chance asked.

"You mean the same way most fellas would, including you and me?"

Chance snorted. "We're chivalrous enough that we at least *try* not to stare too much. I know, sometimes it's difficult. Like when she was coming down the stairs wearing that dress . . ." Chance cleared his throat, took a deep breath, and turned his attention back to his cards.

"McPhee worries me," Ace said after a moment. "A man like him is used to getting what he wants. And anytime he doesn't, he probably just takes it."

"Yeah, I thought the same thing. But he should have gone back to his ranch by now. Sheriff Maddox was doing a pretty good job of trying to run him out of town."

"The sheriff was outnumbered," Ace pointed out.

"Remember, Deputy Calloway said that basically, McPhee's law-abiding. I don't reckon he'd let his men shoot Maddox just because they don't get along."

"We can hope not," said Ace, "but sometimes men get carried away and do unexpected things . . . especially when there's a beautiful woman involved."

"And Ling sure fits that description," Chance said, nodding slowly. "Maybe one of us should go check and see if McPhee and his men are still in town."

"We can do that later. As long as we're sitting here in front of her door, I suppose she's safe enough."

They played for a while longer, then set the cards

aside and stood up as they heard footsteps coming along the second-floor corridor. Ace went to the open door, leaned on the jamb, and looked along the hall to see Deputy Ernie Calloway approaching.

"Deputy," Ace said with a friendly nod. "Get tired of sitting down in the lobby pretending to read the newspaper?"

"I was just doing what the sheriff told me to do," Calloway said. "That's my job, you know."

"What brings you up here now?"

"Checking on you," the deputy replied in a straight-forward manner. "Making sure you hadn't snuck out the back way."

"And taken Ling with us, you mean?"

Calloway glanced toward the door on the other side of the hall. "Well . . . I reckon she's in there?"

Ace nodded. "She told us she was going to lie down for a while. I believe her. But if you don't, I reckon you can knock on the door and see for yourself. Of course, if you do, you're liable to wake her up . . ."

Calloway waved off that suggestion. "No, I don't reckon there's any need to disturb her."

"Listen, there's no reason for you to go back down and sit by yourself in the lobby. If you're supposed to keep an eye on Chance and me, why don't you come on in? We're just playing cards. We can play three-handed."

"You're sure? It *is* pretty boring down there, listen-ing to Cyrus Heimerdorf snore."

"That's the clerk's name?"

"Yeah. And he can sleep twenty hours a day if you let him."

Ace chuckled and motioned with his head. "Come

on in." He told Chance that Calloway would be joining them.

Chance grinned. "Good. I don't know that I've ever played cribbage for money before, but there's always a first time."

"Not today," Calloway responded instantly. "My wages aren't good enough to risk any of them gambling with a—" He stopped speaking and shook his head.

Chance cocked an eyebrow. "You were about to say something insulting?"

"No. Let's just say I'm not a gambling man."

"Fair enough. It'll just be a friendly game. Of course, if you decide to make a friendly wager . . ."

"I won't."

Once they had settled down and started playing, Ace asked, "What happened between the sheriff and that fella McPhee?"

"Oh, they snorted at each other and pawed the ground for a while like a couple old bulls, then McPhee and his men rode out, taking that new safe of his with them. They'll be doing good if they make it back to Rimfire without that big old thing busting down the wagon they were hauling it in."

"McPhee doesn't trust banks, eh?" drawled Chance.

"Angus McPhee doesn't trust much of anybody or anything, I'd say," Calloway replied. "But he was one of the first ranchers in these parts, back in the days when there wasn't anything around here except hostile Indians and lobo wolves and blizzards. He's survived and prospered this long, so I reckon you can't find too much fault with what he does."

"Did he convince the sheriff to release those three prisoners?" Ace asked.

Calloway shook his head. "No, sir. Sheriff Bud's just as stubborn as McPhee is. Those men are still locked up, and they will be for a few days, until the judge schedules a hearing."

"I'll bet McPhee didn't like that."

"Oh, he was just bellering out of general principles, I think. He doesn't really care that much about Kiley, Doakes, and Stebbins. They fancy themselves hardcases, but McPhee's got a lot tougher men than them riding for him."

They continued to play while they were talking, but the game and the conversation came to an abrupt end when the door of the room across the hall opened and Ling peered out curiously. Instantly, the Jensen boys and Calloway were on their feet.

"Everything is all right?" she asked.

"Everything is fine," Chance assured her. "Did you have a good nap?"

"This one is very rested." If she had been lying down, it wasn't possible to tell by looking at her. Not a hair was out of place, and there wasn't a crease in the silk dress.

Ace took his watch from his pocket and flipped it open. "Be time to go get supper in a little while. How's the food in the hotel dining room, Deputy?"

"It's fine," Calloway said.

Ling smiled at him and asked, "You will join us again, Deputy Calloway?"

"Uh . . . no, I reckon not. It's obvious by now that nothing else is gonna happen, so I think I ought to go back to the sheriff and tell him he can stop worrying about you folks."

"See, once you get to know us, we're not so bad," said Chance.

Calloway looked like he wasn't convinced of that, at least where the Jensen brothers were concerned. He took off his hat and told Ling, "If you need anything while you're in Fort Benton, ma'am, you just send for me. I'll be glad to take care of any problem you might have."

She nodded. "This one is grateful to you, Deputy."

Calloway was clearly reluctant to leave, but he did anyway, clapping his hat on and heading for the lobby.

Ling asked, "Have you decided what you will do with this one, Mr. Chance?"

He frowned. "That's not my decision to make. You can do whatever you want, Ling. That's the way it works here."

"And if this one wants to travel with you and be your servant?"

"Well"—Chance sighed—"I don't reckon there's much I could do about it."

"Good. That is settled, then. Let us go and eat." She smiled at the brothers. "This one is hungry!"

They ushered her ahead of them, and as they went down the stairs, Ace whispered to Chance, "You just agreed to let her ride with us. That's a terrible idea!"

"Try telling *her* that."

CHAPTER SEVENTEEN

The roast beef in the hotel dining room was all right, as Deputy Calloway had said. The other guests who were eating there kept trying not to stare at Ling, Ace could tell, but they weren't doing a very good job of it.

She either didn't notice or pretended not to. Judging by the amount of dignity she displayed, she was more like a princess than a slave.

When the meal was over and they walked into the lobby, she asked, "What will you do now?"

"What would you like to do?" Chance asked her. "It's not like Fort Benton has a lot of opportunities for entertainment unless you like hanging out in saloons."

"That is what this one's master always did."

"Haggarty?" Chance grunted. "I'm not surprised."

"How about you?" asked Ace. "What did you do while he was playing poker?"

"Whatever needed done. Sometimes there were clothes to wash or mend. Mostly this one just waited until her master required something of her."

"Well, that's over and done with," Chance declared. "You can do whatever you want now."

"Really? This one thinks she would like to—" Ling stopped speaking as the need for a yawn came over her. She lifted a hand to her mouth and covered it daintily.

"How about turn in early?" Ace suggested. "After that long riverboat trip, you're bound to be worn out. Why don't you get a good night's sleep, and in the morning we'll figure out our next move."

"That has already been decided. This one will go wherever Mr. Chance goes."

"Now hold on." Chance shook his head. "No, there's no point in arguing about that now. Like Ace said, we'll talk again in the morning."

"Very well." Ling bowed to him. "Good night, Mr. Chance."

"You don't have to—"

She had already turned to Ace and repeated the bow. "Good night, Mr. Ace."

"Good night, Ling," Ace told her. "Sleep well."

"This one is sure she will."

The brothers stood there and watched her go up the stairs. So did Cyrus Heimerdorf, behind the desk.

After a moment, Chance snapped at the clerk, "What are you looking at?"

The man turned away and busied himself by fussing with the hotel register.

"I guess now we can go spend some time in one of those saloons," Chance said once Ling was gone. "It'll be nice to play a real game instead of cribbage. Makes me feel like an old English lady."

Ace grinned and waved a hand toward the door. "After you, Duchess."

It was a profitable evening. Ace and Chance returned to the Western Lodge some eighty dollars richer than when they left, thanks to Chance's skills at the poker table and a timely bit of good luck here and there.

Ace had spent the time nursing a beer and watching the goings-on in the saloon. Several times, townsmen had come up to him and congratulated him on the fight he and Chance had had with the trio of McPhee men.

"Those fellas are used to comin' in here, swaggerin' around, and doin' whatever they want," a bearded old-timer had said. "They can get away with that down in Rimfire, since McPhee durned near owns the place, but this ain't Rimfire. 'Bout time somebody give 'em what they had comin' to 'em."

"We didn't really do anything except defend ourselves and the lady with us," Ace explained.

"That China gal? I didn't lay eyes on her myself, but I heard plenty! Fellas say she's one o' the purtiest things ever stepped off a riverboat."

Ace smiled. "I can't argue with that."

Other men slapped him on the back heartily and told him to pass along their good wishes to his brother, since they didn't want to interrupt Chance in the middle of the game. Ace accepted the sentiments graciously, but he was just as glad when the poker game wrapped up and he and Chance were able to head back to the hotel.

They paused in the dimly lit upstairs hallway to look at the door of Ling's room.

After a moment, Chance said, "I hope she's doing all right in there."

"She's sleeping, more than likely," Ace said. "We don't want to disturb her."

"Yeah, you're right. I know that. I'd feel better if we were certain she didn't need anything, but I don't see how we can do that without waking her up."

"Let's just turn in," Ace suggested. "You'll see in the morning that everything's fine."

Chance shrugged and went on in when Ace unlocked the door of their room.

For somebody who had claimed to be worried, it didn't take Chance long to fall asleep. He was snoring softly, but Ace lay there awake, thinking that maybe his brother had been right. Maybe they should have knocked on Ling's door and called out to her to make sure she was all right.

If he did that now, though, Chance would never let him hear the end of it.

Eventually Ace dozed off, although his sleep was light and restless. He didn't know how much time had passed when something roused him.

He opened his eyes. The room was still dark, with only a bit of faint starlight creeping in through the slight gap in the curtains over the window.

His eyes were adjusted to the darkness and were naturally keen enough for him to pick up a hint of movement over by the chairs where he and Chance had piled their clothes.

Ace's gun belt was over there, but his Colt wasn't. It lay on the small table beside the bed. Moving in absolute silence, he reached out and closed his hand around the revolver's walnut grips then used his other arm to push back the covers.

A floorboard creaked, making a tiny sound as the intruder moved.

Ace might not have heard it if some instinct hadn't already awakened him. He glanced toward the door. It was closed, but that had to be how their nocturnal visitor had gotten into the room. They would have heard the window being shoved up. The door had been locked when they turned in, but it wouldn't take much skill to defeat that.

Ace had no idea who the intruder might be. A sneak thief, maybe. He decided that was the most likely explanation. It crossed his mind that Angus McPhee might have sent one of his gun-wolves after them to take revenge for his men being locked up but discarded that idea as too far-fetched.

Whoever the varmint was, he intended to get the drop on him. He sat up slowly so the bedsprings wouldn't shift and make too much noise, and swung his legs off the mattress. Barefooted and wearing only the bottom half of a pair of long handles, he stood up and raised the Colt, ready to call out to the intruder and warn him not to move.

Ace sensed as much as heard the sudden threat beside him and tried to twist in that direction, thinking wildly, *There are two of them!*

Something crashed against his head with stunning force, driving him to his knees. He felt the gun slip from his fingers and heard it thud to the floor, then the second intruder hit him again and he pitched forward into oblivion.

The first thing Ace was aware of as consciousness seeped back into his brain was the sound of somebody moaning.

At first he thought maybe he was the one making that noise, but then he realized that wasn't the case. It was coming from somewhere else in the room.

Ace tried to move. Pain exploded in his head and radiated out to fill his body. He had a terrible taste in his mouth that threatened to make him sick. He fought it down, thinking that if he had to throw up, it might just kill him.

Gradually, the pain and the sickness subsided. He risked opening his eyes and saw that he was still in the hotel room he shared with his brother. Gray light came in around the curtain. The hour was somewhere around dawn.

He remembered waking up to find someone in the room. As he recalled being hit on the head and knocked out, a feeling of alarm raced through him. He had to know if Chance and Ling were safe.

Ace was lying on the floor next to the bed. He moved his hands under him and pushed himself up. For a few seconds, the room spun crazily as if the world had started turning the wrong way. Then it settled down and he was able to lift his head and take a better look around.

Chance was sprawled on the bed, moving around a little as another moan came from his mouth. His eyes were closed. He was trying to regain consciousness but hadn't quite made it yet.

When Ace was propped up in a stable sitting position, leaning against the bed, he raised his hand and tentatively explored the side of his head where the wallop had landed. He found a tender lump, but it wasn't sore or swollen enough to explain why he had been out for hours. He should have come to in minutes after being knocked out.

The light at the window made it clear that wasn't the case. What in the world had happened to him and Chance?

Carefully, Ace struggled to his feet. His head swam again. He swallowed hard, clinging to one of the posts at the foot of the bed until everything settled down.

Chance was lying on top of the covers as if he had been trying to get up but had collapsed back onto the bed. He had a small lump on his forehead where he'd been hit.

Ace reached down, grasped his brother's bare foot, and gave it a good shake. "Chance. Hey, Chance. Wake up!"

"Wha . . . whazzat . . ." Chance struggled to open his eyes. When he had them half open, he tried to lift his head. He let out a loud groan as his head fell back.

"You'll feel better in a minute," Ace told him.

"I could feel better . . . and still be dying." Chance's voice was thick and sleepy.

"You're not dying." An idea occurred to Ace. "I think we've been drugged."

"Drugged . . . ? What?" Chance opened his eyes, winced, and went on. "Feels like somebody . . . hit me."

"Yeah. Somebody clouted both of us, knocked us out, then gave us something to make sure we stayed out for a while." Ace's voice was stronger, and he didn't feel as much like he was about to collapse. "It's nearly morning."

"Who in blazes . . . would've done something . . . like that?"

"I've got an idea," Ace said grimly. "You saw the way McPhee looked at Ling. What if he came back for her?"

"Son of a—" Chance rolled onto his side and then sat up to swing his trembling legs off the bed. He tried to stand up but swayed and would have fallen backward if Ace hadn't caught hold of his arm to steady him.

"We've got to find out if she's all right," Chance said.

"Yeah." Ace looked around for the gun he had dropped and spotted it lying on the floor. Bending over to scoop it up wasn't easy, but he managed.

Chance's shoulder holster and gun were with his clothes. He got the revolver and turned toward the door. Both brothers were clad only in their long underwear, but they didn't want to take the time to get dressed. They were too worried about Ling.

The corridor was empty when they stepped out into it. Ace went across the hall and knocked on Ling's door. He called her name and asked, "Are you in there?"

No response came from the room.

"Damn it!" said Chance. "Try the knob."

Ace twisted the knob with his free hand. It turned, and the door moved in an inch or so.

Ace and Chance leveled their guns and moved back a little. Ace kicked the door open, ready to fire if anybody shot at them from inside the darkened room.

Nothing happened.

After a moment, he said, "I'll go in first. You cover me."

"Go ahead," Chance told him.

Ace moved quickly into the room, crossed to the window, and thrust the curtain back to let in more of the predawn light, then swung around toward the bed. It was empty, although the rumpled covers showed that someone had slept in it. The room wasn't that big, and it took only a second to look around and make certain there was no sign of Ling. "Blast it! She's not here."

"McPhee got her," said Chance as he lowered his gun. "That's the only explanation."

"It looks like all her things are gone," Ace went on. "He must have had some of his men sneak into our room to take care of us, then grabbed her. He probably threatened to kill us to keep her from causing too much of a commotion."

"Yeah, that makes sense." Chance turned back to their room. "Come on. We need to get dressed and roust out the sheriff. Maybe we can pick up their trail before they get too far."

Ace hoped so, but he knew the kidnappers probably had a pretty big lead on them already.

Still, where else could they have gone except McPhee's ranch? The problem was that McPhee might be smart enough to hide her out somewhere else for the time being.

The Jensen brothers started to pull their clothes on, then Chance stopped abruptly. "Wait just a damn minute!"

"What is it?" asked Ace.

"The money belt's gone!"

Ace stiffened in surprise. "Are you sure?"

"Of course I'm sure!" Chance pointed at the chair. "It was right there, along with the rest of my things."

"And all of our stake was in it?"

"Yeah, except for a few bucks in my pocket and whatever you've got on you." Chance checked his coat. "That's still there, but the rest of our money's gone!"

Ace felt almost as disoriented as he had when he first regained consciousness. The theft didn't make sense . . . but then it did. "After they knocked us out, McPhee's men must have grabbed the money belt, too. McPhee sent them after Ling, but that made a nice little bonus for them."

"Yeah," Chance agreed. "That's one more reason to go after them as fast as we can."

They didn't waste any more time and pulled their clothes on. As they clattered down the stairs, the noise made the clerk dozing behind the desk start awake. Ace would have asked the man if he'd seen anything but figured that would be futile. McPhee's men would have gone in and out the hotel's rear entrance, and the clerk would have slept through the whole thing.

As they emerged from the building, Ace said, "You go to the sheriff's office and let whoever's on duty there know what happened. I'm going to head for the livery stable and get our horses saddled. We may not wait around for Maddox to form a posse."

"Good idea," Chance agreed. He trotted off toward the sheriff's office.

Ace hurried to the livery stable. The big double doors were closed, but he pounded on them with his fist and called, "Open up!"

After a couple minutes of knocking, one of the doors swung back a foot or so. Joe Patterson, a lanky, rawboned man with a thatch of dark, gray-shot hair peered out sleepily. "What in tarnation do you want, son? Do you know how early it is? How many times am I gonna get dragged outta bed this mornin'?"

"My brother and I need our horses."

"Yeah, yeah, that's the life of a liveryman, I reckon. Any hour o' the day or night, we get folks needin' their horses." Patterson swung the door open wider. "Well, come on in." He pulled his suspenders up over the red long handles he was wearing. "I'll give you a hand gettin' 'em saddled."

Ace started into the barn, then stopped short as something the livery owner had said soaked into his brain. "This isn't the first time somebody woke you up this morning?"

"Naw." Patterson scratched his beard-stubbled jaw. "O' course, the first time wasn't 'cause somebody knocked on my door. My dog pitched a fit in the middle o' the night and woke me up when somebody rode by. I looked out anyway, just to make sure it wasn't anybody lookin' to stable their horses."

"It was some of Angus McPhee's men, wasn't it?" Ace asked excitedly. "How many of them were there? Did they have a girl with them?"

Patterson held up his hands. "Slow down there, young fella, slow down. It was only a couple o' riders, and neither of 'em work for McPhee." The liveryman frowned. "One of 'em *was* a girl, though. How'd you know that?"

"Never mind that," said Ace. "Who was she with?"

"Some well-dressed fella. Must've been middle-aged, 'cause he had white hair and a little mustache."

That description rocked Ace back on his heels. It matched Jack Haggarty, who they hadn't seen since the fire on the *Missouri Belle* the day before.

"Haggarty," Ace said. "He came back and kidnapped her."

"Kidnapped?" Patterson shook his head. "I reckon you got that wrong, kid. The way those two were laughin' and talkin' together as they rode by, I'd say they was the best of friends."

CHAPTER EIGHTEEN

By the time Chance reached the livery stable with a sleepy-looking and clearly angry Sheriff Maddox accompanying him, Ace was sitting on a stool just inside the doors with a glum look on his face.

"What are you doing?" demanded Chance. "You were supposed to be getting the horses ready so we can go after McPhee!"

"The horses are saddled," Ace said, "but we're not going after McPhee."

"What are you talking about? He kidnapped Ling, or at least he had his men kidnap her!"

Ace shook his head. "Nobody kidnapped her, Chance. She double-crossed us."

"Double-crossed us? What in blue blazes are you talking about?"

"She left here of her own free will," Ace explained. He had gotten enough of a description from Joe Patterson to be sure that the young woman the liveryman had seen was indeed Ling. "From the sound of it, the man she rode out with was Jack Haggarty."

"Haggarty!" Chance looked stricken as he immediately grasped the implications of what his brother was telling him.

Sheriff Maddox spoke up. "Haggarty's the gambler from the boat, the one you figure started that fire so he could get away from you, right?"

"That's right," said Ace. "It looks like he and Ling were working together all along."

Chance held up a hand, palm out. "Wait just a damn minute. You don't know that. After Haggarty made it off the riverboat, he could've lurked somewhere around here until last night, then snuck into the hotel and kidnapped Ling. Maybe we were right about what happened but were wrong to blame it on McPhee."

Patterson was standing nearby, leaning on the jamb of the open door that led into his office and living quarters. A big yellow dog sat at his feet, tongue lolling from its mouth. "That gal I saw didn't look to me like she'd been kidnapped. The fella she was with wasn't forcin' her to do anything against her will."

"You can't know that for sure," insisted Chance. "He could've had a gun on her . . ." His voice trailed away as he saw the way Patterson was shaking his head.

"I know you don't want to believe it," Ace said. "Neither did I, at first. But there's really no getting around it, Chance. That was Ling and Haggarty sneaking around in our room. Haggarty knocked us out and drugged us—although I guess it might have been her—and then they stole our money belt." A bitter note crept into his voice as he added, "She probably felt you wearing it when she hugged us and figured that's where most of our stake would be. Haggarty knew it was a pretty good amount of money, too. He'd seen how much you won on the riverboat."

"But . . . but blast it, that would make her nothing but a thief!"

Ace nodded glumly. "I reckon that's about the size of it."

"That business about how she was Haggarty's slave . . . ?"

"Probably just a lie, so she could get close to us, find out where we kept our money, and steal it."

Chance looked a little sick. "I believed her. I believed every word out of her mouth."

"So did I."

"Yeah, well, that doesn't make me feel any better about being tricked!"

Sheriff Maddox said, "A kidnapped woman's one thing. A thief's another. I'm not sure I can round up a posse that's willing to go after somebody who stole a little money from a couple foolish youngsters."

"It wasn't just a little money," said Chance. "It was two thousand dollars."

Patterson let out a low whistle of surprise. "That's a heap of dinero."

Maddox shook his head. "Doesn't matter," the sheriff declared. "It's still just theft. I'll file a report, but I'm not about to go chasing across the territory after a couple thieves."

"What about the fact they knocked us out?" asked Ace. "That's assault, isn't it?"

"Legally, I suppose it is. Most folks in these parts

don't rely on the law to handle problems like that, though. They stomp their own snakes."

"We know that," Chance snapped. "We're not greenhorns, no matter what you think of us, Sheriff."

Maddox shrugged. "Then you understand why I'm not gonna get all worked up about this. You track those two down and bring 'em back here, I'll lock 'em up for you and put 'em in front of a judge. That's about all I can do."

"You mean all you're *going* to do."

"Same difference," Maddox said. "Now, if you'll excuse me, the sun's nearly up, and I ain't had any coffee yet." He stalked off, leaving Ace and Chance at the livery stable.

The brothers looked at each other.

Chance said, "We're going after them, aren't we?"

"We're sure going to try." Ace turned to the liveryman. "Mr. Patterson, did you see which way they went when they left town?"

Patterson shook his head. "No, not really. After they rode by, I closed the door and went back to bed, where I stayed until you came along and started bangin' on the door."

"Did they notice you looking at them or that the stable door was open?"

"Well, now, I can't really answer that, can I? I don't know what they saw and didn't see. But I'll say that they didn't act like they knew anybody was watchin'. In fact, the gal leaned over in the saddle and gave the fella a little kiss."

Chance let out an exasperated growl.

Patterson went on. "The door was open just a crack,

and I didn't light a lantern. I reckon there's a good chance they didn't know anybody was around."

"Which means they probably think they got away free and clear," said Ace. "If your dog hadn't barked and woke you up, we wouldn't have any idea what happened to Ling. She would have just disappeared."

"We would have blamed it on McPhee," said Chance. "We tried to, until we found out different."

"If they were smart enough to figure that out, they might have thought we'd start looking for them by heading for McPhee's ranch. That means they'd go the other direction. North instead of south, right?" Ace looked to Patterson for confirmation.

The liveryman nodded. "Rimfire and McPhee's Tartan spread are south of here, all right."

"What's north?" asked Chance.

"The Canadian border, if you go far enough. Not much between here and there except open range. Some of the spreads hereabouts use it for grazin', but there's no civilization to speak of."

"What about on the other side of the border?" Ace wanted to know.

"More of the same for a long way."

Ace looked at his brother. "It doesn't sound like there'd be anything in that direction to appeal to them. At least in Rimfire there are saloons where Haggarty could gamble."

Patterson said, "Oh, yeah, there's several saloons in Rimfire. It's a pretty wide-open town."

"We should at least check for fresh tracks leading south," Ace went on.

Chance nodded. "That sounds about like the only choice we have."

"You boys are goin' after 'em, then?" asked Patterson.

Both Jensen brothers looked at him, grim-faced and determined, and Chance said, "Was there ever any doubt?"

Rimfire was a long day's ride to the south, but according to Patterson, Ace and Chance would be able to reach it by nightfall . . . or thereabouts, anyway. They were thankful for that because it meant they wouldn't have to lay in enough supplies for a longer journey. They bought some extra biscuits at Plummer's Café and some jerky at the general store. That would serve as their midday meal.

They had a good breakfast before they set out, although the time spent doing so chafed at the brothers. Every minute that passed was a minute Ling and Haggarty were using to build a bigger lead. Yet with it likely they were heading for Rimfire, time wasn't quite as much of the essence as it might have been otherwise.

Finally they were ready to ride out. They started by crisscrossing the area south of town, searching for fresh hoofprints left by two riders. They found several such trails, but without knowing anything about the horses Ling and Haggarty had been riding, it was impossible to be sure which of the tracks belonged to them—if any of them did.

"We're just going to have to head down there and see what we can find," Ace said as they reined in and sat staring at some of the tracks they had found leading south.

"Yeah, you're right." Chance thumbed back his hat. "The only thing we've got going for us is that they don't know we figured out what happened. They may be just moseying along and taking it easy. They might not be planning on getting to Rimfire until sometime tomorrow."

"In which case we might catch up to them today," said Ace.

"Yeah. So we'd better do some riding, hadn't we?"

By way of answer, Ace heeled his big chestnut into motion again. Chance was right beside him on the cream-colored gelding. Both horses had plenty of strength and stamina, and they moved out smartly in ground-eating lopes.

The Jensen brothers were accustomed to long days in the saddle, although it had been a while since they'd made a fast ride. They stopped occasionally to stretch their legs and let their mounts rest, and at midday they paused longer. Riding the horses into the ground wouldn't accomplish anything, and the halt gave them a chance to eat the food they had brought along, washed down with water from their canteens.

Most of the time, however, they were on the move, and the miles rolled past. A few mountains were visible in the distance, but the terrain where they rode was grass-covered prairie with a few sparsely wooded hills. Now and then a dry wash or a rocky ridge blocked their path and they had to find ways around the obstacles, which slowed them down and increased their frustration.

"I still don't want to believe it was all a lie," Chance said at one point during the afternoon.

"You mean the things that Ling told us?"

"Yeah. All that stuff about her father selling her, and the things she's had to go through since then."

Ace shrugged. "All that might have been true. There may have even been some truth to the story about Haggarty winning her in a poker game. Seems like he hasn't exactly been keeping her a slave ever since then, though. From the sound of what Mr. Patterson told us, they're more like partners than master and slave."

"Lovers, more like," Chance said with a disdainful grunt.

"Well, could be. It wouldn't surprise me if they've run this little game before. Haggarty loses Ling in a poker game, then she passes word to him about when to rob the unlucky fella she winds up with."

"I'll bet she doesn't even talk like that," Chance said bitterly. "'This one' this and 'this one' that. Calling herself a humble servant. Bowing to us, for God's sake!"

With a rueful smile, Ace said, "You've got to admit, it worked pretty well."

"Yeah, but they're not going to get away with it. We'll catch up to them, either before we get to Rimfire or there in the town, and then we'll settle things. Haggarty's not gonna get away this time."

"What about Ling?" Ace asked. "If we're right, she's as much a part of it as he is."

"She ought to go to jail, that's what!"

"It won't be easy, sending a woman to jail, no

matter what she's done. Sort of goes against the grain, doesn't it?"

Chance frowned. "Well . . . maybe. If we could get our money back, and if she promised not to try to fool anybody else like that . . ."

"You'd believe her if she made a promise like that?"

"If Haggarty's in jail where he belongs, she won't have much choice, will she?"

"We'll see." Ace had a hunch things wouldn't work out that neatly. They seldom did. But at least he and his brother could try to recover their money without ruining the rest of Ling's life, if it was at all possible.

They saw quite a few grazing cattle during their ride but no other people until, in the middle of the afternoon, they topped a long, gradual rise and spotted a line of wagons stretched out across the prairie about half a mile ahead of them.

"Look up there," Chance said. "It's a wagon train. I didn't think there were any of those around anymore."

"There are plenty of places left where there's good homesteading land, but the railroads don't go there yet. Wagon trains are still the best way to get there."

"But this is all ranch land around here."

"It's open range. The government opens up some of it for filing on, now and then, and farmers or smaller ranchers move in. That's what leads to range wars, which you'd know about if you ever read a newspaper."

Chance waved off that suggestion. "If there's anything really important going on in the world, I figure you'll tell me about it. There haven't been any range wars around here, have there?"

"Not yet. But if those are farmers in those wagons up there, there's no telling what might happen."

Having gained on the wagon train since their horses could move considerably faster than the teams of oxen hitched to the big, canvas-covered vehicles, they were only about a quarter mile behind the lumbering wagons. That was plenty close enough for them to hear the sudden roar of gunshots as a group of riders boiled up seemingly from out of the ground and charged at the wagons, firing as they went.

CHAPTER NINETEEN

Ace figured out instantly that the attackers had been lurking in one of the dry washes that slashed across the range, out of sight of the approaching wagons. Whether they were thieves who'd just been waiting for unwary travelers to come along, or whether they were targeting this wagon train specifically, Ace didn't know, nor did it matter.

What was important was that innocent people were in danger, and the Jensen boys couldn't stand by and do nothing. They weren't made that way.

Ace yanked his Winchester from the sheath strapped to his saddle and called, "Come on!" as he heeled the chestnut into a run. Chance had pulled his rifle, too, and was right beside him.

Both brothers were excellent riders, and their mounts were well-trained. They were able to guide the horses with their knees while they lifted the Winchesters to their shoulders.

The wagons had come to a halt. The people on them had scrambled for cover as bullets started to fly. Some of the pilgrims had retreated into the canvas-covered backs of the vehicles while others crouched underneath the wagons. Booming reports floated across the prairie, along with clouds of powder smoke as the immigrants began putting up a fight.

Unfortunately, the attackers were mounted on fast-moving horses, and that made them difficult targets as they raced around throwing lead at the wagons. In an earlier time period, Indians had attacked wagon trains in the same manner, trying to drive the white settlers from their land, but the high point of native resistance on the plains had come almost a decade earlier when George Armstrong Custer and members of the Seventh Cavalry had been wiped out at Little Big Horn. Since then, danger from Indians had declined until it wasn't a real threat anymore.

The white riders circling the wagon train with guns blazing rode fast, crouching low in the saddle to make themselves smaller targets, and directed a steady fire against the wagon train. In the first few seconds of the Jensen brothers' charge, Ace had already seen several of the defenders fall.

He and Chance opened fire on the attackers. One of the riders threw his arms in the air and pitched off his horse. He landed hard, rolled over a couple times, and came to rest in a limp sprawl of arms and legs that indicated he was probably dead.

The raiders became aware that they were under assault from a different direction. Several of them peeled off and galloped out to meet the charge. Smoke and flame spouted from their guns as they raced toward Ace and Chance.

Ace saw dirt spurting up where bullets plowed into

the ground in front of them. He stayed calm, drew a
bead, and squeezed the Winchester's trigger. One of
the men rocked back as the bullet smashed into him.
Another man dropped his gun, twisted in the saddle,
and clutched his shoulder where Chance had drilled
him. He pulled his horse into a looping turn away
from the fight.

A bullet whipped past Ace's ear, the closest any of
the flying lead had come so far. Ace fired again, and
from the way one of the horses leaped, he figured
he'd creased the animal. The rider had to grab the
saddle horn to stay mounted and forgot about shooting as the horse sunfished away to the side.

Evidently, the two men left didn't care for a battle
with even odds. They wheeled their horses and raced
back toward their companions, who were still gallop-
ing around and firing on the wagon train.

The clouds of dust and gun smoke in the air made it
difficult to know how many were involved in the
attack. Ace estimated at least twenty. He and Chance
peppered them with slugs as they continued their
charge.

One of the men suddenly broke away from the
others, shouting and waving an arm above his head.
He galloped back in the direction they had come
from. The others wasted no time in following him.
They were giving up the attack on the wagon train.

Bullets hurried them along as they disappeared
one by one into the wash where they had been hiding
earlier. Ace wasn't surprised when he saw spurts of
powder smoke from the edge of that gully. The men
had dismounted and taken cover but hadn't given up
on their assault, after all.

"They can keep those wagons pinned down until they've picked off everybody!" Chance shouted.

"I know! Let's see if we can flank 'em!" Ace swung the chestnut to the left and rode wide around the wagons.

Chance did likewise as a couple men on horseback left the wagon train and angled out to join them.

Bullets whined around them as the men in the wash tried to keep them from splitting away from the wagons. The four riders were moving so fast it was hard to draw a bead on them. They converged on the wash a few hundred yards away from where the attackers had gone to ground.

Ace barely had time to glance at the men from the wagon train as he swung down from the saddle. One was older, one younger, that was all he saw.

Then he and Chance slid down the bank to the bottom of the gully, each holding his rifle at a slant across his chest. The other two followed. When they reached the bottom, they didn't bother with introductions, just gave each other curt nods, then trotted toward the spot where the attackers were holed up.

As the defenders rounded one of several bends, bullets suddenly flew past them. A force had been sent to meet their flank attack. Ace flung himself behind an outcropping of dirt and fired at the darting figures ahead of them. Chance and the pair from the wagon train sought cover, as well, and returned the fire. Quickly, it turned into a standoff as bullets flew back and forth in the gully.

Ace spotted a leg sticking out from behind a rock and instantly drilled a rifle round through it. The wounded man howled in pain and flopped out into the open. Almost before he hit the ground, his body jerked as a couple slugs punched into it. He spasmed a couple times, then lay still as death claimed him.

Ace looked across the gulley at the older man from the wagon train, who waved and gave him a friendly grin, seemingly not that concerned about the deadly battle in which they found themselves. The man reached inside his shirt and pulled out something that made Ace's eyes widen in surprise.

The man was holding a stick of dynamite with a short fuse attached to it. "You fellas make them rifles sing and dance!" he called to Ace as he fished a match out of his pocket.

"Pour it on 'em!" Ace shouted. He and Chance and the young man fired as fast as they could.

The older man lit the fuse, stepped out away from the bank, and threw the dynamite along the wash. It turned end over end as it flew through the air. Guns fell silent and men shouted in alarm as they spotted the pinwheeling cylinder. Then the dynamite dropped out of sight.

A split second later, a thunderous explosion rocked the ground. A column of dust and smoke rose into the air. Gravel pattered down like rain.

As the echoes of the blast rolled away across the prairie, the defenders heard pounding hoofbeats moving away fast. With no way of knowing whether more dynamite was about to come sailing in at them, all the attackers could do was light a shuck out of there as fast as they could.

The younger man from the wagon train let out a triumphant whoop. "That did it, Uncle Dave! Those varmints won't stop runnin' until they get to Kansas!"

"Don't count on that, Rufe," said the older man. "But at least we spooked 'em for now. We'd best make sure they didn't leave any wounded behind. A crippled predator's the most dangerous critter out there."

The defenders all moved out from the banks where they had taken cover.

The older man, whose jaw was covered with silvery beard stubble, nodded to Ace and Chance. "We're mighty obliged to you young fellas for your help. My name's Dave Wingate. That strappin' youngster is my nephew Rufe."

"We're the Jensen brothers. I'm Ace, he's Chance."

"Pleased to meet you," said Wingate. "We're gonna check on the damages up ahead."

"We'll come with you." Chance reached under his coat and pulled the revolver from his shoulder holster. If there was any more gunplay, the odds were that it would be close work.

Ace drew his Colt, too. The four men moved forward along the wash, past the dead man lying next to the bank, and on around the next bend.

The explosion had left a good-sized crater in the gully floor, along with gouging out part of the bank. The bloody remains of several men were scattered around, indicating just how devastating the damage had been.

The grisly scene made Ace a little sick. He could tell that Chance and Rufe were feeling green around the gills, too. Wingate seemed to take the carnage in stride, though. Given his age, it was likely he had served during the war, and no doubt had seen worse things on the battlefield.

"Wish I knew whether Mitchell was among those blowed-up carcasses," the older man commented. "If he is, we might not have to worry about the rest of that bunch. Without him to lead 'em, there's a chance they won't bother us no more."

"You know the men who attacked you?" Ace asked.

"I know one of 'em—Clade Mitchell. He signed on as one of our guides, but he was just leadin' us out here so he could signal the rest of his no-good bunch when to jump us."

"I caught him usin' a mirror to signal to somebody yesterday," Rufe put in. He was a tall, broad-shouldered young man with a shock of curly black hair under his wide-brimmed hat. "When I asked him what he was doin', he pulled his gun and walloped me." Rufe pointed to a bruise on his forehead. "I reckon the only reason he didn't shoot me was because he didn't want to alert the rest of the wagon train. He figured on killin' me quiet-like. But Uncle Dave come along and spooked him. That's the only reason I'm still alive."

"Mitchell lit a shuck outta there, rather than explain what he was doin'," Wingate said. "I knew then we were in for trouble, that it was only a matter of time before outlaws hit the train. There was nothin' we could do except press on, though. Sure couldn't turn around and go back to Missouri, not after comin' this far."

"That's where you're from, Missouri?" Chance asked.

"Well, it's where those pilgrims are from. Rufe and me, we ain't from anyplace in particular these days.

I've been guidin' and scoutin' for wagon trains for nigh on to twenty years now, and Rufe's come on the job with me lately, since his folks passed on."

"There aren't many wagon trains anymore," Ace pointed out.

"That's for sure." Wingate grinned. "I didn't say it was a *good* job. But it's better 'n trudgin' along behind a plow all day or standin' behind a store counter."

Neither of the Jensens could argue with that sentiment.

"Anyway, after Mitchell took off for the tall and uncut all suspicious-like, I told the cap'n of the wagon train it might be a good idea to find someplace we could fort up for a while, but he wanted to push on ahead and I can't say as I really blame him. Never been the sort to sit and wait for trouble to come to me."

"We're kind of the same way," Chance said with a smile.

"You're sure this fella Mitchell had something to do with the men who attacked you?" asked Ace.

"I got a good look at the no-good scalawag, ridin' right out in front," Wingate replied. "I figure he's probably the boss of the whole gang."

"That's why you said that if he's dead, the others might scatter instead of trying to attack the wagon train again."

"Yep. Between us, we killed more 'n half a dozen of his men, but if he's still alive, I don't reckon that'll stop him. If anything, the dirty polecat'll be more determined than ever to steal everything those pilgrims have."

Ace and Chance exchanged a glance. They had already spent some time helping out the members of the wagon train, while Ling and Haggarty were getting farther ahead of them. They didn't want to be delayed any longer than necessary.

On the other hand, it would be difficult to ride away from the wagon train as long as the immigrants might be in danger. That would go against the grain for both Jensen brothers.

"Where are those wagons bound for?" Ace asked.

"Town called Rimfire, startin' out," said Wingate. "There's some government land on the far side of the settlement that's just been opened up for home-steadin'. That's where they figure to stake their claims."

"Why don't you fellas come with us?" Rufe suggested. "We've seen for ourselves that you're good fightin' men, and if those outlaws come back, we could use a couple extra guns."

"We've never been to Rimfire," said Ace, "but we were headed there ourselves."

"Well, that works out fine!" Rufe said with a grin.

"You'd be welcome to throw in with us," the elder Wingate added.

Ace rubbed his chin and frowned in thought. They weren't that far from Rimfire. The wagons could make it there the next day. And since Ling and Haggarty didn't know that anybody was on their trail, there was at least a chance they would stay in the settlement for a few days before moving on.

They might even try to cheat somebody else out of his hard-earned money.

Ace looked at his brother. Chance shrugged and nodded. If the bandits returned, a couple extra defenders could come in mighty handy for the wagon train.

"All right," Ace said. "We'll ride with you to Rimfire. And if that varmint Mitchell and his friends show up again . . ."

"We'll all give 'em a mighty warm welcome," said Wingate. "A hot lead welcome, in fact!"

CHAPTER TWENTY

After they explored the gully for another hundred yards to make sure no wounded outlaws were hiding in it, the four men climbed out of the gash in the earth. Rufe took off his hat and waved it over his head to signal to those waiting with the wagons that everything was all right.

Ace whistled for his horse, and as it trotted along the edge of the wash toward him, the other three mounts trailed along as he'd hoped. The four of them mounted up and rode to join the wagons.

A white-mustached man in a black suit and hat strode out to meet them. He carried a Spencer carbine and greeted them by asking curtly, "Was it Mitchell and his bunch, like you suspected, Dave?"

"Yes, sir, Cap'n, it was," drawled Wingate. "Don't know if we killed Mitchell or not, but I'd sure like to hope so. The rest of the varmints lit a shuck after I blew a few of 'em to Hades with that stick o' dynamite I grabbed 'fore I rode out."

"That was smart thinking." The man smiled, which relieved the grim cast of his rugged face. "I'm glad I decided to bring along a box of the stuff, just in case we have to blast out any stumps while we're establishing our homesteads."

"Comes in handy for blastin' owlhoots, too," Wingate said with a chuckle

The man looked at Ace and Chance. "Who are these fellows?"

"Couple o' brothers named . . . Johnson, was it?"

"Jensen. I'm Ace and this is my brother Chance."

"Edward Fairfield," the white-haired man introduced himself. "I'm the elected captain of this wagon train." He half-turned and gestured toward the line of wagons.

Now that things weren't quite so hectic, Ace was able to count them. There were fifteen of the big, canvas-topped prairie schooners. He caught a flash of bright red hair in the late afternoon sun and saw that a young woman was on the driver's seat of the lead wagon, holding the reins in her slender hands. She returned his scrutiny with an open, direct gaze. Ace looked away, slightly embarrassed that she might have thought he was staring.

He was just a little surprised. Hair such a bright shade of red wasn't often seen in nature.

"How many men did we lose, Cap'n?" Dave Wingate was asking.

"Two men were killed," Fairfield replied grimly. "Seamus Dugan and Arch Tennison."

Wingate clicked his tongue, shook his head, and said solemnly, "Damn shame. They was good fellas."

"Yes, they were. The only blessing is that neither of them was married, so they left no families behind.

Four more men were wounded, but as far as I know, none seriously. And two oxen were killed."

"You've got more livestock. You can replace 'em."

"Indeed." Fairfield looked at Ace and Chance again. "You gentlemen are welcome to camp with us this evening. We would have extended our hospitality to you anyway, but since you risked your life to help us, you'll be honored guests."

"We're obliged to you, Mr. Fairfield," said Ace.

"Those Jensen boys are doin' more than that," Wingate said as he nodded toward Ace and Chance. "They're throwin' in with us for the rest o' the trip to Rimfire."

"Really? That's excellent news."

"Well, it's not all that far," Ace pointed out. "In fact, we ought to be there tomorrow."

Fairfield's bushy white eyebrows rose in surprise. "We're that close? I didn't realize that." He looked at Wingate. "Did you, Dave?"

"I knew we were close. Didn't rightly know if it'd be tomorrow or the next day when we got there."

"If we're that close, perhaps we should do ahead and make camp for the night. I know that people are quite shaken up by the attack."

"I dunno. You might want to push on a mite farther." Wingate used his thumb to point upward, where black dots wheeling through the sky signified that buzzards were already starting to circle. "You could leave a couple fellas behind to dig graves for the two men we lost." He leaned to the side and spat. "I figure draggin' the other carcasses over to that gully and dumpin' 'em in will be good enough for owlhoots."

"Yes, of course," Fairfield said, nodding. "That's a good idea."

"Me and Rufe will ride on ahead to find a good place and make sure there ain't no more ambushes." Wingate looked at Ace and Chance. "You young fellas mind bringin' up the rear and keepin' an eye on our back trail?"

"We can do that," Ace agreed.

Wingate looked around. "Where'd that blasted Rufe get off to?"

Ace could have answered that. Still mounted, Rufe Wingate had drifted his horse over to the lead wagon, where he was talking to the young redheaded woman. It seemed to be more than idle conversation. Both of them were smiling as they talked animatedly.

Wingate spotted his nephew and called, "Rufe! Come on, dadgum it! We got work to do. You can court Cap'n Fairfield's granddaughter later."

Rufe scowled, and the redhead looked uncomfortable at being singled out. After saying something else to her, he swung his horse away from the wagon and trotted over to join the others. "You don't have to be so doggone contrary, Uncle Dave."

"Just statin' the fact," said Wingate. "We need to scout out a good spot for the train to camp tonight. Let's go."

The two men rode out. Ace and Chance nodded to Fairfield and turned their horses toward the rear of the wagon train. Both of them nodded politely to the captain's granddaughter as they rode past her. Close up, she was freckled and pretty in a wholesome way. She was blushing furiously, too.

Chance said, "I've got a hunch ol' Rufe's not going

to stay in the scouting business for long. When this bunch of pilgrims gets where it's going, I'll bet he stays there and tries to marry Miss Fairfield."

Ace grinned. "No bet."

They dropped back far enough behind the wagons to avoid the worst of the dust being raised by the vehicles' wheels and the hooves of the oxen. On a few occasions in the past, the Jensen brothers had worked on cattle drives and knew what it was like to ride drag. The wagon train wasn't that bad, but it did create quite a bit of dust.

They checked behind them frequently for any signs of pursuit and kept an eye on the flanks, as well. Everything seemed peaceful after the earlier battle. It was late afternoon, and they knew the wagons would be stopping soon.

The train halted when it came to a creek with some scrubby brush and a few cottonwoods growing along its banks. The stream meandered through a shallow valley between two ridges. Wingate and Rufe were waiting on the north bank, sitting their saddles easily.

As Ace and Chance saw the wagons coming to a stop, they rode forward quickly to join the scouts and Edward Fairfield, who had been riding in front of the lead wagon on a big, sturdy roan.

Wingate was saying, " . . . maybe not the best place to fort up, but this is good water and if we draw the wagons in a circle like we usually do, I reckon we'll be fine."

"I trust you, Mr. Wingate." Fairfield turned in the

saddle and bellowed, "Circle the wagons, folks! Circle the wagons!"

From the way the immigrants went about the task, they had experience at it, as Wingate had indicated. By the time the sun had set, the wagons were drawn up end to end. The teams, the other livestock, and the saddle mounts were all inside the rough circle and restrained by a rope corral strung across the circle, dividing it in half. On the other side were the cooking fires, which soon blazed brightly.

Those fires would be visible for a long way out here on the prairie, thought Ace, but he wasn't sure that mattered. They didn't have to worry about hostiles, and Clade Mitchell doubtless knew approximately where the wagon train was, anyway.

Edward Fairfield asked the brothers to have supper with him and his granddaughter. Laura Fairfield had a pot of stew simmering over a fire as Ace and Chance walked up.

She smiled at them. "Welcome to our home, such as it is."

"We'll have a real home soon, girl," boomed her grandfather. "These lads say we'll reach Rimfire tomorrow, and the range that's our destination lies within a day's travel of the settlement, according to the documents we received."

"Did you make arrangements with the government to homestead out here, Captain?" asked Ace while Laura began ladling stew into bowls for him and Chance.

"That's right. We had to pay a fee back in Missouri to reserve our claims. Once we establish our homesteads, prove up on them, and maintain them for five years, the land will be ours free and clear. Fine farming land, I'm told."

"Well, it's probably decent farming land." Ace took the bowl Laura handed him. "It won't be like Kansas or Nebraska, though. This has been ranching country so far, and there's a reason for that."

Fairfield frowned. "I've seen the land we've been traveling over. With proper irrigation, it will grow excellent crops."

"Yes, sir, I believe it will. There'll be a lot of hard work involved, though."

"Don't waste your breath cautioning me about hard work," rumbled Fairfield. "I've known nothing else my entire life, and most of the people in our party are the same way."

"Yes, sir, I'm sure that's true. I meant no offense."

"That's all right," Laura told him. "Grandfather has to growl a little now and then. It's his nature. There's plenty of coffee in the pot, there at the edge of the fire."

Once they were sitting cross-legged on the ground, enjoying the meal, Ace went on. "There's something else you ought to be aware of, Captain, if you're not already. I mentioned that this has been ranching country, and some of the fellas who own those spreads may not take it kindly when folks like you and your friends come in and start claiming land they always considered open range."

"It's not open range," Fairfield said. "The government owns it and wants people to settle on it."

Chance said, "Yeah, but that may not mean much to fellas who have been fighting Indians and rustlers and blizzards for the past twenty or thirty years. They're sort of used to getting their own way."

"I'm sure once they know what the situation is, they'll understand."

"We can hope so," said Ace. "Were you folks all neighbors back in Missouri?"

Laura said, "Some of us were, but not all. Really, we came from all over, and what we have in common is the desire to start over."

Gruffly, as if to hide his own emotion, Fairfield said, "Laura's parents—my son and his wife—died of a fever last year. Poor girl didn't need to stay where there are so many bad memories, so I sold my farm and we decided to come on out here. Nothing like an adventure to take your mind off your sorrows."

"No, sir, I suppose there's not." Ace had a hunch that Fairfield wanted to get away from his own sorrows as much or more than Laura did . . . but that was all right, too.

A big figure loomed up in the firelight, trailed by a smaller one. Rufe Wingate wore a smile on his face as he said, "Evenin', Miss Laura. We ain't too late for vittles, are we?"

"Not at all," she told him. "There's plenty of stew in the pot, and it's still hot. You and your uncle help yourself."

"Thank you kindly, Miss Laura." Smoke curled up from the old briar pipe Dave Wingate held in his hand. He clamped the stem between his teeth while he filled a bowl with stew and carried it over to sit on the ground next to Edward Fairfield. He grunted as he lowered himself. "My rheumatiz sure does act up after a long day in the saddle."

"One of the perils of getting older, Dave," said Fairfield. "The aches and pains seem to multiply into a veritable cascade."

"The way you talk, Cap'n, it's easy to tell that you was a teacher at one time, as well as tillin' the soil."

"I tried to plant a crop in fertile young minds, yes."

"There you go, makin' my point for me." Wingate looked over at Ace and Chance. "Happen to see anybody trailin' us while you were ridin' behind the wagons a while ago?"

Ace shook his head. "No, there wasn't any sign of anybody."

"They could have been hanging back out of sight, though," added Chance.

"That's what I was thinkin'," Wingate said with a solemn nod. "I'd like to hope them bandits would think twice about hittin' us again after we blasted 'em the way we did, but I sure can't guarantee it."

"There are few guarantees in life," Fairfield agreed.

Rufe said, "I can think of one. Miss Laura cooks up the best-tastin' mess of vittles west of the Mississippi! Probably east o' there, too."

Laura blushed prettily. "Rufe, you do go on."

"Yes'm, I do."

As they continued eating and washing the food down with swallows of black coffee, Fairfield said to Dave Wingate, "These two young fellows seem to think we may be in for trouble from the ranchers who live in the area we're going to homestead."

"Well, I won't lie to you," Wingate drawled. "I've seen it happen before when sodbusters—I mean, homesteaders—come into an area where cattlemen are used to havin' things their own way. There's been some shootin' wars."

"Grandfather . . ." Laura said worriedly.

"But not lately, and not in these parts," Wingate hastened to add.

"You don't have to worry, Miss Laura," Rufe put in. "Uncle Dave and me won't let anything happen to you folks. You got our word on that."

"Hold on, boy," said Wingate. "I don't remember sayin' we were gonna settle down in these parts. I figured we'd drift on once these folks get where they're goin', maybe do some prospectin' or scout for the army. I hear tell that down Arizona way, they're campaignin' against the Apaches again, and they can probably use some good muleskinners and packers."

"Well, sure," Rufe said. "I just meant until things are calmed down hereabouts."

Ace wasn't sure he believed the young man. As he and Chance had mentioned earlier, it seemed likely that Rufe had something more permanent in mind.

The wagon train had to get to where it was going first, though, and that would take another couple days. Whether or not the Jensen brothers accompanied the wagons all the way to their destination depended in large part on whether they picked up the trail of Ling and Haggarty in Rimfire.

After supper, Ace and Chance thanked Laura for the food, then excused themselves to go check on their horses.

They hadn't reached the makeshift corral yet when Rufe Wingate came up behind them and took hold of their shoulders. "I got somethin' to say to you fellas."

Ace didn't like being grabbed that way. He shrugged off Rufe's hand. Chance did likewise.

Ace kept his voice neutral as he asked, "What do you want, Rufe?"

"I seen the way both o' you were lookin' at Miss Laura earlier. You think she's a pretty gal, don't you?"

"Of course we do," Chance replied. "Any man with eyes in his head would think that."

"Well, don't you get any notions about her. She's my gal, you understand. I won't take it kindly if either of you fellas starts tryin' to court her."

Ace said, "We may not even see her again after the wagon train reaches Rimfire tomorrow. We were grateful to her and her grandfather for their hospitality, that's all. So you don't have anything to worry about, Rufe . . . except convincing Laura that she's your girl."

"Oh, she's convinced of it, all right!"

Chance grinned. "Although, if I was to take it into my mind to let her know just how admirable I find her . . ."

That was Chance, thought Ace. Unable to resist a challenge, even when he didn't actually care about the objective.

Rufe balled his hands into fists and stepped closer to Chance. "You better just forget about—"

A startled yell from somewhere else in the circle broke into the warning. All three young men looked around. Their eyes widened in surprise as they saw a ball of fire arcing through the sky toward the camp. It plummeted down, struck the canvas cover on one of the wagons, and instantly the flames began to spread.

CHAPTER TWENTY-ONE

More flaming arrows swooped down toward the wagons, lighting up the sky. Fortunately, they weren't aimed as well as the first one. One of the arrows struck another wagon and set it afire, but the others either fell short or landed inside the circle.

Those misses created dangers of their own, however, catching the grass on fire from the arrows that landed outside the wagon train.

Inside the circle, not far from where Ace, Chance, and Rufe Wingate stood, one of the falling arrows struck a man in the shoulder, lodging there and setting his shirt on fire. He screamed as the flames began to spread.

Ace acted instantly, lunging at the man and tackling him from behind. Ace knew he might be making the arrow wound worse as he rolled the man in the dirt, but putting out the burning shirt was more important at the moment.

A couple blazing arrows landed inside the gathering of livestock, spooking the animals and making them mill around nervously. The oxen surged against wagons and made them rock back and fort. The horses were skittish and threatened to push down the rope corral.

In a matter of seconds, the rain of fire from the sky had thrown the camp into complete chaos. The immigrants ran around, screaming and shouting, and then the sudden boom of guns added to the racket.

"Those outlaws are back!" Chance yelled as he jerked his gun from its holster and whirled toward the outside of the circle. He saw a muzzle flash from the prairie beyond the wagons and triggered two swift shots at it. Then he shoved Rufe toward the nearest wagon and snapped, "Take cover!"

A few yards away, Ace slapped out the last of the flames leaping from the shirt of the man he had tackled. The man groaned in pain from the burns and the arrow stuck in his shoulder, but those injuries would have to be dealt with later.

Ace leaped to his feet and drew his Colt. He glanced around, spotted Chance crouched at the corner of a wagon as he fired at the attackers, and hurried to join his brother. "Must be Mitchell's bunch again!" Ace said as he dropped to a knee behind the wagon tongue and leveled his revolver at the darkness.

"Can't be Indians!" Chance squeezed off another shot. "They wouldn't have missed with so many of those arrows!"

Ace triggered the Colt at a muzzle flash. The fires started by the arrows that landed outside the circle were spreading, but luck was with the immigrants. The wind was from the south, so it blew the flames *away* from the wagons and back toward the men who had launched the arrows.

That tactic had backfired on them, literally, thought Ace.

As the fire spread, so did the glaring light it cast over the plains. They began to see the outlaws crouching out there, and once they had targets at which to aim, their rapid fire became even more deadly. Their bullets scythed through the raiders, spinning them off their feet.

At the front end of the wagon, Rufe Wingate emptied his revolver at the outlaws, then knelt to reload. His eyes were wide as he snapped his revolver's cylinder closed. "I gotta find Laura and make sure she's all right!"

"Go ahead," Chance told him.

Rufe loped away into the confusion. Most of the immigrants had taken cover. Some of the men had recovered enough from the shock of the attack to start putting up a fight. Rifles cracked and shotguns boomed from various places around the camp.

Suddenly, Ace heard a new sound—the drumming of rapid hoofbeats growing louder. He thumbed fresh cartridges into his gun and called to his brother, "Here they come! They're charging the camp!"

Horses loomed up out of the darkness. The firelight behind them cast monstrous shadows as they closed in on the wagons. Outlaws bent forward in the saddles and slammed shots toward the defenders. Ace had to throw himself desperately to the side as one of the horses leaped over the wagon tongue he had been using for cover.

The horse landed inside the circle. The man on its back hauled on the reins and pulled the animal around in a tight spin. Ace rolled over and came up on one knee in time to see the outlaw's gun swinging toward him.

Both irons roared at the same time. Ace felt the wind-rip of a slug's passage close beside his ear. His shot was more accurate, striking the raider in the throat and angling up into his brain. The impact flipped the man off his horse. Blood sprayed in a grisly arc from a severed artery.

Another of the mounted outlaws reached the gap between wagons where the Jensen brothers had stationed themselves. He leaped from the saddle, landed with one foot on a wagon tongue, and pushed off from it to crash into Chance and drive him to the ground. The collision jolted Chance's gun from his hand.

The outlaw tried to bring his revolver to bear, but Chance grabbed his wrist and thrust it up as the man pulled the trigger. The bullet went harmlessly into the air as the gun exploded deafeningly. The outlaw's weight pinned Chance to the ground, but his arms were still free. He hung on to the man's gun wrist with his left hand and rocketed his right fist up in a short but powerful punch to the outlaw's chin.

Chance's head was spinning. The impact had knocked the air out of his lungs, and he struggled to draw in a breath. At the same time, he was fighting off the man who wanted to kill him. He hit the raider twice more and finally knocked the man off to the side. Chance rolled away from him, scooped his gun from the ground, and came up firing just as the outlaw caught his balance and triggered a shot of his own.

The raider's bullet plowed into the ground only

inches from Chance. Chance's slug lanced into the man's chest and knocked him over backward. The outlaw's revolver boomed again as his finger jerked the trigger spasmodically. His back arched and then he slumped as he died.

Ace got to his feet, hurried over to his brother's side, and reached down to grasp Chance's arm. He helped Chance up and they both turned toward the gap where the attackers had breached the wagon train's circle. Ace expected to find more of the outlaws trying to get through, but he saw only the fire burning across the prairie. A few shots still rang out here and there. For the most part, however, the fight seemed to be over.

The rope corral had held, and the livestock were starting to settle down. Ace spotted Rufe Wingate's tall figure and started in that direction. Chance went with him, still breathing heavily as he caught his breath.

As the brothers came up to the Fairfield wagon, they saw that Rufe, Dave Wingate, Edward Fairfield, and Laura all appeared to be unharmed.

Fairfield asked, "Are the outlaws gone?"

"They ain't shootin' at us anymore," Wingate said. "I reckon that's all that matters."

"They must have gotten more of a fight than they expected," said Ace.

"And that prairie fire blowing right back in their faces didn't help matters for them," added Chance.

Wingate said, "Reckon we must've killed another half dozen of the varmints, at least. We're whittlin' 'em down. Maybe they'll give up and go away."

"I need to see how many of our people were hurt," said Fairfield.

"I'll come with you," Wingate volunteered.

As the two older men walked off, Rufe put his hands on Laura's shoulders and gazed intently down at her. "You're sure you ain't hurt?"

"I'm fine, Rufe. How could I be anything else, the way you hovered over me and shielded me with your own body?"

He shook his head. "I don't reckon I could've stood it if anything ever happened to you, Miss Laura."

She put her arms around his waist, rested her head against his chest, and hugged him. "You're sweet."

Rufe looked a little surprised and embarrassed, but he managed to put his arms around her and awkwardly embrace her.

Ace chuckled and said quietly to his brother, "Looks like things weren't quite as settled between those two as Rufe made them out to be."

"Yeah, I'd say this is the first time he's hugged her like that," Chance agreed. "Probably won't be the last, though."

"No, probably not."

Edward Fairfield and Dave Wingate returned a short time later to report that another of the immigrants had been killed in the attack. The party had suffered several more injuries, as well, including the man who'd been struck by the flaming arrow.

But once again, Clade Mitchell and his band of outlaws definitely had come out second-best in the clash. Four of the raiders had made it into the circle, only to be killed. It was unknown how many of them had fallen out on the prairie, fatally wounded.

"We'll keep them four horses," Dave Wingate declared. "Rufe, get some other fellas and drag the bodies of those dead owlhoots outta camp. We don't want 'em in here with us overnight."

"We'll have to bury them in the morning," said Fairfield. "I didn't feel right about dumping those other men in that gully and leaving them there."

Wingate spat. "Better 'n what they deserved."

"That may well be true, but I won't leave them for the scavengers."

"Suit yourself," Wingate replied with a shrug. "If we're as close to Rimfire as these Jensen boys say, takin' the time to bury those skunks won't keep us from reachin' the settlement tomorrow."

Once the bodies had been carried out of the camp, Wingate and Fairfield set up extra guard shifts for the night. It didn't seem likely that the remaining outlaws would return, but they couldn't be sure of that.

Out on the prairie, the fire had burned itself out, but the smell of smoke still hung in the air, mixing with the acrid tang of burned powder. It was a vivid reminder of just how dangerous life out on the frontier could be.

Ace and Chance took one of the extra turns at standing guard, but nothing else happened. By morning the smell from the charred prairie wasn't as bad, but it hadn't gone away completely.

There would be no service for the dead outlaws,

only a quick burial as soon as a single large grave could be dug. Ace thought Edward Fairfield didn't like that much and would have preferred individual graves, but the wagon train captain didn't make any objection.

When that grim chore had been taken care of, everyone got busy preparing to pull out for the last stretch of the trip to Rimfire.

Whether the immigrants would proceed immediately on to the range where they planned to settle was still unknown. Ace supposed it would depend on how long it took the wagons to reach the settlement.

The creek was shallow enough, with a rocky bed, that they had no trouble fording it and pushing on south. At Wingate's request, Ace and Chance rode up front with him, Rufe, and Fairfield.

Rufe kept glancing back over his shoulder, looking at Laura as she handled the team of oxen hitched to the lead wagon.

"Rufe, watch where we're goin'," his uncle scolded him. "If you want to look at what's behind us, you can drop back and ride drag with them other fellas I put back there."

"Sorry, Uncle Dave," Rufe muttered. He tried to keep his eyes pointed ahead of the wagon train, but it wasn't easy for him.

A range of low but rugged peaks rose to the east. Those were the Highwood Mountains, Ace recalled. Another range, the Little Belts, was visible to the south. Between them lay a broad, fertile valley evidently watered by numerous streams, judging by how green it was as the wagon train entered it. He could see why cattlemen had been drawn to it. It was good range for grazing. The small hills that rolled across the valley would make farming more difficult, but certainly not impossible. There were a number of wide, level stretches where fields could be plowed and planted.

In the vast country with its huge, arching sky, it seemed like there ought to be plenty of room for everybody.

Unfortunately, some people didn't see it that way.

By midday, the wagons had penetrated several miles into the valley and had passed hundreds of grazing cattle. Angus McPhee's Tartan Ranch was south of Rimfire, Ace recalled, so those cows probably didn't belong to him. He didn't ride close enough to check their brands.

Edward Fairfield pointed and said excitedly, "Look up there! I think I see some buildings."

"Yep, you do," drawled Wingate. "I spotted 'em a couple minutes ago. Reckon that's Rimfire. See that line o' trees this side of it? That's where a creek's runnin'. Anybody with any sense who starts a town is gonna put it where there's water."

"Do you think we can reach our homesteads today as well?"

Wingate shook his head. "Don't know about that, but there's a chance, unless you decide you want to spend the night in town and then push on. Ought to get there tomorrow if we do, for sure."

Fairfield frowned in thought. "I'm not sure what to do. If we stop, it will be a chance for our people to stock up on supplies and rest a bit. But we're so close!"

"Reckon you could put it up to a vote."

"No, the people elected me captain. I'll make the decision. But let's wait until we've reached the settlement."

"Seems fair enough," Wingate said with a slow nod.

There was no real road between Fort Benton and Rimfire, but the wagons had been following a rough trail. It curved to the southeast and led to a bridge over the creek that ran beside the settlement. The bridge appeared to be wide enough for the wagons, Ace thought as they approached, but not by much. The drivers would have to be careful not to let the vehicles stray too far to one side or the other. If that happened, a wheel might drop off the side, and then the wagon would be stuck there, blocking the bridge.

"Come on, fellas," Wingate said to Rufe, Ace, and Chance. "Let's ride on ahead and make sure everything's all right before we let those wagons start across."

They nudged their horses into a quicker gait that carried them out ahead of the wagons. As they neared the bridge, Ace spotted a large number of men on horseback coming from the other direction.

Chance saw the riders, too, and said to his brother, "I don't like the looks of that."

"Neither do I," Ace agreed. "That big fella in front, isn't that Angus McPhee?"

"Yeah, I think so."

The two groups reached the opposite ends of the bridge at the same time. The bunch on the south side reined in, blocking the trail that turned into Rimfire's main street about fifty yards farther on. Angus McPhee was out in front, right in the center of the group and their obvious leader. Ace and Chance could see him clearly.

"Hold it right there!" shouted McPhee. He had approximately twenty men with him, all of them armed. Beside him was a man with a dark, narrow mustache.

As Ace, Chance, and the Wingates reined in at the north end of the bridge, Dave Wingate muttered, "Damn."

"What is it?" asked Ace.

"See that mean-lookin' hombre next to the big blowhard who just hollered for us to stop? That's Clade Mitchell."

CHAPTER TWENTY-TWO

Angus McPhee walked his horse a few feet out onto the bridge. The iron shoes rang like gunshots on the thick planks. "Those wagons aren't coming across this bridge," he called as he reined his mount to a halt. "You might as well turn 'em around and take 'em back where you came from."

"How dare the man act like that?" exclaimed Edward Fairfield, who rode up to join them. "This isn't his private kingdom."

Ace said, "From what we've heard about McPhee, he probably feels like it is."

"That's Angus McPhee?" asked Wingate.

"Yeah," said Chance. "We saw him in Fort Benton, acting all high and mighty with the sheriff. It didn't get him anywhere there . . ."

"But McPhee pretty much owns Rimfire," Ace concluded.

"Good Lord!" Fairfield exclaimed. "That's Clade Mitchell with him!"

"Yeah," Wingate said dryly. "I was just explainin' that to Ace and Chance."

"What's Mitchell doing here? He's an outlaw."

"McPhee may not know that."

"It doesn't matter. This is a public bridge," Fairfield insisted. "He can't deny us the use of it."

"Reckon he thinks he can," said Wingate.

"Wonder what his connection is with Mitchell," mused Ace.

McPhee's already florid face flushed even darker with impatience and irritation as the men talked. He yelled, "Quit yammering amongst yourselves and get those wagons out of here! You're not welcome in Rimfire!"

"This is absurd," Fairfield said. "I'm going to talk to the man. Surely he can be reasoned with."

Ace wouldn't have bet on that, and he was about to say as much when Fairfield nudged his horse forward and rode out onto the bridge. Instantly, Clade Mitchell's hand hovered over the butt of the gun on his hip.

"Hold it, Mr. Fairfield," Ace said quickly. "Don't crowd them."

"Yeah," put in Dave Wingate. "You don't want to give that snake Mitchell any excuse to slap leather."

Fairfield stopped where he was and sat there on his horse looking confused and angry. He turned to frown at the others and ask, "What are we going to do, then?"

"Lemme have a talk with 'em." Carefully, Wingate drew his revolver and handed it to Rufe. "Hang on to that hogleg, boy." He pulled his rifle from its sheath and passed it over to Ace. "I'll leave this with you."

Then Wingate urged his horse forward and held up his empty hands. "I ain't armed!" he called to the men at the other end of the bridge. "Just want to palaver with you, McPhee."

Clade Mitchell said something in a low voice to McPhee. Ace couldn't make out the words, but he knew they probably weren't anything good.

Wingate walked his horse to the center of the bridge and stopped. "How about meetin' me halfway, McPhee?"

The cattleman didn't respond immediately, but after glaring at Wingate for a moment, he started ahead. His men watched tensely.

Ace could tell that they were keyed up and ready to fight. It wouldn't take much to start the ball.

McPhee jerked his horse to a stop facing Wingate and demanded, "Didn't you damn sodbusters hear me? You're not wanted here in Rimfire." His angry voice was loud enough that Ace and the others had no trouble understanding him. They could make out Wingate's answer, too.

"Now hold on there, mister," the scout said. "I'm no homesteader. My nephew and I just signed on to guide these pilgrims here." Wingate nodded toward Clade Mitchell, who had remained at the other end of the bridge. "The same as did that no-account, double-crossin' varmint yonder, name of Mitchell."

"Don't listen to that old fool, Mr. McPhee," Mitchell called. "He's soft in the head."

Wingate ignored that and went on. "You ain't doin' yourself any credit by associatin' with an outlaw like him. He and his gang attacked that wagon train twice in the past twenty-four hours. They killed three of our folks and wounded a good deal more."

"That's a damned lie!" Mitchell yelled.

McPhee lifted a hand and motioned imperiously for Mitchell to be quiet. He said to Wingate, "Whatever trouble there is between Mitchell and your bunch, it's none of my business. He came to warn me that a wagon train full of homesteaders was on the way to Rimfire. All I care about is keeping a bunch of dirt-grubbing farmers off my range!"

From the north end of the bridge, Edward Fairfield called, "It's not your range, sir. It's government land, designated for homesteading."

"It's open range!" McPhee shouted back at him. "Open range meant for grazing, and by God, it's going to stay that way! If you think I'll allow you to tear it up with your plows and fence it off from my stock, you're mad!"

Wingate rubbed the silvery stubble on his chin. "I've seen the papers these folks have. The government done give 'em the right to claim land in a parcel south o' Rimfire, betwixt here and the Little Belts, and homestead it. You may not like it, Mr. McPhee, but those are legal documents and the law says that's the way it's gonna be."

"Don't throw the law in my face," snapped McPhee. "Where was the law when savages tried to wipe me out? Where was the law when rustlers nearly stole me blind? Where was the law when the temperature was forty below, the wind was so hard the snow was falling sideways, and my cows were freezing to death? I'll tell you where—nowhere!" McPhee clenched a fist and thumped it against his chest. "*I* fought off all those things! No government, no law, no fancy papers! Just one man with blood and guts and sweat!"

"I appreciate that, Mr. McPhee, and I admire you

for what you done. I purely do. But that don't change a thing here. These folks got a right to come into town, and they got a right to homestead that land."

"All those guns behind me say they don't," replied McPhee.

It was shaping up to be pretty bad, thought Ace. The immigrants were tough and had plenty of backbone—they had proven that by the way they had fought off Mitchell's gang not once but twice—and they outnumbered McPhee's crew, but the cattle baron's gun-wolves were hardened killers. If it came down to a full-fledged battle between the two sides, McPhee's men might well wipe out all the men from the wagon train. Maybe a United States marshal might come in someday and hold McPhee responsible for what he'd done . . . but those pilgrims would still be dead, one way or the other.

"Mr. Fairfield," Ace said quietly, "maybe you'd better hold off here."

"You mean not cross the bridge? You're telling me we should back down?"

"It sticks in my craw, too," admitted Ace, "but the way it shapes up, you're about to get a bunch of your people killed."

"My God, it's an injustice!"

"Yes, sir, it is," said Chance, "but Ace is right. McPhee's got you outgunned."

Clearly, Fairfield was torn between outrage and caution. After a moment, caution won—but just barely. "Dave, come on back. We're not going to get anywhere arguing."

Wingate looked around, obviously reluctant to follow Fairfield's order. He sat silently on his horse for a moment, as conflicted as Fairfield had been, then sighed and turned his mount.

"That's right," McPhee sneered. "Turn and run."

Wingate stiffened.

Ace saw the reaction and eased his hand closer to his Colt. He halfway expected Wingate to go after McPhee, even though he was unarmed.

Then Wingate said, "There'll be another day."

"Aye, that there will. And this town and this valley will still belong to me on that day, too."

Slowly, Wingate walked his horse back toward the north end of the bridge. McPhee stayed where he was, alone in the center of the span, sitting straight and haughty in the saddle.

Fairfield's shoulders slumped in despair as Wingate reached the group. "What do we do now, turn around?"

"Nope." Wingate took his gun from Rufe and pouched the iron, then reclaimed his rifle from Chance. "Circle the wagons and make camp here on this side of the creek."

"What good will that do? That reprobate's not going to let us go through the town to get to our land."

"Ain't no rule says you have to go *through* the settlement," Wingate pointed out.

"You mean . . . we should go around?"

"I reckon the important thing is where you're goin', not how you get there."

"But Uncle Dave," said Rufe, "I ain't sure we can get these wagons across that crick without usin' the bridge. The banks are too steep for that."

"Right here they are. But we're scouts, ain't we,

boy? We'll find another place where the wagons can ford that stream. Then, if we pull out in the middle of the night and be quiet-like about it, we might be able to get these folks to that stretch of range 'fore McPhee knows about it."

That seemed like a risky plan to Ace, but he knew it stood a chance of success. However, even if Wingate was able to pull that off, it wouldn't mean that the trouble was over. "McPhee will still try to run you off of what he considers his range."

"He'll have a harder time of it once folks are dug in," Wingate countered.

Fairfield took off his hat, raked his fingers through his thick white hair, and scowled. "I don't like this. I don't like anything about it. But I won't just abandon all of our plans. I won't turn tail and run. We'll make camp here, at least until we've considered all our options."

Ace looked across the bridge. McPhee had ridden back to join his men. Most of them headed south along the settlement's main street, although three riders remained behind, probably to keep an eye on the bridge and probably at McPhee's order. They would alert the others if the immigrants tried to take the wagons across.

Fairfield and the Wingates started toward the wagons to spread the word that they were making camp. Ace and Chance stayed where they were at the head of the bridge.

"What do you think?" asked Chance. "We threw in with these folks, but we're not actually part of their bunch. Do we stick with them?"

"We came to find Ling and Haggarty and that money they stole from us."

"That's what I was thinking. And maybe, if we can get into town, there might be something we could do to help those pilgrims after all."

"The thought did cross my mind," Ace admitted.

Rufe Wingate paused and turned in his saddle to call to the Jensen brothers, "Are you boys comin' with us?"

"You go ahead," Ace told him. "Maybe we'll see you later." He heeled the chestnut out onto the bridge and Chance followed suit on his gelding.

The three guards had dismounted. With rifles in hand, they stepped up onto the bridge.

One of them called, "Stop right there, you two!"

Ace kept his horse moving but raised his hands slightly. "We're not looking for trouble."

"Mr. McPhee said not to let any of you sodbusters set foot on this side of the creek."

"Do we look like sodbusters to you?" Chance inclined his head toward the wagon train. "We rode with those folks for less than a day. Never laid eyes on any of them before yesterday afternoon. My brother and I just happened to be riding in the same direction they were headed. We've got business of our own in Rimfire."

"Yeah?" challenged the gunman as the Jensen brothers reined to a halt near the southern end of the bridge. "What business is that?"

"Poker," Chance said with a smile. "I can see several saloons from here. You think I can find a good game in one of them, and maybe a few pretty girls?"

McPhee's men relaxed slightly.

The spokesman said, "I got to admit, you two don't look like farmers. You're gonna have to wait right here, though, until I've checked with Mr. McPhee." He jerked his head at one of the other men, who mounted up and galloped along the street, even though he didn't have very far to go. The man reined in, swung down in front of a saloon called The Branding Iron, and disappeared through the batwings.

Ace and Chance waited as several minutes ticked by. On the north side of the creek, the immigrants had begun pulling the wagons into a rough circle, as they had the previous night.

One of the guards said in a surprised voice, "Them sodbusters ain't leavin'."

"McPhee didn't tell them they had to," said the man who'd been doing the talking earlier. "He just said they couldn't cross the creek. They're probably gonna sit over there and stew for a while until they realize there's nothin' they can do except go back where they came from."

Ace hoped that all of McPhee's men felt that way and would continue to do so. That would make it easier for Dave Wingate's plan to succeed, provided that Wingate and Rufe could find a place for the wagon train to cross the stream.

The man who had ridden down to The Branding Iron emerged from the saloon, mounted up again, and returned to the bridge. "The boss said it was all right for these two to come into town."

"Good," said Chance. "I could use a drink, too."

"In fact," the hardcase went on, "Mr. McPhee said he wants to talk to you fellas. I'm supposed to take you to him right now."

"Wait a minute," said Ace. "We don't have anything to say to McPhee."

The man put his hand on the butt of his gun. "That don't matter. He's the one who has words for you."

Ace and Chance looked at each other.

Chance said, "What the hell does McPhee want with us?"

"One way to find out," Ace replied with a shrug.

CHAPTER TWENTY-THREE

The Jensen brothers rode along the street toward the saloon with McPhee's gunman following them. Rimfire looked like a fairly decent little town with a number of businesses in addition to the saloons—a couple general mercantile stores, a hotel, two cafés, a livery stable, a blacksmith shop, a saddle maker's, a doctor's office, and even a newspaper, the *Rimfire Herald.* If what Ace and Chance had heard was true, Angus McPhee either owned or held a note on most, if not all, of those establishments.

They reined to a halt in front of The Branding Iron and swung down from their saddles.

Chance looked at their escort and asked dryly, "Will our horses be all right here?"

The man flushed angrily. "We ain't horse thieves, if that's what you're gettin' at. Nobody'll bother your horses."

Ace looped his reins around the hitch rail and nodded to Chance. "Let's see what McPhee wants with us."

"Better call him *Mister* McPhee," the gunman warned. "Show some respect."

"Fine. Mr. McPhee." Chance's tone didn't sound very respectful, however.

Ace pushed through the batwings first, followed by Chance. They stopped just inside the saloon and looked around. The Branding Iron bore a distinct resemblance to dozens of other saloons they had visited during the time they had been roaming the frontier, although it was cleaner and more opulently appointed than many of those places. Ace thought it was likely McPhee owned the saloon outright and made it his headquarters while he was in town.

At the moment, the rancher was sitting at a large table in the back of the barroom. Clade Mitchell was with him, as were a couple other hardcases. McPhee saw Ace and Chance and gestured curtly for them to come over.

"You reckon we're walking into a trap?" Chance asked under his breath.

"Maybe, but I don't think so," replied Ace. "McPhee's so confident he's in complete control around here, he wouldn't try anything tricky. He'd just go ahead and shoot us if that's what he wanted to do."

From behind, McPhee's man prodded them. "Go on over to the boss's table."

The saloon wasn't very busy. A few men stood at the bar, nursing drinks, while a card game was going on at one of the tables. Chance cast a wistful glance in that direction. Even under the odd circumstances, the lure of the cards was strong.

All of the men in the place cast glances at the Jensen brothers as they crossed the room. So did the lone woman, an attractive blonde in a low-cut dress who stood at the end of the bar. An air of tense expectation filled the saloon, as if trouble could erupt without warning at any second.

With Angus McPhee's volatile temper, wherever he happened to be probably felt like that, thought Ace as they came to a stop in front of the table.

McPhee's hat was pushed back on his head. He toyed with a glass of whiskey. The half-full bottle sat close by his hand. He looked up at Ace and Chance and said, "I know you boys."

Ace didn't see any point in denying it. "We were in Fort Benton when you were talking to Sheriff Maddox and his deputy."

"Yeah, but that's not the only way I know you."

Ace glanced at Chance. Neither knew what McPhee meant by that.

The cattleman didn't offer to explain. He lifted the glass and threw back the drink, then splashed more whiskey into it. "What are you doing with those damned homesteaders?" he demanded. "You don't look like farmers."

"We were on our way to Rimfire when we came across them yesterday afternoon," said Ace. "They were under attack from a gang of outlaws led by this man." He nodded toward Mitchell.

"That's a damn lie," Mitchell rasped as he leaned forward in his chair.

Chance asked coolly, "Are you denying that you signed on with them as a guide?"

"Sure I did. I did the best job I could for them, too. But then that big lug Rufe Wingate jumped me. He claimed I was paying too much attention to the

Fairfield girl, so I knew I had to either leave the train or kill him." Mitchell shrugged. "I don't like getting blood on my hands unless there's a good reason, and a prissy little thing like Laura Fairfield doesn't qualify. I prefer my women a little more . . . earthy, let's say."

Ace frowned. He and Chance had seen Rufe's jealous anger for themselves. It was easy to imagine him blowing up at Mitchell if he thought the man had been looking lustfully at Laura.

"After that happened," Mitchell went on, "I felt like I didn't owe any particular loyalty to those immigrants anymore, so I rode here to Rimfire to warn Mr. McPhee about them. Figured I'd throw in with folks who are more like what I'm used to."

"Owlhoots and hired killers, you mean?" asked Chance.

"Shut your mouth, boy," growled McPhee. "My men are plenty tough when they need to be, but they're not outlaws."

"The wagon train was attacked twice," Ace insisted. "My brother and I were there for both fights. Edward Fairfield said he saw you leading the wolf pack yesterday, Mitchell."

"Fairfield's a liar," responded Mitchell smoothly. "He's holding a grudge against me because of what happened with Wingate and his granddaughter. I was nowhere near that wagon train yesterday."

"Can you prove that?" asked Chance. "Were you already here in Rimfire?"

McPhee said, "Clade didn't ride in until late last night, but that doesn't prove a damn thing. Anyway, this isn't a courtroom, boy, and you're not a blasted lawyer, so stop acting like one. This is a saloon—*my* saloon."

"From what I hear, this is your *town*," said Ace.

"That's right." McPhee downed the second glass of whiskey without displaying any reaction to the fiery liquor. It might as well have been water. "Rimfire damn sure is my town, and I want to know why you two were headed here. Forget those sodbusters and Mitchell here. My business is with *you*."

Ace shook his head. "I don't know what you're talking about, Mr. McPhee."

"I reckon you do."

"No, I—"

The cattleman lifted a hand.

Ace heard footsteps behind him and Chance as the other men in the saloon shifted around. He remembered what Chance had said a few minutes earlier about a trap, and he suddenly realized that maybe his brother had been right.

McPhee leaned forward and said harshly, "I know why you're here, and you're never going to get what you're after. In fact, you're going to pay for what you've already done. I'm going to teach you a lesson you'll never forget." He surged up out of his chair and shouted, "Get 'em!"

A rush of footsteps told Ace and Chance the real threat was behind them. They whirled around to see half a dozen of McPhee's men, the ones who had been at the bar earlier, charging them. The men who had been playing poker were on their feet as well and had guns in their hands. Ace knew that if he and Chance slapped leather, McPhee's men would fill them full of holes.

Their only option was to meet the attack head-on.

Ace sprang at the nearest man, ducked under a roundhouse punch that came at his head, and hooked a hard right into the hombre's belly. As the man bent forward, Ace lowered a shoulder and rammed it into his chest, knocking him back into the path of the other men. A couple stumbled over him, and all three fell to the sawdust-littered floor.

Chance went on the offensive, too, blocking a punch with his left forearm and jabbing his right fist into his opponent's face. Blood spurted hotly over Chance's knuckles as the man's nose flattened under the impact.

With three of the attackers momentarily tangled up together on the floor, Ace turned his attention to the other two still on their feet. They came at him together. He weaved aside from a punch, letting the fist go over his shoulder, and brought an elbow up under the man's chin, snapping his head back.

Ace couldn't stop the second man from landing a blow on the jaw and driving him to the side. He almost lost his balance and fell but caught himself in time to stay upright. He slammed a punch to the second man's chest.

A few feet away, one of the men on the floor recovered enough to reach out and grab Chance's ankle. A quick jerk upended him. Chance tried to catch hold of a nearby table as he fell, but all he succeeded in doing was overturning it. A couple of McPhee's men scrambled after him, obviously intent on pinning him down.

As one of the men tried to jump on him, Chance kicked him in the belly and threw him aside. The other one grabbed Chance by the throat with both hands and started banging the back of his head on the floor.

Ace was still trading punches with his opponent, standing toe-to-toe with the man as they pounded away at each other. The outcome of that slugging match was interrupted when the third man who had fallen made it to his feet.

He seized Ace from behind, grabbing both of his arms. "Got him!" the man shouted. "Give him hell, Chuck!"

Ace tried to writhe free, but he couldn't get enough leverage. Fists crashed into his face and body again and again, until a red haze seemed to drop over his eyes and fill his vision. His head spun crazily and his muscles no longer responded to his commands.

Chance was in bad shape, too. He knew if the man kneeling on top of him and choking him managed to slam his head into the floor a few more times, he would pass out. He summoned up what little strength he had left and brought his hands up, cupping them as he slapped them hard against the man's ears.

It was painful enough to make the hardcase howl and caused his hands to slip a bit. Feeling the tiny relief, Chance bucked up from the floor. The man lost his hold and fell off to the side. Chance rolled the other way, gasping for breath and blinking rapidly as he tried to clear his vision that had gone dangerously blurry.

Also on the verge of passing out, Ace finally managed to get one foot up and plant it in the belly of the man who was hammering him. He shoved the man away and at the same time went limp. The unexpected weight caused the man who was holding him to stagger and let go. Ace slid to the floor.

He wound up lying next to Chance, who was red-faced and gasping. Their eyes met, and they knew they had only split seconds to get back up before McPhee's men were on them again.

They didn't make it. Vicious kicks thudded into the ribs of both brothers. Numbing pain washed through them. Ace got his hands underneath him and tried to push himself up, but he couldn't find the strength. Then another booted foot caught him in the back and savagely drove him back down. All the Jensen brothers could do was lie there and groan.

The brutal punishment seemed endless. After it had gone on for an eternity, Ace heard McPhee call out, "All right, boys, that's enough." The cattle baron's voice seemed to come from far, far away.

Ace's breath rasped in his throat as he lay there on the saloon floor, huddled in pain. He heard harsh breathing beside him and knew it came from Chance. He was a little surprised that McPhee's men hadn't stomped them to death, but for the moment anyway, both of them were still alive.

Ace hurt so much he wasn't sure how grateful he was for that.

Footsteps thudded heavily on the floor as someone approached them. Ace opened his eyes and through the gauzy red curtain that hung over them, he saw a pair of feet in expensive boots come to a stop. The small part of his brain that was still working figured those feet belonged to Angus McPhee.

That was confirmed a moment later as the cattle-man said arrogantly, "You boys never should have come to Rimfire. You should have known that I wouldn't let you get away with what you did."

Ace wanted to ask him what in the world he thought they had done, but his swollen, bleeding lips wouldn't form the words. All that came out of his mouth was an incoherent grunt.

"There you are," McPhee went on. The tone of his voice told Ace that McPhee wasn't talking to them anymore. "I'm sorry you had to see this, my dear, but you have to admit, these two had it coming to them."

"Yes, Mister Angus, this one is so grateful to you for what you have done," replied a familiar voice.

Ace groaned as he lifted his head and turned it to look, unable to resist the pull of that voice. He gazed up the staircase that rose on one side of the room to the saloon's second floor. Ling stood at the top of those stairs, smiling down at the bloody, sprawled bodies of the Jensen boys.

It was the last thing he saw before his vision faded out entirely.

CHAPTER TWENTY-FOUR

The next thing Ace was aware of was a sound that he gradually recognized as the grunting of hogs. As he realized that he was lying in thick, sticky mud, terror shot through him like a bolt of lightning.

McPhee had had him and Chance dumped in a hog pen where the vicious tuskers would tear them apart and eat their bodies!

Ace gasped and got a mouthful of mud for his trouble. He jerked his head up. Pain thundered inside his skull like somebody was pounding on a giant drum stretched between his ears. He tried to see where he was, but to make things even worse, he seemed to be blind, to boot!

Then he realized that his eyes were caked with mud. He lifted his hand, felt it tremble, and pawed at his eyes, but that didn't help any. As he forced his stunned brain to think, he figured out that his hand was probably covered with mud, as well.

He concentrated on pushing himself up to a sitting position. As he did, harsh laughter came from somewhere close by.

"What's the matter, boy?" asked an unfamiliar male voice. "You think them porkers are about to get you?"

Ace wiped the mud off his hands as best he could, then went to work scraping it away from his eyes. He blinked painfully because it felt like both sockets were filled with grit. With maddening slowness, his sight began to clear. Everything was gray, but that was because the sun had set and dusk was settling down over Rimfire.

He looked around and saw a pole fence beside him, only a couple feet away. On the other side of that fence, a huge hog stared at him. The mud from the swamp-like wallow inside the pen extended outside the fence, and that was where he and Chance were.

Chance was sprawled on his belly, which meant his face was in the mud. Fearing that his brother had drowned in the stuff, Ace reached over and grabbed hold of Chance's shoulder to roll him onto his back. Chance coughed and sputtered, which indicated that he was alive, anyway.

Ace pulled Chance up and helped him lean against one of the fence posts. When the massive hog came up to reach his snout through the fence and snuffle Chance's arm, Ace swatted the animal's nose and yelled, "Get away from him, damn you!"

That prompted another outburst of laughter.

Ace turned his head and saw that four of the men who had given them that awful beating were standing nearby, grinning in the twilight. Their thumbs were hooked casually in their gunbelts.

"You two are just about the sorriest, most pathetic-lookin' specimens of humanity I ever laid eyes on," one of them said.

"I ain't sure they even look human anymore," said another. "More like tar babies, the way they're so covered with mud."

"You reckon this'll learn 'em not to mistreat womenfolks?"

That didn't make sense to Ace at first, but then his brain began to grasp a possible explanation. That answer could wait, though, until he found out what their enemies planned for them. "What . . . what are you going to do with us?"

The gunman who had spoken first said, "I don't reckon anybody would've raised a fuss about it if we'd strung the both of you up from a tree limb. The boss ain't a murderer, though, so he said to let you go with a warnin' to rattle your hocks outta these parts and never come back." He chuckled. "It was us who came up with the idea of throwin' you in the mud and lettin' you lay there until you woke up. Figured it might scare the hell outta you, and it sure looked like it did."

Ace wasn't going to give the man the satisfaction of admitting that an instinctive terror had filled him for a moment upon awakening. What had been done to them was already bad enough without adding that humiliation. *How much more humiliating can things get?* he asked himself.

"Wha . . ." Chance muttered. "Wh-where . . . ?"

Ace gripped his brother's shoulder. "Take it easy, Chance. We're all right." It was true. He hurt all over and knew that by morning his bruised muscles would ache even more. The pain in his head had subsided to a dull throb, though, and he could tell that he didn't have any broken bones. He hoped the same held true for Chance.

"Where are . . . our horses?" Ace managed to ask.

"We've got 'em," the hardcase replied. "You can climb in the saddle and go on back to those sod-bustin' friends o' yours. Just don't ever show your faces in Rimfire again." The man's tone hardened. "If you do, I reckon the boss will give us the go-ahead to kill you."

"What for? We didn't do anything!"

"You kidnapped that gal the boss is sweet on and tried to turn her into a whore!"

That was the answer Ace expected, or some variation on it, anyway. He knew that Ling must have spun some pack of lies to McPhee when she and Haggarty arrived in Rimfire and she set her sights on the cattleman.

She had been in Fort Benton when Sheriff Maddox was talking to McPhee about that new safe. She knew McPhee had a lot of money and that he kept it on his ranch, not in a bank vault where she and Haggarty couldn't get their hands on it.

"Let me guess," Ace said. "McPhee won her from a gent named Haggarty in a poker game."

"What?" The gunman sounded genuinely surprised. "What the hell are you talkin' about? That fella Haggarty is the gal's father."

Ace could only stare and say, "What?"

"Well, her adopted pa, anyway. Miss Ling is one of them Celestials, you can tell that by lookin' at her, but Haggarty took her in and raised her after her folks were killed by an avalanche in the Sierra Nevada while they were workin' on the Central Pacific Railroad."

Ace stared at the man in the fading light for a couple seconds longer, then leaned his head back against the fence post behind him and began to laugh. It made his sore muscles hurt like blazes, but he couldn't stop himself. He shook with bitter hilarity.

Another of McPhee's men said, "What in blazes is he laughin' at? He sounds like he's gone plumb crazy!"

"I don't know," said the first man, "but he'd better stop it. He's startin' to get on my nerves."

Ace lifted a shaky hand and got himself under control. "If . . . if you'll bring us our horses, we'll get out of Rimfire."

"Now you're talkin'." The gunman turned to one of his companions. "Fetch those nags."

The man came back a minute later leading the two horses. Ace used the hog pen fence to hang on to as he climbed slowly and painfully to his feet. Chance still seemed mostly out of it, so Ace braced himself, reached down, and took hold of his brother's arm. It took most of the strength he could muster to help Chance to his feet.

"Come on," Ace told his brother. "We've got to get out of here."

"Yeah. Don't . . . don't like this place," mumbled Chance.

"You and me both," Ace agreed.

He got Chance's foot in the stirrup, then boosted him up into the saddle. Chance grabbed the horn to keep from toppling over the other way. Once he was sure Chance was steady enough to stay mounted, Ace climbed onto the chestnut's back.

The man who'd been holding the reins handed them to him. "I wouldn't look back if I was you."

"Just point us toward the bridge," said Ace.

The men got them turned in the right direction.

Ace hesitated. "One more thing. What's McPhee going to do with the girl?"

"She and her pa went out to the ranch house with him to visit for a spell. They're gonna be his guests there for a while."

"Yeah," said Ace. "Sure they are."

The gunman scowled and demanded, "What do you mean by that?"

Ace didn't answer. He dug his heels into the horse's flanks and started it walking forward. He reached over and grabbed hold of the reins of Chance's mount. He had to lead the horse because Chance's head had sagged forward and he didn't seem to know what was going on.

Ace prayed that his brother hadn't suffered any permanent damage from the beating.

They rode slowly toward the bridge, which was still visible in the dim light but wouldn't be for much longer. Across the creek, the glow from the fires at the wagon train camp could be seen.

Those would be his guide, thought Ace, hoping they could make it that far.

The destination seemed like it was a million miles away.

Edward Fairfield and Dave Wingate had done the smart thing by posting guards around the camp. As

Ace and Chance approached the wagons, a couple men holding rifles stepped out of the gathering darkness. They couldn't see very well in the gloom, and one of them called, "Hold it right there, you two. Who are you?"

"It's Ace and Chance Jensen."

The ride out of Rimfire, across the bridge, and on to the wagon camp seemed to have taken a lot longer than it really had. At least Chance had been able to stay in the saddle and hadn't passed out. If he had started to fall, Ace wasn't sure he could have caught him.

The guards recognized the brothers' names and hurried forward.

One of them exclaimed, "Good Lord! What happened to you fellas?"

The other man said, "You look like you been rollin' with the hogs."

That was closer to the truth than Ace liked to think about. "We need to see Captain Fairfield and Mr. Wingate . . . but I'm not sure . . . we can make it that far."

"Get off those horses and sit down. Ben, go fetch the cap'n!"

One of the guards hurried off. The other helped Ace and Chance dismount and sit on the lowered tailgate of a wagon. Less than two minutes later, Fairfield, Wingate, and Rufe hurried up and stared at the brothers in surprise.

"I wasn't sure we'd see you fellows again," Fairfield said. "To be honest, I thought you'd abandoned us."

"We just tried to see about the business that brought us here," Ace explained. "But McPhee grabbed us . . . and had something else in mind."

"Whoo-ee, you smell bad," said Rufe. "Maybe you should've come through the creek to get here, instead of over the bridge. Might've washed some of the stink off you."

"Hush up, boy," snapped Wingate. "In case you can't tell, these fellas have been through the wringer. McPhee must've sicced his wolves on 'em."

"That's what happened, all right," said Ace. "Rufe's right about the stink, though. I can smell it on myself."

"Once you've got some of your strength back, you can wash up."

Now that he and Chance had at least solved the mystery of where Ling and Haggarty had gone—although they were no closer to recovering the money stolen from them—Ace forced his thoughts back to the problems facing the homesteaders. He looked at Wingate. "Were you able to find . . . a place where the wagons can get across the creek?"

"We sure did," the old scout replied. "Rufe and me faded back a ways on the trail, then swung wide around the settlement so none o' them varmints would be likely to spot us. We found a spot about two miles upstream where the banks are shallow enough for the wagons to get down to the creek. They'll be able to get across there. We just need to wait until it's the darkest hour of the night and McPhee's men are more likely to be asleep."

"And then we'll head for the range we're going to homestead as quickly as we can," Fairfield added. "I just hope we can find it in the dark."

"I can steer by the stars well enough to put you in the general vicinity," said Wingate. "As soon as it starts gettin' light in the mornin', we'll look around and find them landmarks you showed me on your map. You can have your claim stakes hammered in before McPhee even knows what's goin' on."

Chance spoke up. "Claim stakes aren't going to stop McPhee. He'll just have his men pull them up and gun you down."

Relieved to hear his brother's voice sounded relatively strong and clear, Ace disagreed. "Maybe, maybe not. You heard what his men said about him. He's not a murderer."

"He came damn close with us," Chance said.

Ace couldn't argue with that.

"What are you two fellas gonna do now?" asked Wingate.

Ace hadn't had an opportunity to talk things over with Chance and explain what he had found out and guessed about Ling and Haggarty's current scheme. It was certain, however, that they weren't in any shape to go back into Rimfire and raise any hell tonight.

Besides, their holsters were empty and their rifles were gone. McPhee's men had disarmed them.

"It looks like we're going with the wagon train," Ace said. "If you'll have us."

Fairfield said, "I won't lie to you, there were some hard feelings when you left and went on into town. But you weren't actually part of our group, and that didn't stop you from risking your lives and helping us fight off those outlaws, not once but twice. In fact, I think there's a distinct possibility we wouldn't have been able to defeat them if not for the two of you. So you're welcome to come with us, and if anyone doesn't like it, they can take up the issue with me."

"We're obliged to you for that," Ace said, nodding.

Dave Wingate rubbed his chin. "I'm a mite surprised you boys don't want to take off for the tall and uncut and put Rimfire and this valley as far behind you as you can."

"Not just yet," Chance said in a voice that was flat and hard with anger.

"We already had one score to settle when we got here," added Ace, equally grim. "Now we have another one."

CHAPTER TWENTY-FIVE

Laura Fairfield brought cups of hot coffee to Ace and Chance, trying not to wrinkle her nose in distaste as she handed the cups to them.

"We know we smell pretty bad," Ace told her.

"No, it . . . it's fine."

Chance laughed. "The only way we'd smell fine is if you were another hog." He sounded more like himself.

Ace was glad of that. As he sipped the hot, strong brew he felt it restoring more of his strength and hoped it was having the same effect on his brother.

Dave Wingate came over to the wagon where the Jensen boys were still sitting. He had a silver flask in his hand. "Hold out them cups, fellas, and I'll fortify 'em a mite." The old scout poured a little whiskey in each cup.

As Ace drank, he felt the bracing kick of the liquor. He still hurt like hell, but at least he was beginning to feel human again. "We've got some spare clothes in our saddlebags. I reckon we ought to go over to the creek and try to wash this mud off before it dries any more than it already is."

"We'll need guns, though," Chance said. "The sons of . . . the varmints stole ours."

Laura said, "You can call them whatever you want, Mr. Jensen. You don't have to spare my delicate feelings. I've been driving oxen all day for the past couple months, so I've probably said a few things myself that maybe I shouldn't have."

"Anyway," Wingate added, "if anybody ever deserved some good old-fashioned cussin', it's those fellas who ganged up on you like that." He paused, then said, "Speakin' of gangs . . . did you see Clade Mitchell in town?"

"He's thick as thieves with McPhee," Ace said.

"Good choice of words," Chance put in.

"He denies having anything to do with those attacks on the wagon train, and McPhee believes him," Ace went on. "They seem like they've thrown in together."

"McPhee's done taken a viper to his bosom, as the Good Book says," commented Wingate as he nodded his head. "He'll come to regret it, sooner or later."

Clade Mitchell wasn't the only viper involved, thought Ace. That description fit Ling and Jack Haggarty, as well. He didn't know exactly what that duo was planning, but he would have bet a brand-new hat that it involved stealing every bit of Angus McPhee's money they could lay their hands on.

The Jensen brothers finished the spiked coffee and felt strong enough to head for the creek. Carrying the extra clothes, Wingate and Rufe went with them to stand guard. Ace and Chance stripped off the mud-covered clothing, left it on the bank, and waded into the stream.

Rufe said, "Them duds oughta be burned. I don't reckon you could ever get the stink out of 'em."

"That's fine with me," said Chance. "Although I really did like that suit."

"You can get another one," Ace told him. "After we've done everything that needs to be taken care of."

It was a warm night, but the creek, fed by springs and snowmelt from the mountains, was cold. The chill actually felt good. It helped numb some of the aches from the beating. They soaked for a long time and scrubbed off the mud caked on their skin. By the time they emerged from the stream, they might not have smelled like roses, but they didn't smell like a hog wallow anymore.

As they dressed, Dave Wingate held out a couple pairs of boots. "Cap'n Fairfield went around the wagons askin' folks if they had any spare boots. These may not fit perfect, but they're better 'n what you got. The cap'n is lookin' for some extra guns for you, too."

"We're sure obliged to you," Ace said.

"Like the cap'n said, you put your lives on the line for us, so helpin' you out now is the least we can do."

Chance said, "We'll do whatever we can to help these folks get their claims established, too. Anything that sticks in Angus McPhee's craw sounds good to me."

A few minutes later, Edward Fairfield brought them each a revolver. One was a single-action Colt .45, which Ace claimed because it was like the gun he usually carried and he had cartridges for it. Chance took the long-barreled Remington and the ammunition for it. Their holsters had been ruined by the mud, so they tucked the weapons in their waistbands, butt forward on the left side for a cross-draw. It wasn't what they were used to, but it was the best they could do for the moment.

With that taken care of, the five men returned to the camp. Ace and Chance cleaned as best they could the mud on their saddles, since they couldn't afford to lose the saddles. When they were satisfied they had done everything possible under the circumstances to rid themselves of the stench, they went to find Fairfield and Dave Wingate.

The wagon train captain and the scout were conferring near Fairfield's wagon.

Ace nodded to the two older men. "We're ready to pull out whenever you folks are."

"Are you sure you want to cast your lot with us?" asked Fairfield. "There's bound to be more trouble with McPhee and his men."

Chance grunted. "That's what we're counting on, Mr. Fairfield."

"Well, then, we're glad to have you join us. But I'm afraid that since you weren't with us when the group formed back in Missouri and didn't pay any fee, you won't be able to claim any land. . . ."

"That was never our intention," Ace assured him.

"We don't plan on settling down," Chance added. "We just want another crack at McPhee and his bunch of gun-wolves."

"Reckon you'll get that, more 'n likely." Wingate looked at the sky. "Give it another couple hours, and it'll be dark enough for us to move out."

Fairfield nodded. "I'll pass the word, then, and make sure everyone knows to be ready."

The delay finally gave Ace and Chance an opportunity to sit down and talk about what had happened in Rimfire.

"Did you see Ling in the saloon after McPhee's men stomped us?" Ace asked his brother.

"What?" Clearly, Chance was surprised. "You mean she was there?"

"Yeah, standing at the top of the stairs, watching."

Chance took several deep breaths. "I could say something right now, but I don't like to talk that way about any woman, even a double-crossing one like her."

"I asked McPhee's men about her later on, while we were out there by that hog pen, but I think you were still too groggy to understand what was going on."

"You're right about that," said Chance. "I don't remember any of it."

"As far as I can tell from what they said, Ling told McPhee that you and I kidnapped her from her father and were holding her prisoner in Fort Benton, that we planned on turning her into a prostitute. Just like those three men of McPhee's assumed before that ruckus we had with them."

"Wait a minute. Who the hell is her father?"

"Well, stepfather, actually. She claims Haggarty adopted her and raised her after her real parents were killed working on the railroad in California."

There was enough light from the moon and stars that Ace could see Chance staring at him in amazement.

"You mean to tell me that McPhee actually believed that crazy yarn?" asked Chance.

Ace nodded. "Evidently he did. He invited Ling and Haggarty out to his ranch to stay there for a while as his guests."

"They're after his money," Chance declared flatly. "They heard what he said about getting a new safe, and he wouldn't be doing that unless he had a lot of money to put in it."

"Yep. That's sure the way it seems to me."

"McPhee's taken with Ling. Can't really blame him for that, the way she looks and acts when she wants to worm her way into a fella's affections. Is McPhee married?"

Ace frowned. "I haven't heard anybody say anything about a wife."

Chance waved a hand. "Well, it doesn't matter. He's not very likely to marry a Celestial. He wouldn't mind keeping her around as his mistress, though, and Haggarty will go along with that. They'll do whatever they have to in order to string McPhee along until they get their hands on that loot. The question is . . . what are we going to do about it?"

"They should still have most of the money they stole from us, maybe even all of it. They haven't been gone from Fort Benton long enough to spend it."

Chance frowned. "Yeah, but how are we going to get it? They'll be sitting pretty, out there on McPhee's ranch surrounded by all his hired guns. We wouldn't stand a chance of getting within half a mile of the place."

"Once these immigrants stake their claims, McPhee's going to have his hands full dealing with them."

"Hmmm," Chance said as he rubbed his chin.

"That might give us a chance to slip in and confront Haggarty and Ling."

"Except that we promised to help Mr. Fairfield and his people," Ace pointed out.

"Yeah, that's true, and I don't like going back on my word. I don't like being broke, either. Or letting thieves get away with stealing from us."

Ace agreed. "I feel the same way. So we just have to come up with ways of solving both problems—and keep from getting ourselves killed while we're doing it."

"Yeah. That's all."

The moon was already slipping down toward the horizon. Once it had vanished, only the light from the stars was left, but it was enough for the drivers to see where they were going as the wagons pulled out of the camp. Anybody watching from across the creek wouldn't notice that the wagon train was leaving. That was the hope, anyway.

Fairfield had passed the word for everyone to be quiet, too, but it was impossible to move oxen and horses and heavy wagons without making some noise. Rimfire lay dark and silent on the other side of the creek. With any luck everyone in the settlement was asleep and wouldn't realize that the immigrants were gone until the sun came up in the morning.

Ace and Chance rode at the front of the wagon train with Edward Fairfield and Dave Wingate. Rufe was riding beside the lead wagon where he could protect Laura if any trouble broke out. Everyone was tense. Rifles and shotguns were loaded and handy.

Wingate led the wagons back up the trail for about half a mile, then swung west. The terrain was rougher but not bad enough that the wagons with their enormous wheels couldn't handle it. It made for slow going, however.

The night seemed fleeting to Ace and Chance.

When the wagons had covered a couple miles, Wingate turned them south again. Ace pointed out a break in the trees as they approached the creek again.

"That's where the banks slope down enough for the wagons to make it," said Wingate. "We're far enough from the settlement that we'll be able to go all the way around and then make a beeline for that land folks are claimin'. It's five miles due south o' town, accordin' to that map you've got, Cap'n."

"Yes, there's a large, relatively flat stretch there, between some camelback hills on the eastern end, low piney ridges on the north and south, and a rocky basin to the west."

"We can find that with no trouble," Wingate assured him. "There gonna be room for all your people there?"

"Plenty of room," said Fairfield. "Good water, too. There's a smaller creek than this one we're about to cross, but enough water for us to irrigate our fields, especially if we dam it at the lower end."

Ace said, "No offense, Mr. Fairfield, but if you do that, you'll have a range war on your hands for sure. No cattleman's going to put up with having a running stream dammed, no matter how reasonable he is. And Angus McPhee doesn't seem to fit that description."

"You seem awfully sure of yourself for a young man."

Wingate said, "I reckon the boy's right, and I'm far from young myself. You're used to life back east, Cap'n. Folks out here do some things different, and they don't give a damn how you used to do 'em back where you come from."

"If we use the creek for irrigation, it's liable to cause it to dry up downstream anyway, just the same as if we'd dammed it."

"You'll have to figure out a way around that," Ace said. "Maybe divert some of the water so that you're only using part of it and the rest flows on downstream for McPhee to use."

"Well," Fairfield said with a frown, "that seems reasonable enough, I suppose. Do you really think McPhee is the sort to compromise, though, or is he going to insist on getting his way completely?"

Wingate pursed his lips. "He didn't exactly strike me as a reasonable fella."

"That's what I thought, too. We're going to have a fight on our hands."

"That's what I been tellin' you all along, Cap'n. But at least we're gonna have surprise on our side this time."

The four men rode down the bank and splashed across the creek.

Wingate was right, thought Ace. It was a good spot to ford the stream.

One by one, the wagons made the crossing and rolled up the bank on the south side. Wingate told Laura to drive far enough that the others could line up behind her and then stop. She did, waiting with Rufe to keep her company until all the wagons were across.

Then Fairfield, Wingate, and the Jensen brothers led the way again, swinging west into the valley that represented new homes for the pilgrims.

But like anything else worth having, they might have to fight for those homes and pay for them with blood and tears.

CHAPTER TWENTY-SIX

By the time the eastern sky began to turn gray with the approach of dawn, the wagons were rolling through the broad valley. From what Ace could see of the landmarks in each direction, the map that Edward Fairfield had brought from Missouri was accurate.

The train came to a halt beside the creek Fairfield had mentioned. It was shallow and only about ten feet wide, but it had a nice, steady flow to it, Ace found when he dismounted and dipped his hand into the water. He cupped some of it and brought it to his mouth. Cool, clear, and good, as most streams in the high country were.

"Better circle up again," Wingate advised. "I know you folks are anxious to roam around and look at the land so you can figure out which spots you want to claim, but you'll be a lot more vulnerable if you're scattered."

"How do we go about staking our homesteads, then?" asked Fairfield.

"Maybe you should work in bigger groups," Ace

suggested. "One man can find a parcel he likes and stake it while the others with him keep an eye out for McPhee's gunmen."

Chance said, "Once McPhee knows you're here and realizes you've stolen a march on him, it won't take him long to come calling with every gun at his disposal. It would be a good idea to get as much done today as you can, even though everybody's tired after traveling most of the night."

Wingate's leathery face creased in a grin. "You youngsters got good heads on your shoulders. I reckon you've already been to see the elephant a time or two, ain't ya?"

"We've run into our share of trouble," Ace agreed.

"And we expect to run into more," said Chance. "If we live long enough."

Working quickly, the immigrants began setting up the camp that would serve as their base while they were staking out their claims. The eastern sky turned rosy, then golden sunlight washed across the landscape as the fiery orb peeked above the horizon.

With enough light to finally look around, Edward Fairfield decided he didn't need to search for a claim. "This will do fine for me, right here where we're camped," he declared.

"The livestock's gonna trample down the grass," Wingate cautioned him.

"It will grow back." Fairfield hunkered on his heels and dug up a handful of dirt. "This is fine soil. Rufe, would you mind helping me with my stakes?"

"No, sir," Rufe answered without hesitation.

"I'll come along, too," Laura said, which made Rufe's smile widen into a happy grin.

"Boy's like a big ol' puppy dog," Dave Wingate said quietly to Ace and Chance as he watched his nephew walking away with several wooden stakes in his arms. "That gal's got him plumb wrapped up. Lucky for him she's mighty pretty, and a decent sort, to boot. Her grandpa's a good man, too. A mite stuffy, that's all."

"I've got a hunch Rufe may not be moving on with you, Mr. Wingate," said Ace.

The old scout sighed and nodded. "I been startin' to realize the same thing. Well, it don't matter. Long as he's happy, that's all I care about. I just hope he don't expect me to put down roots with him. I been lettin' the wind carry me along for too many years to stop now." Wingate looked over at Ace and Chance. "Ain't known you boys long, but I get the feelin' you're the same way. Just too fiddle-footed for your own good."

Chance laughed and admitted, "That pretty well sums us up, all right."

"Thing is, you might still grow out of it. I'm too old and set in my ways." Wingate hitched his trousers up. "Well, come on, let's get ready to ride again. We're gonna have a whole heap o' pilgrims to keep an eye on."

Once the camp was established, Fairfield assembled the entire group to explain to them how they would proceed.

Before leaving Missouri, the men in the company had drawn lots to see in what order they would claim land once they reached their destination. The men on the first half of that list would leave camp first to explore the valley and stake their claims, one at a time as the others in the party watched for trouble.

The others would remain in camp with the Wingates to guard it. When the first group had completed their work, they would return to the wagons, and the other men could go out to stake their claims.

While this was going on, the women and children would remain at the camp, as well as the older boys who could also help guard the wagons.

"I'm going to ask Ace and Chance Jensen to ride with the groups staking the claims," Fairfield continued.

That came as a surprise to the Jensen brothers and didn't sit too well with some of the immigrants, evidenced by muttering coming from the crowd.

Fairfield raised his hands to quiet them. "All of you know that Ace and Chance risked their lives to help us fight off Clade Mitchell's gang, and just because they had to go into Rimfire yesterday to take care of some business of their own doesn't change that. We're lucky to have such valiant young men on our side!"

"I'll second that," drawled Dave Wingate.

Ace didn't feel particularly valiant at the moment. He figured Chance didn't, either. Stiff, sore muscles from the beating they'd received made both of them hobble around like they were considerably older than they were. They could still ride and handle guns and knew these people still needed help, so none of the rest of it mattered.

Fairfield, who was standing on the tailgate of a wagon to address the crowd, turned to them and said,

"I suppose I should have asked you fellows about that before announcing it . . ."

Ace shook his head. "No, sir, that's all right. Chance and I will be happy to go with your folks."

"Yeah," said Chance, "if there's going to be another run-in with McPhee's men, my brother and I want to be there for it."

With that settled, plans proceeded quickly. The sun was up, and McPhee's men might stumble across the camp at any time. Ace and Chance ate a hasty breakfast, swallowed cups of hot coffee, and then mounted up to ride out with eight of the pilgrims who had come to settle in the valley.

Naturally enough, the men wanted to be close to the creek so their farms would have a good source of water. They stayed near the stream as they picked out their claims one by one and drove in their stakes.

Ace and Chance kept their eyes open, scanning the countryside around them on both sides of the creek for any sign of McPhee's men or anyone else who might pose a threat to the immigrants. As they rode, they saw a few cattle grazing here and there, but no vast herds.

"Given the time of year, McPhee probably has most of his stock up in higher pastures right now," Ace commented. "He'll move it back down here during the winter, where there's more protection from the weather."

Chance nodded. "So he probably doesn't have a lot of hands riding this range right now. Maybe that bunch of pilgrims will be lucky and can get dug in good before McPhee even knows they're here."

"We can sure hope so."

A few minutes later, Ace wondered if he and his brother had jinxed things by saying that as they spotted several riders in the distance coming toward them.

Ace looked around and saw that the men from the wagon train were widely scattered. His gaze fell on a small stand of trees about a quarter mile away. "Round up the others and gather them in those trees, just in case we have to fight," he told Chance. "I'll see who those fellas are and maybe stall them a mite, if I need to."

A lot of times, if the stakes were low, Chance would argue with his brother's decisions. Ace was convinced he did it just for the love of arguing. In times of real danger, however, Chance tended to defer to Ace's judgment.

On this occasion, he said, "I don't like you facing them alone . . . but I'll do what you say. Just be careful, Ace."

"I won't start any trouble," Ace promised. Of course, he couldn't speak for what those other hombres might do. . . .

Chance galloped back the way they had come while Ace rode toward the strangers at a more leisurely pace. He didn't want to hurry a showdown along. Better to give Chance as much time as possible to gather the other men.

Ace could tell when the other riders spotted him. They spurred their horses faster, closing in on him. He wished he still had his Winchester. The repeater would have gone a long way toward evening the odds.

As it was, he was facing four men while armed only with a single revolver. He took the Colt from his waistband, thumbed a round from his pocket into the empty chamber where the hammer had been resting, and tucked the gun away again.

The men were close enough that he could see their rugged faces and well-worn range clothes. They appeared to be cowboys, and Ace had a hunch they rode for the Tartan spread, which was the biggest ranch in that part of the valley. At first glance, he didn't recognize any as McPhee's men he had seen in Fort Benton or Rimfire. That didn't mean much, though, since he had probably laid eyes on only a fraction of McPhee's crew.

Since they were hurrying to confront him, he didn't see any reason to keep riding toward them, reined in, and waited. The reins were in his left hand. His right rested on his denim-clad thigh, ready to make a fast grab for the Colt if he needed to.

The men hauled back on their reins and slowed down, coming to a halt about twenty feet from Ace. One of them, a blocky man with a slab of beard-stubbled jaw, eased his mount forward a step and demanded, "Boy, what are you doin' here? This is McPhee range!"

"Actually, it's not," Ace replied calmly. "The government owns this land, and it's been opened up for homesteading."

The man turned his head and spat contemptuously. "Yeah, we heard somethin' about that. It don't make no sense. The gov'ment is thousands of miles away in Washington. What some damn paper pusher back there says don't mean squat here in Montana."

"You're wrong about that," said Ace. "You can ask the army and the U.S. marshals if you don't agree."

One of the other men said, "Quint, there's more of 'em over there in those trees." The words had a slightly worried tone to them.

The punchers were outnumbered, and from where they were they couldn't tell if the men Chance was gathering together in the trees were armed with rifles.

"Some of those damn sodbusters the boss sent word about?" asked Quint. "How 'n the hell did they get down here? They're supposed to be camped up by Rimfire!"

The man's reaction told Ace that McPhee was probably still at the settlement and hadn't returned to the ranch yet. He had sent word to his men, though, to be on the lookout for the immigrants.

Quint didn't wait for his companions to answer his question. He edged his horse forward another step and glared at Ace. "You get off this range right now, boy, and take your friends with you. You ain't welcome, and you got no right to be here. We'll take it easy on you this time, but if we can catch you on Tartan range again, you'll get a tarrin' and featherin'—if you're lucky!"

"We're not going anywhere," Ace said. "Those men are staking their legal claims, and they're going to continue to do that."

Quint stiffened. So did the men with him. Bluster was one thing; driving stakes into the ground was another. Those stakes were physical proof that the homesteaders were not going to be denied their rights.

"Kid, I'm about two seconds away from shuttin' your big mouth with a bullet."

"You try that and the rest of our group will blow you all out of your saddles." Ace summoned up a smile that was a lot cooler than he felt inside. "I'm sure by now there are half a dozen rifles lined up on you." He hoped he was right about that.

A man said, "Quint, looks like that bunch has taken cover in the trees. We're out in the open. It ain't shapin' up to be a good fight."

"You reckon any man who pushes a plow can handle a gun worth anything?" Quint demanded harshly.

"I'd just as soon not find out. The boss has got other men ridin' for him who are more used to this sort of thing than I am."

"Yeah, that goes for me, too," agreed one of the other men. "Let's go back to the ranch, get a bunch of the fellas together, and then come see what we can do about this."

"Damn it!" Quint snapped. "Shut your big mouth, Cooper."

"What does it matter? You can tell this youngster's smart and coolheaded enough to have figured out already what's gonna happen."

Ace might have appreciated that compliment under other circumstances, but he just wanted to get out of the situation without any lead flying. The immigrants had been tested by the battles with Clade Mitchell's gang and it was likely they could hold their own against McPhee's men, but nobody needed to die today if it could be avoided.

Finally, Quint growled, "All right." He pointed a blunt finger at Ace. "But this ain't over, kid. I'll see you again, and then I'll teach you not to mouth off to me."

"I was just telling the truth," Ace said.

Quint grunted a curse and jerked his horse around. He galloped furiously back the way they had come from, taking out his anger on the horse. The other men turned and followed him, casting wary glances at Ace as they left.

When the McPhee men were gone, Ace rode back to join Chance and the others at the trees. Chance's gun was in his hand as he rode out into the open. The immigrants were dismounted and still held their rifles at the ready.

"I was hoping you'd have the sense to hit the dirt if those cowboys pulled iron," Chance said. "We had beads on all of them."

"That's what I told them," Ace said. "One of them didn't much want to listen to reason, but the other three just wanted to get out of here without getting ventilated."

"Where are they going?"

"Back to McPhee's ranch," Ace replied grimly. "I'm sure they'll gather the rest of his men and head over here to drive off the wagon train." He looked at the homesteaders. "I think we've staked all the claims that are going to get staked today. We need to get back to camp and warn everyone to get ready for trouble."

CHAPTER TWENTY-SEVEN

The men who hadn't staked their claims yet were reluctant to abandon the effort, but they understood that their families back at the wagon train might soon be in danger, so that made all the difference. They mounted up and rode hard along the creek toward the camp.

The people there heard the horses coming and turned out to greet the riders. Edward Fairfield and Dave Wingate hurried forward.

As the newcomers reined in, Fairfield asked, "What happened? Are you finished already?"

"No," said Ace. "Some of McPhee's men stumbled across us, just like we knew they might."

"I didn't hear no shootin'," Wingate commented.

"It wasn't far from that . . . but we had them out-gunned and they decided to head back to the ranch and get reinforcements."

"Then they'll be here in a little while."

Ace nodded. "All they have to do is backtrack along

the claims that are already staked. That will lead them right to the camp."

"We'd best be gettin' ready, then." Wingate went to start the preparations while Ace, Chance, and the other men dismounted.

Fairfield asked, "How many of the claims did you get staked?"

"Five, I think," Ace replied. "With your claim here where the camp is located, that makes six."

"Not a bad start, I suppose . . . although I wish they hadn't discovered that we're here until we had finished." The older man sighed. "Now we may not get to."

"Don't go thinking that," said Chance. "You folks just want what's rightfully yours. McPhee's got to be reasonable enough to see that, sooner or later."

Ace hoped his brother was right . . . but he wasn't going to count on it.

The wagons were still in a circle. The livestock had been allowed to wander and graze, but they were quickly driven back inside the enclosure formed by the vehicles. Mothers gathered up any children who had gone exploring, and men made sure rifles and shotguns were loaded and ready before they took up defensive positions behind the wagons.

Once that was done, there was nothing else for the immigrants to do except wait to see what was going to happen next.

It didn't take long for them to find out.

Ace and Chance waited at the Fairfield wagon, along with Dave and Rufe Wingate. The Jensen brothers and the elder Wingate spotted a cloud of dust in the distance at the same time.

"Yonder they come," Wingate said as he nodded in that direction.

"From the looks of that dust, it's a pretty good-sized bunch, too," said Ace.

Rufe turned to Laura. "Don't worry, honey. I won't let nothin' bad happen to you."

She pushed her red hair back from where the breeze had moved it into her face. "You be careful and don't let anything happen to *you*, Rufe."

"When they get here, I'll do the talking," Fairfield said.

"You sure you want to do that, Cap'n?" asked Wingate. "I ain't sure you and these fellas speak the same language."

"Well . . . maybe it would be better if you tried to convince them that we have a right to be here. But I *am* the duly elected captain of this wagon train, and I'll handle whatever I need to handle."

"I know you will, Cap'n. I ain't sayin' you won't." Wingate let out a grim chuckle. "Anyway, I got a hunch it won't make a heap o' difference who does the talkin'. Those fellas'll be lookin' for trouble, and they'll likely be bound and determined to find it."

The riders came into view a few minutes later, pounding toward the wagons. Ace estimated there were at least twenty men in the group, making the odds close to even, but McPhee's men had more experience when it came to fighting. Ace could sense the tense, nervous air that hung over the camp.

"I'll go on out there and talk to 'em." Wingate stepped over the wagon tongue.

"We'll go with you," Ace said.

"Just to back you up," Chance added. "You're doing the talking."

Wingate nodded to them. "Appreciate that, boys." He looked past the Jensen brothers to his nephew. "Rufe, you stick close to Miss Laura and her grandpa. I'm countin' on you to look after 'em."

Rufe swallowed and nodded. "I'll sure do it, Uncle Dave," he vowed.

Wingate, Ace, and Chance walked out about a dozen yards from the wagon and waited for McPhee's men. The scout carried his Winchester in both hands, slightly slanted across his body. Ace and Chance drew their revolvers and stood holding the guns at their sides.

The riders didn't slow down until the last minute. Ace knew they were trying to be intimidating. He, Chance, and Wingate didn't flinch, however. Dust swirled as the group of Tartan punchers hauled their horses to a stop about twenty feet away.

Quint was still in the lead. About half of the men with him looked like typical cowhands, tough enough but not professional gunmen. The others had the stamp of the hardcase on them, like Quint.

He rested his hands on the saddle horn and leaned forward with a sneering grin on his heavy-jawed face. "I told you there'd be another time, kid," he said to Ace. "I'll bet you didn't think it'd be this soon, though."

"You're talkin' to me now, mister," snapped Wingate.

Quint glared at him and demanded, "Who are you, besides a scrawny old pelican?"

"Name's Dave Wingate. I'm the chief scout for this wagon train."

"Then you're the one who led them onto Tartan range. You should've known better than that, old man."

"This ain't Tartan range," said Wingate, "but I figure you already know that."

"It's open range and always has been! It's Angus McPhee's land by right of use. He's been grazin' his stock in this valley for nigh on to twenty years!"

Wingate shook his head. "That don't matter. It's gov'ment land and has been ever since ol' Thomas Jefferson bought it off the Frenchies eighty years ago. Up until now, nobody really cared if fellas like McPhee grazed their stock on it, but that don't mean things'll stay like that forever. Back in Washington, they're wantin' homesteaders to come out here now and help civilize the frontier."

"Do you even hear what you're sayin'?" asked Quint. "The frontier don't need civilizin'. It's just fine the way it is!"

Wingate scratched at his jaw and sighed. "You know, son, I sort of agree with you. I come out here even before the men like your boss. I seen this country the way it once was, when there was nobody around but the Injuns and the place was full o' antelope and bear and moose and buffalo. Didn't have to worry about towns clutterin' up the landscape or railroads stinkin' up the air or anything else like that. You could wake up in the mornin' and breathe deep and watch an eagle soarin' overhead without a care in the world. Plenty of times I wish it was still that way. But it ain't, and there ain't a damn thing you or me or anybody else can do to put it back like it was. The world just don't work that way."

Quint sat there glaring for a long moment after Wingate fell silent. Finally, he said, "That was a pretty speech, old-timer. But words don't change nothin'. Get those wagons and them damn sodbusters outta here now or there'll be trouble, bad trouble. We won't be responsible for what happens, either. It'll be on your head."

"Well, you're right about one thing," drawled Wingate. "Won't nobody be able to hold *you* responsible . . . 'cause you'll be dead."

Quint stared at him for a couple heartbeats, then his hand stabbed toward the gun on his hip. He was fast. His gun came out and blasted just before the rifle that Wingate snapped to his shoulder went off with a wicked crack.

Wingate staggered a step to the right, hit by Quint's slug, but the blocky gunman rocked back in the saddle, dropped his revolver, and clapped a hand to his chest where Wingate's round had drilled into him. His eyes rolled up in their sockets and he pitched to the side, out of the saddle.

Everyone else seemed frozen for the second it took for those things to happen, and then all hell broke loose at once. The other men on horseback grabbed for their guns, while the immigrants crouching behind the wagons opened fire on them.

Unfortunately, Ace, Chance, and Wingate were in the middle.

Wingate was still on his feet and even had the rifle up, blazing away at McPhee's men. A bloodstain was spreading on his shirt, however.

"Get him back to the wagons!" Ace called to Chance as he triggered the Colt. He didn't want to kill anybody—some of these men were just ordinary cowhands riding for the brand. He sent slugs whistling around their heads, making them duck as he and Chance retreated toward the wagons. Chance had taken hold of Dave Wingate's arm to keep him from falling.

They only had to cover a few feet, but the distance seemed much longer when bullets were zipping through the air around their heads. Chance and Wingate dived over a wagon tongue and rolled behind the wheels. Ace vaulted after them, feeling a slug pluck at the sleeve of his shirt.

He scrambled to his feet and hurried behind the corner of the wagon bed. The thick planks of the vehicle's frame offered considerable protection. Peering around the canvas cover, he saw that McPhee's men were scattering. Quint was down and so was another man, but none of the rest seemed to be hurt too badly.

Dave Wingate was lying on the ground with Rufe and Laura kneeling beside him. Chance stood over them, shielding them as he peppered shots at the gunmen.

"Uncle Dave!" cried Rufe. "Uncle Dave, can you hear me?"

Wingate cracked an eyelid, raised his head, and then pushed himself up on an elbow. "Of course I can hear you, boy. You're bellerin' like an ol' bull. That bullet dug a hunk outta my side. It didn't make me deaf."

"You're bleeding quite a bit, Mr. Wingate," Laura told him. "You'd better lie still and let me tend to it."

"You know, I'm feelin' a mite puny all of a sudden, so I reckon I'll do that, missy." Wingate sagged back to the ground.

Laura ripped his shirt open to see how bad the wound was.

Ace turned his attention to the fight. The Tartan punchers had retreated across the creek into some trees and brush. Wreaths of powder smoke hung over the vegetation as they continued firing at the wagons.

The immigrants kept up a steady barrage of their own. Ace looked around the camp and saw that a couple men had been wounded, but it didn't appear that anyone had been killed yet. That was pretty lucky, considering how much lead had been flying around in the first explosion of violence.

The battle appeared to be on the verge of settling down into a stand-off. The immigrants might have a slight advantage because they had more food and ammunition than McPhee's men. They had water barrels on the wagons, too, while the enemy wouldn't dare venture down to the creek for a drink, which would make easy targets of them.

The problem was that McPhee's men were probably better shots, and the defenders had their families with them. No man wanted to see his wife and children put in danger. The safest thing would be to call it off and leave, even though trying to return to Missouri might ruin them.

But if they didn't have the pioneer spirit, they wouldn't have ever started out here in the first place, Ace thought. It took a heap of courage and determination to venture into thousands of miles of unknown territory in the hope of finding a better life.

His Colt's hammer clicked on an empty chamber. He opened the gun and thumbed fresh rounds from his pocket into the cylinder.

Just as he closed the weapon, Edward Fairfield hurried up to him and asked, "Are you and your brother all right, Ace? I couldn't tell exactly what happened right after the shooting started. There was too much dust and gun smoke in the air."

"Yeah, we're fine," Ace answered. "Mr. Wingate caught a slug, though. Your granddaughter's tending to him."

Fairfield nodded. "I know. I just spoke to her. She thinks Dave will be all right, as long as nothing else happens to him." Fairfield paused. "Do you think we're going to be overrun?"

"Doubtful," Ace replied. "The sides are pretty evenly matched, and without that fella Quint egging them on, I'm not sure the rest of the bunch will want to charge right into your guns. In fact, I'm pretty sure they'll be content to sit over there and take potshots at us, at least for a while."

"Which is plenty dangerous in itself—" Fairfield stopped abruptly and his eyes widened as he gazed back to the west.

The dust boiling up there told Ace that another large group of riders were headed toward the wagon train. He didn't know who they were, but since the immigrants didn't have any friends in those parts, it was more likely the newcomers were the rest of McPhee's men.

The wagon train was caught right in between.

CHAPTER TWENTY-EIGHT

With Dave Wingate wounded and out of action, Ace knew that someone had to take charge of the camp's defense. He didn't particularly want the job, but more than likely, he and Chance had had more experience in such matters than any of the immigrants. He told Chance, "Keep those fellas in the trees pinned down. We've got more trouble on the way."

Chance looked around, saw the approaching riders, and bit out a curse. "McPhee?"

"I don't know who else it could be," Ace answered grimly. He motioned for Fairfield to come with him and hurried along the circle, crouching low to make himself a smaller target. He picked out several defenders to come with him and positioned them on the other side of the camp. "Don't open fire until I give the word. We don't want to fight a battle on two fronts unless we have to."

One of the immigrants spoke up. "Captain, do we have to take this kid's orders?"

"Ace is in charge of our defense," Fairfield replied without hesitation. "We haven't known him for long, but Dave Wingate trusts him and his brother and that's enough for me!"

"I appreciate that, sir," Ace said. "You fellas be ready but hold your fire for now." He checked his pocket for more cartridges. He was running low, but Fairfield had assured him there were plenty in one of the wagons.

The newcomers were close enough for Ace to be able to make out individual riders. He wasn't surprised when he spotted Angus McPhee's big, broad-shouldered figure among the leaders. Ace recognized three of the more than dozen men with McPhee—Kiley, Doakes, and Stebbins, the trio in Fort Benton. Evidently, the justice of the peace had fined them for disturbing the peace and let them go and they'd had time to catch up to McPhee in Rimfire.

As the men approached the camp, McPhee held up a hand in a signal for them to stop. They slowed and then came to a halt, but McPhee kept riding in a slow lope now.

"Hold your fire!" shouted Ace. He called across the circle to his brother. "Chance, have the men stop shooting over there!"

All the immigrants' guns fell silent, including those of the men in the trees across the creek. A tense silence fell over the landscape, broken only by the thudding hoofbeats of the horse Angus McPhee was riding.

McPhee rode around the camp to the creek and ordered, "You men over there hold your fire and come on out!"

"Mr. McPhee!" a man called from behind a tree. "Those sodbusters killed Quint and Johannson!"

"Quint was a hotheaded fool," snapped McPhee. "Did he slap leather first?"

The uneasy silence from the trees was answer enough.

McPhee turned his horse and walked the animal toward the wagons. "Wingate!" he said sharply. "Come on out and let's talk."

Edward Fairfield was kneeling behind a wagon wheel. He raised up enough to call, "Mr. Wingate is wounded. I'm the captain of this company."

McPhee motioned curtly with his head. "Come on. We've got to hash this out before more people die."

"I couldn't agree more," replied Fairfield as he rose to his full height.

Ace was stiff with worry. He didn't think McPhee was treacherous enough to be trying to trick Fairfield into an ambush, but he couldn't be sure of that. He wanted to hurry across the camp and go with Fairfield, but he held off. McPhee already had it in for him and Chance. Seeing the Jensen brothers might just anger McPhee and make things worse.

Unobtrusively, Ace moved closer so he could take action in a hurry if he needed to.

Fairfield stepped over the wagon tongue and walked out to face the cattleman. "I'm Edward Fairfield, Mr. McPhee. We saw each other in Rimfire. Why don't you get down from that horse so we can talk man to man?"

"Reckon I'm fine where I am," McPhee said. "What are you sodbusters doing down here where you don't belong? I told you that you're not welcome in this part of the country."

"That's not your decision to make. We have every

right to stake claims on this land. This area has been opened for settlement, and we intend to settle it."

"I graze cattle along this creek every winter," barked McPhee. "How am I gonna do that if there are a bunch of farms here?"

For a moment, Fairfield didn't answer, then the former schoolteacher said, "All of our people who have staked claims so far have done so on this side of the creek. If the others in our party do that as well, you could graze your stock on the other side."

"What's to keep 'em from comin' across? *Fences?*" The utter contempt McPhee put into the word made it clear how he felt.

"Some fences, yes," Fairfield admitted. "But during the winter we won't be growing as many crops, so your cattle wouldn't be able to ruin our fields. We can always drive them back across the creek if they stray."

"You mean butcher 'em. I never saw a sodbuster yet who wasn't a thief at heart."

From where Ace stood, he saw the wagon train captain flush with anger at the ugly accusation.

Fairfield managed to control his temper. "We're honest folks, Mr. McPhee. I give you my word on that. Any losses you might have, I'll make them good personally. You have my word on *that,* too."

Before McPhee could come up with some other objection, Fairfield went on. "There's something else to consider that I don't believe you've thought of. Winter grass grows in this valley, but it's not as abundant as what grows during the summer. My people could devote part of their land to hay, which you could then use to help feed your stock during the worst part of the winter."

McPhee frowned in surprise. "Buy hay from you, you mean?"

"At a fair, reasonable price. None of us want to do anything except get along and raise our families, Mr. McPhee. The last thing we want to do is try to cheat our neighbors."

McPhee's frown deepened as he leaned forward in the saddle as if he didn't like being described as a neighbor to the immigrants. "There have been some mighty rough winters in these parts over the past twenty years," he admitted after a moment. "Sometimes I lost stock because there wasn't enough graze to go around, even in these protected valleys. You really think you could harvest enough hay to help feed my herd?"

"It's something I've been thinking about," said Fairfield. "It's too late in the season to be of much help to you this winter, but give us a year to get established and the next winter should be easier for you. For all of us."

McPhee's eyes narrowed as he said, "It goes against the grain to give up something that's mine in the hope of getting something back. Hope is fleeting."

"Indeed it is. But you won't be giving up range as much as making better use of it."

"For *farming*." Again McPhee's voice was filled with contempt, as if the word tasted bitter in his mouth.

"The time has come for the cattleman and the farmer to work together," Fairfield insisted. "I know it's a change and change is never easy, but the world won't stand still for either of us, Mr. McPhee, no matter how much we might like for it to."

The man who had told McPhee about Quint and

the other Tartan rider getting killed called to the rancher. "Don't listen to him, Mr. McPhee! They gunned down two of us! They gotta pay for that!"

"Yeah," another man growled. "Sodbusters are like lice. You gotta wipe 'em all out or else they keep spreadin' and spreadin'."

McPhee hipped around in the saddle and glared at the men. "I'll decide what I do, not a bunch of hired guns," he snapped.

"You reckon you can hold this land without us, McPhee?" the first man said, his tone defiant and challenging.

"By God, Sherman, I'll hold it without *you*. You're fired!"

"Fine by me," the gunman snapped. He started toward his horses. "I'll go by the ranch and draw my time."

"No need for that," said McPhee. "I'll give it to you right here and now!" He reached into his pocket and brought out a double eagle, then flung the gold piece toward the man. It bounced off his chest and fell to the ground. Instead of going for the coin, the man snarled and yanked his gun from its holster.

The blast of a shot came before Sherman could bring the revolver level. His arm jerked and the gun flew from his hand as he cried out in pain. He staggered and used his left hand to clutch his bullet-drilled upper right arm.

McPhee looked around in surprise to see who had fired the shot. So did Fairfield.

Slowly, Ace lowered the gun. He had stepped out in the open to stop Sherman from shooting McPhee.

The rancher looked at him in surprise, then a red, angry flush began to spread over McPhee's face.

"Sorry, Mr. McPhee," Ace said. "I didn't know if you could take him or not, so it seemed like a good idea to stop him."

"You!" McPhee exploded. "I suppose your brother is here, too."

Chance stepped out from behind one of the wagons and drawled, "Yeah, I am. No thanks to your boys who stomped us and then tried to feed us to the hogs."

"If I'd wanted you dead, you'd be dead." McPhee looked at Fairfield again. "I was about to work a deal with you, mister, but I won't do business with anybody who shelters worthless scoundrels like these two!"

Fairfield looked at Ace and Chance in utter confusion. He didn't know anything about the situation with Ling, and Ace figured it was too much of a complicated mess to explain at the moment.

"Don't let Chance and me stop you from settling things with these folks," he said to McPhee. "We're not part of their group, and we don't have any intention of settling down here. We just gave 'em a helping hand or two, that's all."

Fairfield said, "Ace, I appreciate what you're trying to do, but it's not necessary. You boys are welcome to stay here as long as you like, and if that's a problem for Mr. McPhee—"

"Damn right it is," said the cattle baron.

Ace shook his head. "It doesn't have to be. Chance and I will move on right now, if that's what it takes."

"But where will you go?" asked Laura Fairfield. She had come up with Rufe, who stood beside her with his arm around her shoulder.

Chance grinned and shrugged. "Ace and I have never worried all that much about where we're going. As long as we're on the move, that's all we care about. Right, Ace?"

"Right," Ace agreed. He tucked the gun back in his waistband. "We'll ride out right now." He was running a risk by making that offer, and he knew it.

McPhee honestly didn't seem to want a battle with the immigrants, but he might change his mind once Ace and Chance were gone and couldn't help them anymore. Not only that, but once the Jensen brothers were away from the wagon train, McPhee might come after *them*, and they would be on their own.

But he and his brother had been on their own for quite a while and had always managed to take care of themselves. It seemed like a worthwhile gamble if it would keep any more bloodshed from occurring.

Several seconds crawled by, and then McPhee rasped, "Get your horses and get out. If you're worried about me coming after you, I won't. And there won't be any more trouble here, either. Fairfield and I will hash this out and come to an arrangement."

"I can't tell you how glad I am to hear you say that, Mr. McPhee," Fairfield said.

"You've never seen the frozen carcasses of cows that starved to death in the dead of winter," snapped McPhee. "I have, and if there's something I can do to prevent it, I will, by God. Even if it's putting up with a bunch of sodbusters and their damn fences."

"We don't have to like each other," Fairfield pointed out. "We just have to work together."

McPhee snorted. He turned his horse and spoke to the men on the other side of the creek. "Saddle up and head back to the ranch. Take those bodies with you. I know you don't like it, but that's the way things are for now." He looked at Fairfield. "I'll ride back over here tomorrow. We'll talk some more. In the meantime, my men will leave you alone." McPhee pointed at Ace and Chance. "And those two had better be gone, or any deal we might make is off and that creek's liable to run red with blood!"

Chapter Twenty-nine

Since Ace and Chance didn't have much—horses, saddles, borrowed revolvers—it didn't take long for them to get ready to depart from the wagon train. They would have liked to recover their own guns, but it didn't seem likely Angus McPhee would cooperate with that goal.

McPhee's men withdrew as the rancher had ordered, but McPhee himself drew rein and turned his horse around when he was a couple hundred yards from the camp. He sat there by himself, watching as if he intended to make sure that the Jensen brothers actually left.

Rufe came over to Ace and Chance. "My uncle wants to talk to you fellas before you ride out."

"How's he doing?" Ace asked.

"Uncle Dave?" Rufe made a scoffing sound. "He'll be all right. He's tough as whang leather. It'll take more 'n a bullet graze to do him any real damage."

Ace was glad to hear that was the extent of Wingate's injury. He and Chance walked across the camp with Rufe.

Laura met them at the back of the Fairfield wagon. "Mr. Wingate is inside."

Ace and Chance climbed into the wagon and found the old scout propped up in one of the bunks.

Wingate grinned at them. "That little gal insisted on havin' Rufe and the cap'n put me in here so I could rest better, and once she makes up her mind about somethin', you can't talk her out of it. Just like any woman."

From where she was standing beside the lowered tailgate, Laura snorted.

Ace said, "We're glad you're all right, Mr. Wingate."

The older man was shirtless, but he had bandages wrapped around his torso, holding a thick dressing in place over the wound. "Yeah, I bled like a stuck pig and I'll be pretty stiff and sore for a while, but that little crease didn't really amount to much. As skinny as I am, I reckon I can't afford to lose too much meat from these old bones."

"You've got enough to last you for a while," said Chance.

"Dang right. Anyway, the cap'n tells me you boys are leavin'."

Ace nodded solemnly. "That seems like the best thing to do. I think McPhee actually wants to work out a deal with these folks, but he's got a grudge against Chance and me and won't settle things as long as we're around."

Wingate waved a knobby-knuckled hand. "You don't have to explain nothin' to me, son. I don't know what it's about and it don't matter." He extended the hand. "All I care about right now is thankin' you fellas for all your help."

"We were glad to pitch in," said Ace as he shook hands with the scout.

"And don't forget, you helped us after McPhee's men gave us that thrashing," added Chance as he gripped Wingate's hand.

"Speakin' of which, I guess I ain't the only one who's a mite sore," Wingate said.

"We'll be carrying around some bruises for a while," Ace said. "But we like to keep moving, so that'll keep us from stiffening up too much . . . I hope."

"Yeah, that's the plan," Chance agreed.

"Whereabouts are you headed?"

The Jensen brothers exchanged a glance. They hadn't had a chance to discuss it, but the whole problem of Ling and the money she and Haggarty had stolen from them still hung over their heads.

"We don't really know yet," said Ace. "Sort of figured we'd head on south, though. That'll take us away from McPhee's ranch and Rimfire, and we're sure not welcome in either of those places."

Edward Fairfield was listening from the back of the wagon. "If you fellows would like for me to put in a good word for you with Mr. McPhee, I'd be glad to. He's shown a few glimmerings of being a reasonable man."

"No, that's all right, Mr. Fairfield," said Chance. "You don't want to do anything that might complicate coming to an agreement with him about settling here in the valley."

And it wouldn't do any good for Fairfield to speak up on their behalf anyway, thought Ace. McPhee was smitten with Ling, that was obvious, and when a man fell for a woman, common sense usually went out the window. The Jensen brothers might be young, but they were old enough for Ace to have grasped that fundamental truth about the universe.

"Suit yourself," said Fairfield. "You'll be taking our best wishes with you, wherever you go."

"And if you ever come back this way, you have to stop and say hello," added Laura.

Ace and Chance said good-bye to Dave Wingate, then stepped down from the wagon, shook hands with Rufe and Fairfield, and returned the impulsive hugs that Laura gave them as Rufe scowled a little.

As the brothers headed across the camp toward their horses, more of the men shook hands with them and slapped them on the back. Several of the women hugged them.

One woman handed them a burlap sack, explaining, "These are some supplies that everyone pitched in on for you. There's enough food and ammunition in there to last you for a while."

"We're mighty obliged to you, ma'am," Ace told her, "and to everyone else, as well. We'll miss you folks."

"You risked your lives to help us," said one of the men. "None of us will ever forget that."

Ace tied the bag onto his saddle. He and Chance could transfer the contents to their saddlebags later, after they left the camp. Waving to the pilgrims with whom their trails had intertwined for the past few days, they heeled their horses into motion and rode south.

"We're not really leaving this part of the country, are we?" asked Chance as they put the wagon train behind them.

"While Ling and Jack Haggarty still have that money they stole from us?" Ace shook his head. "Hell, no."

They rode south for about a mile and stopped on top of a small hill where there were enough pine trees and rocks to give them some cover if they needed it. As McPhee had promised, none of his men had come after them so far, but neither Ace nor Chance would put it past some of the rancher's gun-wolves to seek vengeance on their own.

They dismounted and stood looking at the landscape around them, alert for any sign of trouble.

Chance said, "If McPhee's back at his ranch, it's likely Haggarty and Ling came out from Rimfire with him."

"Yeah, he's going to let them stay there as guests," said Ace, "but I reckon we both know what that means."

"How long do you think it'll be before the two of them make their move?"

"As soon as they figure out how to get into McPhee's safe and clean it out," said Ace.

Chance laughed. "Do we really want to save him from that? Wouldn't it be easier to let them steal his loot, then take it from them along with our money?"

"Which would make us thieves just like they are," Ace pointed out.

"Well, not *exactly* like they are. McPhee owes us something for that beating his men gave us, and they stole our guns, too." Chance shrugged. "But you're right, I suppose. Doc didn't raise us to be outlaws."

"No, he didn't. Maybe what we should do is wait

until Haggarty and Ling clean him out, then grab them and take them and the money back to McPhee."

Chance gave his brother a skeptical look.

"If we did that, Ling would come up with some wild story about how it was *us* who stole McPhee's money, and he'd swallow it hook, line, and sinker. You know he would."

Ace nodded glumly. "You're right. He'll almost have to catch them red-handed before he'll believe anything bad about Ling."

"Maybe . . . maybe if we wait until they have the loot, then trail them until they hole up somewhere, one of us could keep an eye on them while the other went back to lead McPhee to wherever they're hiding."

"That might work," said Ace. "For now, it looks like we're going to have to find a place to watch the ranch headquarters without being spotted ourselves. That way we'll know when the two of them try to sneak off."

"And not get caught by McPhee's men while we're doing it."

"Well, yeah. As many warnings as McPhee has already given us, he wouldn't be happy if he found out we were spying on his ranch house."

"I can't help but think Doc would be disappointed in us for getting mixed up in a mess like this."

"Doc got mixed up in plenty of messes of his own. Remember Janey?"

"Oh, yeah," Chance said. "Who could forget Janey?"

They decided to wait until nightfall, then use the cover of darkness to approach the headquarters of the Tartan ranch. They didn't know exactly where it was located, only the general vicinity, but Ace was confident they could find it. The trick would be to locate the ranch house without giving away their presence nearby.

While they were waiting, they transferred the supplies from the burlap sack to their saddlebags and ate some jerky and biscuits that were among the provisions. The afternoon was long and boring, so Chance passed the time the way he often did when he had the opportunity. He stretched out under a tree and slept.

Ace kept watch, which was his usual pastime, too.

They didn't set off for McPhee's ranch until dusk had settled over the Montana landscape. It would have been nice to build a fire and brew a pot of coffee, but they couldn't afford to give away their location. More jerky and water from their canteens made for a grim supper, but it was better than nothing.

With so few cattle grazing down there at that time of year, Ace didn't figure McPhee would have any nighthawks out riding the range, but he and Chance moved cautiously and quietly anyway. They stayed well south of the area where the wagon train was camped and then worked their way eastward through the broad valley, sticking to the shadows as much as possible. It made for slow going, but they had all night, Ace supposed.

A couple hours after full dark had fallen, he spotted some dim spots of light ahead in the distance.

At the same moment, Chance said, "Look up there."

"I see 'em," said Ace. "Looks like several windows."

"Must be McPhee's place."

"I don't know of another spread in these parts."

Several times the lights disappeared, blocked by trees or higher ground. On each occasion, Ace and Chance rode back and forth until they picked up the distant glow again. Gradually they came closer, until they decided it would be a good idea to dismount and go ahead on foot.

They tied the horses to a couple thin-trunked aspens, drew the revolvers, and catfooted forward. The ground sloped up slightly until they found themselves on a small ridge overlooking a wide pasture. On the other side, visible in the light from moon and stars, the ground rose again, but only a few feet to a bench where the ranch buildings sat.

Light shone from a couple windows in the ranch house, which was a sprawling, two-story frame structure. It had started out as a small shack, back in the days when McPhee had first come out to establish his spread, and had been built on to over the years.

Off to one side was a long, low bunkhouse, also with a lighted window. A huge, dark, looming shape had to be a barn. Smaller buildings were likely a cook shack, blacksmith shop, maybe a smokehouse. Several large corrals were scattered around the place, including a round pen most likely used for breaking horses.

Ace and Chance had seen a number of similar spreads and had even worked on a few of them.

They knelt on the rise and Chance whispered,

"How are we going to make sure Ling and Haggarty are here?"

"I can't imagine those two riding out from Rimfire on horseback," replied Ace. "I'll go take a look in the barn and see if there's a buggy there. If there is, we'll have a pretty good idea the two we're looking for are in the house."

"You're not gonna go by yourself."

"Yes, I am. That way, if anything happens to me, you'll still be out here on the loose, so you can pull my fat out of the fire."

"Makes sense, I suppose," Chance said with a shrug. "Doesn't mean I have to like it, though."

"No, it sure doesn't." Ace rose to his feet and dropped a hand on his brother's shoulder, squeezing for a second. "I'll be back."

"Be careful."

"Always am," Ace lied.

The way Chance grunted indicated that he knew it was a falsehood, too.

Ace moved along the ridge for a hundred yards and then slid down it so he could circle around the buildings and approach the barn from the rear. The route he followed skirted wide around the bunk-house. He didn't want to bump into some cowhand on his way to or from the privy or even one who was just restless and out for a walk.

The night was quiet enough that he could hear the horses shifting around in their stalls and swishing their tails back and forth. Over in the bunkhouse, voices spoke too low for him to make out the words, and then a man laughed. Even after all the drama earlier in the day, the Tartan appeared to be at peace.

A small door in the back wall of the barn stood open about a foot. Ace eased it back a few more inches and slipped through. Inside the barn, the darkness was almost complete. Only a faint gray light seeped in here and there. It was enough to allow him to make his way around slowly and carefully. As he moved toward the front of the barn, he saw something sitting motionless in the wide center aisle. When he was close enough, he reached out and touched it. His fingertips encountered the cool smoothness of metal. He slid his hand along what felt like a rail of some sort and realized it was part of the frame of a buggy, just like he'd expected to find.

He supposed it was possible McPhee could have a buggy parked in his barn without Ling and Haggarty being at the ranch headquarters, but it was one more bit of evidence to indicate that they were there.

Ace felt around on the thing until he was absolutely certain it was indeed a buggy, then turned to go back the way he had come. As soon as he rejoined Chance, they could withdraw from the immediate vicinity of the ranch and start looking for a place to hole up.

What they would do after that, he still didn't know. If the opportunity presented itself, if McPhee rode off and left Ling and Haggarty at the ranch house without too many men to guard them, maybe he and Chance could grab the two thieves and force them to confess to McPhee. That would be a long shot at best, but it might be the only chance they would have to recover their money and convince McPhee of the truth.

Those thoughts were going through Ace's brain as he slipped out the barn's back door, and they might have been distracting enough that he didn't hear the man who stepped up behind him. Or maybe the man was just that good.

At any rate, Ace was surprised when he felt the cold ring of a gun muzzle press against the back of his neck as a man's voice whispered in his ear, "Don't move, mate, or I'll blow your spine clean in two."

CHAPTER THIRTY

Ace stayed where he was, sensing that his life hung by a thread. The hard, icy undertone in the man's voice told him the words were no idle threat. The man would kill him without hesitation.

Even so, Ace didn't like having a gun pulled on him, so he was alert for any opportunity to turn the tables on him.

"Ah, you're gonna be sensible," the unseen man continued. "I like that. Never enjoy spillin' blood without a good reason."

The man had an accent, and after a moment Ace placed it as Australian. Ace and Chance had encountered a few natives of that continent in the South Pacific while they were in San Francisco with Doc Monday, years earlier. According to Doc, at one time there had been an Australian gang among San Francisco's underworld, and some of their descendants were still along the Barbary Coast.

The likelihood of Angus McPhee having an Australian gunman working for him seemed pretty remote, but Ace couldn't rule it out entirely. If his captor dragged him before McPhee, there was no telling what the rancher might do.

"I'm not looking for trouble—" Ace began.

"Hush now. You're one of McPhee's men, aren't you? What are you doin' out here at this time of night?"

Ace took a deep breath. From the sound of those questions, the man behind him wasn't one of McPhee's hands, although he might be trying to pull some sort of trick. Ace didn't think so, though. He trusted his instincts and spoke just above a whisper. "I'm no more one of McPhee's men than you are, mister."

"Then who are you?"

"Just a fella who's got a score to settle." That answer was simpler than trying to explain about Ling and Haggarty and what they had done. Let the Australian draw his own conclusions.

That was just what the man did. "A score to settle with McPhee? What are you plannin' to do, ambush him? Burn down his barn?"

"Just taking a look around," Ace replied. "Seems like he's got visitors. I found their buggy in the barn."

"Visitors, is it? And you've got an interest in them?"

"I might," Ace allowed cautiously.

For a moment, the man didn't say anything.

Ace sensed that he was thinking things over.

Then the man said, "I think you'd best come with me, mate."

"I don't know if that's a good idea—"

"Maybe not, but I'm the one with the gun at your neck, so your opinion ain't really relevant, is it? Stand still. Budge an inch and I'll pull the trigger."

"If you do that, McPhee's men will come running

to see what the shooting's about, and I'm guessing *you're* not supposed to be here, either."

"Don't get too full o' yourself, lad." The man reached around Ace and plucked the gun from his waistband. "That's all I wanted, just to make sure you don't get any foolish ideas in your head. Fact of the matter is, I'm startin' to get a feelin' we may be on the same side." He pulled the gun away from the back of Ace's neck. "Now, you're comin' with me, all right? No trouble."

To Ace, cooperation seemed like the fastest and easiest way to find out what was going on. "All right."

The man put his hand on Ace's shoulder and steered him away from the barn. They skirted one of the corrals and moved through the darkness toward some trees a hundred yards away. The place where Chance was waiting for him was in the opposite direction and Ace hated leaving his brother behind, unaware of what had happened at the barn, but there was nothing he could do about it at the moment.

From the barn Ace hadn't seen anyone hiding in the trees, but as he and his captor entered the grove, several dim shapes appeared, surrounding them.

A man asked, "Who the hell is this, Clancy?"

"Don't know, Mr. Belmont, but he claims that he's no friend to Angus McPhee."

From the slight deference in the Australian's voice and the way he addressed the questioner, Ace figured Mr. Belmont was the boss and spoke right up. "My name is Ace Jensen, Mr. Belmont."

"Is that supposed to mean anything to me, son?"

"No, sir, I don't imagine it does. I just figured you'd want to know who you're dealing with."

Belmont's voice held a trace of amusement as he said, "So we're dealing now, are we?"

Ace gave a short nod. "Could be. Depends on whether our goals agree with each other."

"And what would your goal be?"

Under the circumstances, until he found out more, Ace figured he had to play it straight. "I just want to recover what was stolen from me." He still didn't say anything about Chance. He wanted to protect his brother, and also wanted him to remain on the loose for the time being . . . same as he had explained earlier when they'd split up.

"McPhee stole something from you, did he?" asked Belmont. "Cattle, maybe? Are you telling me the man's a rustler?"

"No, sir. From everything I've heard about him, McPhee's an honest man. But that doesn't go for his guests. They're the one who are thieves."

"Guests? Who do you think that might be?" Belmont had him backed into a corner.

Ace could lie, but that might just get him deeper in trouble. He answered honestly, "A man named Jack Haggarty and a young woman called Ling."

"They're the ones you're after?"

"That's right," Ace replied, knowing the answer might get him a swift bullet if it turned out to be the wrong one.

Instead, the dark shape that had been addressing him stepped closer, right in front of him, and a hand clapped down heartily on his shoulder. Belmont chuckled. "We need to go somewhere and talk, young man. I think you may have found yourself some allies."

Outnumbered as he was by at least six to one, Ace had no choice but to accompany Belmont, Clancy, and the other men through the trees until they reached the other side of the grove, where a man was waiting with horses and a buggy.

When they emerged from the trees, the light was a little better, and Ace was able to get a look at the men. They appeared to be a mixture of types, some wearing range clothes, others dressed in city garb like Belmont, who turned out to be a thick-bodied man in a suit and a stylish derby hat. He took a cigar from his vest, stuck it in his mouth, and left it unlit as he asked, "Where's your horse, Ace?"

"I left him tied up in some trees," Ace replied, which was true as far as it went.

"You can retrieve him later . . . if our conversation goes well."

That sounded a little ominous, and Ace felt certain Belmont meant it to sound that way. He didn't say anything to that.

After a moment Belmont went on. "Tell me what happened with Haggarty and the woman."

"I met them on a riverboat—"

"No, wait," Belmont interrupted. "Let *me* tell *you*. You got in a poker game with Haggarty and wound up cleaning him out, right?"

"Yeah, that's what happened," said Ace, continuing to leave Chance out of the story.

"So then Haggarty wagered this Oriental treasure he claimed to have," said Belmont. "Only it turned out to be the woman."

"No offense, Mr. Belmont, but you sound like you're speaking from experience."

Belmont rolled the cigar from one corner of his mouth to the other and said around it, "Bitter experience, my boy, bitter experience. But I suppose I should let you tell your own story."

"There's not much more to tell. You're right about what happened with Haggarty. I 'won'"—Chance paused and gave Belmont a "signifying" look— "the woman, although I reckon he let me win, and Haggarty dropped out of the picture. Then, after we got where we were going, which happened to be Fort Benton, Ling disappeared with all my money, and I found out that she rode out of town with a man matching Haggarty's description. That's what happened to you, isn't it?"

"Some of the details don't quite match up, but basically, yes," said Belmont. "And I daresay they stole considerably more from me than they did from you."

"They got two thousand dollars."

Belmont took the cigar out of his mouth. "Their take from me was ten times that."

Ace let out a low whistle. He couldn't stop the reaction. Twenty thousand dollars was a hell of a lot of money, more than he had ever seen in one place. Even Doc Monday had never played for stakes that high.

"If they had that much, why did they even bother stealing from me?"

"Because they're thieves, and stealing is what they do," said Belmont. "It just comes naturally to them. You wouldn't expect a rattlesnake not to bite, would you?"

"No, I reckon not," Ace admitted. "Still, it seems like they should've just laid low somewhere."

"They may have gone through the loot they took from me. It's been a while. I wasn't able to get on their trail right away. I had to hire detectives for that." Belmont nodded to a couple of the men with him.

"And they led you here?" Ace asked.

"That's right. I assume you trailed Haggarty and his accomplice from Fort Benton?"

"Yeah." Ace paused. "You called Ling an accomplice. You reckon Haggarty's the one behind the whole scheme?"

"That seems reasonable to me. Ling's a young woman. I'm not sure she has the experience to come up with the game they play. Her job is simply to blind the chosen victim with her beauty and charm."

"And to actually steal the money."

"Which Haggarty ordered her to do," said Belmont.

The way he defended Ling told Ace that the older man had fallen for her just the way McPhee evidently had. She hadn't had to go that far with the Jensen brothers and make either of them fall in love with her because she had gotten her hands on their money so quickly. However, Ace had no doubt that she would have done whatever was necessary to get what she wanted.

"So you came all the way from San Francisco to catch up to them, even though you may not be able to get your money back?"

"Who told you I'm from San Francisco?" Belmont asked sharply. "You recognized my name? Leo Belmont. Clancy, did you say anything?"

"Nary a word about where we're from, Mr. Belmont," Clancy replied. "I swear it."

"I've been to San Francisco a few times," Ace explained. "I recognized Mr. Clancy's accent as Australian and figured that maybe he was from there."

"Ah, because of the Sydney Ducks, you mean," said Clancy. "My father was a member, back in the old days. Just a lad he was, but he managed to survive those damn vigilantes."

"That's enough," said Belmont. "No need to bore young Ace here with a lot of history. It's true that I'm from San Francisco. I brought some of my employees with me and hired a few more men when we got out here in Montana Territory. It seemed like some men who were more familiar with the area might come in handy."

"That's a good idea," said Ace.

"I'm glad you agree," Belmont said dryly. "Do *you* know the area?"

"Not that well, but I can find my way around."

"How handy are you with a gun?"

"I'm a fair hand with one," said Ace. That was an understatement. He and Chance had been born with a natural ability to get a gun out fast and fire it accurately. Neither of them was in the same league with the famous gunfighter Smoke Jensen—who had the same last name but was no relation as far as the brothers knew—but they were better than most men when it came to gunplay.

Belmont put the cigar back in his mouth and said, "I can always use a good man."

"To do what, exactly?"

"Help me get back what's mine, or at least to settle the score with Haggarty."

"You don't plan on hurting Ling?"

"I don't make war on women," Belmont said curtly. "Besides, like I told you, I'm convinced that Haggarty is the mastermind of that duo."

"I wouldn't want to see her get hurt, either. The main thing I'm interested in is getting my two thousand back."

"I can make that happen if you throw in with us."

Clancy said, "Boss, you don't really know this dodger . . ."

"We have something in common, though. Two things, actually . . . an enemy and a goal. So what do you say, young Mr. Jensen? Are you with us . . . ?" The unspoken remainder of that question was obvious, and it left room for only one answer.

"I'll throw in with you, Mr. Belmont," Ace said.

"Excellent! You can go back and get your horse."

Ace's spirits rose. That would give him an opportunity to tell Chance what was going on.

Belmont added, "Clancy, you go with him. Meet us back in Rimfire."

That dashed Ace's hopes and added another complication. He and Chance had planned to avoid Rimfire in case some of McPhee's men were there. McPhee might have given them orders to shoot on sight if the Jensen brothers showed up in town.

He would deal with that when the time came, he decided. Outnumbered as he was, all he could do was play along with Belmont's plans and try to find a way to tip off Chance as to what was going on.

"Here you go, mate," Clancy said as he handed Ace's gun back to him.

Ace wrapped his fingers around the Colt's smooth walnut grips and felt a little better about the situation.

If things went to hell, at least he could put up a fight.

CHAPTER THIRTY-ONE

Belmont climbed into the buggy and grasped the reins while the rest of his men mounted up, with the exception of Clancy.

The Australian took the reins of one of the horses but didn't swing up into the saddle. "I'll lead the beast. Quieter that way. Well, let's go, lad. Take me back to where you left your horse."

Ace set off through the night, circling wide around the ranch headquarters. As they walked, he asked, "What is it you do for Mr. Belmont?"

Clancy laughed shortly. "Whatever it is that he needs done."

"What business is he in?"

Clancy's tone hardened. "Now you're diggin' into things that are none o' your concern, my young friend. I thought you frontiersmen made a habit o' not asking about a gent's past."

"You're right. It's none of my business, and we'll just leave it that way."

"Aye, 'twould be wise."

Clancy's reaction told Ace that the hunch he had

was probably correct. Having a grandfather in the notorious criminal gang known as the Sydney Ducks didn't make Clancy a crook, but the possibility certainly existed. The fact that Belmont would hire detectives to track down Haggarty and Ling and then come all the way up to Montana to seek vengeance told Ace that the man was ruthless and accustomed to getting his own way. Taken together, those things told him that odds were, Leo Belmont was a shady character at best, a member of San Francisco's underworld at worst.

And that was the man who'd become Ace's newfound ally, although not exactly by his own choosing.

Clancy and Ace approached the spot where he'd left Chance. Coming at it from a slightly different direction, Ace wasn't exactly sure where his brother was. Not wanting the gunman to stumble over Chance, Ace raised his voice a little. "That horse of mine ought to be around here somewhere."

"Not so loud," warned Clancy. "You don't want McPhee's men to hear you. We can't be sure that everybody's asleep."

"No, I reckon not, Mr. Clancy."

The Australian snorted. "Clancy's my first name, and it's the only one you need to know. No mister about it."

"Sure."

If Chance was in earshot, that exchange was bound to puzzle him considerably. Ace could only hope that his brother would realize he was trying to tip him off.

He heard a noise ahead of them as something

shifted in the brush, and then a horse made a snuffling sound. "There he is."

A moment later, he spotted a dark shape under the trees that he took to be his chestnut. The horse nudged his nose against Ace's shoulder as the young man walked up. He didn't see Chance or the other horse but suspected they were still nearby.

Acting on that assumption, Ace said, "Mr. Belmont told us to head for Rimfire, right?" That would tell Chance where they were going.

"Aye. We should be there before mornin'."

"That's good. McPhee's men know who I am, and they've got a grudge against me. I may have to lie low and stay out of sight until Mr. Belmont's ready to make his move against Haggarty and Ling."

Ace was filling in his brother as best he could. He knew Chance was quick-witted enough to grasp the situation from the seemingly innocuous comments.

"You just do what the boss says, and you'll be all right," Clancy told him.

The two of them mounted up.

Ace said, "I could use a gun belt for this Colt, and I'll need a rifle, too. McPhee's hardcases stole my Winchester."

"I reckon we can fix you up with those things. You can pay Mr. Belmont back once you've recovered what that slant-eyed witch stole from you."

"Sounds like you must not have cared very much for Ling," Ace commented.

Clancy spat. "I never really trusted her, I'll say that much. But the boss, once he laid eyes on her, well, he couldn't really think straight where she was concerned. You've seen the girl. You know what I'm talkin' about."

"Yeah, I do. I surely do."

They rode off, heading north toward the settlement. Chance was somewhere behind them, and Ace couldn't help but wonder what his brother would do next.

Chance waited until the sound of hoofbeats had faded away completely before he emerged from the thick shadows under the trees where he had retreated when he'd heard Ace approaching and talking to somebody. He had stood there with his hand over his horse's nose to keep the animal from whinnying while he listened to the puzzling conversation between his brother and the man with the Australian accent.

Who in blazes was Clancy, and why did Ace sound like they were partners? he wondered. And who was that fellow Belmont? Somebody who had a grudge against Haggarty and Ling, obviously, but Chance didn't know any more than that.

He had no answers for those questions, but he'd been able to tell from Ace's tone of voice that his brother was trying to warn him. As far as Clancy and Belmont knew, Ace was alone, and he wanted to keep it that way for the time being. Chance had to play along.

Once Ace and Clancy had ridden off, Chance mounted up and proceeded slowly in the same direction.

If Ace was headed for Rimfire, that was where Chance was going, too.

* * *

It was well after midnight by the time Ace and Clancy rode into town. They went to the livery stable, where a sleepy, grizzled old hostler took their mounts without seeming to pay much attention to who they were.

Ace got his first good look at Clancy while they were in the livery stable. The man's rawboned frame was an inch or two taller than Ace. He had a rumpled thatch of rusty red hair under a pushed-back plug hat. He also sported a handlebar mustache of the same shade. He wore a brown tweed suit and a collarless shirt with no tie. He looked like a bruiser, but Ace recalled that Clancy was able to move almost soundlessly when he wanted to. That took a surprising amount of grace for a big man.

They went from the livery stable to the Dobbs House hotel, which was across the street and a block down from the Branding Iron Saloon, McPhee's headquarters whenever he was in the settlement. The saloon was still lit up and piano music spilled from it. There was a good chance some of McPhee's men were inside, but there was also a good chance they wouldn't encounter any in the hotel.

"We'll go in the back," said Clancy as he turned down the alley beside the hotel.

Clancy led up the rear stairs to the second floor and along the corridor. "The boss has a suite up here. I want to let him know that we're back."

"Sounds like a good idea," Ace agreed. He wanted to get a better look at Leo Belmont, too.

Clancy stopped at one of the doors and rapped softly on it.

From the other side of the panel, Belmont called, "Who's there?"

"It's me, boss," Clancy replied. "I've got that Jensen boy with me."

"Come on in."

Clancy opened the door. As they stepped inside, Ace saw Belmont slip a small revolver back into the pocket of the jacket he wore. He was a careful man who greeted visitors with a gun in his hand.

Belmont was stocky, with a beefy face and tightly curled salt-and-pepper hair. His eyes were set in pits of gristle and tiny scars around them and his mouth showed that he had been in plenty of fights in his time.

Whatever position in life Belmont occupied now, thought Ace, he had risen to it the hard way.

It was no wonder that he hadn't felt in a forgiving mood when Ling had disappeared with twenty thousand dollars of his money. Forgiveness probably wasn't in his nature.

"Any problems?" Belmont asked.

"Not for us," Clancy reported, "and everything looks quiet here in town."

"It is," Belmont agreed. "For now."

Ace said, "If you don't mind me asking a question, Mr. Belmont . . . ?"

"Go ahead," the man said with a wave of his hand.

"How many men do you have working for you?"

"Fifteen," Belmont answered without hesitation. "Why?"

"McPhee has at least twice that many, probably

more if you count all the regular hands who work on his ranch."

Belmont didn't seem impressed. "I'm not worried about a bunch of cowboys."

"No offense, sir, but a lot of those fellas who ride for McPhee aren't what you'd call cowboys. They're gun-wolves, plain and simple. And they're probably a match for anybody you have working for you."

Clancy snorted contemptuously. "Nobody's tougher than a Barbary Coast man," he boasted.

"Maybe not, but they'll have you outnumbered."

Belmont took out another cigar. Unlike earlier, he clipped the end off and lit it, turning the cylinder in the match flame until it was burning evenly. He dragged in a deep breath and blew out the smoke. "What are you getting at, Jensen?"

Several thoughts were percolating around in Ace's brain, possible ways he could turn this complication to his and Chance's advantage. "If you plan to make any sort of move against Haggarty and Ling, you're liable to lose if you go up directly against McPhee." He glanced at Clancy. "No matter how good you are, it's hard to win when you're outnumbered and outgunned."

Clancy glared at him.

Belmont asked with an arrogant smirk, "What would you suggest, then?"

"Haggarty and Ling are guests at McPhee's ranch. If you could get him into town on business, he'd probably bring some of his men with him. The odds against your men would then be better if they made a move on the ranch."

Belmont frowned and seemed to be taking Ace more seriously as he asked, "You think McPhee would leave the two of them out there?"

"I believe there's a good chance he would. They don't have anything to do with his business, after all. As far as he knows, it's just a social visit they're making."

Belmont chewed on the cigar a second before he said, "They're after his money. She will use her wiles on him, and he won't know what's going on until it's too late."

More than likely, Belmont was describing exactly what had happened to him back in San Francisco, although he either didn't realize it or didn't care.

"What you really need to do if you can get McPhee away from the ranch," Ace said, "is to send just a few men out there—three or four—to grab Haggarty and get him out without anyone knowing. Then you could force him to give your money back to you. Or however much of it he has left, anyway."

"And I suppose you think you should be one of those men," scoffed Clancy.

"As a matter of fact—"

"Wait a minute." Belmont held up a hand to stop him. "That's actually not a bad idea."

Clancy objected. "Boss, I don't know—"

"It's starting to become pretty clear to me that Jensen has a good head on his shoulders," Belmont went on as if he hadn't heard the objection Clancy had started to raise. "And he's familiar with this part of the country."

"You've known him two hours!"

Belmont didn't look happy that one of his employees would speak to him that way. He snapped, "I can size up a man in two minutes, if I need to. Besides, at least half of our men are ones that I hired in Denver. I don't really know any of them, either. Besides, Jensen's got a personal stake in this. He wants to get his hands on Haggarty almost as much as I do."

"That's true, I reckon," said Ace.

Clancy didn't look happy about it, but obviously there was a limit to how much he was willing to argue with his boss. "You're callin' the shots, Mr. Belmont. I'll go along with whatever you decide, and I'll make it work, too."

"Yes, I know I can count on you, Clancy." Belmont turned his attention back to Ace. "What do you say, young man?"

"I need a gun belt and a Winchester. Clancy said you could probably fix me up."

Belmont nodded. "Of course. We'll see to it first thing in the morning. What else?"

Ace started to shrug and say that was all, but then he suggested, "Can you guarantee I get my two thousand back?"

A bark of harsh laughter came from Belmont. "Two thousand dollars? Yes, I think I can guarantee that. Getting my revenge on Jack Haggarty is worth more than that to me. A lot more." One of Belmont's hands clenched into a fist. "I don't like being betrayed. I won't tolerate it."

Figuring that anger was directed more at Ling than at Haggarty, Ace worried what he was letting himself in for by throwing in with Belmont. He wasn't going to allow Belmont to harm the young woman, no matter what she had done.

Knowing he stood a better chance of being able to protect her by pretending to work with Belmont, he realized he needed to keep up the ruse. "In that case, I reckon I'm in."

CHAPTER THIRTY-TWO

As second in command, Clancy had a room of his own at the Dobbs House, and he insisted that Ace share it with him. "It ain't that I don't trust you, mate, it's just that I want to be sure you won't be tryin' to pull any sort o' tricky double cross."

"Like you said before, Clancy, we're on the same side," Ace assured him.

"We'll see."

The night passed quietly, and in the morning Clancy had one of the other men bring some breakfast up from the dining room for both of them.

"You said you wanted to stay out o' sight, so that's what we're doin'," Clancy explained. "I told one of the boys to fetch you a gun belt, too, and to put a rifle with your saddle and other gear over at the livery stable."

"Sounds like you've got everything under control," Ace commented.

"That's my job," Clancy said flatly. "I take care o' things for Mr. Belmont. You'd be well advised not to forget it."

"I don't figure you'll let me," said Ace with a faint smile.

When the man arrived with the gun belt, Ace buckled it on and slipped the Colt into the holster. Having the gun's weight back on his right hip where it was supposed to be felt good. Despite his relatively young age, he had been packing iron for quite a few years and had gotten used to having it there.

"So, now you're a gunfighter again," said Clancy in a slightly mocking tone.

Ace shook his head. "No, I'm not a gunfighter. I've met some of them, and I'm not on their level. I do all right, though."

The man who had brought the gun belt handed a flat-crowned black hat to Ace. "Thought you might like this, too."

"Thanks. My head was feeling a mite bare." Ace put on the hat. "How does it look?"

"Jaunty as all hell," Clancy said dryly. "Come on. Let's go talk to Mr. Belmont."

The man from San Francisco was having breakfast in his room, too. He had an empty plate in front of him on the table and was leaned back in a chair, wearing a silk robe and sipping coffee from a china cup. "Good morning," he greeted Ace and Clancy. "The hat and the gunbelt make a different, Jensen. You're starting to look like a hardcase."

Ace hadn't shaved in a couple days, so he was sporting a considerable amount of dark stubble. It wasn't an image he usually cultivated—normally he was so clean-cut it was annoying, according to Chance—but it might come in handy.

Ace nodded curtly to Belmont. "Feel a lot better packing iron the right way."

Belmont didn't offer them any coffee. Ace supposed the thought never even occurred to the man.

Belmont said, "I did some thinking about what you suggested last night, Jensen. I've written a note to Angus McPhee, introducing myself and asking him to meet me here in town. I told him I'm looking to start a ranch in the area and that I'd like to talk to him about buying some cattle to start my herd." Belmont laughed. "I tried to come across as a bit naïve about such things. If McPhee's like every other Scotsman I've ever met, he'll jump at the chance to get the best of someone in a business deal. I'll send a man out to his ranch with the note, and I won't be surprised if McPhee comes into town this afternoon to try to rook me."

Ace nodded. "That sounds like it ought to work, all right. And while McPhee's here in Rimfire . . ."

"You and Clancy and a couple other men will be out at his ranch, grabbing Jack Haggarty. Don't kill him, though. I want him alive until I get my money back. As much of it as I can, anyway. *And* I want him to suffer for thinking he can steal from me and get away with it."

"What about the woman?" asked Clancy.

Ace had been about to ask the same thing, but it was probably better that the question came from Clancy, he thought.

"She's just Haggarty's pawn," responded Belmont with a shrug, "but bring her along with you if you can. If McPhee has reacted to her the same way most men do, he won't want any harm coming to her. As long as she's in our hands, he'll be less likely to make a move against us."

"Makes sense, boss," Clancy said, nodding. He glanced at Ace. "You got that, Jensen?"

"Clear as can be," Ace told them.

"We'll have to wait to get word from McPhee, so we'll know what his plans are," Belmont said. "I'll let you know as soon as I hear anything."

Ace and Clancy returned to the room where they had spent the night. Clancy dug a greasy pack of cards out of his bag and slapped it down on the room's small table. "I fancy a game of blackjack," he said in a tone that didn't allow for any argument. "Nickel a hand."

"All right," said Ace. Chance was better at blackjack than he was, the same as all the other card games, but Ace knew how to play and didn't mind doing so to pass the time. "I may have to give you an IOU, though, since I'm just about broke until I get my money back from Haggarty and Ling."

"I don't mind takin' your marker." Clancy's lips pulled back from his teeth in a grin that was half-snarl. "I know where to find you if you try to run out on me, mate."

In some trees about a quarter mile from Rimfire, Chance had made camp the night before and spent some restless hours dozing in his bedroll. He didn't like not knowing for sure that his brother was all right.

Riding openly into town would be asking for trouble, though, so all he could do was keep an eye on the settlement. If it was at all possible, Ace would tip him off about what was going on. Until then, Chance would have to be patient.

Once the sun was up, he risked a tiny, almost smokeless fire, knowing that it wouldn't be seen behind the screen of trees, so he was able to boil coffee and fry some bacon. That made him feel a little better.

As he hunkered on his heels next to the now-cold fire and sipped the last of the coffee, he rasped a hand over his unshaven chin. He didn't like wearing the same clothes day after day and being scruffy. His appearance mattered to him. He had always enjoyed being sharply dressed and well-groomed.

At the moment, however, there were a lot more important things to consider, such as both of them surviving and getting their hands on the money that had been stolen from them.

Chance was confident that Ace was working on that.

Belmont's messenger was back from the Tartan Ranch by early afternoon.

Belmont summoned Ace and Clancy and told them, "McPhee's going to come to Rimfire this afternoon, and he wants to have dinner with me here at the hotel this evening. This is perfect. He'll probably spend the night. In fact, I'll string him along enough that he'll *have* to spend the night."

"What if he brings Haggarty and the girl into Rimfire with him?" asked Clancy.

"When he's coming to talk business?" Belmont shook his head and waved off that idea. "Not likely.

But if he does, we'll wait and come up with some other plan. I've put off settling the score with those two for this long, I can let it go for a while longer if need be." His voice hardened. "But not too much longer. Judgment Day's coming for Jack Haggarty."

Ace noticed that once again Belmont didn't include Ling in his vow of vengeance. He might be angry at her, but he blamed Haggarty for what had happened. It sounded like Belmont didn't intend to hurt her. Ace hoped that was the case.

Belmont went on. "You can pick out the other two men you want to take with you, Clancy, then the four of you go ahead and slip out of town. You can ride out to McPhee's ranch while he's on his way to Rimfire. Just be careful that you don't run into him on the way."

Clancy nodded. "I understand, boss. I'm taking Whistler with me."

"A good choice," agreed Belmont. "What about the other man?"

"I'm thinking that fella you hired in Denver named Robertson."

Belmont frowned. "I don't recall the name. Which one is he?"

"Stocky fellow, close-cropped beard." Clancy grinned. "You'd never look twice at him, that's why you don't remember him. But I like his eyes. Cold as ice, they are. He'll do whatever needs to be done and won't hesitate, just like Whistler."

Clancy glanced at Ace, who read the challenge in the Australian's gaze. Clancy was asking him if *he* would do whatever needed to be done. He returned the look coolly and levelly.

After a couple seconds Clancy sneered and turned his attention back to Belmont. "We're to bring Haggarty and the woman here?"

Belmont shook his head. "Too risky, with McPhee in the hotel. Take them to the livery stable and keep them there. Send word to me when you get back with them. If Haggarty cooperates and gives my money back to me, there won't be any reason to hang around here. We can start back to San Francisco . . . as soon as I've taught Haggarty a lesson."

Considering the marks of past brutality on Belmont's face, Ace was convinced the man intended to deliver that lesson to Haggarty himself.

They left Belmont's suite and went along the corridor to one of the other rooms. Clancy rapped softly on the door. The man who opened it had a lean, foxlike face with shaggy blond hair hanging over his ears. His pale blue eyes had a predatory look to them.

"Get your gear and come to the livery stable, Whistler," Clancy told him. "We're ridin' out in ten minutes."

Whistler nodded but didn't say anything.

Clancy knocked on the door of another room. The man who opened it matched the description Clancy had given Belmont.

"Robertson, you're comin' with Jensen, Whistler, and me," Clancy told him. "Be ready to ride in ten minutes."

"Sure," Robertson replied. His voice was mild and unthreatening, just like his appearance, but Ace felt

a slight shiver go through him when he looked in
the gunman's eyes and saw a frigid emptiness that
made him think Robertson's soul must be an arctic
wasteland.

"Need anything else?" Clancy asked Ace as they
started toward the stairs.

"Except for my horse and saddle and that new
rifle, everything I own is on me," said Ace.

"It's a smart man who travels light."

They went down the rear stairs again and headed
for the livery stable, sticking to the back alleys so if
any of McPhee's men were in town, they would be less
likely to catch sight of Ace.

Whistler and Robertson walked in while Ace and
Clancy were saddling their horses. Clancy had made
good on his promise. There was a Winchester with
Ace's saddle, not a new weapon but one that appeared to be in fine shape. It fired the same round as
his Colt, and there was a full box of cartridges, too.

Ace kept the hat pulled low over his eyes to obscure his face as the four of them rode out of Rimfire.
No one yelled behind them, and no shots rang out,
so he assumed they had been successful in keeping
him from being spotted.

Once they were out of the settlement, Ace looked
around at the Montana landscape, not really expecting to spot Chance but wishing he could know for
sure that his brother was out there somewhere, keeping an eye on him. As twins, there had always been
some sort of mysterious connection between them
that went beyond their occasional habit of finishing
each other's sentences. Usually, Ace could sense it
whenever Chance was around, and vice versa. Ace felt

a faint stirring of that, but it wasn't as strong as it usually was.

He was confident that Chance was alive, though. He would know it if anything ever happened to his brother. He was sure of that.

As Chance lowered the field glasses he'd fetched from his saddlebag, a smile tugged at the corners of his mouth. Ace looked like he was all right as he rode out of Rimfire with three hardcases. In fact, he looked better than he had the last time Chance had seen him. He was wearing a hat again and had a gun belt strapped around his waist with the holstered Colt attached to it. A rifle butt stuck up from a sheath strapped to the chestnut's saddle, too. Ace was well-armed again.

The smile disappeared. All Chance had was the old Remington.

He shrugged off the frown. That didn't matter. He would put it to good use when and if he had to.

It didn't take him long to throw his saddle on the cream-colored gelding and set off after his brother and the other men, hanging back enough so the others wouldn't be able to spot him easily. It appeared that they were headed in the direction of Angus McPhee's ranch.

Were they on their way to a showdown of some sort? Chance found himself hoping that was the case.

Ace suggested that they cross the creek and angle toward the northern side of the valley. "We'll be a lot less likely to run into McPhee that way, since his ranch headquarters lies south of the creek."

Clancy looked narrow-eyed at him. "This isn't some trick you'd be pullin', is it, mate?"

Ace didn't bother trying to hide the exasperation he felt as he said, "Haven't you realized by now that we're after the same thing, Clancy? All this constant suspicion is getting old."

"Can't be too careful, that's all. Anyway, it's your own interests I'm lookin' out for, boy. If you double-cross us, I'll turn you over to Whistler here, and you wouldn't like that. You know why they call him Whistler?"

Ace glanced at the lean, shaggy-haired man. "I don't have any idea."

"Because he likes to whistle a little tune while he's workin', and the work he does best is with a knife. I've seen him practically skin a man alive . . . and *keep* him alive while he was doin' it. No, sir, the Apaches don't have a thing on our pal Whistler here."

Ace kept his face impassive. If Clancy's lurid comments were true—and Ace had no reason to believe they weren't—that pretty much eliminated any doubts he might have had that Belmont and his men were criminals.

And he had willingly thrown in his lot with them, he reminded himself . . . but only because that represented the best chance he and his brother had of recovering the money stolen from them.

Clancy turned his horse toward the creek at the next spot where it looked easy enough to ford. "The kid's right, I suppose. We don't want to run smack-dab into McPhee."

Belmont planned to kill Haggarty, Ace mused as they rode east through the valley. Could he stand by and allow Haggarty to be murdered? Ace didn't think so. He certainly couldn't let Ling come to any harm if he could prevent it. More and more, it looked like he was going to be put in the position of having to help those two escape from Belmont's vengeance.

And then Belmont, Clancy, and the rest of that pack of killers would be after *him*.

It was a hell of a lot of trouble for two thousand dollars, thought Ace. Maybe it would be better if he lit a shuck out of there before they ever reached the Tartan. He could find Chance, and they could put Rimfire, McPhee's spread, and the whole valley behind them.

But that would mean abandoning two people— not two *innocent* people, to be sure, but still human beings—to whatever Belmont had planned.

At the moment, the odds were not great—Clancy, Whistler, and Robertson against Haggarty. If Ace waited until they got their hands on Haggarty and Ling, he might be able to turn the tables, especially if Chance was nearby and could take a hand, as he hoped. Then he could try to convince Haggarty and Ling to give up whatever plans they had of robbing McPhee and get out of there instead.

They would still have Belmont after them, but there was a limit on just how many problems one man could fix, Ace told himself.

"What the hell are you broodin' about, mate?" asked Clancy, breaking into Ace's grim thoughts.

"Nothing," Ace replied with a shake of his head. "Just hoping that Haggarty and the girl don't go into

Rimfire with McPhee. I'd just as soon get this over with tonight."

"I hear what you're sayin'. We've come all the way from San Francisco—well, Whistler and I have, anyway—and I'm ready for the boss to settle things with those two."

"He's going to kill Haggarty, isn't he?"

Clancy snorted. "He stole from Mr. Belmont. What do *you* think is gonna happen to him?"

"And the girl?"

"He's got a soft spot for that witch," Clancy said with a sigh.

Whistler spoke up for the first time. "But that won't stop him from givin' her to us, will it, Clancy?"

His voice reminded Ace of a snake slithering through the grass.

Clancy just grunted, but he didn't deny what Whistler said.

A ball of cold sickness formed in Ace's belly. From the sound of it, things were even worse than he thought. He had to find some way to make them right.

Or more likely . . . die trying.

CHAPTER THIRTY-THREE

By late afternoon, Ace and the other three men were hidden on a wooded hilltop in sight of the Tartan headquarters. Clancy took a spyglass from his saddlebags, extended it to its full length, and peered through the lenses at the cluster of buildings.

"Better be careful not to let any sunlight reflect off that glass," Ace cautioned him. "If anything glints up here, some of McPhee's men are liable to spot it and investigate."

Clancy gave him a disgusted look. "Don't tell me how to do my job, mate. I've been spyin' on people longer than you've been alive."

"I don't doubt it, but I know the sort of men McPhee has working for him. They've always got their eyes open for trouble."

"And trouble's what they're gonna get," muttered Clancy as he resumed his surveillance of the ranch.

Ace had field glasses of his own and used them to watch the house, making sure to stay in the shadows under the trees where the sun's slanting rays couldn't reach the lenses. After a while, his scrutiny was rewarded.

A man stepped out of the ranch house onto the wide front porch, took a cigar from his vest pocket, and lit it, puffing contentedly.

Ace recognized Jack Haggarty immediately.

The gambler wasn't dressed as flashily as he had been on the *Missouri Belle*, but the prematurely white hair and neat mustache were unmistakable. If Haggarty was there, then Ling had to be, Ace thought. It was nice to know that the pursuit he and Chance had launched had finally borne fruit.

Of course, the presence of those murderous criminals who were currently his "partners" complicated things considerably, Ace told himself.

Clancy had spotted Haggarty, too. "There he is. That means the Chinese girl is here, too. The boss was right. McPhee didn't take them to Rimfire with him."

Ace wondered if Haggarty and Ling had already found McPhee's safe, managed to break into it, and looted its contents. If that was the case, they were probably waiting until nightfall before slipping away and making a run for it. If not, they would be patient, biding their time until they could clean out the safe.

It didn't really matter. Their plans were about to take an unexpected—and potentially deadly—twist.

After a few minutes that he spent smoking and

looking satisfied with himself, Haggarty turned and went back into the ranch house.

Up on the hilltop, Clancy pointed and gave directions to the men with him. "Once it's good and dark, we'll slip down there, keepin' well away from the bunkhouse. Whistler, you and Robertson will stay on the porch and cover the bunkhouse. If there's an alarm raised and those cowboys start to come out, you cut 'em down as soon as they set foot in the open, understand? It'll be your job to keep 'em bottled up while Jensen and I grab Haggarty and the girl."

"Sure, Clancy," said Whistler. "We can do that."

"I'm going in the house with you?" asked Ace.

"Aye. And before you can say anything . . . yeah, it's because I still don't trust you, kid. I want you where I can keep an eye on you. If you're tellin' the truth about wantin' to get even with those two, just like the boss, you'll do as I say and won't cause any trouble."

"You'll see," Ace said.

In reality, he was glad that Clancy had decided to split their force. He would only have to deal with the Australian once they were in the house. He might still have to face off against Whistler and Robertson before the night was over, but at least the odds would only be two to one.

Or even, if Chance was able to take a hand.

Ace wondered where his brother was.

Chance had seen Ace and the other three men riding up the back side of the hill, shielded from the ranch house by the trees and the hill itself. Even though he lost sight of them when they disappeared into the thick growth of pines, he had a hunch they would go to ground there and keep an eye on the ranch headquarters while they waited for night to fall. He didn't know what they were after, but the odds of them making a move in broad daylight seemed pretty slim.

So if they could wait, he could wait, too.

But when darkness settled over the ranch, he intended to sneak down there so he would be close by if his brother needed his help.

Haggarty didn't put in another appearance during the remaining couple hours of daylight. Ace felt his impatience growing as the shadows of dusk began to gather. Someone in the house lit the lamps. A warm yellow glow of light filled the windows.

The men wouldn't make their move until it was completely dark, and as they waited for that, time seemed to drag with maddening slowness.

Finally, Clancy said, "All right, let's move out. We'll lead the horses."

Robertson said, "We should have brought extra mounts for Haggarty and the girl."

The same thing had occurred to Ace back in Rimfire, but he hadn't pointed it out, not wanting to make it easier for Clancy to succeed in kidnapping Haggarty and Ling. The mustachioed crook might know everything there was to know about surviving on the Barbary Coast as part of San Francisco's criminal underworld, but he wasn't experienced when it came to handling trouble on the frontier.

The thought that Ace might help the two thieves get away had already been stirring in the back of his brain, even then.

"Why the hell didn't you say something about that back in Rimfire, Robertson?" snapped Clancy.

The stocky gunman shrugged. "Belmont don't pay me to think. Just to shoot."

"And you're a city boy like me, Whistler," Clancy said to the shaggy-haired killer. "What about you, Jensen?"

"I just didn't think about it," Ace lied easily.

Clancy cursed for a moment, then said, "All right, it's too late to do anything about it now. If we can, we'll steal a couple horses from the barn. If not, Haggarty and the woman can ride double with us. Whistler, you take Ling."

"Glad to," said Whistler.

Ace couldn't see him, but he could hear the leering quality in Whistler's voice.

"Jensen, you keep up with Haggarty."

"All right," Ace agreed, hoping that it would never come to that.

"Everybody know what your job is?" Clancy didn't wait for answers. He just added, "Let's go."

They led the horses and moved slowly and quietly down the hill, angling away from the bunkhouse where lights still burned.

It might have been smarter to wait until even later in the night before making their move, mused Ace, but he supposed Clancy felt the same sort of impatience he did.

Because of the caution with which they proceeded, it took almost half an hour to get down the hill and circle toward the ranch house. By the time they reached the bottom, the lamps downstairs had been blown out, although a couple windows on the second floor still showed light.

Ace guessed that meant Haggarty and Ling hadn't turned in yet.

They tied the horses to some small trees at the side of the house and catfooted toward the porch. All four men had drawn their guns.

As night fell, Chance moved closer to the hill where Ace and the other men were waiting. He thought about trying to get close enough to overhear whatever they were saying, so he would understand more about what was going on, but he was convinced that Ace didn't want his companions to know his brother was anywhere in the vicinity. Ace could skulk around like an Indian and nobody would know he was there, but Chance doubted that his own skills were up to that task. He would step on a branch and break it, or trip and fall down, or do something else that would alert the men to his presence.

Better not to push his luck, he decided. It was a wise man who knew his own limitations.

He was close enough, however, to know when they left the hilltop and started sneaking down to the ranch headquarters. He had been expecting them to do just that, so he was ready to follow them.

Deep in some shadows under a tree, he watched as the four dim shapes crept closer to the ranch house.

When they reached the end of the porch, Clancy stepped up onto it first. One of the boards creaked faintly under his weight. He eased aside and found more solid footing. Ace, Whistler, and Robertson avoided the plank that had made the slight noise.

When Clancy reached the door, he wrapped his left hand around the knob and carefully tried it. The knob turned. He swung the door open. Ace waited to see if the hinges would make any noise, but they were silent. Evidently McPhee or someone who worked for him kept them well-oiled.

Clancy turned and gestured to Whistler and Robertson. The two men split up, one going to each end of the porch to stand guard. Clancy lifted his left hand and crooked the fingers in a summoning gesture to Ace, then stepped into the house.

Ace followed.

Chance saw them split up. One man moved to each end of the porch, evidently to stand guard, and the other two went inside. There was enough light for him to see their silhouettes as they passed through the door. Chance recognized Ace by his shape.

Haggarty and Ling had to be in there. That was the only thing that made any sense to Chance. Ace was going after them.

But were the men with him allies . . . or was Ace their captive?

Sticking to the shadows, Chance worked his way closer, hoping to find out the answer to that all-important question.

Without any starlight, it was even gloomier in the house and it took a few seconds for Ace's eyes to adjust. He saw Clancy stalking cautiously toward a staircase and followed the Australian, staying close to the wall as they ascended so the likelihood of a board creaking would be less.

Ace wasn't sure that would matter, since his heart was slugging so heavily in his chest it seemed to him that everybody on the ranch ought to be able to hear it thundering.

The hallway at the top of the stairs was illuminated dimly. Ace lifted his head high enough to look past Clancy along the corridor and saw that light was spilling through an open door at the end of the hall.

They approached it as quietly as they could, but it was unlikely any slight noises they made would be heard anyway since two people in the room were talking to each other and their voices would obscure any other sounds.

Those voices were familiar, too. Ace recognized the silky tones that belonged to Ling as the young woman said, "Don't you have it yet, Jack?"

"Don't get impatient," replied Haggarty. "This safe is one of the best they make. But I never yet met a combination lock I couldn't crack, and this one won't beat me, either."

So they had found Angus McPhee's safe, thought

Ace, and were trying to break into it at that very moment. They must have considered it an unexpected stroke of luck when McPhee received the note from Leo Belmont and decided to go into Rimfire for the night, so he could talk business with the man from San Francisco. That gave them the perfect opportunity to realize their goal.

"Anyway, we've got all night," Haggarty went on, unconsciously echoing the thoughts that were going through Ace's head. "McPhee won't be back until tomorrow sometime."

"And I want to be long gone by then," snapped Ling. "The longer we have to stay here, the harder it's going to be to keep McPhee at bay."

"Well, if you have to let him into your bed . . . it wouldn't be the first time, would it?"

"Shut up and work that lock," Ling told her partner.

Out in the hallway, Ace reflected grimly that although Ling's voice was unmistakable, she had completely lost the singsong cadence of her speech she had displayed when she had been with him and Chance, not to mention all the self-deprecating references to herself as "this one." In fact, she sounded very much American and as hardboiled as a trail town soiled dove, to boot. Ace suspected that her true personal history was much different from the heartstrings-tugging story she had told him and his brother.

None of that mattered at the moment.

When Chance reached the side of the house, he dropped to hands and knees, then stretched out on his belly and crawled toward the porch. Normally he wouldn't want to get his suit dirty, but in the clothes borrowed from the immigrants with the wagon train, that didn't matter as much.

Besides, Ace was in there, so Chance didn't really care how dirty he got.

As he got closer to the porch, he heard the man at that end of it moving around a little. Chance froze where he was. He thought the shadows at the side of the house were thick enough to conceal him, but he didn't want to risk getting any closer until he had to.

In the hallway, Clancy leveled his revolver and stepped through the door. "Don't either of you move!" he warned. "Haggarty, stay right where you are or I'll blow your kneecap into a million pieces. Jensen, watch the girl!"

Close behind him, Ace's eyes took in the scene in a fraction of a heartbeat. They were in a large room that appeared to be a combination of library, study, and office. Two sides of the room were covered with bookshelves filled with leather-bound volumes, telling Ace that Angus McPhee was a reader. Even under those circumstances fraught with danger, Ace wished he had time to study the titles.

A huge rolltop desk dominated one side of the room, and near it was a smaller set of shelves. They had been swung into the room to reveal a small chamber that normally would be hidden. Squatting in the chamber like a big iron toad was the safe McPhee had brought from Fort Benton. Jack Haggarty was on one knee in front of the safe, leaning close to it so he could press his ear to the combination lock and listen for the tumblers to click as he slowly turned the knob.

Ling stood beside the desk. Wearing high-topped boots, whipcord trousers, and a green silk blouse, she was dressed for riding, appropriate since she and Haggarty had planned to loot McPhee's safe and make their getaway tonight. Her raven-black hair was pulled into a ponytail that hung down her back.

Following the split second in which Ace took note of all that, Haggarty gasped a startled curse. He started to turn and stand up, but he froze when Clancy thrust the pistol at him.

Ling was impassive, except for a slight widening of her almond-shaped eyes as she looked at Ace. She had to be shocked to see him . . . or maybe she wasn't. If she and Haggarty had been playing their crooked games for a while, it probably wasn't the first time one of their victims had come after them. Her lips tightened just the least little bit.

Her hand moved slightly toward her waist. Ace didn't know if she had a knife or a small gun hidden somewhere. The trousers were tight enough that it didn't seem likely.

But he didn't want to take any chances with her and said sharply, "Don't do it, Ling."

She smiled. "Mister Ace! Thank God you are here. This one was so frightened . . ." At the look on his face, her voice trailed off and she went on. "Oh, hell. I'm wasting my time, aren't I?"

"I'm afraid so," he told her.

From where he knelt in front of the safe, Haggarty said, "It appears these gentlemen have the drop on us, my dear." He looked at Clancy. "I know you, don't I? You work for Leo Belmont."

"That's right. Mr. Belmont wants to have a word with the both of you—"

Ace didn't see any point in letting it go on. He took a quick step, raised his Colt, and brought it crashing down on Clancy's head.

CHAPTER THIRTY-FOUR

Clancy's caution and skepticism about Ace's loyalty had kept him on edge or some instinct warned him and he'd started to twist away from the blow. Even though Ace's gun smashed into the side of Clancy's skull, it didn't knock the Australian out or even drive him off his feet.

Clancy kept turning and tried to bring his revolver to bear on Ace, who brought the barrel of his gun cracking down on Clancy's wrist. The gunman cried out in pain but held on to the gun. Haggarty surged up from the floor and tackled him from behind, sending Clancy forward to ram into Ace. All three men sprawled on the floor, but Ace was on the bottom and the hard landing jolted the air out of his lungs. For a second, his head swam dizzily as Haggarty and Clancy wrestled on top of him.

They rolled a little to the side, and he heaved his body up to throw them off the rest of the way. He started to get up just in time to see one of Ling's boots streaking toward his face as she launched a vicious kick.

Ace jerked his head aside. The heel of Ling's boot thudded into his left shoulder and knocked him off balance again. As he fell backwards, he reached out, grabbed her foot that was still in the air, and heaved. With a startled cry, she fell, too, and landed hard on her rear end.

Thankfully, no shots had gone off yet. A gun blast would bring Whistler and Robertson racing into the house and up the stairs. Ace wanted Clancy taken care of before he had to deal with the other two killers.

Haggarty was putting up a good fight—a better fight than Ace would have expected from a dandy and a gambler—but Clancy had him outclassed. The Australian's fist slammed into Haggarty's jaw and rocked his head back.

An instant later, Clancy chopped at Haggarty's head with the gun he held in his other hand and landed a glancing blow that opened up a deep cut on Haggarty's temple. Blood welled from it and ran down the man's face. The blow stunned him long enough for Clancy to hit him again. Haggarty sagged to the floor, limp and unconscious.

On his hands and knees, Ace pushed off with his feet and came up in a diving tackle that sent him flying toward Clancy. He planted a shoulder in the man's back and carried him forward. Clancy toppled toward the safe. His head struck the door with a resounding thud and bounced back.

Clancy crumpled and landed facedown on the floor, out cold, if not worse.

Ace got up on his knees and remained there for a moment, breathing heavily. He was about to get to his feet when he felt the touch of a razor-sharp blade against his throat.

"Stay where you are," warned Ling. "I don't want to slit your throat, Ace, but I will if I have to."

Ace froze in place. Ling's deft pressure on the knife made the blade barely break the skin, but he knew it wouldn't take much to open up his throat and slice through his veins and arteries. Death would be swift after that.

"That's good," Ling said softly. "I had the idea that you were the smarter of the brothers. That's why we made sure that Chance wound up winning me."

Haggarty groaned and began stirring around.

Ling nudged him with a foot. "Jack! Jack, are you all right?"

Haggarty blinked his eyes open, sat up shakily, and used his hand to wipe blood from his face. "Damn!" he exclaimed. "Am I killed?"

"Don't be a fool," Ling told him. "That man hit you on the head and opened up a cut. You know head wounds always bleed so much they look worse than they really are."

"Yeah, I guess. Feels like somebody's banging a drum inside my skull, though." He looked over at Clancy's senseless form. "Who in blazes . . . ?"

"Don't you remember him? He works for Leo Belmont, you said so yourself a few minutes ago. His name is . . . Clancy. That's it. Just Clancy. One of those damn, dirty Australians. The vigilantes should have cleaned them all out of San Francisco thirty years ago when they had the chance."

"Yeah, yeah," Haggarty said, sounding irritated. "I just got hit in the head and knocked out. I'm a little

addled. But I remember Belmont, that's for sure."
Haggarty chuckled. "One of the best jobs we ever
pulled."

"Belmont must not have thought so, if he sent
Clancy all this way after us." Ling looked down at Ace
and added, "What I don't understand is what this boy
is doing here."

"Take that knife away from my throat and I'll explain," Ace said tightly, trying not to let his Adam's
apple move too much. "You'd better listen to me.
Clancy didn't come here alone."

Ling hesitated, but only for a moment. She lifted
the knife and took a step back. "Don't try anything.
I'm quicker than you."

"And so am I," said Haggarty as he scooped up
Clancy's fallen gun and pointed it at Ace. "Drop that
Colt."

Ace set the revolver on the floor.

"Slide it back to me," ordered Ling.

He did so, then asked wearily, "Is it all right if I
stand up now?" He heard Ling pick up the gun.

She nodded. "All right. No tricks."

Ace climbed to his feet while Haggarty did likewise. The gambler managed to get up without ever
letting the gun barrel budge from being pointed in
Ace's direction.

Once he was upright again, Ace said, "There are
two more of Belmont's men downstairs, standing
guard just outside the house. Belmont didn't just
send them after you, though. He came himself. He's
in Rimfire tonight, meeting with Angus McPhee."

Ling's carefully controlled exterior was shaken.
"Belmont's in the settlement?"

"With about a dozen more men," said Ace. "He's the one who sent the note that lured McPhee into town."

"We'd better think about packing up and getting out of here," Haggarty said to Ling. "I've heard plenty of stories about Belmont and the men who work for him." A little shudder went through him. "Some of them are lunatics, if you can believe even half the things that are said about them."

"We knew that when we targeted him in the first place. The risk was worth it."

"Maybe at the time." Haggarty shrugged. "Now I'd just as soon forget about whatever might be in McPhee's safe and put some distance between us and Belmont."

She glared at him "For God's sake, Jack, have you lost all your nerve? I'll cover Jensen. You go back to seeing if you can get that safe open."

"The way my head is spinning and ringing from being pistol-whipped, you expect me to be able to hear those tumblers ticking over?" Haggarty shook his head. "It doesn't matter if we have all night. I won't be getting this safe open anytime soon, Ling."

She stared at him, clearly angry and impatient, but after a few seconds she heaved a sigh of resignation. "All right, but you know how I hate leaving money behind. I suppose it's better to give it up, though, than to let Belmont catch us."

The past few minutes had been very educational for Ace. Every assumption that Leo Belmont had made about Haggarty and Ling appeared to be wrong. Ace had made some of those same assumptions himself.

But now he knew the truth. Ling was the leader

of the duo. She was probably the mastermind who decided who they would go after and how they would do it, too.

"It's not going to be as easy as just saddling up and riding away," he told her. "Don't forget, there are two more of Belmont's men downstairs. And I'll bet they're getting pretty restless by now, wondering what's taking Clancy and me so long."

"Men don't scare me," Ling said with a disdainful sneer.

"Those two ought to."

Haggarty said, "You'd better listen to him, my dear. I don't really understand *why*, given our history with him and his brother, but I'm starting to think the young man actually wants to help us."

"I don't want to see anybody go through what Belmont has planned for you, even a couple thieves," said Ace. "I'll help you, all right."

Ling squinted at him. "But you want something in return."

Ace nodded. "Our two thousand dollars."

Ling's lips drew back from her teeth in a snarl. "No!" she spat. "Once I take money from a mark, I never give it back!"

"You probably still have some of the loot you got from Belmont. Just think of it as giving me some of that money, instead," Ace suggested.

Ling scowled at him for a moment, then demanded, "You think you're so damn smart, don't you?"

"No, but I'm stubborn. And I can help you get past Belmont's men, if you're willing to work with me."

Haggarty had taken a handkerchief from his pocket

and was tying it around his head to stanch the bleeding from the cut. As he finished, he laughed. "You have to admit, there's more to the boy than you thought there was. I didn't expect him to be quite such a hardcase, either."

Ling regarded him coolly and asked, "If I agree about the two grand, what are you going to do in return?"

"I'll go downstairs and tell Whistler and Robertson—those are Belmont's men—that we've captured the two of you but that we need help with you."

"Are they going to believe that?"

Ace smiled. "I reckon they'll believe it if I tell them you'd gotten McPhee's safe open just before we nabbed you, and we're going to split up the money."

Haggarty said, "You can never go wrong appealing to a man's greed. Or his lust. We've learned those things, haven't we, my dear?"

"Shut up." Ling nodded to Ace. "All right. We'll give your plan a try."

"I'll need my gun back," he pointed out. "If I show up down there with an empty holster, it's going to make them suspicious."

With a practiced ease that told him she had handled many weapons, Ling opened the Colt's loading gate and shook out the cartridges one by one. Then she snapped it closed and handed the revolver to him. "I know you have more bullets, but at least this way you can't double-cross us until you're out of the room, anyway."

Ace pouched the iron. "I don't intend to double-cross anybody except Belmont and his bunch, and I reckon they've got it coming. Now, about that two thousand . . ."

Ling sighed then snapped at Haggarty. "Give him the money."

One-handed because he was still holding Clancy's gun, Haggarty reached inside his shirt and started fumbling with a money belt around his waist.

Ace asked, "Is that my brother's money belt?"

"As a matter of fact, it is," Haggarty said. "Do you want it back, too?"

"No, that's all right. Just the two thousand." Chance could always get another money belt, thought Ace, and they were running out of time.

Haggarty took a wad of greenbacks from the belt, riffled through them, and stuffed some of them back. "I appreciate you not holding us up for more," he said as he handed the bills to Ace.

"For God's sake!" Ling exclaimed. "Do you have to be so damn genial, Jack?"

"It's my nature," Haggarty replied with a smile.

"And I'm not a thief," said Ace as he stuffed the money in his shirt. "We just wanted what's rightfully ours. Now that I've got it, I don't mind helping you two get away." He paused. "You realize, though, Belmont's probably not going to give up. In fact, I reckon you can count on that. Once he realizes you've escaped, he'll just come after you again. He won't care how long it takes or how many detectives he has to hire."

"We'll take our chances," said Ling confidently.

"I've been thinking that Mexico sounds nice," added Haggarty. "There are places down there where a man can disappear and never be found. And I'm not talking about a Mexican prison, either."

Ace nodded toward Clancy, who was still unconscious.

"You'd better tie him up while you still can. You don't want him coming to while we're trying to get out of here. That would be a complication you don't need."

"You're right." Haggarty bent to the task while Ace went to the door.

Ling met him there and said quietly, "If you try any tricks, it won't matter if you get away. Betray us and I'll hunt you down and make you wish you'd never been born."

"Don't worry. I want to put those hombres out of action just as much as you do." He stepped out into the hall.

Ling eased the door almost closed behind him, leaving it open just enough to provide sufficient light for him to see where he was going. As he walked toward the stairs, he took cartridges from the loops on the shell belt and clicked them one by one into the Colt's chambers. When the cylinder was full, he slid the revolver back into leather.

He didn't have to be as quiet going downstairs as when he and Clancy had crept up, but he tried not to make much noise anyway. When he reached the first floor he ghosted across the foyer and noiselessly opened the front door.

"Whistler!" he called in a half-whisper as he stepped onto the porch. "Robertson!"

* * *

Way too many minutes dragged by. Chance worried about spiders crawling on him or some snake slithering along and bumping into him. Whatever Ace was up to, he wished his brother would go ahead and—

He stiffened as he heard Ace's voice calling softly to the men on the porch.

Two shadowy shapes appeared, one at each end of the porch, and moved toward Ace.

"Jensen?" Whistler asked. "Is that you? Where's Clancy?"

"Upstairs with Haggarty and the girl," Ace replied as he jerked his head toward the staircase. "He sent me to get the two of you."

"What for?" asked Robertson, sounding suspicious. "Can't you handle a couple prisoners?"

"It's not that," Ace said. "Haggarty was able to get McPhee's safe open. There's a pile of loot in it, and he figured the right thing to do would be to cut you boys in on it."

"Is that so?" Robertson said, sounding interested. He started toward the door.

"Wait just a damn minute," Whistler said sharply. "I've known Clancy for a long time. That greedy owlhoot would have stuffed as much money in his pockets as he could and never said a word to anybody else if he didn't have to." His gun started to come up. "This kid's lying!"

CHAPTER THIRTY-FIVE

As the guard closest to him turned and walked toward the front door, Chance seized the opportunity to crawl closer. When he reached the end of the wall, he stood up silently and pressed his back against it, holding the Remington up close to his head as he edged forward to peer around the corner.

Ace stood just outside the front door with the other two men. They were talking in low voices, when suddenly one man got louder and sounded angry. Chance could tell that trouble was imminent. With no warning it erupted elsewhere, namely inside the house. Several shots suddenly blasted out from upstairs, taking him and all three men on the porch by surprise.

The time for stealth was over. He put his left hand on the porch and vaulted up onto it.

At the sound of the shots, Whistler and Robertson both jerked toward the door. Ace didn't know what was going on upstairs, but he could make a guess— Clancy had come to while Haggarty was tying him up and was putting up a fight or he'd been shamming and waiting for an opportunity to jump Haggarty.

Either way, all hell was breaking loose, and Whistler and Robertson were both distracted. Ace knew he wouldn't get a better chance to turn the tables on them.

He whipped his gun out and fired at Whistler, knowing that with the racket from the house there was no need to worry about being quiet anymore.

Whistler twisted aside and his own gun spouted flame. Ace felt the wind-rip of the bullet as it screamed past his ear. He triggered again, and the slug punched into Whistler's chest and knocked him backwards. He hit the railing that ran along the front of the porch and flipped up and over it.

Ace had taken too long to dispose of Whistler. He turned toward Robertson, expecting to feel the smash of a bullet from the man's gun, but a shape came flying out of the shadows just as Robertson pulled the trigger.

The collision jolted Robertson's arm upward, so the geyser of flame from the revolver's muzzle pointed toward the porch roof. Ace heard a soggy thud, then Robertson pitched forward to land on his face.

Chance stood over him, holding the Remington he had just used to knock Robertson out.

Ace had seldom been so happy to see his brother. He would have liked to explain everything, but at that moment Whistler surged up from the ground in front of the porch. He had his left hand pressed to his chest where he was wounded, probably mortally, but he was still alive, and hatred gave him the strength to raise his gun and fire.

The bullet whipped between Ace and Chance. They pivoted toward him. Shots roared from their guns at the same instant. The smashing force of the slugs lifted Whistler off his feet and threw him backwards. He landed in a limp sprawl of death from which he wouldn't be getting up.

"Come on!" Ace barked at Chance as he lunged toward the door. The guns had fallen silent inside, which was worrisome. Ace wanted to get up there to McPhee's study and find out what had happened.

Colt flame bloomed from the top of the stairs before Ace could reach the bottom of them. A slug chewed splinters from the banister. Ace jerked his gun up and would have returned the fire, but in the dim light he caught a glimpse of Ling struggling in Clancy's grip as the man started down the stairs with her. His left arm was clamped around her waist like an iron bar, and the gun in his other hand swung from side to side and blared raucously as he charged toward the ground floor.

Ace and Chance dived out of the line of fire, Ace going left, Chance going right. Ace hit the floor and rolled over, coming up on a knee with his Colt thrust out. He couldn't risk a shot, though, as long as Clancy was using Ling as a human shield.

Outside, men shouted, no doubt some of McPhee's riders as the gunshots brought them hurrying out of the bunkhouse. As Clancy galloped between the Jensen brothers and out onto the porch, Ace heard one of them yell, "Hold your fire! He's got that Chinese gal!"

Clancy didn't have to be cautious. He emptied his

gun toward the ranch hands, scattering them as he ran along the porch and then leaped off.

Ace lunged out the front door, intending to go after Clancy and Ling, but at that moment the same man who had given the order to hold their fire bellowed, "There's more of 'em! Get 'em!"

A storm of lead screamed through the night and smashed into the front of the house. Glass shattered. Ace flung himself backwards through the doorway as bullets sang their deadly song all around him. It was pure luck that he was untouched.

He scrambled up from where he fell but stayed low, crouching as he moved toward one of the windows. From the other side of the foyer where Chance knelt came the question, "Ace, are you all right?"

"Yeah, for now," Ace replied as bullets whined through the broken windows and slammed into the walls. He didn't want to have to fight a gun battle against Angus McPhee's men, but it looked like he might not have much choice in the matter. The Tartan hands didn't know what was going on, but they knew their boss was gone and there were intruders in the house, so they were pouring lead at it.

"I don't reckon you'd want to explain exactly what's going on here," Chance said dryly over the roar of the gun blasts.

"I'd like to, but I don't know if there's time."

"I don't think we're going anywhere for a while, unless it's to be carried out feetfirst."

Ace knew that Chance's grimly humorous comment was accurate. They were pinned down. When he risked a glance through the shattered window, he caught a glimpse of men running through the shadows toward the back of the house, cutting off that possible avenue of escape.

It seemed likely that sooner or later McPhee's men would rush the house, probably sooner. They would recognize the Jensen brothers and know that McPhee had ordered them shot if they set foot on Tartan range again. Ace figured those gun-wolves wouldn't waste any time following that order.

The sound of a groan from the staircase distracted him from those bleak thoughts. He swung around, gun ready, and saw Jack Haggarty staggering down the stairs with his right hand clamped to his upper left arm. Blood from a bullet wound welled between his fingers.

"Better stay back, Haggarty! There's a lot of lead flying around down here!"

Haggarty stopped and peered at Ace in the gloom. "Jensen?" he muttered. His gaze turned the other way and he spotted Chance. "And the other Jensen? You're both here?" He paused. "Of course you are. You wanted your money. I remember now." Haggarty had to lean on the wall next to the stairs. "By the way, I'm shot."

"You're McPhee's guest," said Ace, thinking furiously. "You reckon his men would hold their fire if you asked them to?"

"Possibly. They have no idea why . . . Ling and I are really here." Haggarty caught his breath. "Ling! Clancy has her—"

"He got away with her," Ace said, "but we can go after him if we can convince McPhee's men to stop trying to ventilate us."

"Wait there. Keep your heads down. I'll try to make

them listen." Haggarty turned around and started struggling back up the stairs. He disappeared, and then a few moments later he called from a second floor window, "Hold your fire! Hold your fire out there! Listen to me, you men! This is Jack Haggarty!"

The shots continued blasting. Haggarty kept shouting until the gunfire started to tail off.

One of McPhee's men yelled, "Stop shootin' for a minute!"

"Thank God!" said Haggarty. "You men know me. I'm Jack Haggarty. I'm your employer's guest. And I'm wounded!"

"Stay where you are, Mr. Haggarty!" called the spokesman for the Tartan crew. "We'll clean out those skunks down below and come up to get you!"

"You don't understand!" Haggarty insisted. "Those men you're shooting at are friends of mine."

Flanking the ranch house's front door, Ace and Chance looked at each other.

Chance raised his eyebrows. "We're his friends now?"

"He figures I know where Clancy took Ling," said Ace. "And as a matter of fact, I've got a pretty good idea."

"Well, I'm glad somebody does, because I don't even know who the hell Clancy is."

"He works for a man named Belmont. He trailed Haggarty and Ling here from San Francisco because they stole a bunch of money from him."

"Ah, now things are starting to make sense," Chance said, nodding.

"Belmont is in Rimfire, pretending to talk business

with McPhee. He set that up so I could sneak in here with some of his men and grab Haggarty and Ling."

"You've thrown in with this fellow Belmont?"

"Not really. I was just playing along with him. Actually, I was going to try to help Haggarty and Ling get away from him . . . once I got our two thousand bucks back, of course."

"And did you? Recover our money, I mean?"

"I sure did," said Ace.

Upstairs, Haggarty shouted to McPhee's men, "If you'll hold your fire, I'll come down and explain everything! And I'm going to need some medical attention, too!"

Ace heard low-voiced conversation outside, then the spokesman replied, "Come ahead, Mr. Haggarty. We won't do any more shootin' . . . for now."

Chance said to his brother, "I suppose that means we should hold our fire, too."

"Seems like the only way we're going to get out of here alive," Ace replied.

A moment later, Haggarty reappeared at the head of the stairs and started down them.

Now that the air wasn't filled with bullets, Ace holstered his gun and hurried to help the gambler. "How bad are you hit?" he asked as he slipped an arm around Haggarty's waist.

"Clancy just winged me, but on top of all the blood I'd already lost, it made me pass out," Haggarty explained. "He was only pretending to be unconscious. As soon as you left the room and I went to tie him up, he jumped me. I put up the best fight I could, but he was too much for me. He got his hands on the gun and shot me."

When they reached the bottom of the staircase, Haggarty went on. "You'd better let me go out first. They know how taken with Ling their boss is, and I'm supposed to be her stepfather. They won't shoot me."

"We can hope not," muttered Chance.

Haggarty took a deep breath and stepped out onto the porch. With a rush of rapid footsteps, McPhee's men closed in on the house.

"It's all right," Haggarty told them as he glanced at the bodies of Whistler and Robertson. "I don't know who these two men are, but I suspect they're accomplices of the man who kidnapped my daughter. We can't waste any time going after them."

"Who are those hombres we chased inside?" asked one of the men.

"Friends of mine. They tried to help Ling. You know them, but you've got them all wrong." Haggarty turned to look through the open door at Ace and Chance and motioned with his head for them to come out.

"Put that gun away," Ace told his brother. "We'd better go out with empty hands."

Chance looked like he didn't care for that idea, but he did what Ace said. Holding their hands in plain sight, the two of them stepped out onto the porch.

"It's those Jensen boys!" exclaimed one of McPhee's riders.

Haggarty said, "There's been a fundamental misunderstanding about these lads. They're actually friends of ours, and they just want to help. Ace, you know where Clancy took Ling?"

"To the stable in Rimfire," Ace replied. "He and the others were supposed to take both of you there and turn you over to Belmont."

"Who in Hades is Belmont?" asked one of the men.

"Our real enemy," Haggarty assured them. "And now we need to mount up and head for Rimfire—"

Before he could go on, he swayed, his eyes rolled up in their sockets, and he pitched forward to land on the porch in a senseless heap.

CHAPTER THIRTY-SIX

The next few minutes were tense but busy ones. McPhee had told his men what to do if they found Ace and Chance on the Tartan spread, and they didn't disregard those orders easily. It didn't help that Kiley, Stebbins, and Doakes were among those left behind at the ranch when McPhee went into Rimfire. Those three hadn't forgotten about their run-in with the Jensen brothers in Fort Benton, and they sure hadn't forgiven it, either.

In fact, Ace could hear the three men trying to stir up the others while he knelt beside Jack Haggarty and ripped the man's sleeve open to reveal the bullet wound in his arm. It looked like the slug had passed through cleanly without breaking the bone, which was lucky. Damage to the muscles and blood loss were the main things Haggarty had to worry about, along with blood poisoning.

"I need some whiskey," Ace said as he looked up from what he was doing. He ignored the rabble-rousing from Kiley, Stebbins, and Doakes.

"I could use a drink, too," one of the men said.

"I need it to clean this wound." Ace tried not to sound too impatient.

One of the ranch hands took a flask from his pocket and handed it to Chance, who passed it along to Ace.

"Good Scotch whiskey," the man said. "Mr. McPhee won't allow anything else on the place."

Ace had to chuckle a little at that, despite the circumstances. He poured the fiery liquor into the bullet hole in Haggarty's arm. Even though the gambler was unconscious, he stirred and groaned a little at the whiskey's bite.

Then Ace tore strips off the bottom of Haggarty's shirt and bound up the wound as best he could. That was all he could do for now. Haggarty needed the attention of a real doctor.

And they needed to get to Rimfire as quickly as they could if they were going to save Ling from Leo Belmont's vengeance.

"A couple of you load Mr. Haggarty in a wagon and take him to town so the doc can tend to him," Ace said as he stood up. "The rest of us need to mount up and get there as soon as we can."

"You hear that?" Kiley practically yelped. "The kid's givin' orders now! He ain't even supposed to be here, but he thinks he can waltz in and start bossing us around!"

"Shut up, Kiley," another man growled. "You heard what Haggarty said. The whole thing's been a big misunderstanding. And if that gal the boss is sweet on is in danger, I'll be damned if I'm gonna sit around on my hands and not try to help her."

Stebbins said, "Aw, he never shoulda got mixed up

with one o' them Celestial gals, anyway. They ain't fit to be nothin' but washerwomen or soiled doves."

"You let Mr. McPhee hear you say that and he'll whip your tail from now till next Sunday," a man warned him.

Ace turned to Chance. "Come on. Let's get our horses. These hombres can keep squabbling if they want to, but we're heading for Rimfire."

Kiley asked, "Are we gonna let 'em just leave like that?"

"No, we're going with them," another hardcase said. "Come on, men."

Ten minutes later, Ace, Chance, and ten more men from the Tartan spread were riding hard toward Rimfire. Trailing a considerable distance behind them was the wagon carrying Jack Haggarty. Ace hoped they would all get to town in time to keep anyone else from dying tonight.

He sure wasn't going to count on it, though.

Most of McPhee's men were professional gunmen, so Ace didn't actually expect them to let him take the lead, but since he knew more about what was going on than anyone else in the group, they seemed to be willing to follow his suggestions.

As they rode, he filled them in on Belmont's desire for revenge on Haggarty and Ling. The men were skeptical at first.

"The boss won't want to hear any of that," one of them cautioned. "He's plumb taken with that girl."

"I don't doubt it," said Chance. "She's very charming. And Haggarty is as slick as can be. But they're thieves, all right. They stole two thousand dollars from my brother and me."

"But you want to help 'em, anyway."

"Belmont's a criminal," said Ace, "and his men are murderers. Haggarty and Ling are crooked, but as far as I know they're not killers."

Although he wouldn't put that past Ling, he thought, if she was cornered. However, he was still convinced they weren't as bad as Leo Belmont and his bunch.

As they neared the settlement, Ace signaled for the riders to stop. "I think one or two of you should go to the hotel and find Mr. McPhee—whoever he's the most likely to believe. The rest of us will go to the stable, since that's probably where Clancy took Ling. If Belmont and his men have her there, we'll hold off on attacking until Mr. McPhee and the rest of his men who are in town show up. The two sides ought to be pretty evenly matched then."

"Kid, you better not be leadin' us into some sort of trap," warned one of the men. "If you do, you won't live to see mornin', I can promise you that."

"Chance and I have told you the truth. About everything. You'll see for yourself when you get to the stable."

Men riding into town, even that late at night, weren't going to draw too much attention in a frontier settlement, but such a large number of riders might. Ace suggested that they split up even more— move into Rimfire one or two at a time—and then converge on the stable. The others agreed and rode off in different directions, leaving Ace and Chance walking their horses toward the edge of town.

Chance said quietly, "You realize we're about to go to war over one woman, don't you?"

"The Greeks and the Trojans fought a whole war over one woman," Ace pointed out.

"Yeah, but Helen wasn't a thief, and she never threatened to cut anybody's throat, either."

Ace had told his brother about what had happened in McPhee's study. "I know Ling's a pretty shady character, but we can't let Belmont kill her . . . or whatever else he's got in mind for her, which might be worse if Whistler was right."

"Even if we rescue her, McPhee's liable to hold a grudge against us. I don't know if he'll ever believe the truth about her."

"Maybe not," Ace agreed. "But we got our money back, and there's nothing stopping us from riding away when this is over and letting everything else sort itself out."

"If we live through it, you mean."

"Well, yeah, there's that to consider," Ace said.

After a few minutes, Chance said, "You know, we might want to head south. Winter's not that far away, and we don't want to be up here in this part of the country when it gets cold. We could take our time, wander down through Colorado and New Mexico, maybe find a nice little border town where it'll stay warm."

Ace nodded. "We haven't spent that much time down there. Sounds like a good idea."

"It's a deal then. Assuming we live through this mess."

"Yep."

By that time they were in the settlement and

turned their horses down one of the side streets and then cut into the back alley that ran behind the livery stable. They dismounted, left the horses tied behind a store that was closed for the night, and eased through the shadows on foot.

They came up behind the livery stable and found four of McPhee's men waiting for them. The other six drifted up in the next few minutes.

"We heard voices inside there," one of the men whispered. "Couldn't make out what they were sayin', though."

Ace looked up. A small door in the back wall of the barn was high enough that it had to open into the hayloft. It was closed at the moment, but it might not be fastened. "A couple of you boost me up there," he said as he pointed at the door. "If Chance and I can get into the loft, we can find out what's going on."

Quickly, two of the men took hold of his legs and lifted him so he could reach up to the door. Bracing himself with his other hand against the wall, he pulled the door back slowly, not knowing if it would make any noise. When it didn't, Ace whispered for the men to raise him higher. He got both arms hooked over the edge of the opening and hauled himself up and through it.

They boosted Chance up, too, while Ace was crawling toward the front of the hayloft. He reached a spot where he could look down into the barn's broad center aisle. What he saw made his guts clench with fury.

Ling was strung up to one of the barn's crossbeams. She had a rope around each wrist, and they were pulled tight enough that her arms were stretched over her head and her feet barely touched the ground. She had to be in pain, but she wasn't making a sound. Ace knew she was conscious. Her head was up, and she appeared to be looking straight ahead at Leo Belmont, who paced back and forth in front of her with a smirk on his brutal face.

Belmont's men, including Clancy, were gathered around watching. A few of them seemed a little uneasy about what was happening. Western men, even the most hardened ones, tended not to like seeing violence carried out against women.

The others had eager, avid looks on their faces, especially the gutter trash Belmont had brought with him from San Francisco. From what Whistler had said, Belmont had promised to turn Ling over to them when he was finished with her, and they were eager to get their hands on her.

"Haggarty's dead," Belmont was saying to Ling.

Ace supposed that was what Clancy had told him.

"You might as well tell me where that money is hidden. Things will go a lot easier for you if you do."

"Go to hell," Ling said in a low voice.

Chance crawled up beside Ace in time to hear that exchange and whispered, "Damn it. Is that Belmont?"

"Yeah," Ace breathed.

"He's as bad as you said he is."

"Maybe worse," Ace said.

Belmont turned to one of his men and extended a hand. The hardcase placed a coiled whip in it.

"Last chance," Belmont told Ling as he turned back to her. "You can die quickly and painlessly . . . or I can spend the next half hour introducing you to the pleasures of the lash. I promise, before I'm done you'll be begging to tell me what I want to know."

Chance leaned close to Ace's ear. "He's just threatening her, right? He won't really do that?"

"I don't know," Ace answered honestly. From the demonic look on Belmont's face, the man was capable of almost anything.

Ling said something Ace couldn't make out. It made Belmont move closer to her. Suddenly, she thrust her head forward and spat in his face.

Belmont jerked back. He slashed the still-coiled whip across her face, knocking her head to the side. Then he let the whip uncoil and stepped behind her, raising his arm to bring the lash down on her back.

Before that blow could fall, shots blasted outside the barn.

Someone crashed into one of the double doors, making it swing back. Guns spurted flame as men began charging in from the street.

Angus McPhee was in front, Colt in hand, shouting, "Ling! Ling!"

McPhee's men who were behind the barn, hearing their boss yelling inside, crashed through the rear door, eager to get in on the action.

Any plans Ace and Chance might have made didn't matter. All that was left was to fight as chaos erupted inside the livery stable. They leaped to their feet and dived off the edge of the hayloft.

Ace landed on Leo Belmont's back. The impact drove him to his knees and knocked the whip out of his hand, but the strength in his thickly built body kept him from going all the way to the ground. He reached back, got hold of Ace, and heaved the younger man off him.

Chance landed feetfirst, with his heels driving into Clancy's back. They went down in a tangle of arms and legs and flailing fists.

Belmont's men were caught in a crossfire as the two groups working for McPhee opened up on them. For a few mad seconds, gun-thunder filled the barn along with spurting muzzle flames and clouds of powder smoke.

Then McPhee's bellow rose over it. "Hold your fire! Hold your fire! You might hit Ling!"

Ace was glad to hear that. He and his brother were caught in the middle of that lead storm, too, as they battled with Belmont and Clancy.

Belmont slashed at him with the whip. It cut his cheek and his hand as he tried to ward off the worst of the blows. Then he was able to catch hold of the whip with his left hand and wrap it around his wrist. He jerked Belmont toward him and rocketed out a straight right-hand punch that slammed into the older man's jaw with such force that Ace felt it shiver all the way up his arm to his shoulder.

Belmont collapsed.

Ace swung around in time to see that Chance had his hands full with Clancy. The big, mustachioed man was on top of Chance, driving punch after punch into his face and body. Ace leaped toward them, and since he still had hold of the whip, he looped it around Clancy's neck from behind, grabbed it with his other hand, and drew it tight across Clancy's throat. Ace dug in with his feet and dragged Clancy backwards, off Chance.

Clancy struggled ferociously, kicking out with his feet and trying to reach back and hit Ace, but he couldn't get any leverage or work up any force. Ace kept up the pressure, grunting with the strain as he summoned all his strength and made the whip dig deeper and deeper into Clancy's throat. He was pulling back so hard he lost his footing and sat down, but the death grip in which he had the larger man never slipped.

Finally, Clancy spasmed several times and went limp, either dead or passed out. Ace didn't know which, and at the moment, he didn't care. His chest heaved from his terrific exertions as he looked over at Chance, who seemed to be all right, just battered and groggy as he lay a few feet away.

With an incoherent cry of rage, Belmont surged to his feet and lunged at Ling. He had pulled a knife from his pocket and drove it at her chest. She was strung up so tightly she couldn't move out of the way, and McPhee, who watched in horror, couldn't risk a shot for fear of hitting her.

Out of nowhere, another shape leaped in front of Ling. Belmont's knife went into Jack Haggarty's chest, driving deep. As Haggarty cried out, he lifted the pistol he held, jammed the barrel under Belmont's chin, and pulled the trigger. A mass of blood, brain, and bone fragments exploded from the back of Belmont's skull.

He and Haggarty hit the ground at the same time.

"Jack!" screamed Ling.

"I'm sorry, boss." The man was one of the ranch hands who had brought Haggarty into Rimfire from the Tartan. "As soon as we got to town, he stuck a gun in my side and made me bring him here instead of the doc's place!"

The shooting was over. Those of Belmont's men who had survived the ruckus had surrendered.

"Cut me down!" Ling cried. "Jack!"

One of McPhee's men stepped up and used a bowie knife to sever the ropes holding her. She fell to her knees and crawled to Haggarty, sobbing as she pulled his head into her lap and cradled it.

With his face set in grim lines, McPhee went over to Ace and Chance. "You boys were telling me the truth about those two, weren't you? He's not her stepfather, is he?"

"No, and earlier tonight we found them trying to break into your safe." Ace studied the look on McPhee's face for a moment, then said, "But you don't care about that, do you?"

"I feel what I feel for her, no matter what she is," said McPhee heavily. "There's nothing else a man can do where a woman's concerned." Wearily, he scrubbed a hand over his face. "But I'll see to it that Haggarty gets a decent burial, and after that . . . well, what Ling does after that will be up to her, I suppose." He sighed. "And if you two want to stay around here, I reckon there's no reason for me to forbid it."

"You're not going to cause any more trouble for Mr. Fairfield and the rest of those settlers?"

McPhee grunted. "No reason to. That fella Fairfield actually has some pretty good ideas. I can work with any man who's reasonable."

"Then there's no reason for us to stay around these parts." Chance looked at his brother. "Isn't that right, Ace?"

"It sure is." Ace smiled. "As a matter of fact, I think we're going to be heading south. . . ."

The next morning, that was exactly what the Jensen brothers did, with new guns for Chance, new clothes for both, and plenty of supplies, all paid for by Angus McPhee.

As they reached the edge of town, Chance commented. "McPhee had better be careful if he's going to keep Ling around. That girl's going to take him for everything he's worth. He'll be lucky if she doesn't kill him. She ought to be in jail."

"Maybe so, but I'm not going to take on McPhee's whole crew of gunmen to try to put her there," said Ace. "She's his problem now, and at least we won't ever have to deal with her again."

Chance looked over at him, narrow-eyed. "You probably shouldn't have said that. You may have just jinxed us."

Ace laughed. "I'm not that superstitious."

"All card players believe in luck . . . and sometimes it's bad."

"I reckon we'll find out," said Ace.

"If we live long enough," added Chance.

The Jensen brothers rode south, leaving Rimfire behind them.

THE GREATEST WESTERN WRITER
OF THE 21ST CENTURY

*The MacCallister family is legendary in the
American frontier . . . and wherever a MacCallister travels,
the legend—and the guns—follow.*

USA TODAY AND *NEW YORK TIMES*
BESTSELLING AUTHORS
WILLIAM W. JOHNSTONE
with J. A. Johnstone

TEN GUNS FROM TEXAS
A Duff MacCallister Western

When Duff MacCallister journeys to Texas to deliver
100 head of Angus cattle, he finds a land on fire.
Unruly, lawless teams of cattle rustlers, branded
Fence Busters by the locals, are rampaging across
grazing land and cutting fences in the name of an
eastern land company. The ranchers are fighting back,
and Duff joins the fray. The fight leads to Austin
and into an even deadlier mission.

The governor's daughter has been kidnapped by
Fence Busters. Duff and his partner Elmer are willing
to go after her, but they're going to need more men
and a lot more firepower . . . The best the governor
can do is give them the names of three outlaws who
once served honorably in war. Now Duff MacCallister
is going up against a fanatical, highly trained enemy,
riding with gunmen he cannot fully trust. Once the
shooting starts, there is no turning back—because
Duff and his posse are heading straight into the
bloody depths of hell.

CHAPTER ONE

Chugwater, Wyoming

Duff MacCallister was having a Scotch with Baldy Johnson at the Fiddler's Green saloon when Wang Chow came in.

"Hey!" someone shouted. "What's that Chinaman doin' in my drinkin' bar?"

"This isn't your drinking bar. It is mine," Baldy said. "You may have noticed on the sign out front, just under the name Fiddler's Green. It says Baldy Johnson, Proprietor."

"Yeah? Well, it seems to me like you would have more consideration for your customers than to allow a stinkin' Chinaman to come into a bar where white men are drinkin'. I think you should throw him out."

"Throw him out yourself," Baldy replied, smiling across the table at Duff.

"Really? You mean it's all right with you if I throw him out?"

"Sure, go ahead."

Wang Chow looked at Duff, who, with a smile, nodded at him.

"Hood, you really plannin' on throwin' that Celestial outta here?" one of the other saloon customers asked.

"Yeah." With a malevolent smile, Hood left the bar and started toward Wang Chow. "What's your name, Chinaman?"

"My name is Wang Chow."

"Well, Wang Chow, you got two choices. You can either turn around and leave now, or you can let me mop up this floor with you and throw you out. Which will it be?"

"I do not wish to do either," Wang Chow replied.

"Well, then, we'll do it my way." Hood swung, putting everything into a wide right cross.

Wang Chow ducked easily under the wild swing, then shot out his hand, palm forward, striking Hood in the chest. The return blow surprised Hood, and drove him back several steps.

"Why, you—!" Hood swung again, missing as badly as he did the first time.

Wang Chow hit Hood on his forehead with the heel of his hand.

"Stop playing around with him, Hood," someone said.

Hood decided to try a straight jab and shot his left fist forward. Wang Chow moved his head to one side easily, and with no show of effort, hit Hood in the side, just under his arm.

Hood punched and swung again and again, never once making contact with Wang Chow, who with movements as graceful as those of a dancer, responded to every one of Hood's attempts with a counterpunch that scored. It soon became very evident that Wang Chow was carrying Hood and could, at any time, have dealt him a fight-ending blow.

Hood was getting more and more frustrated, and more and more exhausted. Finally, breathing heavily, he stopped, and held up his hand. "What did you say your name was?"

"I am Wang Chow."

"Well, Wang Chow, come over here and let me buy you a drink. I need to make friends with anybody who can fight the way you do."

"Why don't the two of you come over to my table?" Baldy called out to them. "I'll get the drinks. You've probably worn yourself out."

"You've got that right," Hood said.

The two men walked over to sit at the table with Duff and Baldy.

"Where did you learn to fight like that?" Hood asked.

"I am a priest of the Shaolin Temple of Changlin," Wang Chow replied.

"A priest? I'll be damned if I've ever seen a padre who could do that."

"Wang Chow isn't the kind of priest you are thinking of," Duff said. "A Shaolin priest is a most unique individual. Wang Chow entered the temple as a boy of nine, and left when he was twenty-eight years old, a master of the Chinese martial art of *Wushu*."

"How did you wind up in America?" Hood asked.

"Some evil men killed my mother and my sister," Wang Chow said. "When I went to the temple to burn incense to honor my family, the master of the temple told me to seek no revenge. I was told that if I did so, it would bring dishonor to the temple."

"Damn, but you done it anyway, didn't you?" Hood asked.

"Yes. I cut the topknot to my hair, which distanced me from the temple, then I went to the tong of the men who had done the evil thing. Six men were there, laughing about having killed my family." Wang Chow stopped.

"Well, go on," Hood said. "What happened?"

"I killed them."

"Wait a minute. You said there were six of them."

"Yes."

"And you killed all six?"

"I am ashamed to say that I let my temper control me."

"So you shot all six of them?"

"I do not use guns," Wang said.

"Then how did you kill them?"

"I killed them with the sword."

"What happened then?"

"I was expelled from the Changlin Temple and the Empress Dowager Ci'an issued a decree ordering my death. I left China with a group of laborers, and came to America to work on the railroad," Wang said in conclusion.

"Damn," Hood said. "I'm glad I didn't really make you mad."

Duff and Baldy laughed.

"Say, Duff, is it true you're going to be taking some of your beeves to Texas?" Baldy asked.

"Aye, 'tis true. I've been dealing with a man named Jason Bellefontaine. He owns the Slash Bell Ranch at

Merrill Town, which is near Austin. He wants some Angus to improve his herd."

"How soon will you be going?"

"I expect it'll be at least another month before we've got everything worked out. I've checked with the railroad. 'Tis five hundred of the creatures I'll be takin', so 'tis twenty cars I'll be needing."

"You're takin' cows to Texas?" Hood laughed. "Here, now, 'n if that ain't 'bout the funniest thing I've ever heard. I thought cows come out of Texas, not go in."

"These are Angus cattle. 'Tis a special breed from Scotland they are, and far superior to the Longhorns 'n aye, even the Hereford."

"Superior how?" Hood asked.

"Oh, in about ever' way you can count," Elmer Gleason said, joining the conversation. "They have lower calf weights, so the birthin' is a lot easier, which means you don't lose as many during calving season. They produce a quality carcass, 'n that means a better beef.

"But now, you take a Hereford, they have a higher birth weight, 'n they got white faces, which could cause the pinkeye. Also, they ain't as calm as the Angus is, neither."

"What about the Longhorn?" Hood asked.

"Anyone who is still raisin' Longhorns don't even deserve to be called a cattleman," Elmer said.

"What do you know 'bout bein' a cattlemen?" Hood teased. "I mean, seein' as you ain't nothin' but a cowboy your ownself."

"Oh, on the contrary, Mr. Hood," Duff said. "Mr. Gleason owns a substantial piece of Sky Meadow. He is every bit a cattleman, and has a personal stake in the safe delivery of these cows to Mr. Bellefontaine."

Near Phantom Hill, Texas

As Duff and the others were having a pleasant gathering in Fiddler's Green, some eight hundred and fifty miles south, two outlaws, Al Simmons and Hugh Decker, were on the run.

"They're a-comin'. I can feel it in my gut. They are out there, and they're close." Simmons climbed down from a rock and walked over to his horse, where he slipped his rifle out of the saddle holster.

"What is it you're a-plannin' on doin' with that rifle?" Decker asked.

"When they get here, I'm goin' to commence shootin'. It looks to me like we don't have no other choice."

"Yeah," Decker agreed. "Yeah, you're prob'ly right."

With rifles in hand, the two men climbed back up onto the rock that afforded them not only a good view of the approaching trail but also some cover and concealment. They checked the loads in their rifles, eased the hammers back to half-cock, then hunkered down on the rock and waited.

"Let 'em come up to about fifty, maybe seventy-five yards away," Simmons suggested.

He and Decker weren't career outlaws. Until earlier that day, they had never done anything against the law. But they'd held up the Abilene stagecoach. During the robbery they took nothing from the passengers, stealing only the money being transported by the coach. They believed they had every right to do that because, until the week before, they had worked for the stage company, keeping the coaches in good repair. However, their supervisor had come in drunk and offensive. They'd gotten into a row with him, and he fired them. When they took their case to the station manager, he upheld his supervisor. To make things worse, they were each due two weeks' pay, and the company withheld their pay, claiming it was a *fine*.

They had moped over the unjust treatment for a few days. When they learned that the bank was expecting a shipment of money, they made up their mind to rob the coach.

Even though they had worn masks during the holdup, the driver had recognized them and a posse, hastily formed, had chased them into a dead-end canyon.

As the thieves waited, the posse came into view over a distant rise.

"There they are," Decker said.

"I see 'em!" Simmons raised his rifle to his shoulder.

"Wait a minute," Decker cautioned. "Don't shoot!" He reached up to pull Simmons's rifle down. "They don't have no idea we're here."

"You're right. I'll wait until they get closer," Simmons agreed.

They waited as the distant riders came closer, sometimes seeming not to be riding, but rather floating as they materialized and dematerialized in the heat waves rising from the ground. On they rode, across the long, flat plain.

"It's takin' 'em forever to get here," Simmons complained.

"Yeah, well, what else have we got to do?" Decker asked with a chuckle.

"Nothin', I suppose," Simmons replied, also chuckling.

The two men waited until the posse closed to less than one hundred yards.

Simmons lifted his rifle again and rested it carefully against the rock, taking a very careful aim. "Wait until they get just a little closer," he said quietly. "I'll give you the word, then we'll both fire at the same time."

"No," Decker said.

Simmons looked at him in confusion. "What do you mean, no?"

"Think about it, Al. Do we really want to do this?"

"What do you mean, do we want to do this? Seems to me like we don't have no choice. 'Case you ain't noticed, this here is a dead-end canyon. We ain't got no way out 'cept through them."

"There's at least twenty of them. There's two of us," Decker said. "What difference does it make how many we shoot? We'll still be dead in the end."

Simmons nodded. "That's prob'ly true."

"And consider this. Some of them men is our friends," Decker said. "Hell, me 'n you had Thanksgiving dinner with Phil Burke and his wife. And how many times have we pitched horseshoes with Danny Mitchell? If we start shootin' now, we'll wind up killin' some of our friends. I don't mind goin' to meet my Maker as a thief, but damn if I want to meet Him with murder on my conscience."

"What do you propose that we do?"

"I say we give up."

"We'll be goin' to prison."

"Yeah, well, at least we'll be alive, 'n we won't be murderers. Besides, they'll feed us there, 'n we'll have a place to sleep. It ain't like we don't know no one that's there. How bad can it be?"

"Yeah," Simmons said. "Yeah, you're right. So, what do we do now?"

"We give up. I'll call down to 'em." Decker cupped his hands around his mouth. "Phil!" he shouted. "Phil Burke!"

Burke, Burke, Burke echoed back from the canyon.

"What do you want?" Burke called back.

"Me 'n Al want to give up!" Decker shouted.

Give up echoed several times.

"That's up to the sheriff!" Burke called back up.

"Sheriff, tell them boys not to shoot. We're comin' down," Decker shouted.

Down, down, down echoed.

"All right. Toss your guns out, then come down with your hands up," the sheriff replied.

Simmons and Decker responded to the sheriff's order, then, with their hands up, climbed down from their perch behind the rocks.

Two weeks later, tried and convicted, they were delivered to the prison at Huntsville.

CHAPTER TWO

Slash Bell Ranch—Travis County, Texas

Six mounted men materialized out of the darkness, riding slowly and quietly. Of the six men, only their leader Dirk Kendrick was not carrying a large wire cutter tool. When they reached a long stretch of barbed wire, he held up his hand. More than a hundred calves were on the other side of the wire. Most were sleeping, but many were moving around anxiously, searching for their mothers, for though they had been physically weaned away from the teat, they were not yet emotionally ready to be alone.

"Cut from here to there," Kendrick said, pointing to locations on the wire fence. "Cut all five strands."

When the wires were cut, five horsemen looped their ropes around the posts standing between the two cuts and urged their mounts on. The horses easily pulled the posts from the ground then dragged the section of fence away, leaving a twentyfoot opening.

Aware that something had happened, even the calves that had been asleep were on their feet.

"All right, boys, let's get the creatures out of there," Kendrick ordered.

All six men went into the pen and, within less than a minute, every calf had been moved out, each content to move as long as all the others were moving.

Merrill Town, Texas

When Jason Bellefontaine, owner of the Slash Bell Ranch, left the theater, he decided to have a few drinks over at the CSS *Alabama* Saloon before returning home. Owner Ken Prescott had been a crewman onboard the Confederate raider and had honored his saloon with the name. He had lived in Mobile before the war and was signed on to the ship by Admiral Semmes, who, at the time, was also a resident of Mobile.

"Tell me, Ken, do the folks back in Mobile actually live in houses?" Bellefontaine teased.

"Not just houses, my friend, but mansions," Prescott replied. "You will find some of the most beautiful mansions in all of America on Adams or St. Anthony, Claiborne or Conception Streets, right there in Mobile."

"Then why did you leave, if there are such beautiful homes in Mobile?"

Prescott smiled. "Because I didn't live on any of those streets. I lived on Telegraph Road."

Bellefontaine laughed. "Good enough reason. Besides, if you had stayed in Mobile, we wouldn't have the *Alabama* Saloon, and where would I go when I have a thirst for a beer?"

"You could always go to the Hog Pen," Prescott suggested, mentioning one of the other saloons in town. Whereas the CSS *Alabama* was a very pleasant saloon with a convivial atmosphere, the Hog Pen catered to a considerably more crude clientele.

"Ha. I would be real welcome in the Hog Pen now, wouldn't I?" Bellefontaine finished his drink, then set the glass down on the bar. "Take care, my friend. I'll see you later."

"Bye, Jason," Prescott said as Bellefontaine started toward the door.

Bellefontaine rode through the dark to return home, thinking of the unbranded calves that had been rounded up over the last two days. Tomorrow his crew would be branding them, then turning them back into the herd. It promised to be a busy day, so reason told him he would be better served by returning to the ranch and going to bed.

It took him no more than half an hour to cover the five miles between his ranch and Merrill Town, and though he had no watch, he was certain it had to be after eleven o'clock by the time he dismounted in front of the barn. He was about to unsaddle his horse when someone came toward him, moving out of the shadows. It was so dark he couldn't see who it was, and for a moment he thought the worst. Cautiously, he let his hand slip down to rest on his pistol.

Recognizing Sam Post, his foreman, he relaxed. "Hello, Sam. I thought sure you and the others would be in bed by now. Especially given how hard you all worked today," Bellefontaine said as he returned to the job of unsaddling his horse.

"We've got a problem, boss."

"What kind of problem?"

"When I stepped out of the bunkhouse about an hour ago, I heard the calves we had cut out for brandin' today all bawlin' 'n such, so I rode out to check on 'em just to make sure they were all right."

"And?"

"They're gone, boss. Ever' damn one of 'em."

"Damn. How did they get away? Did the fence fall?"

"No, sir, the fence didn't fall. It was cut."

"Cut? You mean by the Fence Busters?"

"Oh, it was the Fence Busters, all right, Mr. Bellefontaine. Ain't no doubt in my mind about it."

"Dirk Kendrick?"

"Yes sir. That's what I figure all right. That's why I've got all the men up and dressed," Sam said.

"What for?"

"So we can go after him. Don't forget, boss, those were some of the newly born Hereford calves. You don't want to lose any of 'em, do you?"

"Sam, suppose we did go after them. What good would it do? Remember, we aren't dealing with your average rustler here. The Fence Busters are as well organized a group of men as I have seen since Robert E. Lee surrendered my regiment to the Yankees at Appomattox. If we go after them with no more than a handful of cowboys, we're are going to wind up getting a bunch of good men killed."

"Does that mean we don't do anything at all?"

"We can go see Sheriff Wallace," Bellefontaine suggested.

"Dirk Kendrick has Sheriff Wallace in his pocket, you know that. Deputy Bullock is so slimy I don't see how even Wallace can put up with him."

"Yeah, well, I tend to agree with you," Bellefontaine said. "But right now, what other choice do we have?"

"You've got those Angus beeves comin' in before too much longer," Sam said. "I'd hate to see some of them get stole like these was."

"We'll just have to be extra careful," Bellefontaine said.

"How many?" the ranch owner asked.

"One hundred and nine," Kendrick replied. "Eighty-five are Herefords and twenty-four are Longhorns."

"It will cost you five dollars a head to keep them here, same for the Longhorns as for the Herefords."

"The Longhorns are worth only half as much as the Herefords," Kendrick complained.

"Whatever the cattle are worth on the market means nothing to me," the ranch owner replied. "I run the same risk in holding stolen Longhorns that I do stolen Herefords. The law makes no difference, so far as stolen property is concerned."

"I didn't say I wasn't going to pay it. I need someplace to keep them, and right now your ranch is the only place I have."

"Yeah, it is. Listen, I was thinkin'. Maybe you had better cut some of my fence and run off a few head of Longhorn. I'll claim I had several head of Herefords stolen. I wouldn't want people getting suspicious because my fence wasn't cut 'n I wasn't losin' cattle just like ever'one else is."

Kincaid chuckled. "I see what you mean. It is to our mutual benefit to maintain a degree of secrecy with regard to our business arrangement. All right. Soon as we get the cattle we acquired tonight remanded to an area that offers the least chance of discovery, we run off a few of your Longhorns."

"Just what is it you expect me to do?" Sheriff Wallace asked when he was approached by Bellefontaine the next morning.

"Well, you are the sheriff and I did have some of my cattle stolen. The correct thing to do when you have some of your property stolen is to report it to the sheriff."

"Yeah, well, first of all, how do you know your cows was stole?"

"What do you mean, how do I know? The calves were gathered in a pen to be branded. They were there, now they aren't there."

"And you say it was the Fence Busters?"

"It had to be. The fence was cut."

"Was the fence on public or private land?"

"It was on public land. I run a lot of my cattle on public land and fence off my cattle to keep them separated from other brands. All the cattlemen do that. The only thing we do is make sure that everyone has equal access to the water. Hell, you know that, Wallace."

"Yes, I do know that, and therein lies the rub," Sheriff Wallace said.

"What do you mean?"

"You know damn well, Bellefontaine, that there is no law against cutting fences that are on public land. If it was the Fence Busters, there's nothing I can do about it. They have every right to be cutting the fences. In fact, they have been hired by a legitimate company in New York to do that very thing."

"Yes, but I don't think they have been hired to steal my cattle," Bellefontaine replied. "No legitimate land company would do that. Besides which, I'm not the only one having cattle stolen. I checked with some of the other ranchers before I rode in here this morning, and a few of them lost cattle last night, too."

"You said it was calves, didn't you?"

"Yes."

"Then how do you know they were stolen? If it was calves, it's more 'n likely they just wandered off on their own, lookin' for their mamas. That's what calves do, you know."

"It wasn't calves that were taken from Chris Dumey or Tom Byrd or Donald Dobbins. It was cows, full grown and ready for market. Whether you are willing to admit it or not, the Fence Busters are nothing more than cattle thieves. They might try and pass themselves off as legitimate businessmen, but nobody in the entire state believes that."

"I wouldn't be so quick to make that accusation, if I were you," Sheriff Wallace replied. "You may not realize it, but you are setting yourself up for a lawsuit. Big companies like the New York and Texas Land Company have lots of money, and they can afford very expensive lawyers. It wouldn't be good for them to be accused of association with cattle rustlers. I'd lay off if I was you."

Bellefontaine sighed. "Sam told me I was wasting my time coming here, and he was right."

"Even if what you say is true, how do you expect me to do anything about it? There are at least forty Fence Busters. I've just got Deputy Bullock."

Disgusted, but not really surprised, Bellefontaine left the sheriff's office and rode back out to his ranch.

"What did the sheriff tell you?" Sam asked when Bellefontaine returned.

"You were right. He isn't going to do anything."

"We need to get rid of him come the next election," Sam said. "He's worthless as tits on a steer."

"I would suggest that you run for sheriff . . . except that you are too good a foreman, and I wouldn't want to lose you."

Sam grinned. "I'm not goin' anywhere, boss. I like ridin' for the brand."

CHAPTER THREE

Blowout, Texas

The town was a scattering of flyblown, crumbling
adobe buildings laid out on the east side of the Blanco
River about three miles below the origin of Blanco
Creek. The name came from Blowout Cave, located
in a hillside east of the river about a mile above the
spring. At one time, the cave had been home to thousands of bats, and over at least a hundred years, a
huge deposit of guano had accumulated. Ammonia
and other gases from the decomposing guano had
built up to such a degree in the cave that it was impossible for anyone to breathe, thus no one could even
stand to be there long enough to mine it for fertilizer.

During a thunderstorm, lightning struck at the cave
mouth and ignited the gases. The resultant explosion
carved away almost one third of the mountain and
gave the town its name.

It had no city marshal nor sheriff and had trouble
filling those positions since three law officers had
been killed over the last two years. Those hapless

victims of Blowout's lawlessness lay buried in a part of the cemetery known as the "Lawman's Corner."

Blowout wasn't an outlaw town as such. There were still decent citizens and merchants who were trapped in the town by circumstances. Occasionally, they would hold secret meetings and plan ways to attract someone willing to put on a badge.

At the moment, such a meeting was taking place.

"Who is going to give his life to be the sheriff in this town?" asked Wes Long, owner of the mercantile. "We didn't do anything to help any of the previous lawmen stand up to Kendrick, and we aren't likely to show any more courage for the next sheriff."

"Besides, we already got law." Fred Matthews owned the wholesale and freight company.

"What are you talking about, Fred? You call Dirk Kendrick law?"

"Yeah, I do. I mean, when you think about it, he keeps his men sober 'n won't let any of 'em run roughshod over the citizens of the town. He keeps the peace."

"It's a hell of a peace is all I've got to say," Long added.

As had all previous meetings, that one ended in frustration and failure. They had not been able to come up with one suggestion to deal with the problem at hand—the occupation of the town by Dirk Kendrick and the Fence Busters.

Wheatland, Wyoming

Wheatland was twenty-five miles north of Chugwater and more than twice as large. The greater population had brought Duff to town, for it was there that he was able to make arrangements to have enough cattle cars delivered to the railhead in Chugwater to accommodate the cattle he would be shipping.

Once he had completed all the arrangements, he stopped at Nippy Jones Tavern to have a beer before he started home to Sky Meadow Ranch. Only one other customer was at the bar, standing at the opposite end. Duff got the distinct impression that the man was looking at him. More than looking, the man was studying him.

Duff started to walk down and introduce himself, but before he could do so, the man left the saloon. He also left a beer mug that was more than three quarters full.

As Duff was mulling this over, Nippy Jones, the owner of the saloon, came down to speak with him. "Hello, Duff. What brings you to town?"

"Hello, Nippy. I came to town so that I might lease twenty stock cars."

Over the years since he had arrived in the United States, Duff had done a considerable amount of business in Wheatland. As a result, he knew several of the local businessmen. As it so happened, Nippy Jones and Baldy Johnson, owner of Fiddler's Green, were also very good friends.

"Ah, shipping some stock to Kansas City, are you?"

"Nae, to Texas. I've sold some cattle to a rancher there."

"Ha, it's about time Texas started improving their ranches with good Wyoming cattle."

"Scottish cattle," Duff corrected. "'Tis true that

they'll be coming from Wyoming, but the breed is from Scotland."

Nippy laughed. "I'll not argue with you. By the way, how is the old Sergeant Major doing?" Nippy asked.

"Baldy is doing quite well, and 'tis his own regards he asked that I bring you."

"And give him my best as well," Nippy replied.

"Nippy, the gent that just left your establishment, would ye be for knowin' his name?"

Nippy shook his head. "I never laid eyes on 'im 'til he come here today." Suddenly he brightened and held up hand. "But I think he must know you. No more 'n fifteen minutes before you came in, he asked about you."

"What did he ask?"

"He asked if you came here often. He said he was wantin' to meet you. And that's funny, now that you think about it. If he actually did want to meet you, I wonder why it is that he didn't stay and talk?"

"'Tis enough to make a man wonder now, isn't it?"

"Don't you find that a little peculiar?" Nippy asked.

"Aye, 'tis peculiar all right, but I've lived long enough to have seen many a peculiar fellow. If ye nae mind, I'll be for takin' my drink over to the table."

"Go find your table, 'n I'll bring your drink m'self," Nippy offered.

Shortly after Duff's drink was delivered to him, two men came into the saloon, talking with each other as they stepped in through the swinging batwing doors. Once they were inside, they separated. The big bearded man went to one end of the bar, while the smaller of the two, who had a handlebar mustache but no beard, went to the opposite end. Both of them appeared to take no notice of Duff, but he couldn't help but notice that both were studying him in the mirror.

To most people, the fact that those two men had come in together, talking as if they were old friends, then taking up positions far apart from each other would mean nothing. But for Duff, it activated a little signal of alarm. He had the feeling they were setting up an ambush, and he had an even stronger feeling that he was the target.

Deliberately and as unobtrusively as he possibly could, Duff slid his pistol out of his holster, then held it on his lap under the table. He had never developed the skill of the fast draw, which seemed so prized by all Westerners, but did whatever needed to be done to give him an even chance anytime he was forced into a confrontation. For that reason, he held the pistol on his lap.

He had one additional advantage, one that required no manipulation of the situation in order for it to be effective. He was an exceptionally accurate shot, and his prowess extended with equal skill to the pistol and the long gun.

Even as he wondered about the strange behavior of the two men who had just come in, the same man who'd left a few minutes earlier returned and walked right to the center of the bar.

He was met by Nippy Jones. "You left your beer more 'n half full last time you was here, Mister. I can replace it if you like, but it'll cost you the price of a new beer."

"I'll do my drinkin' after," the man said.

"After?"

"After me 'n this feller over here finish up with our business." The man turned to face Duff.

Here it is, Duff thought. He almost felt a sense of relief, not only because it was proof positive that his natural instincts were still active and correct in the assessment of danger, but also because the threat was imminent and he could deal with it right away.

"Would you be the Scotsman they call Duff MacCallister?" the man asked.

"Aye, Duff MacCallister 'tis my name."

"Is that a fact? Well, Mr. Duff MacCallister, my name is Deekus Pollard, and I'm calling you out, now."

With that announcement, a sudden repositioning of all the other patrons in the saloon occurred as most everyone moved to get out of the line of fire, should shooting begin.

Duff noticed that neither of the two men who'd come in just before Pollard had moved. In fact, they seemed to be studying their beer, which seemed very strange, given the possibility that they might be in the line of fire.

"Mr. Pollard, would you be for telling why you wish to pick this fight with me?"

"What difference does it make? You'll be dead in another couple minutes, 'n once you're dead, how or why you was kilt won't make no difference at all."

"Ah, so you are a philosopher, as well as a gunman. I have found that philosophers are some of the most interesting men I have ever encountered. 'Tis a shame I'm going to have to kill you."

Pollard's smile disclosed crooked, yellow teeth.

"I ain't the one that's goin' to be kilt. You see, I got me what you might call an edge."

"An edge, you say? Do you think that's fair?"

"Fair? What do you mean, fair, you damn fool? I'm here to kill you. Fair ain't got nothin' to do with it."

"Well, in that case, I shall feel nae compunction about acquiring my own edge, and you'll have nae cause for complaint, seeing as you have already established the parameters for our *tête-à-tête*."

"For our what?"

"You're right, *tête-à-tête* would nae be the correct word, would it? I mean, of course, because a *tête-à-tête* normally refers to a head-to-head encounter between two people, and 'tis obvious that isn't to be the case here."

"I don't know what you're a-talkin' about, but I can tell you right now, you won't be a-drinkin' no tea."

Duff chuckled, though instead of humor, there was a raw, almost dangerous edge to his laughter. "This is a life-or-death situation, wouldn't you agree?"

"Yes."

"And in a life-or-death situation, one should take every advantage, should they not?" Duff cocked the pistol he was holding under the table.

"Yeah," Pollard said.

"I'm glad to hear you say that. Oh, and you two gents standing at either end of the bar . . . I suspect that you are a part of this. If you are, you will die along with Mr. Pollard. If you aren't, then you need to leave now, while you can."

"Draw!" Pollard shouted.

Duff didn't squeeze the trigger until Pollard had his gun in hand.

Pollard's victorious smile changed to an expression of shock when he heard the roar of a gunshot and felt the bullet tear into his stomach. He dropped his own unfired pistol and slapped his hands over the bleeding wound in his stomach.

"What the hell? Where'd that gun come from?" shouted the big, bearded man standing at the bar. He put his hands up, as did the smaller man standing at the opposite end of the bar.

"Don't shoot, don't shoot!" the bearded man shouted. "We ain't in on this!"

Duff pulled the still-smoking pistol out from under the table. "Would the two of you be good enough to take your guns out of your holsters 'n lay them on the bar?"

"Why? I told you we ain't goin' to do nothin'"

Duff cocked his pistol, the sound of the hammer drawing back making a loud, metallic click in what had become a very silent room. "I'll nae be askin' again."

"All right, all right. I'm a-doin' it!" the bearded man said. As he slowly drew his pistol to put it on the bar, the other man followed suit.

Duff nodded to the owner. "Mr. Jones, if you would be so good as to remove the bullets from the two guns, I would appreciate it."

Nippy Jones did so.

"Now, if you two gentlemen would be for joining me, I would like to buy you a drink."

"You want to buy us a drink?"

"Aye."

"Why?"

"Have you ever heard the expression, *Keep your friends close, but keep your enemies closer?*"

"Nah, ain't never heard nothin' like that," the bearded man said as he and his companion joined Duff at his table.

"Well, 'tis an old Chinese proverb. To that end, would you be for tellin' me your names?

"I'm Tremble," the larger of the two men said. "He's Harrison."

"Mr. Tremble, Mr. Harrison, why did you want to kill me?"

The two men looked at each other for a second, then Harrison spoke. "We didn't want to kill you. There ain't neither one of us ever even heard of you before today. It was Pollard that wanted to kill you. He seen you when you was down at the depot, 'n he said he'd give us twenty dollars apiece if we'd come along with him."

"Oh, that's most disheartening to think that my life would be worth no more than forty dollars."

"Yeah, well, here's the thing," Tremble said. "We wasn't supposed to have to do anythin' but just be standin' there 'n sort of back him up. Pollard said he'd be able to kill you all by his ownself."

"And why is that? Why did he want to kill me, I mean."

"He said you kilt his brother."

Duff shook his head. "He was mistaken. I have nae killed anyone named Pollard."

The sheriff and his deputy had arrived, and after interviewing several eyewitnesses, informed Duff that the killing of Pollard was justifiable homicide, and that he needn't be present for the official inquiry.

"What about these two?" Duff asked, indicating Tremble and Harrison. "Can we charge them with attempted murder?"

"I'm not sure that we can," the sheriff replied. "As I understand it, neither of them actually even drew their guns. I think it would be hard to make a case against them."

"That's right, Sheriff. We just happened to be standin' there when it all happened."

"Uh-huh," the sheriff replied, showing his disbelief. "I'll say this for you. You are a couple very lucky men."

"You mean 'cause you can't charge us with nothin'?" Tremble asked.

"No. I mean you are lucky that you didn't actually take part in the shooting. I know you didn't, because if you had been a part of, it you would both be dead now."

"What makes you think that?" Tremble charged. "I mean, don't get me wrong, we wasn't a part of it, but if we hada been, there woulda been three of us to his one. More 'n likely, MacCallister would be the one that would be dead now."

The sheriff chuckled cynically. "Of course he would be," he said, sarcastically. "Now, I want you two to get out of my town before I change my mind."

"You got no right to run us out of town," Harrison said.

"I don't have to run you out of town. I can put you in jail."

"How are you goin' to put us in jail? We ain't neither one of us done nothin'. You ain't got no reason."

"I'll keep you in jail till I think of a reason," the sheriff replied.

"No need for that," Tremble said. "We're leavin'."

"Hey, Tremble," Harrison said as the two men rode out of town. "Why don't me 'n you wait here, 'n when MacCallister rides by, we'll shoot 'im."

"What would be the advantage of that?" Tremble replied. "Pollard's dead. We wouldn't make any money from it."

"Yeah, well, maybe not. But we could get some satisfaction out of it."

"How about getting satisfaction and a lot of money?" Tremble suggested.

"What do you mean? Do you have an idea?"

"Yeah."